Last Exit

Peri Jean Mace Ghost Thrillers #11

Copyright © 2018 Catie Rhodes.

All rights reserved.

Published by: Long Roads and Dark Ends Press

No part of this book may be reproduced, scanned, or distributed in any printed or electronic form without express written permission from the publisher. The scanning, uploading, and distribution of this book via the internet or any other means without the permission of the publisher is illegal and punishable by law. Please do not participate in or encourage piracy of copyrighted materials in violation of the author's rights. Purchase only authorized editions.

This is a work of fiction. Names, characters, businesses, places, events, and incidents are either the products of the author's imagination or used in a fictitious manner. Any resemblance to actual persons, living or dead, or actual events is purely coincidental.

Cover artwork by Book Cover Corner

Content Editing by Word Webber Press

Copy Editing by Julie Glover

Proofreading by Deborah Digrispino

ISBN Ebook: 978-1-947462-21-2

ISBN Print: 978-1-947462-22-9

First Printing, 2018

Rhodes, Catie.

Last Exit/ Catie Rhodes. — 1st ed.

Visit the author website: www.catierhodes.com

SERIES LIST

Forever Road (Book #1)

Black Opal (Book #2)

Rocks & Gravel (Book #3)

Rest Stop (Book #4)

Forbidden Highway (Book #5)

Rear View: Prequel (Book #6)

Crossroads (Book #7)

Dead End (Book #8)

Dark Traveler (Book #9)

Wrong Turn (Book #10)

Last Exit (Book #11)

LAST EXIT

PERI JEAN MACE GHOST THRILLERS BOOK 11

CATIE RHODES

Another for my sweetie. I could not have done this without your love and support.

1

————

I struggled to get the "Closed" sign open. It popped out of my hand and clattered to my feet. Damn Cecil and these cheap-assed open/closed signs. I had warned him. Told him you get what you pay for. He'd gone behind my back and bought them anyway.

Calm down. Cecil and the signs weren't the whole problem. They weren't even that big of a deal in the grand scheme of things. The tension aching between my shoulder blades came from another source. I cut off the train of thought. *Not now.* I'd have to live through the dreaded event soon enough.

I focused on the night sky. A cloud cover rendered it starless and murky. It had been one of those blustery, windy days with a high chance of rain in the weather forecast. If my poor aching bones were right, this storm would usher in the first cool weather of autumn. We needed the break.

That gorgeous Texas Hill Country sky blazed hot enough to melt glass by the end of summer.

But I wished the rain could wait until tomorrow, after Tanner and I finished our little errand. The flood of worries came again. I slammed the door shut on them. Best not to dwell on it. It wouldn't do any good. I picked up the sign to try again.

Wind whipped my hair into my face, delivered stinging lashes to my cheeks. I ignored it and put some muscle into my task. The wind strengthened. It caught the sign and slammed it closed on my thumb. I bit back an ugly word and let the sign fall to the dirt again.

Injured finger clutched to my chest, I glanced around to see who'd been watching. A few Summervale revelers glanced in my direction. None showed any interest.

They had other things on their minds. Though Samhain was still five days away, many wore costumes. Their excitement lent a mystical charge to the air. Everyone had a spring in their step, drawn by the moon and the shadows that lurked in the darkness.

A woman wearing a red leotard, tail sewn on the ass, came toward me. She'd attached manufactured goat horns to her head. She held the chubby hand of a toddler wearing a purple and gold satin costume and a pointed hat with bells on it.

I smiled at the kid. She—or he, the costume made it hard

to tell for sure—gave me that wide-eyed stare kids give strangers. I nodded to the mother.

"Too cute." I pointed at the kid.

She giggled her thanks and kept walking, probably afraid I was going to try to pull her into my tent and take her money. If only. I stared at the tent where Tanner ran his arcane items business. Usually I loved hanging out with my scorching hot boyfriend. But I had a bad feeling about what we had planned for tonight.

My worried thoughts swelled. They tapped at my defenses and begged to come out to play. I gave up and let them come.

Some friends of Tanner's from California were in Texas. Staying at a hotel in Austin, not too far away. Tanner and I would be going to visit them shortly.

But that wasn't what worried me. It was the way Tanner had acted about the whole thing. He had told me just that morning over breakfast. After everybody was at the table. So I couldn't ask many questions. Worse, his invite to tag along was half-hearted.

I could have just refused to go. But no woman can resist that sort of bait. We live on curiosity. And we have to know the whole story, even when it would be best if we didn't. I had a gut feeling this whole adventure would end badly. But there was nothing I could do other than play it out.

So I did the only thing I could. I snatched that el-cheapo

sign off the ground and put my anxiety into it, forcing it open, even bending the frame a little. I attached it to the little pole that would keep it from blowing away.

A loud clap of thunder forced my attention off the blasted sign. I stared into the impenetrable night. Lightning flashed. Carnival goers shrieked and gasped. They scattered like a pack of buzzards surprised by a car. The dirt throughway emptied. Except for one person. Her eyes locked with mine.

Time stopped. My heart crawled into my throat and lodged there. I held up my hands in a warding off gesture.

"No. You're dead," I whimpered. Unable to stand it another second, I scooted back into my tent and closed the flap. Mouth cotton dry, I went back over what I had seen.

Barbie. Standing there giving me that evil glare she reserved for when I'd committed a mortal sin. My mother had been a bitch, a thief, and a murderer. She had abused me and abandoned me as a child. Was she my personal boogieman? Probably.

Acknowledging the havoc and pain my own mother had wreaked in my life put me back in control. The logical side of my brain took over. Barbie was dead. I had watched her die. If I had really seen her, she was a ghost. In which case, I had the upper hand.

Not only was I a powerful spirit medium, I was a witch. And not just any witch. Mohawk—that sleaze bucket— had called me the Gregorius Witch. I didn't know quite what that meant but the name gave me a tingle of power unlike anything I had ever experienced.

I, Peri Jean Mace, would go back outside my tent and banish Barbie. I would fling her into the deepest, darkest pit, and she would never find her way out. Then I'd go with Tanner to meet his friends. Get the mystery over with. I pushed my shoulders back and marched toward the tent flap. Just as I reached it, someone came inside.

I screamed and backpedaled. My feet tangled together, and I pitched to the ground. I landed with a grunt and raised my arms to protect my head. Now it would happen. My mother's ghost would kick me. She would pound me with freezing fists.

"Are you okay, honey?" The voice didn't belong to Barbie. Relief flooded me.

I raised my head to see who my visitor was. Queenie, a witch from Natchitoches, Louisiana. Someone I trusted way more than my mother's ghost. I climbed to my feet, brushing off my pants and trying to retain my dignity. Impossible task. I'd just busted my ass in front of her.

So I sucked it up and forced a smile to my face. "Miz Queenie! What are you doing so far from Natchitoches?"

She gripped me in a hug and kissed both my cheeks. "All week long, I had a feeling I needed to come see you."

She let go of me and set her quilted bag on top of my séance table. From it she withdrew a smaller cloth pouch, which she laid on the table. She turned back to me, smiling, but it wasn't a comforting smile. Her faded eyes, darting around my tent, said she had serious business with me.

"Are you here about the Wanderer?" Nervous tendrils spread through my stomach. This was even worse than meeting Tanner's friends.

I didn't know who—or what—the Wanderer was. But Cecil and Queenie both seemed to think he could relieve me of the spell blocking me from the full power of Priscilla Herrera's mantle. No telling what kind of horror that experience had in store for me.

"I think it might be," Queenie smiled. From the cloth pouch she pulled a deck of Tarot cards. "I'll pass on his message by reading your cards. Are you game?"

I glanced at my cell phone. Two minutes until it was time to meet Tanner. Any other time, I'd have messaged him and told him to go on without me. But I wanted to see firsthand what he didn't want me to see. On the other hand, whatever Queenie had for me could save my life. I shoved the phone back in my pocket.

"Of course I have time." I went to the séance table and sat down.

Queenie took the chair across from me. The two candles I kept on the table flamed to life. I jerked with surprise. Queenie, acting as though she hadn't seen, calmly shuffled the cards three times. She set them in front of me. "Cut them, please."

I did as she said, and she directed me to do it two more times. Queenie laid out a spread of three cards in front of me.

"You choose which one to turn over first."

I let my hand hover over each card. The one on the left made my eyeballs burn. I pointed at it and Queenie turned it up.

The image of a burning tower, a man and woman falling to their deaths in a tossed ocean greeted me. I recoiled. My scant knowledge of Tarot included the meaning of the Tower. My skin tightened.

"Upheaval, clearing the way for something new." Queenie's voice raised the hair on the back of my neck. "Turn the next card."

Again, I passed my hand over the two remaining cards. The one on the right sent a charge of bright energy flowing through me. I pointed to it. Queenie gestured her permission for me to see what waited.

The image on the card turned my stomach. A man lay prostrate, ten swords sticking out of his back. I didn't know the meaning of this card offhand, but the image was clear enough. Bad shit coming down the sewer pipe.

Queenie stared at me across the table. Her lips trembled.

She licked them and spoke. "Ten of Swords. Betrayal. Loss. Ending. Turn over the final card, please."

I did as she asked. After the Tower and the Ten of Swords, the sight of the skeletal horseman with his scythe didn't surprise me. Still, I jumped when Queenie spoke.

"The Death Card. You clear away what is old and used up so that something else can regrow in its place." She swept a hand over the three cards.

I did my best to stay calm, but worry fogged my brain. "What would you say the Wanderer's message is?"

The candle sputtered. Queenie watched it as though it was talking to her. She gulped. Just as I suspected. Nothing good. She took a deep breath and began to speak.

"A storm is coming." Thunder clapped, underscoring her point. "You're going to lose things that are very important to you right now. If you survive, you will become someone new."

Upheavals, losses, death. There'd been so much over the past couple of years. I had lost almost everything there was to lose. The idea of more tragedy coming down the road, headed for me, invoked wild terror. I didn't see how I could withstand more hardship. I wiped at my face, surprised to find sweat there.

Queenie reached across the table and squeezed my hand. "None of us relishes upheaval. But it is something each of us must endure. You must learn to believe that you will come out on the other side." She took her hand off me. "Now as for what it has to do with the Wanderer, he won't lend his help to you until you reach this point." She tapped the Death card.

Wordlessly, Queenie packed her tarot cards back into their pouch, which she dropped in her large, quilted bag. She stood from the table. She was done.

"I have a flight out of Austin to Mexico City late tonight. I winter in Mexico each year." She winked at me. "If I want a quick visit with Cecil and Shelley, I'll need to hustle."

She turned and hurried out of my tent. I clambered after her. But by the time I got outside, she was already gone.

I sent her a silent well wish. The early Samhain revelers jostled past me. They had forgotten the coming storm and were back to the business of having fun. Just the few minutes Queenie and I had been inside our tent had called forth even more in costume.

My cell phone vibrated in my pocket. I pulled it out. There was a text message from Tanner on the screen.

"I waited on you a few minutes, but you must've changed your mind. See you in a few hours."

No way. He wasn't getting off that easily. I ran through the crowd, determined to catch him before he left. Urgency drove my short legs through the pre-Samhain carnival goers, earning more than a little ire. I flashed them glares but didn't back up my silent threat. Right now, catching Tanner mattered more.

Just about the time my smoke-damaged lungs set up a true protest, I saw Tanner's broad, squared shoulders going through the carnival exit.

I followed at a dead run, no idea that tonight was the last night I'd ever work for Summervale Carnival. Or that years would go by before I passed through its gates again.

———

I raced through the carnival's parking lot, side aching, and grabbed at Tanner. He spun, face set in hard lines. His lips pressed together when he realized it was me.

"I waited. Where were you?" Embarrassment or anger tinted his broad cheekbones.

"I had a last minute visitor." The few short words came out in a rushed gasp. I really needed to quit smoking.

Rather than ask who my visitor was, Tanner turned and marched to the back of the lot where I usually parked my truck. I had no choice but to follow or be left behind. I marched along, mind churning.

This was the first time Tanner had blown me off. It stung. I didn't know how to take this departure from his usual kindness. Should I force a confrontation or simply try to ride it out?

One thing was for sure. I wouldn't say a word about Queenie. My gut said it wasn't the right time. We needed to get this visit to his friends behind us. Save Queenie's bad news for later.

Tanner quickened his step, leaving me behind.

"Wait just a damn minute." I yelled at his back.

Tanner stopped so fast, I walked right past him and had go back. He waited, hands on hips, lips pressed into an angry slash. "What now? We're going to be late."

"Then you need to start talking." I jammed my hands on my hips and stared into his glittering eyes. *Careful, Peri Jean. This man is a tornado when he's angry.*

Tanner narrowed his eyes, gave his head a frustrated toss. "All right. What do you want to hear?"

Oh, no he didn't. I wasn't going to stand there and act reasonable while he patronized me.

I closed the distance between us. "You're going to tell me why you're acting like somebody poured a shot of hot sauce up your ass, and you're going to do it right now."

He let out one of those long, put-upon sighs. "Can we not? You wanted to come with me to see Dave and Neecie. Fine. You're going."

I took a step away from him. My fingers found the ends of my shoulder length hair and twisted the strands. I didn't get it. Tanner and I lived together, shared everything. He knew everybody I knew. Why didn't he want me to meet these people? Was he ashamed of me?

Though I'd thought I left all those old insecurities behind, tears burned my eyes. Maybe he was ashamed of me. Tanner had lived an affluent life with his deceased wife and two daughters. Not only that, his wife, Bea, had been drop-dead gorgeous. One of those lithe, California blondes.

These friends of his, this Dave and Neecie, might be less than impressed with short, dark-haired me. Maybe Tanner didn't want to see their reaction to me first hand. I backed away, shaking my head.

"You don't want me to go. I won't." I swallowed back the raw tide of hurt.

The anger left Tanner's face. He dropped his gaze to his feet. For several seconds, his shoulders rose and fell with his breaths. When he raised his head, the harsh glare of anger was gone. His eyes had softened.

"Come here." He held out both hands.

I shook my head. "It's okay."

I turned to walk back to the carnival, already calculating the money I could make if I reopened my tent for the evening. The carnival was about to close, but people wait until the last minute to act on their most forbidden desires. No matter how we progressed as a society, how enlightened and accepting we got, a sèance still seemed forbidden and a little scary. The people who came to see me with only a few minutes until closing were the most interesting. I quickened my step. Tanner came after me this time, put one arm around me, and pulled me to face him.

"You probably remember Dave was the one who gave us directions to Black Silas's auction in China Grove." His dusty cowboy boots, ones I'd bought him, kicked at the ground.

I hadn't, but I nodded for him to continue.

"Dave and I used to do business together." Finding and selling magical items made up the majority of Tanner's business. "I suspect he wants to talk about that."

I still didn't understand the problem. Tanner's business was different than mine, but I helped him sometimes and shared in the profits. I shook my head and shrugged. "So? Do you not trust me?"

He rolled his eyes. "You know that's not it."

"Then what is? I'm trying to understand why you're doing everything you can to keep me from meeting your friends." My voice rose with each word. "But all I'm coming up with is that you're embarrassed of me or don't trust me."

I glared at him, cheeks blazing with the admission of my worst fears, and waited for him to tell me how wrong I was. The seconds stretched out.

Tanner nibbled at the corner of his lip. "It's neither of

those things. Dave and Neecie are from a different world than all this."

He swept a hand at the noisy carnival behind us. I turned to look at it, trying to see whatever Tanner saw. Garish lights. Smells of artery-clogging fried food. Throngs of people out for a night of low-brow fun. I faced Tanner.

"You're right. I don't belong with Dave and Neecie." I spun on my heel and started walking back toward the carnival again.

Tanner didn't come get me this time. I tightened my body against frustrated tears. The rumble of my truck's engine came from behind me. Tanner would drive past me in a few seconds. I could give him the finger. That might ensure he'd stay away for the night.

With some men, the fights only made the sex hotter. Fighting with Tanner hurt. It made me sad. Then I'd want to apologize. And Tanner didn't deserve an apology right now. He'd shown his ass for no good reason. The truck pulled up next to me. The window whirred down.

"Please get in." Tanner leaned across the seat, face tight with impatience.

I considered running off like a pissy teenager, making Tanner chase after me. It seemed stupid even in my imagination. A good hint it was a dumb idea. I stopped in my tracks and crossed my arms under my boobs.

"You don't want to show up fighting with your girlfriend.

Especially not a girlfriend who's *beneath* your friends." I took off walking again, hunched over my crossed arms.

He gunned the truck and caught up with me again. "Look at me." He swallowed hard. "I'm sorry, okay? Please just get in. I promise I'll do my best to explain."

I blew out a hard breath. Tanner meant the world to me. Easily the most stable guy I'd ever been with, he was usually the one comforting me and making sure everything was the way I needed. Maybe he needed a turn acting crazy and unreasonable. This was, after all, a glimpse at a life that got violently ripped away from him—not one he chose to leave. He deserved a chance to explain himself. I got inside the truck.

"Don't drive too fast." I buckled my seat belt.

Tanner raced the truck through the sand parking lot. People walking to their cars hopped out of the way, some of them yelling, others giving us the naughty finger. Tanner turned to me and grinned.

"Slow down," I yelled and gripped the oh-shit bar a little harder.

Tanner got us out to the road without running anybody down and sped toward downtown Austin, about a half hour's drive away. We rode in silence for half the drive, and then Tanner reached out and took my hand.

"In no way do I think Dave and Neecie are better than

you." He gave me a quick squeeze and let go to grip the wheel with both hands as he made a dangerous pass.

"Then why do you want me to stay away?" I huddled into my seat. How was it I'd come so far, accomplished so much, and something like this could turn me into an insecure mess in a matter of seconds?

Tanner stared at the traffic for so long, I nudged him. He turned and gave me a smile, a real one. "I'm thinking of the right way to say it."

I contemplated the darkness. Those three Tarot cards came back, their images floating against the night sky. Upheaval. Betrayal. Death. Thunder shook the sky.

Tanner angled his head to stare at the sky through the windshield, almost rear-ending a car in front of us. "I didn't think the forecast called for storms."

"The weather is changing. Lots of times that means thunderstorms." The thunder cracked again, and a bolt of lightning lit the sky. The Tower Tarot card flashed behind my eyes. *Whatever changes will be forever*, the voice sounded like me, only older and more sure of herself. I turned my head to face Tanner. "You've stalled long enough. Say your piece."

He wouldn't look at me. "Appearances are very important to Dave and Neecie. They go to a great deal of effort to be trendy and hip. It's a lifestyle for them."

I nodded and waited for the rest.

Tanner took his hand off the wheel and gripped my hand again. "But you're just you. Profane. Wickedly funny. Sexy as hell. And you make no bones about it. That's what I love about you."

"And you know Dave and Neecie won't like me." This was something I understood. Nobody in the world likes being told something, or someone, they love is less than wonderful.

"It's not that they won't like you. It's that you'll be so different from anybody they know that they'll be analyzing you, trying to figure out what makes you tick." The dashboard lights shone green on his face. "I didn't want to subject you to it."

Some emotion flashed across his face, and he turned away as though watching the traffic. I nodded slowly. Not every word of that was true. But I'd have to let things ride for now. Whatever the truth was, we couldn't show up to Dave and Neecie's hotel arguing. They'd pick up on any tension between us. I didn't want them knowing our business.

"I'm sorry for pushing my way in to the visit." I wasn't really, but an apology would smooth things.

Tanner took his attention off traffic to smile at me. We flew toward the car in front of us. Silently, I pointed. He snapped his gaze back on the road and swerved around them. They rewarded his ace driving skills with a shrill horn honk.

Once we were speeding down the fast lane again, Tanner

spoke. "There's something else I need to tell you about Dave. Bea was his first cousin."

I cringed. Not only had Dave known Tanner's first wife, he'd been family. There was no way he wouldn't be offended to see Tanner moving on.

Tanner continued, oblivious to my growing unease. "Bea and Neecie grew up next door to each other, but Neecie went to private school instead of to public schools with the rest of us. Bea introduced Neecie to Dave. They've been together ever since."

I leaned my head back against the headrest and forced myself not to groan. Neecie would hate me just on principal. She'd see me as an intruder moving in on her best friend's husband.

"Don't worry. Dave and Neecie will love you," Tanner said. "When they called tonight to make sure we were still on, they specifically asked if I was dating again." He smiled.

Dave and Neecie weren't going to love me. Not a chance. They'd size up and catalogue every way I fell short. Maybe tell Tanner what they'd figured out. I kept my lips zipped.

"We're five minutes early," Tanner crowed.

Great. Five extra minutes to hang out with Dave and Neecie. I could barely contain my excitement.

2

____

The made-to-look retro neon sign read Starlight Hotel. It didn't quite match the wall of shrubs grown to hide the property from the street. Tanner parked my big truck curbside between a restored Volkswagen Karman Gia and a shiny new Toyota Prius.

Tanner shut off the truck and got out, but I hung back. Staring into the vanity mirror, I smeared on some lipstick Hannah had given me. My eyeliner had migrated over the course of the evening. I used a tissue to wipe it away and redid it.

Tanner opened my door. "Stop. You look great."

I did stop, but not because I looked great. I stopped because I didn't think it mattered. Tanner's friends were going to think whatever they thought of me.

Tanner led me to an entrance almost hidden in the shrubs. An iron gate barred our way. Tanner punched a few numbers into the keypad next to it. A lock clicked, and we passed onto Starlight Hotel property.

The well-lit grounds looked like a movie set. We walked along bright white sidewalks, past several buildings.

"Dave was right." Tanner led me toward one of the buildings. "It's hard to believe you're in the middle of Austin."

I agreed. The sounds of the bustling city seemed distant. This place felt private, almost isolated. None of this looked like any hotel I'd ever seen.

"Are you sure this is a hotel? Nobody's going to call the cops on us for trespassing?" I asked as we passed under the outstretched limbs of a huge oak.

"It's a hotel, all right. The kind Dave and Neecie enjoy. It's called a boutique hotel." Tanner pulled me close to him and brushed his lips against my cheek. "There's probably fewer than fifteen rooms to rent, and the nightly rate likely runs around one thousand per night. Maybe five hundred for the cheap rooms."

The numbers rocked me. I had a little nest egg from finding the Mace Treasure a year earlier, but I never touched it. It was earmarked for a home someday. A home I hoped to share with Tanner. Tonight made me wonder if we wanted the same things.

Thunder clapped behind us, and lightning briefly lit the sky. We both jumped and then laughed. Tanner took my hand, and I gave him an affectionate squeeze. But the lightning bolt in the Tower Tarot card loomed large in my mind. Nervous acid ate away at my stomach. I wished for a cigarette but didn't quite dare fire one up at such a fancy place.

We passed a long, narrow swimming pool. A neon sign had been placed behind it. One word reflected in the water. Vibe. What did that mean? I glanced at Tanner and wrinkled my nose.

"It's a lap pool. For exercise." Then he realized I meant the sign. "It doesn't mean anything. It doesn't have to. It's hip and unique."

I didn't get it but said nothing. What kind of people had enough money to pay a thousand dollars for one night in a hotel? Tanner had once treated me to a weekend trip at a nice hotel here in Austin, but this place made it look like a rooms-by-the-hour establishment.

Tanner steered me up the steps of an old, whitewashed bungalow. We crossed the porch.

Tanner tapped on the door. "Dave? It's Tanner."

The door swung open. A man with a big, bushy beard and short hair dashed out, holding open his arms. "Tanner!"

The two men embraced, laughing, clapping each other on the back.

I took a few steps back, chest tight and tense, a tangle of negativity crowding my thoughts. The man I guessed to be Dave had tattoos running down both arms. He even had one visible on his neck. The rolled up cuffs of his jeans brushed lace up work boots so worn out they looked ready for the garbage.

Maybe feeling me studying him, he turned to me, smiling, one hand held out. "I'm Dave Stewart. And you are?"

Tanner took a quick step forward. "This is my friend, Peri Jean Mace. The one I was telling you about."

Dave looked confused for a second but covered it well. He grabbed my hand, and pumped it. "Of course, of course."

A squeal came from inside the room, followed by the slap of bare feet on a hard floor. "Oh my god, it's Tanner."

The door slammed open, and a thin woman, also wearing rolled up blue jeans, these with rips in them, jumped at Tanner. He caught her and swung her around. She smacked a kiss on his cheek. Tanner, laughing, set her on the porch. She'd left a smear of her very red lipstick on his cheek.

The squealer turned to me and raised her carefully shaped eyebrows. "I'm Neecie. Did I hear Dave call you Peri Jean?"

I nodded, wishing I could be anywhere else on the planet. Neecie pulled me into a soft hug. I tried not to stiffen and pull away. Strangers don't need to hug me.

She let go of me and headed back inside, motioning over her shoulder. "You have to see our fabulous room."

I followed them all inside, praying I got through this

without doing the wrong thing. My chances were about as good as a pig's in a slaughterhouse.

Dave and Neecie's one thousand dollar room looked like somebody's grandmother's house that had been redecorated by painting all the antiques garish colors and putting some faux fur rugs on the hardwood floors. I smiled and nodded as Neecie showed us all the retro touches, ending with the bed.

"It's the softest bed I've ever slept in." She sat down on it and curled her fingers in the bedspread. Neecie wasn't just thin. She had that delicate, fine bone structure that looked like she'd break if handled roughly. "The guy at the front desk said these beds come from Japan." She said the last few words in a whisper and raising those perfect eyebrows again.

I worked to keep the shock off my face, to act as though I saw beds from Japan every day. Neecie puzzled me. Like Dave's boots, her clothes looked like cast offs. Worn out, frayed blue jeans with holes in the knees. A tunic-style blouse made out of an old flannel shirt and a what looked like a cast off bed sheet. But the ring on the third finger hinted at the kind of affluence I couldn't imagine. So did this room, even with the brash colors.

"So Peri Jean, are you from Austin?" Neecie leaned back on the bed, eyes bright with interest.

"I'm from East Texas. Little town out in the middle of nowhere." I stared at Neecie's fair skinned arms and graceful wrists and glanced at my own hands. Scars across the knuckles from fights. Veins prominent on the backs.

Dave and Tanner joined us at the bed. Dave sat down next to Neecie, tattooed arm brushing her unadorned one. The two of them stared at me so intently I began to squirm.

He asked, "Where is this little town in relation to where we are now?"

"About five hours north and east of here." I began to sweat under the heat of their assessment.

"It's about three hundred fifty miles," Tanner sat on the bed next to Dave. "It's the kind of place you expect to hear banjos and worry that the locals might eat you for lunch."

They all laughed. This was a different Tanner than the one who'd gone to Gaslight City with me one month earlier to watch my uncle Jesse marry Rainey Bruce, one of my oldest and dearest friends. That Tanner had made quick friends with my uncle and remarked on how quaint my hometown was. Which Tanner was the real one?

Tanner, Dave, and Neecie exchanged knowing glances. For one wild second, I thought they were going to invite me to have some kinky sex with them.

Instead Dave said, "Does anybody want coffee? Or I've got beer. Local craft brew."

I had been up since dawn, and the coffee sounded good. I opened my mouth to accept, but Tanner shook his head.

I followed his lead. "No thanks."

Dave ran a hand through his hair, which I noticed looked unwashed. So did Neecie's for that matter. But when Neecie had hugged me, I hadn't smelled dirty hair. She'd smelled soapy and sweet. Did Dave and Neecie use a styling product to make their hair look greasy? I bit my lip to keep from smiling.

"But we bought a Chemex, just to use during our visit," Dave said. "There's this new brewing method that allows you to get all the floral notes. It produces a super fragrant cup."

"It really is good," Neecie said, still kneading the bedspread like a cat.

Tanner shook his head again. "Last time you made me a cup of coffee, it took you an hour. I'd rather hear about this offer you have for me."

I stared at Tanner. He knew all along Dave wanted to talk business. No maybe or might about it. How many more half-truths would I catch him in? He caught me watching him and flushed but didn't drop his eyes.

"Fair enough." Dave pointed at the cigarette pack visible in the breast pocket of Tanner's button down shirt. "How about going outside for one?"

Though we'd just gotten inside, we all trooped back outside. Dave began the process of rolling a cigarette. He caught me watching, winked, and offered the cigarette to me. I shook my head, pulled out my store-boughts, and lit one.

Dave popped his cigarette in his mouth and lit it. I sniffed for the skunky odor of marijuana but only detected tobacco. Dave rolled his own plain tobacco cigarettes?

Dave spoke without taking the cigarette out of the corner of his mouth, making it bounce up and down with each word. "So I told you about the little bungalow we bought in Silver Lake, right?"

Neecie turned to me before Tanner could answer. "That's the Silver Lake area, in L.A."

"You mean Los Angeles?" I said it like a hick on purpose. "In California?"

Neecie nodded, her sharp features creased into an ecstatic smile.

Tanner's mouth twitched at my show. "That the one you sent pictures of?"

"The same." Dave got out his phone, tapped a few buttons, and passed it to me before continuing to talk to Tanner. "I told you it's only a thousand square feet. We decided to turn one of the closets into extra space. When I knocked out the wall, I found this tiny, hidden room."

I'd been flipping through the pictures while Dave talked, but now I stopped. Secret rooms almost always had unsavory things attached to them. Were Dave and Neecie here to recruit Tanner and me to run a ghost out of their cute little house? I halfway wanted to see California. But I wasn't so sure about taking Tanner back there. He might have a full-on regression into mourning his wife and children.

Thunder shook the world. Just beneath its rumbling, I picked up other sounds. Men shouting. Dogs barking. Hoofbeats pounding. And underneath that, blatting engines. A memory flitted at the edge of my mind but passed before I could latch on.

I glanced at Dave, Neecie, and Tanner. They hadn't heard anything past the thunder. They were still talking about whatever Dave found in the house. And I had missed whatever it was.

Tanner rubbed his chin, hand rasping over the short stubble he kept just the right length with a beard trimmer. "You say it's a witch's altar?"

"Or something," Dave nodded. "I saw it, felt that crackle come off it, and I told Neecie 'There's one guy in the world who could tell us what this stuff is and if it's worth anything.'"

"And help us find buyers if it is," Neecie chimed in.

Tanner shrugged. "You know the same buyers I do."

Dave did this thing where he shrugged and wagged his head back and forth. When he spoke, it was in a whiney, wheedling voice. "But without you there to tell me how powerful this altar is or isn't and how valuable it is or isn't, how can I get top dollar?"

"You must fly back with us." Neecie's gaze flicked to me. Guilt passed over her face like a cloud over the sun on a windy day. She dismissed me and focused on Tanner. "We're looking at a commercial space right near the house. Selling these items could really give us the financial push we need to get into it."

Tanner nodded. "I understand that and want to help you, but..."

A heavy heat settled in my stomach, mingling with the shock already filling it. Tanner had come here knowing Dave and Neecie had a proposition for him. That meant he was willing to entertain whatever they had to say. I knew this as sure as I knew to watch for snakes in tall grass. My mind struggled to catch up, but it felt as graceful as running through mud.

Tanner glanced at me out of the corner of one eye and hung his head.

Dave and Neecie, skillfully ignoring me, doubled down on him. They showed him pictures from their phones, pictures of L.A., the city where Tanner grew up and spent most of his adult life. He smiled and exclaimed over places he'd loved. His words didn't upset me. The light behind his jewel colored eyes did. In the months I'd known Tanner, I'd never seen him glow like this.

Then Dave delivered the deathblow. "I ran into Nichole.

You ought to see the kids. They're getting so big. They asked about their Uncle Tanner. Nichole asked about you too."

Tanner stiffened. Nichole was his sister. They had some bad blood between them, something Tanner wouldn't talk about other than to admit he owed Nichole an apology over the way he'd acted following Bea's death.

Neecie put a hand on Tanner's arm, caught my glare, and dropped it. "Come to L.A. See your sister and your nieces and nephew. Visit with all your old friends. Maybe stay."

"Even if you don't stay, we could really use your help selling this altar, or whatever it is." Dave kept his gaze carefully off me.

How could these people stand right here in front of me and try to talk Tanner into abandoning me? And not even invite me to come with him? The nerve of it made me see red.

I forced myself to back up. Tanner had no commitment to me. He'd said he loved me. But people fell in and out of love all the time. I knew that as well as anybody. I curled in on myself and stood staring out at the night, smoking cigarette after cigarette until Tanner said we needed to get back to the RV park where my family was camped.

"You live in an RV?" Neecie nearly screamed.

"Yep. But I own it free and clear." I stepped toward Dave

and Neecie, enjoying the way their eyes widened, and held out my hand. "Nice meeting you folks."

Tanner played grabby hands all the way back out to my truck. I didn't respond the way I usually did. Normally we'd have ended up doing something raunchy right there in my truck. Not tonight. I climbed behind the wheel before Tanner could and held out my hand for the keys.

He handed them over with a sigh. "You drive like an old woman."

I ignored the barb. "Are you going back to California with them?"

He went around to the passenger side of the truck and climbed inside. Any other time, he'd have wanted to go twelve rounds over me driving. That alone told me how bad this was.

Part of me wanted to force Tanner to answer right then. Get the unpleasantness over with. But I tamped down the impulse, started the truck, and drove us back to the little town outside Austin where my family camped in a remote, nearly deserted RV park. This discussion was better had when I wasn't behind the wheel of a huge truck. Tanner must have felt the same way. The entire half hour drive, he said nothing.

As we turned into the RV park and drove past the darkened RVs where friends and family slept, Tanner said, "I think I want to fly to California with Dave and Neecie."

My entire body tensed. I pushed my lips together and locked my jaw. If I opened my mouth, I'd start screaming and not be able to stop.

Tanner put one hand on my arm. "Look at me."

I did, tears gathering in my eyes.

"When Bea got pregnant, neither of our families wanted us to have the baby. We were too young, too irresponsible. Even our friends said we were crazy. I mean, we were kids in high school." Tanner gave my arm a light squeeze. "But not Dave and Neecie. They stuck with us. They babysat. In those early years, they helped us stay afloat."

"You owe them," I muttered. It made sense. Tanner was the most decent, kind man I knew. Of course, he wouldn't abandon his friends.

"And I need to set things right with Nichole. If she's willing to speak to me again, I've got to do this." Tanner leaned close. "Please understand. And know that I am coming back."

I swallowed the urge to cry, shut off the truck, and floated into my RV, barely aware of my movements as I unlocked the door. Tanner followed, head hung. I turned on the lights, wincing at their glare.

I spoke for the first time. "Let's get you packed then. Text them and let them know you'll be there in a couple of hours."

His mouth dropped open.

I turned my back on Tanner, sorrow poisoning my emotions, and went to find his duffel bag.

———

I stood in the doorway of the tiny closet in my RV's bathroom, pretending to assess what belonged to Tanner. But, really, I was fighting to control my bleeding emotions.

Shock radiated through me in dizzying waves. I couldn't believe I didn't see this coming. But Tanner had never let on he was unhappy. Not even a little bit. So how could I have known?

I grabbed Tanner's leather jacket, one of the few things he had from his old life before we met, took it off the hanger, and started to put it in the duffel bag at my feet. My arm stopped midway and just hung there, trembling. I raised the jacket to my face and inhaled deeply.

Tanner's musky, earthy smell. It had come to mean home, happiness, and safety. I took another deep breath. Tonight would be the first night in a long time that I'd sleep without this smell wreathing me, without the weight of Tanner's leg across my body.

My lips trembled. I swiped an impatient hand over them. I would not let Tanner see me cry. Nor would I run around pulling a big, ugly fit. Adults didn't do that. Okay. Maybe some did. But this one didn't. Not anymore. I was better than that.

Tanner and I had had good times. Better than good. If he wanted to go now, he had his reasons. I had to accept them and move on.

"We're not over. I'm no further away than a phone call. I'll be back soon as this stuff sells." Tanner's voice came from behind me.

I sucked in a harsh gasp and let out a little scream. The jacket fell around my feet. I picked it up, folded it, and stuffed it in the duffel bag.

"Did you hear me?" Tanner touched my shoulder. "Call me if you need me. I'll be back before you know it."

I doubted it. Rather than argue, I began pulling his shirts off hangers, folding them, and packing them.

"Get a sack for your shoes," I said without turning around. "You don't want them getting your clothes dirty."

Tanner's light footsteps retreated. A rustling sound came from a few feet away. He reached around me and held the sack in front of me. I shoved his sneakers and his flip flops into it and passed it back.

"Would you just talk to me?" He stood behind me for several long minutes, waiting.

Finally I managed to choke out, "I can't."

He walked away. A few seconds later, the closet next to the bed opened, and the sounds of his rustling around for his things came.

I grabbed a plastic bag and loaded up his toiletries, resisting the impulse to stick his toothbrush in my butt before I packed it.

We had Tanner's things packed within the hour. That was the nice part about living in an RV. There wasn't room to store much. Tanner made one last circuit, making sure he'd left nothing.

I already had my truck keys in my hand, bouncing them. "Do you want me to drive you back to Dave and Neecie's hotel?"

He glanced at the bed and tried to smile. "I thought we could…"

"Absolutely not." I had never been less in the mood in my life. Well, maybe a few times.

Tanner's face fell, but he gave a sad nod of acknowledgment. We loaded the truck in silence. Hannah was right next door, and I didn't want her to come out to find out what was happening. I'd have to explain the whole thing to her soon enough. Right now, I just wanted to take Tanner wherever he wanted and call it done.

The thunder continued to rumble. For the second time, I thought I heard men's shouts, the whinnies of horses, and dogs barking behind it. And that weird sound of engines racing. That memory fluttered again at the edge of my consciousness. Again, it faded before I could assess it.

Lightning cracked, bringing back the brightness of

daylight for an instant. My imagination gave the clouds strange shapes. Almost human.

The radio played to Tanner's and my silence as we drove. The moonless night, still except for the claps of thunder and flashes of lightning, was so dark that the reflection of my headlights on the road's yellow stripes was all we had to light our way.

"I'm coming back," Tanner repeated.

"You've said that." I lit a cigarette and kept my eyes on the road.

"But you don't believe me." His voice rose with indignation.

"Would you believe me?" I stole a glance at him, at the dashboard lights glowing on his face. An ache grew in my chest. I swallowed hard against the rising tide of emotion.

"No. Probably not," he mumbled. "Things have moved so fast between us. That was okay when I was eighteen with a pregnant girlfriend. But now I'm pushing forty. A little perspective won't hurt either of us."

His words stabbed at my deepest insecurities, woke them up, and made them start talking. *Why does he need perspective? I thought we were happy.* I shut down the thoughts, cleanly pushed them out of my mind. There'd be plenty of time for recriminations later. Right now, I wanted to get this man out of my truck, out of my life, so I could have a tantrum in private.

The curbside in front of the Starlight Hotel was full, so I had to drive around looking for a spot. Tanner, maybe seeing the end coming, started talking.

"You're thinking I don't love you, but I do. Hey, look at me." He tapped me, but I wouldn't look at him. Because then he'd see the hurt on my face. My pride couldn't have that.

Eyes forward, I whipped into a parking place. We were blocks from the hotel now, and it would be a helluva walk toting Tanner's worldly belongings. Plenty of time to nag at each other and cause more hurt. Might as well speak my mind before things went any further. I took a deep breath and faced him.

"If you love me so much, why are you doing this?" I gestured at the backseat, full of his stuff.

He dropped his head and spoke to his lap. "I'm scared."

Again, the images of those Tarot cards popped into my memory. The Tower. Death. Ten of Swords. Was Tanner cutting ties and running off the big upheaval predicted in the cards? It made a sick, ironic kind of sense.

He turned to me, eyes bright and wet. "I know I'm hurting you, and I'm so sorry. But I need some time to digest all this."

There was no way to answer. I pulled the keys from the ignition, got out, and began unloading Tanner's stuff.

Two dark figures hurried down the sidewalk toward us. As

they neared, their faces became clear in the glow of the streetlights. Dave and Neecie.

I threw my head back and stared at the murky sky. Could things possibly get any worse? Having this final scene with Tanner in front of them was worse than crapping my pants in public.

"We saw you two drive by." Dave had that asinine smile pasted on his face again.

Neecie hurried around Dave and came straight toward me, a fresh coat of that bright red lipstick on her lips. She put her arms out. I took a quick step backward and shook my head.

I might have to tolerate this scene in a grownup way, but I would not let her humiliate me. Neecie stopped her approach and stared, curiosity evident in her wide eyes and posture.

"Okay, then." She withdrew. "This caught you off-guard. You're hurting. I get that."

Rather than acknowledge her half-assed sympathy, I pulled Tanner's things out of the truck and set them on the sidewalk. He only had two duffel bags of clothes and toiletries. The rest was his stock of arcane and magical items, the stuff he sold at the carnival.

Staring at the pitiful evidence of Tanner's life sitting there on the sidewalk, my throat tightened again. I glanced up to catch Dave watching me, smile gone, lips pulled down.

My fist curled. Furious words, ones I could yell at him, formed in my mind and pushed their way to my lips. *Let it go, Peri Jean. It's not his fault. Tanner is choosing this.* I let my fist relax as a sob built in my chest.

Dave was probably just as uncomfortable as I was. Here he was thrust into the middle of my tense situation. Neecie too. She'd done nothing to me. Not really. Despite how different they were from me, their love for Tanner was obvious. They needed him right now and wanted him with them. And they thought he was better off back in LA.

Tanner's decision to go didn't match his seemingly genuine sadness over leaving or his promises to come back. But Tanner had a good heart. He didn't like hurting people, and he wasn't doing this to hurt me. He wanted perspective. Away from me. My chest began to throb in earnest.

"Need help carrying this stuff to your room?" I spoke to nobody in particular.

Dave rushed forward and grabbed both duffle bags. "Not at all. We've got it." He elbowed Neecie. "Come on. Grab that box, and let's let them say their goodbyes."

Never taking her eyes off the silent drama of Tanner and me, Neecie grabbed one of the boxes of items for sale and followed Dave back down the sidewalk. At the corner, she turned for one last glance at me. Nosy little mouse turd.

Once they were out of sight, I moved toward Tanner. I'd touched him many times over the past months. But tonight

I hesitated. He moved forward and put his arms around me. Our bodies folded together, my head on his shoulder.

I raised my head and untangled my arms from his. Using one finger I brushed his hair out of his face and locked eyes with him. "I love you and wish you all the luck in the world."

"I'm coming back," he whispered, voice quivering.

I let him go, climbed into my truck, and started the engine. Tanner grabbed the last box and walked down the sidewalk, head hung low, tangle of long hair hiding his face.

Once he turned the corner, I pulled out of the parking space headed back the way I came. My route back home took me past the hotel's entrance. I got there just in time to see Neecie holding open the little iron gate for Tanner to pass through.

She fixed her lips back into a sad pout and waved to me. I showed her my middle finger, gunned the motor, and sped away.

———

Thunder crashed and lightning bolted through the night sky all the way back. The storm would bring the first cool, autumn weather to central Texas. Wash away the dismal dog-breath humid summer. Make way for a new season.

But a storm like that created dangers. Out here in central

Texas, roads flooded easily. I could get washed away. Lost on a raging river. Maybe forever.

My mind tripped back to Queenie's Tarot reading. Did the Tower represent Tanner's leaving? Or was it the Ten of Swords? It wasn't Death. I had a feeling I hadn't yet hit bottom.

Every camper in the RV park was quiet and dark when I returned. Good. At least I didn't have to tell anybody about Tanner yet. After Neecie's little show, I couldn't endure any more sympathy for a few hours. No matter how well meant.

I crept into my RV, stripped down, and took a fast shower. The RV's hot water heater provided approximately five minutes of hot water. It wasn't nearly enough to wash away the hurt of Tanner's blow-off. But I doubted anything was.

Body clean, I crawled into my pajamas. I hadn't used them since Tanner came into my life. That brought a little smile, and I slid between the sheets with it still on my lips.

But I couldn't sleep. The pillows smelled like Tanner's hair, and the sheets smelled like sex. I got up and made up the table into a bed. Because my bedspread smelled like Tanner, I got a flimsy lap blanket out of the closet and used that for cover. I fell into a fitful sleep where Tanner's voice endlessly promised, *I'm coming back.*

Three raps on the door broke my thin rest. I jolted awake to hazy, gray light streaming through the windows. Looked like the day was going to match my mood.

Hannah yelled, "Get the hell up and let me in." She banged on the door three more times.

I climbed out of my makeshift bed and opened the door. Hannah stood there holding two cups of coffee and a doughnut box.

"Breakup food," she muttered and shoved her way in. When she saw where I'd slept, she grunted and began stripping the sheets off my bed. "Got any more?"

I shook my head. It was easier to wash them than store a second set.

"Where's your quarters?" She gathered the sheets and bedspread in her arms.

I got my sandwich bag of change and followed her outside. We walked up the little lane of RVs to the overpriced laundromat, empty at this hour. We got the bedding started washing and walked back to my RV.

"How'd you know?" I glanced at Hannah.

"You know I don't sleep well. I saw the two of you loading up the truck, then leaving. When only one of you came back..." She shrugged. There wasn't any need to say more.

I drank the coffee she'd brought and munched on doughnuts. Hannah had bought the custard filled ones.

Tanner's voice kept echoing in my head, "*Call me if you need me. I'm coming back.*" But he wasn't coming back, and he didn't want me to call him.

"What happened?" Hannah made a pained face.

"I don't know." I told her about the visit with Dave and Neecie.

Hannah rolled her eyes at my description. "Oh dear. Hipsters?"

Not completely sure what the term meant, I described what I'd seen, especially Neecie's puzzling worn out clothes but their obvious wealth.

Hannah pealed laughter at that. "That one outfit probably cost more than every garment you've got put together."

I shrugged, still puzzled over the weird outfit. "Hipsters or not hipsters, they had a business offer for Tanner. And he knew they were going to present it. Never said a word to me. What's more, they didn't seem to know about me at all."

Hannah nodded slowly. "I guess I'm not all that surprised."

I put down my coffee and glared at her across the table. What the hell did she mean by that?

She bit into another cream-filled doughnut. "For what it's worth, I also wasn't surprised Leon Blackfox had a wife in South Dakota." She sipped her coffee. "We get back what we put out."

Oh, goodie. Self-help gems from Hannah. Just what I needed.

She put down her doughnut. "Hear me out before you start rolling your eyes."

"I didn't roll my eyes." I ate my doughnut with feigned calmness.

"But you wanted to." Hannah raised her eyebrows and settled her gaze on me. It made her look about a decade older and ten times tougher.

"All right, I'm listening." I said with as much open-minded-ness as I could fake.

"I met Leon when I didn't want to trust any man. He saw that vulnerability and put on a big show of being this protector of women." Her lip quirked down on one side. "But in the end, he was just hanging out with a broken woman while his wife took care of their kids in South Dakota."

"He has kids too?" I curled my lip.

"Of course. The wife called me. Told me the whole story." Hannah stared at me across the table, letting the horror of it sink in.

We sat quietly for several seconds. Then she burst out laughing. I did too. We laughed until my ribs hurt, and Hannah's face was so red I worried she wasn't getting enough oxygen. Hannah stopped laughing first. Picked up her custard-filled doughnut and took a big bite. She smacked while she ate it and swallowed it with gusto.

"That phone call flipped on a light bulb for me. I survived

Michael Gage..." She trailed off, eyes moving back and forth, maybe searching for words to describe what happened to her. She snapped out of it and settled brimming eyes on me. "I survived that. Now I have this-this second chance. It's either make the most of it or waste it slouching around like something pitiful."

Her words hit me hard. I'd survived things too. Nothing so terrible as what Hannah went through with Michael Gage. But I had survived. Losing Tanner was small in life's grand design.

But just thinking his name unleashed a tide of hurt. His laugh. The rough purr of his voice, telling me the stories of his life. All the hours we spent riding in my truck. It had seemed so good. Until he left. Hannah picked up another doughnut, contemplated it, and set it back in the box. She studied me.

"You're thinking about Tanner now, wondering what happened." She didn't phrase it as a question, so I didn't bother to answer. "Want me to tell you?"

I thought about it. Did I want Hannah giving me the self-help digest version of what was wrong with my personality? Honestly? No. I opened my mouth to tell her.

But she rushed to speak before I could. "You don't love yourself. You've come a long way since we started being friends again, but you don't love yourself."

I held out one hand. "Check, please. You're a shitty shrink."

She slapped it away. "Don't make fun of me. I'm telling you the truth."

We faced off across the table. A couple of years ago, when Hannah first came back into my life, I could stare her down. Not now. She carried her share of bad miles.

"Loving a woman who doesn't love herself is a tall order for any man. It's a lot of pressure." She leaned back in her seat and waited.

"Bullshit. I never ask anything of Tanner." I leaned back in my seat, ready to battle.

"Oh? What about when you went to get Mohawk's book?" She watched me, something in her caramel eyes I didn't quite recognize.

"I left his ass here so he wouldn't get hurt." My voice had hardened. I still felt ashamed for the way I had treated Tanner.

"You left him because you wanted to die alone if that's how things went." She pointed one finger at me, pinning me to my seat. "Then he had to come chasing after you to make sure you fought Mohawk and won. Like I said, it's a lot of pressure."

Face heating, I put my elbows on the table and leaned forward. "Pressure? Give me a break."

She mimicked my posture. "It's pressure because his job as your lover is chasing you around, making sure you don't destroy yourself. That's what people who don't love them-selves do."

Heat crept through my body. I opened my mouth to argue with Hannah, but she cut me off.

"The way I know you hate yourself? When you love your-self, you believe you can withstand whatever life throws at you." She paused for a beat. "But you don't. You run around scared shitless of what's going to happen next, what's going to go wrong, even when things are great. That's how people know you hate yourself and your life."

The heat spreading through my body became a flash of anger. "Bullshit. I let Tanner move in with me, even though I was afraid of exactly this."

She scoffed. "You did that out of fear of losing him. You've spent the last few months walking around like a dark cloud is about to burst over your head and piss battery acid all over you."

"I don't do that." I said in flat tone of voice.

"Do too. And because you don't feel confident in your ability to endure, you think it's the end of the world every time you face a frightening challenge. It's exhausting to other people. As long as you're like that, it's going to make you lose people you love." She climbed out of the booth and walked toward the door but paused before opening it and turned back to face me. "I'm saying this because I love you down to the pit of my soul. I wouldn't be alive right now if it weren't for you. You've got more heart and more fight than anybody I know. And I want you to find a way to see how great you are." She slipped outside before I could answer.

I sat with my face flaming, tears brimming my eyes. Hannah was wrong. She had to be. Because the person she described sounded pathetic. She couldn't be me.

3

———

I sat at my table, surrounded by doughnut crumbs, and couldn't quite work up the energy to move. Not even to wipe down the table, or to go take my sheets out of the washer and move them to the dryer.

Had Tanner really cut and run because I was too much trouble? I prided myself on being tough, rolling with the punches. Fighting when needed. I sacrificed myself for others. Put their needs ahead of mine.

But do you do it because you don't like yourself very much?

I shook off the thought before it went too deep and went to get dressed. Get busy and stay busy. That would keep the doldrums at bay.

I wiped down the table, scrubbed the countertops, and picked up the general mess. By the time I finished, I felt pretty good. But when I dropped my pajamas on the pile of dirty clothes in the laundry basket, my forward motion took a rude kick. Crumbled in the laundry basket was one of Tanner's T-shirts.

We didn't even think to check the dirty laundry. Both of us had been too shook up. Worse, the shirt was one Tanner loved. Solid black, it had the words Led Zeppelin and a winged man. I picked it up and put it to my face, inhaling his scent.

Then Hannah's diagnosis of all my problems ran through my head again. Had Tanner left because he was tired of taking care of me? *No. He left because he's a selfish, cowardly bastard.* I slung the shirt back into the laundry basket. I'd wash it and see if my cousin, Finn, wanted it.

From outside my RV came the sound of thumping bass. It came closer, and I could make out Spanish words. Latino rap. The music got even louder, so loud my toiletries vibrated on the counter of the bathroom sink.

This was ridiculous. Somebody was either going to turn down the music, or I'd turn it down for them. I spun, marched to the door, and slammed it open.

An 80s Cutlass Supreme sat in front of my RV. Dark, metallic blue and tricked out to the nines, this was a show-piece. Bass rumbled and thumped from the car.

I'd come out ready to deliver a deluxe knuckle sandwich to the music lover, but now I wasn't so sure. The Cutlass was parked in front of my home as though it belonged here. The music cut off.

I flashed again on Queenie's Tarot cards. The Tower. Death. Ten of Swords. Tanner's leaving had already turned my life upside down. Was this another kick in the ass?

My stomach tightened into a fiery ball. I stifled a sour burp, squared my shoulders, and went to face it head on. Before I walked three steps, the car's door opened.

Weak sunlight filtering through the gray clouds shone on a head of long, curly blonde hair. Tubby Tubman took one last pull on his cigarette, tossed it on the ground, and stomped on it.

"C'mere and gimme some sugar, girl." He held out two skinny, tattooed arms.

Despite the fact that Tubby caused a stink everywhere he went, I considered him a good friend. I ran to him and threw my arms around his bony bod. He hugged me so tight my back made a popping sound. We let go of each other.

"Whose car is this?" I made a face and pointed at the gaudy thing.

"You don't like the late birthday present I got you?" He stuck out his lower lip in a pout.

"You're too cheap to give me a car." I elbowed him.

"Good point. Feller who owed me some money settled the debt with this car." Tubby considered. "After I cut off both his pinky fingers with a pair of bolt cutters."

My stomach, still raw with fear, did a slow flip-flop as I imagined two lifeless, bloody pinky fingers on someone's floor.

Tubby glanced around the camper. "Where's Tanner?"

My two favorite men had met a few times, none very successful. Tubby's unique charm went beyond anything Tanner could appreciate. It was a relief not to have to play referee to them.

"He went back to California." I said it like it didn't matter.

Tubby, who'd known me since I could barely tie my shoes, cocked his head and frowned. "You okay?"

I nodded. No point in analyzing Tanner's leaving further. It brought up too many questions, ones I didn't want to deal with right now.

"Damn that's an ugly car. Can't be anybody but Tubby Tubman." Hannah's voice came from behind us. She hurried around me, grabbed Tubby, and hugged him. He jumped with surprise and flushed.

"You see Rainey and Jesse lately?" I asked Tubby. Rainey wasn't a hands-on person, but that didn't make her any less of a friend.

He nodded. "They're doing good. Jesse works her front desk. She fires him pretty much every day. He comes over to the billiards hall, drinks a beer, laughs about it, and goes back."

My uncle was old enough to be his bride's father. Rainey and Jesse had fallen in love while she helped him get out of prison for a murder he didn't commit. Most of us thought their passion for each other would fizzle once Jesse was released. But the two had surprised us all by marrying several weeks ago.

Rainey's father, Hooty Bruce, had been less than thrilled that one of his old school chums married his daughter, but he'd taken the disappointment with his usual affable dignity. He'd cried in front of me privately and said he worried his daughter was saddling herself with a husband who'd die long before her.

I suspected Jesse was the one man who could tolerate Rainey's tantrums, her mean words, and her drive to be the best without feeling threatened. Rainey gave Jesse back his lost youth, made him feel less like a man who'd spent the best years of his life in prison. They'd found what they each needed.

"What are you thinking so hard about?" Tubby poked me in the ribs, in the spot he knew was ticklish.

I pushed his hand away. "Wondering what kind of trouble you're in, who I'm protecting you from this time."

"I'm always the one who bails your sorry ass out." But Tubby threw a glance at the car, then at Hannah. He lowered his voice. "Truth is, I got some bad news."

Thunder rumbled the sky.

Hannah jumped at the sudden noise, but covered it by turning to Tubby.

"If you pull out your wiener, Tubman, I'm going to make you sorry." She showed him her fist.

He giggled. "Naw. You'd like it too much. Bad news is that somebody who don't like none of us paid me a visit last night."

"Who?" I shifted foot to foot. Names and faces flashed in my mind. I made a lot of people—and things—mad.

"Corman Tolliver." Tubby sank his teeth into his lower lip, frowning. It was as close to expressing worry as he'd get. Tubby prided himself on hiding his fear. If he was this afraid of Corman, that meant I needed to worry.

Hannah gasped at Corman's name. Her hands danced in the air like dying birds. She grabbed my cigarettes from me and lit one. Her hands shook so hard she had to chase the tip of her cigarette with her lighter to get it going. She took a long drag.

"What's that animated turd want?" She grated out words in a cloud of smoke.

"Wade Hill. Said he'd forget about what we did if I gave up Wade." Tubby's blue eyes flicked back and forth, unreadable.

Dark fear broke loose and trampled through me. No. Not this. Not now.

Wade had helped me destroy the Six Gun Revolutionaries Motorcycle Club several months earlier. Corman had been arrested with his father after the incident but quickly released. It made sense for him to be gunning for Wade. Perfect sense.

"What'd you tell Corman?" Anger and fear harshened my voice.

"That I'd give him an answer today." Tubby's calm voice clashed with the blaze behind his eyes.

"Why didn't you kill him?" Hannah stared at the dirt, cigarette clipped between her first and middle finger.

"Can't shit where I eat right now. Got problems with Sheriff Dean Turgeau. Asshole wants to bust me. Murder rap's a good reason." Tubby leaned against the Cutlass and lit his own cigarette.

"So you just disappeared?" I rubbed at my burning stomach. Corman could have followed Tubby to me. He was a sneaky bastard, just like his father.

"He ain't followed me. Don't you think I have better sense than that?" Tubby's voice raised several octaves, and he gestured at the Cutlass. Understanding soured my boiling stomach further. Tubby had used the car to escape Gaslight City under cover. Its owner had been collateral damage.

"What do we do?" I asked him.

"Let's go in your camper and talk about it. I'm 'bout to starve." Tubby's stomach rumbled on cue.

"Come on." I led the way, and the other two followed. My thoughts churned.

Wade had started his life over five hundred miles south and west from Gaslight City, not all that far from where I was camped right then. He lived with his sister and worked in a factory. He'd left his time as an outlaw behind. I'd do everything I could to make sure he got his second chance. Corman would have to be exterminated, and Tubby would help whether he wanted to or not.

I opened the door to my little RV. Dark magic washed over me in a foul wave, bowling me back against Hannah. She caught me under the arms.

"What the hell?" She hoisted me back to my feet.

I couldn't answer her. The box sitting on my table held my full attention. Even if I wasn't one hundred percent sure the table had been empty when I walked outside, I still would have known the box was wrong. It emanated evil.

"What's wrong?" Tubby said from behind me.

"Yeah, what is it?" Hannah gave me a light shove.

I gathered my wits and stepped inside my home. The smell of rotten eggs settled over me. My stomach rebelled, and I gagged, putting my hand over my face to mask the smell.

Tubby shoved around me. "What happened? Your toilet broke?"

He began opening cabinets, hunting for something to eat.

"Get away from it." I gave his arm a hard tug.

"What? Get away from what?" He jerked away from me, grabbed a package of chocolate sandwich cookies, and tore them open. He shoved three into his mouth at once. How could he eat with that smell?

Hannah had backed against the counter and had her hands out in warding off motion. She stared at the box, a sick expression on her face.

"What is it?" She stifled a gag.

Finally. Someone else sensed the danger rolling off this thing.

"I don't know. It wasn't here when I stepped outside." A chill ran over me as the ramifications of my words hit home. While Tubby, Hannah, and I stood not ten feet from my RV's door, someone had snuck in and left this. None of us had heard a thing.

"Think it has something to do with Corman?" I asked Hannah.

She shook her head. "I don't know. But that box holds death. I feel it all over me."

Hannah, who'd gained the talent of predicting deaths after

trying to end her life, had an internal gauge for stuff like this. I'd never doubt her.

"What do I do?" I said to nobody in particular.

"Open the damn thing for starters." Tubby pulled a buck knife from his back pocket and approached the table. His lips parted with a soft pop. He gave his head a slight shake and swallowed hard.

"What?" Holding back my nausea, I approached the table. The box had an address on it written in fancy script.

To: Peri Jean Mace, One Dumb Bitch

From: Oscar Rivera, Lord of Babylon (AKA The Coachman)

Panic raked stinging claws over my nerves and worked its way into my thoughts, chewing and tearing. My breath came a little faster. My mouth dried to the consistency of sandpaper.

A deep, ugly chuckle came from the box.

Hannah and I both gasped.

Tubby, face set in anger, pulled the box open and stared in confusion. "This stuff mean anything to you?"

The stench intensified, but Hannah and I leaned close. She tilted her head to one side. Her mouth opened in slow motion, and she let out a scream.

I snatched the box away and stared at the contents. For a

moment my brain froze. Then it began processing details, one by one, hysteria building at its edges.

Inside the brown cardboard box sat another box. The cheap plastic kind used to store leftovers. The black-painted duct tape sealing it closed had been cut through and dangled in flaps.

"The box we sealed Oscar's runes in." Cold sweat beaded on my forehead. Fear swelled my heart until it ached. I reached for the box and flicked off the lid, even though I knew what I'd find. Sure enough, the runes were gone, all except one.

"But that hole we threw them in was over a hundred feet deep." Hannah yelled in my ear.

I ignored her denial. The proof we'd screwed up sat in front of me. Oscar Rivera had his runes. Somehow, despite my best efforts, I had given them back to him. He now had a gateway to enter back into the living world.

The mark on the one remaining rune glowed red. It pulsed like a heartbeat.

Oscar's voice came from all around me. "I'm coming for you."

A red form came up from the rune and flew at me. Hannah shrieked. Too stunned to make a sound, I scrambled backward, got tangled up with Tubby, and fell on my ass.

Queenie's cards had been right. First Tanner. Now this. And I still felt the same way. Overwhelmed.

"I can't do this again," I sobbed at Hannah and Tubby.

Tubby came a little closer and put one hand on my shoulder. "Baby girl, I'm lost. What is this?"

I sat down at the table, shoved the box out of the way and cried hard. It was just too much for twenty-four hours. When I got control of myself, I used my shirt to wipe my face.

"Go get Cecil and the rest of the family. I only want to tell it once." I stood on shaky legs and walked to the bathroom to splash water on my face. Damned if I'd meet them all weepy-eyed.

———

An hour later, the cloudy day had already darkened to early night. All of Sanctuary gathered in the RV park's common area.

Sanctuary was a traveling community started by Cecil's parents, my great-grandparents. It included people who had supernatural gifts or dealt in the occult. But it also included people who didn't fit into regular society for one reason or another. We were cons. It would have killed Memaw to hear me say that, but it was true.

My family, cousins and my great-uncle and his wife, sat closest to where I'd be speaking. Tubby sat with them. Someone had brought in the cardboard box and set it on the picnic table.

Cecil, my great-uncle, stood and raised both hands. "Everybody? Let's get started."

Illness had weakened his voice. Nobody heard him. Cecil had been ill the last few months. He'd become a shadow of himself, leading the group mainly from behind me.

My cousin, Dillon, handed off her youngest child to her husband and stood on their table. She cupped her hands around her mouth and hollered, "Shuuuut Uuuuuuup."

That did the trick. People quit talking and turned around in their seats to face where I stood in front of the group.

"Thank you, Dillon," I said.

Several people laughed.

"We've called this meeting to let you know of a danger we're now facing. Those with us last February remember our problems with a spirit called the Coachman. His real name is Oscar Rivera." I paused and searched for recognition on their faces.

Thunder crashed in the distance, eliciting a few gasps.

"Not him again. Why can't you people get rid of him?" Anita Johnson stood. She and her husband had once tried to overthrow the Gregg family to lead Sanctuary themselves. Made sense she'd start the squawking. Her husband, Kenny, stood up next to her.

"Yeah. Y'all said you got rid of the threat back in August

after that monster like to've got you." Kenny crossed hairy arms over his chest and slitted his eyes at me.

Cecil coughed into his hand and stood. He had to hold onto the back of his chair.

"Kenny, you're alive because of this little woman right here. You best sit your ass down and do whatever she says." Lecture delivered, Cecil sat with a grunt of relief.

Kenny and Anita stayed where they were.

Tubby nudged Cecil and lifted his shirt to reveal a semi-automatic pistol. He tipped his head at Kenny and Anita, asking Cecil a silent question. Cecil raised his eyebrows at Kenny.

Kenny paled and sat. Almost as an afterthought, he grabbed his wife's arm and forced her to do the same. The two began a whispered argument.

"How do you know Oscar is back?" Gus Martinez stood from the table he'd been sharing with his husband Noah Killebrew.

I reached into the cardboard box and held up the plastic box the runes had been inside.

"Oscar sent this to me." I left out the part where he called me a dumb bitch. It sort of fit, much as I hated to admit it. "The magic Oscar Rivera uses to access the living plane was sealed in this box and dumped in a deep, deep hole. Somehow he managed to get hold of it. He sent the box with a message that he's coming for me."

Noah stood next to Gus. "Where's Tanner? What does he think about this?"

The three men had become quick friends. They attended card games together. Of course Noah and Gus would want to know where Tanner was.

"He's gone back to California." I stared out at the sea of curious eyes, cheeks heating.

"What's going to happen to us?" A dime store psychic who called himself The Mystical Johann called from the back of the commons area.

"Nothing good," Anita Johnson shouted.

"Well, I'm leaving. I joined up with you people for safety. This ain't it." The Mystical Johann flounced out of the pavilion.

I had expected this response. It made me miss Tanner even more. He would have soothed feelings and helped plan. I was too rattled to do anything but run for cover.

"Leaving might be the best option," I yelled over the din, which died down as if a switch had been flipped. When I spoke again, my voice echoed off the shelter's concrete floors. "I suspect we're about to be fighting for our lives." I didn't add that I couldn't protect them all. My titanic pride wouldn't let me.

"Now wait a minute." Cecil half stood, but the room had already begun to rumble with chairs being pushed back and people talking among themselves. They streamed from the little room.

Cecil gripped my arm. He tugged at me until I faced him. He focused his dark eyes on mine, the old leader demanding the new hire perform, and perform well.

"Never dismiss your army," he hissed.

"They're not an army. They're people who don't have any stake in this." I met his gaze, unflinching.

He blinked twice, and I knew I'd won. Boy, I hoped I wasn't wrong telling these people to hit the road. I took off walking. Cecil gave a disgusted grunt and followed.

Bruise colored storm clouds covered most of the sky. The RV park's lights flickered on and buzzed in the quiet. Cecil and I watched as more than a few Sanctuary members raced around their campers, unhooking, getting ready to cut and run. I lit a cigarette and offered Cecil one. His wife, Shelly, no longer allowed him to smoke, but this was dire. Cecil took the cigarette, lit it, and inhaled deeply. He spoke without looking at me.

"Baby, I know Tanner left you without any warning, but you've got to get it together. Come on now. What's next?" He prodded me in the ribs with one bony finger.

I shrugged.

"Don't give me that shit." His voice roughened. "Think."

"What's there to think about?" I spun to face him, eyes

burning. "I don't know how Oscar's going to attack, so there's no way…"

"I know one thing that would help a lot." He stared into my eyes.

The mantle. Of course. Just the thought of my magical core and the scar tissue spell surrounding it made my shoulders ache with unreleased tension. If I could absorb it, I'd give Oscar a fight he wouldn't forget soon. But it wasn't just a finger snap away.

"You're right, Papaw. I have to absorb the rest of the mantle. But Queenie said the Traveler won't see me yet."

"Why?"

"She did a Tarot reading. The cards I got were…" I didn't even want to speak the names of the cards she drew. Somehow that made them seem more real.

Cecil watched my inner battle, face creased with concern. "Go on and tell me. Can't offer you advice otherwise."

I collected myself and did what he said, speaking the words through tight lips. "The Tower. Ten of Swords. Death."

Cecil's olive skin paled to sick yellow, and his mouth slackened. But then he seemed to catch himself. He stood up straight and arranged his face into one of firm, fatherly concern.

"It's not the news you were hoping for. But you're not beat

yet. What are you going to do right now?" Cecil watched a bolt of lightning streak across the sky. The flash of harsh light made him appear nothing but a skeleton. The illusion passed, and I forced my mind into brainstorming mode.

"Oscar sent one of his runes. I might be able use the wheel of life to figure out what he's up to." This was the best I had.

No wonder Cecil was annoyed with me. I should have been planning all this time instead of falling in love and playing house with Tanner.

"How will you do that?" Cecil crossed his thin arms over his chest.

"There's latent magic in that rune. It was glowing earlier. If I can latch onto it, I might be able to channel it. See whatever the rune has seen." The plan began to take shape. I'd have to ask Priscilla Herrera how to do what I wanted, but she'd help. She lived for stuff like this.

"Not bad. Quick thinking." Cecil gripped my shoulder. "Despite my sharp words, I'm proud of you."

Thunder shook the sky. Underneath the thunder came another sound. Men yelling, hoofbeats pounding, and barking dogs. That sound again. What was it?

I turned to Cecil. "Do you hear that at all?"

He shook his head, puzzlement wrinkling his features.

Thunder rumbled again. I lurched toward Cecil and put my arm around him, pouring my power into his worn out body. He stiffened with it. The thunder slammed again. Then came those calls. The hoofbeats. The dogs howling. Underneath the roar of engines at high throttle.

Cecil turned to me, eyes wide. "It's too late. Oscar is coming right now. And he's got an army with him."

I froze, not sure what to make of Cecil's reaction.

"Go," he yelled. "Tell everybody to get ready."

I left my great-uncle, my last elder and source of comfort, standing alone in front of the roiling sky and ran for the nearest camper, which happened to belong to my cousin Finn and his wife, Dillon.

I banged on the door. Zora, their oldest child, opened it. "Hannah's here. She gonna put makeup on me."

"Good," I scooped her up, and set her on my hip.

"I'm a big girl now," she yelled in my ear.

I ignored her and barged inside. Dillon stood over the stove stirring something that looked like stew. Finn sat at the table having a very serious discussion with Hannah.

He spoke without glancing away from Hannah's face. "Zora, I told you to help your mother."

"Finlay." I said his full name in my leader's voice.

He jerked and glanced at me.

I stood over the table, feeling a little foolish issuing orders while I held a squirming little girl. "Papaw and I heard something in the storm. Shouting, voices. Dogs barking. And engines running. Papaw said Oscar's coming and to warn everybody." I paused, trying to figure out how to explain the last part. "Finn, he was scared."

Finn shoved his way out of the booth and headed out the door. "What's the plan?"

"I don't know." I followed him to Brad and Jadine's nice new fifth wheel.

He faced me, dark eyes flashing with fear and anger. He let out a long breath. "All right. We'll figure it out as we go."

Finn spun away from me and ran the last few steps to Brad and Jadine's. Brad answered the door smiling before Finn could knock. He must have been watching us through the window. His eagerness to fit in kept him in a high state of watchfulness. He took one look at Finn's and my faces, and the smile dropped off his face.

"What is it?" He spoke to me more than Finn, but Finn answered.

"Oscar's coming. We've got to fight." My handsome cousin wiped the greasy sweat off his face.

"What do I do?" Brad glanced between Finn and me, face tightening.

"See Papaw standing out there?" Finn pointed to where

Cecil still stood watching the storm come. "Go stand with him. Now. And leave your wife here."

Jadine peeked out from behind Finn. "You don't order me, Finn Gregg. I'll go with my husband."

Finn growled and marched away. I followed him, trying to hoist Zora to a more comfortable position on my hip.

"Let me walk," she yelled in my ear.

I set her on the ground, grabbed her chubby hand, and pulled her along.

"The dead people are coming," She chanted, running along beside me.

I stopped, and she plowed into me. I caught her before she fell.

"What did you say?" I stared into her dark eyes, much as Cecil had done to me not so very long ago.

"The dead men are coming. That mean man who took me from Mommy and Daddy." Her voice wavered.

That was true enough. Oscar was coming. But who were the dead men? Cecil had mentioned an army.

I knelt in front of her and tried to smile. "What do you see?"

Her mouth worked as her young mind tried to interpret the pictures in her mind. I struggled to find words she'd understand while Finn beat on doors and shouted at people to get ready, the monsters were coming.

Dillon appeared next to me. "I'll take her so you and Finn can do what you need to do."

Zora, who'd had her face screwed up as she thought hard, screamed, "I'm helping Peri Jean figure out what do to about the dead men."

"She says there's dead *men* coming. Not just Oscar," I told Dillon what I'd heard—the dogs barking, the horse hooves pounding. The engines. We were facing more than a singular threat.

Dillon turned so pale her freckles stood out like black dots. She marched over, grabbed Zora, and picked her up. "Come with me, little girl."

"I'm a big girl," Zora screamed. A fat tear slipped from the corner of one eye and rolled down her cheek. Her gaze found me. "And I'm helping."

"You can help your mother more than you can help me." I tried to put my hands on her cheeks.

She slapped my hands away. "You're just trying to get rid of me because I'm too little."

Dillon spoke to her older child. "Zander's with Hannah. Don't you want to see him?"

Zora hollered louder.

Dillon gave her head a frustrated shake. "If all hell's fixing to break loose, I want to be near my other kid."

Zora still sobbed as though her heart was about to break.

"Why don't we all go?" I put on a phony smile.

The little girl made a big show of holding back her tears. She rode on her mother's hip like a queen suffering the greatest of indignities.

We walked toward Cecil and Shelly's motorhome. The stuff Zora had said about the dead men coming rolled over and over in my head. There should have been something there that I could use. But this was all happening too fast.

Shelly burst out of her motorhome. "What is this Finn's saying? Oscar is coming now? Can't he just stay in his grave?"

That was when I knew. I was a spirit medium and witch. I had limited powers of necromancy. I should be able to control Oscar to an extent. A crazy plan strung itself together.

"If I can call a circle big enough to cover us all, Oscar might not be able to get through." Fear of failure raced through my bloodstream, making my skin tingle.

Both Shelly and Dillon stared at me, not quite getting it yet.

But Zora yelled, "Yeah. We keep the dead men out with witch magic."

Thunder boomed. Behind it came the shouts and the dogs barking. They were closer than ever.

"I'm going into my camper to get supplies. Tell Brad I need him," I said to nobody in particular.

"I'll get him." Shelly marched off to find her son-in-law.

Dillon, Zora, and I collected Zander and Hannah and went to my RV. We found Tubby sitting at the table eating chocolate sandwich cookies. While we'd all been running around panicking, he'd sat here and finished most of the package. I grabbed my stang and began trying to relax enough to call my magic. I wanted Tanner, needed his calm comfort and his fierce willingness to fight if that's what it took.

Brad pounded on the door and walked in to my camper. "We're making a circle?"

I held up my stang. "I need consecrated dirt. You have anything like that?"

Without answering, Brad ran out.

I spoke to Dillon. "Get everybody in as small of a place as possible. I've never tried to circle this many people." I couldn't admit out loud that I wasn't sure I had the power. "All the holders of the raven tattoo will help me call the circle."

Dillon hurried out, Zora running behind her. Hannah still held Zander. He had both hands on her cheeks and patted them, chanting his favorite words. "Pretty girl, pretty girl, pretty girl." She hoisted the little boy higher on her hip and followed Dillon out of my home.

I motioned at Tubby. "Go help them."

With him gone, I took a long look around, scanning for anything I might need. Then I walked outside and closed the door of my little home for the last time.

4

───────────

Finn had gathered everybody who wanted the protection I offered in a grassy field next to the RV park. Cecil, face pinched with fatigue, stood surrounded by several members of our group, fielding questions. He gave me a relieved wave.

Kenny Johnson jogged out to meet me. "What do you think you're going to do now?"

"Shut up, moron, and get into the circle," I said tonelessly. He wasn't worth wasting energy.

Finn hurried over, "Brad's doing some weird chakra shit over there. What am I supposed to be doing?"

"Get everybody who's not a carrier of the raven mark into the middle of the circle. Mash them together. The rest of us make a circle around them. We're going to try to protect them and ourselves at the same time." Fear tightened my chest.

Thunder rumbled in a cannonade now, one right after the other. Lightning strobed to life a sky full of human shaped shadows. Phantom dogs barked endlessly, snarling and yipping. Behind them droned that sound of engines running. What the hell was it?

I turned to speak to my people. "I've kept Oscar away from me with a circle before. All the Greggs will share power to hold the circle long enough to keep him away."

"What happens if it doesn't work?" Anita Johnson yelled, wrinkled lips creased.

I shook my head at her. If whatever Oscar was bringing down on us looked as bad as it sounded, we'd probably die.

"Gregg family, get ready," I yelled.

Shelly and Cecil took a position in front of the scared group of people we were trying to protect. Dillon and Finn stood next to them, holding hands.

They'd positioned their two children behind them and told Kenny and Anita to keep watch over them. I didn't trust Kenny or Anita any further than I could throw them, but I trusted they knew their lives would end, and badly, if they harmed a Gregg child.

Brad and Jadine worked their way out to the front of the group.

"I've cleansed the ground as best as I can." He shrugged.

I'd worked with Brad for a while now. The shrug meant it wasn't good enough.

Thunder shook the earth. Lightning flashed right after it. The shouts and the dogs barking faded in, and right back out. Behind them buzzed engines. They were close now, too close to quibble.

"It'll have to do," I told him. "Where's the consecrated dirt?"

Brad pointed to several pots of the dirt he and Jadine collected from cemeteries. It was one of their jobs to keep me in the stuff.

"Sprinkle it around the outside of the circle." I motioned at the clutch of horrified people.

Lightning flashed again. I tracked it through the sky and saw something that took my breath away. The shadow of a horseman flitted through the clouds. The whinny of a horse echoed in my head. A memory from a couple of months ago came roaring back in full detail.

It had been the day Tanner and I escaped Devil's Rest in a dead man's convertible. We'd parked the car on an anonymous street in Austin and abandoned it. As we started to walk away, I'd turned for one last look at the horror we'd survived, my mind on what happened to Lot's wife in the Holy Bible. In the gleaming paint, I'd seen a stormy sky, lightning flashing, and a horseman wearing Oscar's face charging toward me, sword raised.

It had been a warning. And I'd ignored it to have a honeymoon with Tanner, who was gone now. What a fool I'd been. Guilt opened a bottomless pit in my conscience. Unfortunately, it wasn't one I could leap into and escape. I had to stay and deal with my mistake.

Dread thudding at my temples, I grabbed another pot of the dirt and hurried to help Brad. When I got to Jadine, I spoke into her ear. "Take two steps forward, and I'm going to position you directly inside the circle. You can step backward, but don't go any further forward."

She nodded and held out her arm for me to direct her to the correct spot, nostrils flaring. She whispered in my ear. "I smell wet dog."

I sniffed the air but didn't have her well-developed sense of smell. "When I call the circle, lend your power. There'll be a sound, but you'll feel it in your body too."

She nodded, sightless eyes staring straight ahead.

I went through the same routine with everybody in our family, save the children, who clustered next to Anita.

Hannah stopped me. "Can I do this too?"

She'd gotten the raven tattoo a month earlier. I nodded. If she didn't help, she wouldn't hurt. Intent went a long way.

I pointed at Tubby. "Stay near Hannah. If things go to shit, help her."

He gave me only a slight nod, flinching as thunder shook the sky.

Once we had everybody in position, Orev flapped into the circle, cawing, his wings stretched wide. He landed on my shoulder and cawed softly into my ear. I didn't speak bird, but I knew the meaning. *Hurry.*

I gripped the stang harder, calling its power. My black opal awoke on my chest, sending waves of sharp magic through my body. The mantle awoke behind the thin layer of scar tissue imprisoning it. It pulsated warmth throughout my body. My fingertips tingled with magic.

The oncoming storm's wind changed and spoke to me. *Now*, it said. Lightning flashed again. The fire inside me latched onto it, channeling some of its wild power.

The rumble of hoofbeats, loud engines, and barking dogs blasted through my head. My magic rose in defense, making me lightheaded. I swayed on my feet.

"Peri Jean?" Brad called from a few feet to my left.

"Let's do it." I raised my stang and drew earth magic through my body, pushed it into the stang, and sent it outward. Light began to radiate from the deer antlers adorning the stang. Its brightness hurt my eyes, but I focused on it and took a deep breath.

"*I call to the power of the North*," I intoned. My family members repeated the line.

My raven tattoo woke up, burning as badly as it had the

day I got it inked onto my skin. Power thrummed through it and reached out to my family members, going deosil around the circle. Brad yelped as it hit him.

I said the next lines.

"I call to the power of the East,

I call to the power of the South

I call to the power of the West

Join me."

My family dutifully repeated each line. The power flowing through us got stronger and stronger with each one. Orev perched on my shoulder, so full of power he shook.

The points of the compass came to life with a flash. The wall of light coming out of my stang passed over my head and connected to each family member.

The thunder slammed closer, and the lightning cracked around us. The shouts of the men and the howls of the dogs warred with the engines behind them. Thunder shook the earth at short intervals.

"I call to the powers above and below," I yelled over the din.

The golden light of my growing circle passed over my body. Time to call the elements.

"I call on the element of water." The dew of humidity misted over me, dampening my clothes.

"I call to the element of air." Warm wind chased through the

bodies gathered in the circle, drawing an uneasy murmur from a few.

"I call to the element of earth." Energy flowed into me from the ground. I breathed it in, letting it flow into the deepest part of my magic. The mantle rose to meet it, twining with it.

"And I call the element of fire," I boomed, Orev cawing beside me.

Lightning cracked down right in front of the circle. Ignoring the screams of my friends and family, I pulled the power into me and fed the mantle with it. It pushed against the scar tissue, stretching it painfully.

I drove the stang into the circle of consecrated earth.

"As above, so below," I called out. *"Let this circle protect us from all harm."*

The golden wall of magic dove under the earth, searching for the roots of the world tree to encircle. I willed it to be so, pouring my already flagging energy into the task.

Lightning flashed in the dark sky. Through the haze of magic and the turbulent clouds, white flashed. I squinted. The clouds moved again. My stomach clenched at what I saw.

A gray horse with red eyes raced toward us. On its back rode a figure with stag horns, not so different from the ones attached to my stang, on his head. He held a sword aloft. The metal caught one of the RV camp's pole lights and illuminated the rider's face for one second. He was nothing but a skull covered with a few bits of dried flesh.

I'm coming for you, bitch, Oscar Rivera's voice boomed in my head. I jolted at the shock. Zora's words came back. *The dead men are coming.* So they were. Oscar had somehow fashioned himself into walking death.

A wall of cold crept up through my feet, sending scrabbling fingers in search of my heart. The horse's hoofbeats shook my whole body. Oscar raised his body off the horse as it sped toward us. I pushed harder at my magic, willing the circle to close.

"Peri Jean, it's not going all the way. There's not enough power." Brad's voice shook with fear.

I pushed with every bit of magic I had. Fatigue darkened the edges of my vision.

Orev let out a distressed screech. *Not working.*

He was right. It wasn't going to work. Without full control of the mantle, I didn't have enough power to encircle and protect this many people.

Thunder crashed, and the clouds opened again to emit another dark figure on a horse, this one white. Horse and rider galloped in the midst of white dogs the size of ponies. The dog's eyes glowed like red searchlights and matched the burning tips of their ears. It looked like they'd been dipped in a vat of hellfire head first. The rider's voice invaded my thoughts.

"*Wanna fuck?*" Michael Gage snickered.

My skin chilled.

The clouds fell open now. As more riders and horses came out of the sky. Their voices threatened to drown out my thoughts. Joey Holze. Nash Redmond. Colton Starr. Camden DeVoss. Veronica Spinelli. Their malicious laughter invaded my mind.

The sound of the roaring engines shook the sky, louder even than the thunder. Finally I recognized it. Motorcycles.

Headlights reflected off the clouds, and motorcycles with their dead riders roared from the sky. King Tolliver rode out front, a skeleton with peeling flesh, only recognizable by his big horse teeth.

His nasty voice vibrated inside my head. "*Bet you thought you'd never see me again.*"

Fear circuited through me, making me even more exhausted.

The other motorcycle riders' presences came into my awareness. Trenchcoat. Other Six Guns I'd helped kill without even knowing their names.

A speckled white horse descended behind them. Its rider had a familiar mane of brown hair flowing from it.

My throat closed. No. It couldn't be. I squinted at the rider. It wore the same peeling skull as the other horseman, making it unrecognizable.

A familiar voice invaded my mind. *"Hey, you little shit. Miss your momma?"*

Sweat tickled my scalp, and my knees went to jelly. I froze.

The blast of a horn shook the earth. Oscar's charge made my teeth vibrate. *"Kill them all, strip them of their power."*

I broke from my thrall.

"Run!" I screamed and yanked my stang from the earth.

———

People scattered all over the RV park. Dillon and Finn ran next to Anita and Kenny, all of them trying to get the kids out of danger. Brad grabbed Jadine, threw her over his shoulder, and ran after Dillon and Finn. I looked for Cecil and Shelly but couldn't see them in the confusion.

Panic settled into my chest, freezing me to the spot. Cecil needed help. He was no longer strong enough to fight anybody. I stood on my tiptoes. The crowd thinned a little more, and I saw Tubby pushing Cecil and Shelly along. He'd defied my order in the best possible way. I let out a breath.

Hannah appeared at my side. We joined hands and ran as hard as we could. Since we both smoked like chimneys, what we did was more like stumble along, gasping and coughing.

A woman's scream cut through the roar of chaos. "No, no, please no."

"That's Lorrie." Hannah yanked me toward the commotion.

We rounded a corner to see a horse looming over Hannah's friend from the face painting tent. Joey Holze. I knew him even though he had the same skull head as Oscar.

Then he raised his sword. As he did, the metal seemed to be turn to white, crackling light. He swung. Lorrie tried to jump out of the way, but the blade dragged across her throat. Hannah screamed as her friend tumbled to the ground, writhing, her neck a gaping wound. Lorrie's life's blood spread on the ground around her.

My stomach dropped. Shock froze me to the spot. Hannah tried to run toward her friend. That cut through my revulsion.

I yanked her back. "It's too late."

And it was. Lorrie's eyes were already glazing over.

Joey Holze swung off his horse and leaned over Lorrie, who'd had a little spark of telepathy. His sides expanded as he inhaled. A glow rose off Lorrie. I squinted at it. What was that? Her soul? Then the mantle flipped over in my chest, and I knew. It was her magical core. Joey inhaled again. Lorrie's magical core went straight into Joey. He stiffened and seemed to expand. When he raised his head, a little more flesh covered his face.

Sick realization flooded me. Joey had eaten Lorrie's magical core, maybe her soul as well, the same way I had consumed Loretta Nell Grimes's a couple of months earlier. And it had nourished him, probably made him stronger.

Another scream came, this one male. Hannah and I turned to see Early Ramey running at top speed, King Tolliver in hot pursuit from the back of his motorcycle. King caught up to Early, pulled a glowing white sword from nowhere, and used it to lop off Early's head. The poor teenager's body fell. His head rolled a couple of feet, hair flopping, and bounced against a tree.

King pushed down the kickstand of his motorcycle, marched over to Early's still form and inhaled the magical core. The same thing Joey had done. Strips of flesh appeared on King's skull. Cold sweat broke out over me.

Despite the fear, a little thread of hate glowed to life. King had cut Early down the same way I'd stomp a roach in my RV. As though sensing my thoughts, King faced us.

We snarled at each other as guilt seeped through me. I'd been responsible for the people who traveled with us. Now I'd failed Early and Lorrie, and judging by the screams around me, many others.

The stitch of hate reddened and grew. It called my magic. I let it come until hot energy vibrated through my body. The black opal burned on my chest. Heat grew in my fingertips until they throbbed. When the pain became so intense I could stand it no longer, I threw it at King.

A flash of light told me my aim had been true. King let out a screech of pain and toppled over. His blue motorcycle landed on top of him. Just as I thought him dead, King pushed the motorcycle off and picked himself up. He turned his skull head to face me, and I swear on my sweet dead grandmother, the fucker was smiling. He mounted the motorcycle and made it roar to life.

What the hell? I'd killed him. If not that, hurt him bad. And here he was acting like nothing had happened.

King raised his sword.

I quit thinking and ran. Hannah and I raced for my camper, not because it was safe but because I was out of ideas. A short distance away, Dillon and Finn ran next to Kenny and Anita. Both men carried a screaming child. My mother leaned forward on her horse as she closed in on the group, sword of doom raised for the kill.

Hannah and I screamed "Dillon!"

Dillon glanced at us, and we both pointed. The young woman saw the problem and tackled her husband, screaming at the same time for Kenny, who carried her other child, to drop to the ground. It all happened in a split second, right as my mother, Barbara Willis Mace, swung her sword.

Anita, for some reason, did not drop to the ground. She

turned to face the horseman, thin lipped mouth open in a scream. She never got it out. The sword completed its arc and sliced cleanly through her neck. Anita's head thumped to the ground. Kenny wailed his grief, let go of Zander, and lunged at the horse. Finn wrestled him away. They all ran for their lives.

I stood frozen among the carnage, barely hearing Hannah's screams for me to keep going. Everything I'd lived for the past few months was being destroyed right before my eyes.

My mother climbed off her horse, skull tilted in a way I remembered from when she smirked. She leaned over Anita and inhaled the poor woman's soul. Even though Anita hadn't had any supernatural abilities, every soul has a little spark of magic. My mother's armor filled out a little at the breasts and hips. Her mane of hair grew thicker and richer in color. She mounted her horse and charged toward us.

My emotions regressed to that of a child. Mommy was mad again and would hurt me. I grabbed Hannah's hand and ran for my life. In my flight to escape my rampaging mother, I saw things that would haunt me forever.

Snarling red-eyed, red-eared dogs attacked an RV and ripped open the sides, the metal emitting pained screeches as it bent. They set upon the elderly couple huddled inside and tore them to bits in a matter of seconds.

A horseman set another RV on fire. This one belonged to Noah and Gus, the couple Tanner had played cards with. I took a few steps toward it. The RV exploded in a burst of fire. Gus and Noah streamed out, engulfed in flames, waving their arms, their pitiful screams thin in the air as they ran in circles and finally fell.

The horsemen lapped up their souls and grew stronger.

My eyes fell on Oscar Rivera in the middle of it all. The antler horns on his headdress vibrated as he laughed.

I searched my power. It was there, but weak. Trying to recover. The failed circle and blasting the horsemen had taken up too much energy. I needed rest, and a lot of it. But I didn't have time for that.

I called to my magic. It felt like scraping the bottom off an empty mayonnaise jar. I pulled at the tiny thread of energy, body aching with the effort. Orev responded from a tree. It would have to be enough. I set my sights on Oscar and started walking.

Hannah yanked me back. "You can't. You're so tired, you're holding your side. You're not strong enough."

I faced her. "But do you see my death?"

Hannah took a deep breath and let her shoulders relax as she called her power of foreseeing death. She searched my face. "No."

"Then go find the rest of the family. Stay with them. If I don't come back, call Mysti." I took off toward Oscar.

Seeming to sense my approach, he turned the horse but

otherwise did not respond. I finally got a good look at Oscar's return to the land of living.

His head, a skull partially covered with tissue and sinew, had living eyes. Jewels sparkled from his antler headdress. Silver armor sparkling with magic protected whatever there was of his body. The metal of his sword flashed pure white-silver.

"Well, well, well. If it isn't my favorite dumb bitch." His beautiful voice caressed my mind. If I allowed it, he could use his voice to lull me into hypnosis. Good thing I was too mad for that.

"I'm going to kill you, Oscar," I hollered, still walking toward him, still calling power.

I called to the power of my ancestors. They surrounded me, witches in blood if not practice. Their whispers tickled at my brain. The energy strengthened, and I channeled it into a ball. I'd throw it at Oscar. It would hurt him, maybe buy me some advantage. I reared back like a star baseball pitcher.

Then I lay on the ground, on my back, staring at the sky and confused as hell. The space in front of me rippled as though something otherworldly was hiding in it. My third eye tingled in the center of my forehead. I opened it.

The hag, the one I'd banished from Hannah and bestowed on King Tolliver came into view. It smiled, barbed teeth slick with spit, and straddled my chest. Its bony hands closed around my neck. Because we'd once shared my body, its thoughts came to me.

King Tolliver wasn't as tough as you thought. He became depressed rather quickly and ate some glass. Took him a while to die. That was fun, but then I had to go find something else to do. And I do hate you with a passion unlike any other.

"Did you let Oscar out?" I thought back.

Of course, stupid. He offered me the world. A place of leadership in his new kingdom. The hag pressed harder, cutting off my air supply.

I plucked at its arms, but there was no way I could overpower a supernatural being. Was there?

From somewhere near Oscar's deep voice intoned, "Choke her out so I can get at the magical core. It's mine, remember?"

The hag redoubled its efforts. The need for oxygen beat at my chest. Black spots danced in my eyes.

The mantle pushed at the scar tissue, straining toward the hag. My chest ached with the force of it. That snapped me awake. The mantle pushed forward again. Pain flashed through me.

The mantle wanted the nasty little hag's power. The knowledge came to me as though it whispered in my ear. I'd eat the hag's magical core instead of it pulling mine out and giving it to Oscar.

I sent a blast of magic into the hag, shocking it. Light flashed behind its awful, black eyes. The ugly little thing screamed in pain.

A hunched figure ran toward me and kicked the hag, knocking it cockeyed on my chest. Cecil reared his shiny old man shoe back and kicked the hag again, this time in the head. Still it clung to my neck.

"Get it, baby," he gasped through his effort, clutching his chest through his shirt. Cecil's heart. His poor, weak heart. Would it get him through this?

I couldn't worry about that right now. Ignoring the need to breathe, I bucked underneath the hag, throwing it off balance. Magic heated every inch of my body. My hands lit. I grabbed the hag's arms and sent the fire into them. The arms blackened and began to smoke. Their owner let out a piercing scream.

Orev cawed from behind me. His wings rustled, both inside my head and out. My hands and Orev's feet hit the hag's chest at the same time. The force of our blow knocked the hag backward and off me. It tried to run.

I sat up and snatched at the scrabbling thing, pulled it to me, and held it down with my knees. Orev and I tore the little monster's chest open as it screamed. Its magic pulsed right next to its heart, black and malignant. Orev darted forward and plucked out the magical core with his beak. He bit it in half and consumed his end like a particularly good snake.

Without letting myself think about it too much, I popped the end he'd left me into my mouth and swallowed. The taste of blood filled my mouth, and the scent of metal filled my nose.

My magic ate what had powered the hag. The beast's power flowed through me, so great it felt as though I'd burst. It blackened the edges of my vision and throbbed inside me like a wound. Then it evened out.

I turned my attention back to the hag's still body. Rubbery skin flayed open to reveal a cracked ribcage. With the magical core gone, all that remained was the heart.

Crystal encrusted, the heart glowed ruby-red. It gave off its own weird light. One that faded with each passing second. Orev pushed around me and plucked it out.

"Don't touch it," I barked.

Orev dropped the nasty organ on the ground, where it rolled, glinting in the weak moonlight. Despite what I'd told Orev, I grabbed the thing and stuffed it in my pocket. Tanner had taught me these things had value.

The hag's small body dried and blackened within seconds. I shoved it away from me, finished with it.

Then I stood and settled my gaze on Oscar. He sat frozen on his mount, sword held at half-mast. Too shocked to move? Good. I'd kill him where he sat.

"I'm gonna kill you, Oscar," I growled and stomped toward him, wiping the blood from my mouth with one arm.

He showed me his bony middle finger. "You're too dumb. Remember where you threw the runes? You might as well have handed them to me gift wrapped." He waited for me to catch on.

My skin went cold. The pieces clicked together. That deep, deep hole where we'd thrown the runes had been the place where Oscar had hidden his soul. Embarrassment burned through me.

Seeing that I'd caught on, Oscar began to laugh. Between guffaws, he managed to gasp, "What kind of moron does that?"

Embarrassment at my colossal mistake burned through me. Fury followed. I might have screwed up once, but I'd make it right.

I called my fire. It came, hotter and more willing than normal, fueled by the hag's inhuman magic. Heat gathered in my hands, burning from the inside out, so painful I wanted to scream. But I couldn't allow myself the luxury of pain. Not in front of Oscar. With a mighty push, I sent the fire to Oscar.

It formed a bright ball and flew right at his head. He spurred his horse and whirled out of its path. The fireball changed directions and followed. Oscar spurred the horse harder, trying to escape the flames. He was too slow. It slammed into his back. Oscar exploded in a flash of light.

The riderless horse galloped away. From somewhere in the

dark night came the sound of a horn. The flat note blasted against my skin, vibrating.

The barking of the dogs stopped. So did the screeches of metal from the other horseman tearing open RVs like sardine cans so they could kill the occupants and absorb their power. The pounding of horse hooves rose as did the motorcycle engines. A flash of lightning caught them disappearing into the clouds, the dogs running behind them.

"How did that not kill Oscar?" I muttered to Orev.

My raven familiar didn't bother to answer. He perched on a post, swaying back and forth. He let out a pained squawk and keeled over on one side. Both legs stuck straight out.

Then I felt it. The hag's poisonous magic swelled inside me like an expanding balloon. The scar tissue spell stretched with it. Pain lanced through me, hot and intense.

I fell to my knees, clutching my chest, the same way I'd seen Cecil do. The agony crested, and my bowels loosened. The buzz from the pole lights got so loud it vibrated my eardrums. Blackness rimmed the edges of my vision and spread until it was all I saw.

5

A cool breeze came out of the blackness to chill my sweat-coated skin. A freezing hand stroked the hair back from my brow. One icy thumb swiped over my forehead.

"You aren't dead, so wake up." Priscilla Herrera's voice sounded almost sympathetic.

I shook off the blackness and blinked. Candlelight jumped on rough-hewn walls. Glassy pain ripped through my chest. I hissed and writhed.

Cool water dripped over my face. A freezing hand delivered light slaps to my cheek.

"Wake up," she said, and slapped some more.

I forced my eyes open. Priscilla Herrera wiped my face with a wet cloth made of some rough material. She dripped more cool water on my face.

"That was a very brave thing you did." Her voice carried

none of the recriminations it usually did. "But now we have to deal with the consequences."

"Where am I?" I took in my surroundings. I lay on a long table surrounded by animal skulls with candles affixed to them.

"You think Samantha is the only one with a hiding place?" Priscilla Herrera raised one thick brow, dark eyes sparkling. "Of course, Samantha with her games and silly fancies created a place out of a story. But I don't work that way. This is a real place, the place I lived with my husband and raised my children."

I took a closer look. Sure enough, we were inside the cabin in Gaslight City where Priscilla Herrera had spent her final hours. My mother murdered my father in front of this house.

The pressure returned to my chest. My insides seemed too big for my body. I curled my legs, barely able to breathe.

Priscilla turned away from me and hurried to the pot hanging in her hearth. She dipped out a ladleful and poured it into a cup.

She hurried back to me and put the cup to my lips. "This will ease it."

The liquid smelled like boiled donkey foreskin mixed with a dash of camphor. I sipped it because anything was better than this pain. The liquid numbed my lips and made my tongue tingle. I swallowed and took another sip.

"That's enough. Now we'll see if that monster's magical core kills you." Priscilla sat down on a stool.

The pain in my chest eased. It was still there, but it seemed further away, less immediate. Without it clouding my vision, I noticed Priscilla wore a smile, a real one that crinkled her dark eyes at the edges. She was pretty in a scary way.

"What are you so happy about? You said I might die." I had never seen Priscilla smile like this.

"You won't die. I was being facetious." She patted my chest.

"Where's Orev?" I hoped we hadn't left him back at that RV park. He'd been sick too.

"He's resting." She gestured at a perch near the ceiling of the cabin. Orev stood still with one leg raised, his usual sleeping posture.

The pain had exhausted me. I fell into a light doze. A while later, Priscilla woke me and gave me more stinky water to sip.

Something popped inside my chest. Relief flooded through me, closely followed by voices. That of the hag. That of Oscar.

This had happened when I ate Loretta Nell Grimes's spirit. I'd seen bits and flashes of her life.

Priscilla's voice broke into my thoughts. "Can you make out what they're saying?"

I listened, but only heard bits and flashes. "Revenge against the entire Gregg family, taking what's mine... nothing that makes sense."

"Try harder," she grumbled.

I concentrated on the voices. It was like listening in on a conversation in another room. I squeezed my eyes shut and pushed myself toward them.

Oscar sat before a fire. The multicolored stars in the night sky told me he was in the dark outposts. He pointed to the deer antler headdress he'd been wearing when he attacked.

He said, "With this, I will rise to the power worthy of me. We will walk the earth as something neither alive nor dead. You'll all rise to power with me. The first thing we'll need is the power of the Gregorius Witch."

I repeated what I'd heard, body chilling. That name again. The one Mohawk called me when I beat him out of making me his brood mare. Hearing it this time, in conjunction with someone wanting to kill me, didn't thrill me the way it had before.

Priscilla's nostrils flared, but she didn't look particularly surprised. She handed me the cup. "Drink the rest of this and listen to me. It's time for you to learn who you are and about your destiny. There's no time left to ease you into it."

I stiffened. "You call the way we've been doing this easy?"

She slitted her eyes at me. "The being you call Mohawk—

you shouldn't make fun of him, you know—called you the Gregorius Witch." She settled her dark gaze on me. "You've never questioned what that meant. Why is that?" Those dark eyes bored into me, chilling me, threatening me.

I shook my head and took another drink of ass water. The term Gregorius Witch both excited and terrified me. Things like that usually stung like a bitch if you prodded them too much.

"Sting like a bitch or not, you're going to find out tonight. You must understand this part of your history so you'll better grasp what is at stake." She brushed strands of hair that had strayed from her bun off her face. It made her look normal, like someone's favorite aunt or grandmother instead of a mean old witch who never cut me any slack.

"The Gregorius Witch was the child of an old god and a human sorceress." She watched my face, her mouth curved in amusement.

"Like Mohawk wanted to have with me." My mouth puckered with the disgust I still felt at the idea.

"Yes, that's why Mohawk wanted to sire a child with you so badly. The child the two of you made together would be even more powerful than one with a full-blooded human." Her eyes sparkled with amusement. "Dark Beings are a randy bunch. It's not so uncommon. But it's not so easy to make it work, either. Most of those children are not viable, mentally or physically."

"But the Gregorius Witch did live." I tried to imagine what

sort of woman she'd have been. My mind supplied a woman with whipping black hair. Maybe she'd had olive skin and dark eyes like mine.

"Live she did. Born in the time of gladiators, she lived for more years than is normal for a human. She was power incarnate, feared and respected. She was a sorceress to emperors and chieftains." Priscilla warmed to her story, face more animated than I'd ever seen. "It was the Gregorius Witch who took on Orev as a familiar. She found him with a broken wing and nursed him back to health. They made a blood bargain, bound themselves to each other for eternity." She sat perfectly still as she told this story, eyes sparkling. "The Gregorius Witch made the bargain with Sol for her power, the mantle, to be passed from generation to generation."

Something occurred to me. "How could you possibly know all this? You're talking about something that happened thousands of years ago. It probably doesn't even exist on record."

Fire kindled to life in Priscilla's dark eyes, and I recoiled, regretting my question immediately.

She leaned into my face, and I smelled grave dust on her breath. "You'll know every detail of this story when the mantle is yours because then your story will be added to it. Only the most worthy take on the mantle. Only the most worthy have their stories added." She turned away from me, sides expanding and contracting.

"I'm sorry." My cheeks flamed. This was the nicest she'd ever been, and I'd screwed it up.

She turned back. "No. I am sorry. It was Leticia, your grandmother, who chose not to prepare you for this. She chose instead to run from it. And here we are."

I thought hard, wanting to please this hard woman again. "So if I can absorb the mantle, I'll have half the power of a half-god?"

A slow smile spread across Priscilla's face. "No. Everything all of us have been before you will belong to you. Everything."

I finally understood what Oscar was up to. "If Oscar manages to take it from me, he'll have it all."

She nodded.

"But how? The mantle can only be passed to one of my descendants. Oscar is not that." If I could get out of this on a technicality, I would.

Priscilla, who'd have normally given me a rough rebuke, only gave me a sad shake of her head. "To pass it to someone living, that is true. It would drive anyone else mad or kill them. But Oscar straddles the realm of the living and the dead. He can't be killed, and, quite frankly, he's already mad."

I hunched over, dug my elbows into my knees, and cupped my cheeks in the palms of my hands. Each new thing I learned made it all a little worse.

Priscilla put a gentle, yet freezing, hand one my forearm. "Take heart. Oscar has had months to work on this. You are only now finding out…"

"Months after I threw the runes right into that hole with him." I nearly shouted. The magnitude of that mistake would haunt me for a long time.

"It's not your fault," she hissed with such fierceness I flinched. "You did the wrong thing, yes. But even I didn't know. Now you'll fix it."

I took the last sip of the nasty water and handed the cup back to Priscilla. She took it with a nod. Pain now gone, I sat up and scooted to the edge of the table.

I had a question. "What happens if Oscar gains the mantle's power?"

Priscilla leaned forward, eyes locked on mine. "After he annihilates everyone you love and steals their power to fuel his mission, he'll bring war to the human race. He will open the gates between veils so *everything* can cross. There'll be anarchy and destruction."

She let that soak in. It would be the end of the world as I knew it. Innocent people. Mothers. Fathers. Their children. Dead because Oscar was an asshole.

Priscilla got off her stool with a grunt. "It's time for you to go back to your body. Are you ready?"

I stood. Orev dropped from the ceiling to land on my shoulder.

Priscilla walked to the door and held it open. I passed into the night and my vision faded to dark.

Something struck my face.

"Wake up," Shelly yelled.

I hauled myself out of the blackness and sucked in a deep breath. The pole lights still buzzed, but the hum was now bearable.

"She's coming around. Don't hit her again," Finn said.

Shelly ignored him and delivered another stinging slap to my cheek.

Not wanting to get hit again, I forced my eyes open. Shelly, Cecil's wife and my great-aunt by marriage, straddled me. The glow from the pole lights bleached her already light hair into a hazy glow floating around her head. She reared back her hand for another slam.

"No," I managed to whisper and shaded my eyes from the harsh light with one shaking hand.

Finn hauled Shelly off me. He leaned into my face, close enough for me to see the tears streaking his cheeks. "Wake up. Please wake up."

"What happened?" My voice came out in barely a whisper.

"You just passed out," he said.

"She stopped breathing," Shelly shouted from the sidelines.

Had I died? The thought sent icicles down my spine. I glanced at Hannah. She gave me an unsure smile and approached. She offered her hand. I took it. Both of us grunting with the effort, she pulled me to my feet. My knees wobbled. Hannah slipped one arm around me to hold me upright. My entire family crowded around me.

Zora ran to me and hugged my legs, staring up at me with that huge grin only kids can pull off. "I touched you so you'd wake up."

I knelt and hugged her back. Zora no longer moved that kind of energy, but her touch might have helped heal me.

"Thank you," I whispered and kissed one velvety soft cheek. She gave me a slobbery kiss on the lips.

From my position next to my young cousin, I said, "I've learned what Oscar wants. The mantle. If he succeeds, he'll ascend to the power of a half-god and open a rift between this world and the dark outposts. He'll bring apocalypse to the human race."

Several mouths fell open.

"How are we supposed to fight against that?" Dillon came forward, took her daughter's hand, and tried to pull her away from me.

Zora let out a screech like an animal caught in a snare. I gave her a light push toward Dillon. She shoved my hand away with another squall. Knowing when to quit, I let her be.

"I don't know how we're supposed to fight, but we're going to figure it out." I turned away and began surveying the wreckage of Sanctuary.

What I saw tightened my throat and made my heart ache. One thought floated through my head: gone, all gone.

———

Cecil came to stand next to me. Side by side, we took in the destruction.

The RV park was small. Owned by friends of Cecil's, it was a no frills, off the grid place. A place for people like us.

Sanctuary, with its dozen and some change RVs took up most of the spots. There'd been a few campers outside our group, but they'd stayed to themselves and seemed to desire the same kind of privacy Sanctuary did. Now they'd paid for being in the same place as us.

Every RV in the park looked like scrap metal, unrecognizable as dwellings. Smoke rose from a few.

I counted my family's heads. "Where are Brad and Jadine?"

As I waited for an answer, my mind helpfully played a movie of the killings I'd witnessed. Bands of fear closed around my heart. Cecil approached.

"They're fine. Just seeing what they can salvage. This isn't Jadine's first rodeo." Cecil spoke with a little smile, proud of his adopted daughter for picking herself up and moving on.

"How many dead?" I'd seen a total of eight people killed. No doubt there were more.

"Everybody's dead except our family, Hannah and Tubby, and Kenny." Shelly pressed her well made up lips into a grim line.

We exchanged shocked glances. Tears blurred the edges of my vision. Faces of the people we'd lost danced through my head, their last pleas for help clawing at my conscience. I gulped back a sob. Oscar and his cronies would die by my hand, and die screaming. Those dead people had been my responsibility. I'd make this right if it was the last thing I did.

Finn picked up Zander. "We gotta get out of here before the cops come. This place is out of the way, but it ain't another planet. You know somebody heard that racket."

"You're right." I nodded my throbbing head.

Hannah stared out over the rubble, her expression sick. "What about police reports? What about insurance claims? I had quite a bit of money in that tore up motorhome over there."

I turned to Cecil. "Papaw?"

Thank goodness he was still the leader of Sanctuary. I had no idea how to balance being an outlaw and collecting insurance money on stuff we legitimately owned.

Cecil stared out at the mess of our lives. Tears brimmed in his eyes. Sanctuary had been his parents' conception. All of it dashed to shards in ten minutes.

He spoke softly, voice trembling. "I'll call my lawyer. Get him on it. But for now, get moving. I got a bug-out plan for us."

He popped me on the shoulder and shuffled away. It was my job to push everybody along.

I raised my voice. "Salvage what you can, see if your vehicle still runs."

"Meet back here in 15 minutes," Shelly yelled.

Tubby and I jogged to the spot where my RV had been parked next to Hannah's motorhome. The top of my RV was caved in as though a giant had stepped on it. The metal on the sides had been pulled back like the top of a tin can. The door hung on one hinge. The step had been torn off and flung who knew where.

Tubby leapt up on the threshold and held out one skinny hand. I used it to climb up. We took in the ruin in silence.

The bed had been ripped to shreds. Pieces of sheet and fluffs of mattress stuffing floated in the air. Dishes, toiletries, clothes covered the floor. The sight reminded me of a landfill. The whole thing carried the strong odor of urine.

I let my shoulders hunch forward. The RV had been my

home only a few months, but I'd loved it because it was the first place I'd ever lived in that was all mine.

After several seconds, Tubby nudged me with one bony elbow. "Come on, girl. Time's wasting."

He was right. I took hurried steps across the sagging floor. "My witch pack is in the closet by the bed. My trunk with my supplies is underneath the board the mattress sat on. That's all I need."

Tubby and I made quick work of getting out the only two things I couldn't leave behind. My truck had deep ruts scratched in both sides. All four wheels had been hosed down with dog pee. All that was okay if it still ran. I went around to the front and had to stop myself from sinking to the ground. The hood stood open, and pieces of the engine scattered the ground.

Miracle of all miracles, Tubby's trashy Cutlass hadn't even been touched. Maybe the raiders hadn't thought it worth their time. He opened the trunk and lifted my things into it.

I put one hand on his arm. "Why don't you go back to Gaslight City? Staying with us is only going to put you in danger."

He snorted and puffed out his chest. "You my friend, ain't you? I ain't going nowhere."

Some emotion, made of equal parts sorrow and gratitude,

swelled in my chest. The muscles, still tender from almost dying of hag poisoning, ached with it.

In my silence, Tubby slammed the trunk shut.

"Let's go hurry Hannah along." I ran the few steps to Hannah's fancy motorhome.

Hannah sat on the ground by the wreck of her motorhome with a blank stare on her face. The metal side of Hannah's motorhome had been ripped off, just as mine had. Long scratches covered the interior walls. Her clothes, much more expensive than mine, lay in a damp snarl on the dirt.

"They dragged my clothes out and *pissed* on them." She raised her head to stare at me. It was too dark to see her eyes, but I knew the way her jaw jutted out. Angry, ready to fight.

"Is anything still usable?" I hated to even ask.

Hannah drew out her two handguns and showed them to me. "I don't even have a vehicle to drive."

"Me either. I'm riding with Tubby." I raised my eyebrows at him.

"We can all ride together," Tubby said quickly.

Cecil, Shelly, and Dillon approached. Shelly had Zora by the hand. The little girl dragged the older woman along, her little face set in determination.

Zora yanked her hand out of Shelly's grip and launched herself at me. I managed to catch and lift her, but I staggered. Tubby kept me upright, but the weakness scared me.

"We're leaving now," she yelled in my face, delighted by all the excitement.

"Looks like it," I told her and turned my attention to Cecil. "Where's Kenny? Shelly said he's still alive. Is that right?"

Another wave of dizziness passed through me. I tried to set Zora on the ground, but she locked her legs around my waist like a wrestler.

Dillon approached me, tapped Zora, and held out her hands. Zora turned her face away. Dillon shook her head at the little girl. "You better mind me, baby."

To me, Dillon said, "Kenny's real upset. Finn and Zander are with him now, trying to get him moving."

Dillon finally pulled Zora off me. The little girl screeched. Dillon pretended not to hear and said, "I think we're gonna have to leave Kenny here."

"We can't leave him for the cops," Cecil snapped. He pointed at me. "Get him to come on or put a bullet in his head. Now."

I froze at the finality of Cecil's orders. He glared at me to let me know he meant every word. I staggered toward the only other voices I could hear in the still night.

I met Brad and Jadine before I'd gone far. Brad carried a laundry basket of personal belongings. Jadine had one hand on Brad's arm and her aluminum cane in the other, but she looked stronger than Brad right then.

Brad looked shell-shocked. The laundry basket shook in his hands. I remembered Mysti telling me about the way she and Brad had moved from foster home to foster home with their worldly belongings in a garbage bag. This must have brought back sad memories.

"Y'all all right?" I peeked into the laundry basket and saw mostly electronics. My head swam from the motion. I needed rest, and I didn't see it happening for a while.

"Everything we had is gone." Brad spoke through tight lips.

"Do you still have a working vehicle?" If everybody's vehicles had been turned to worthless piles of metal, I didn't know how we'd get out of here.

Brad gave his head an angry shake.

"Don't worry," Jadine told her husband. "We'll get it figured out. Papaw'll know what to do." Jadine didn't sound at all concerned. She'd lived this way all her life. Maybe I needed to take a lesson from her.

"*Papaw* can't bring back our home and our truck." Brad started to stomp away.

I grabbed his arm, pulled him back, and spoke into his ear. "Cut the attitude. Nobody plays that crap here."

Brad's head snapped back as though I'd struck him, but he gave me a slow nod and began walking, Jadine following.

Once he got a few steps away, he said something in a sweet tone of voice. Jadine giggled.

Brad had become my family by marriage only a few months earlier. I still wasn't sure this was the right place for him, but I'd promised Mysti Whitebyrd, his sister and my mentor and friend, that I'd make sure he got treated fairly. Most of the help I gave him landed in the "quit acting like a baby" category.

I left Brad and Jadine, hurrying along until I found Kenny crying with both hands over his face. Finn stood next to him, his son Zander on one hip.

Finn waited until I got close and whispered in my ear. "I've got my pistol if it comes to that."

Finn had spent his whole life with Cecil. Of course, he'd know the orders when it was time to bug out.

My stomach somersaulted, and bile rose up the back of my throat. I put on my leader face and sat down next to Kenny.

"I saw what happened, and we're all sorry. Anita was one of us. You are too." I held my breath against the odor of his fear sweat.

Kenny cried harder. I felt for him. If I knew Tanner was dead, it would kill me. Because of that, Kenny deserved what kindness I could manage to give him.

"You have to get up. Cecil says all of us have to go now." I put my arm around Kenny. His b.o. wreathed my head.

Kenny leaned his head on my shoulder, tears immediately soaking through the thin material of my T-shirt. My consciousness wavered again. I squeezed my eyes shut for several seconds. Once I had control of myself, I lit two cigarettes and pressed one between Kenny's lips.

"Cecil said I have to get you moving before the police come." I couldn't quite make myself articulate Cecil's orders. I didn't think I'd ever be able to give that kind of order.

Kenny's tears cut off, and his head snapped up. His eyes searched mine, and his mouth dropped open. He'd been with Cecil long enough to understand too. He seemed to get control of himself and glanced around us, taking in the smoking trashed RVs, and the piles of still bodies.

"What about Anita? Do we have time to find her...body?" He turned to me, dumb eyes wide and almost innocent.

Finn and I exchanged a glance. I raised my eyebrows. He shook his head. I rolled my eyes.

"Listen. Sooner or later—probably sooner—somebody's gonna come nosing around. Once that happens, the blue light special is gonna descend on this place like stink on shit." I hated the way I sounded, but this had been a long, nasty twenty-four hours.

Kenny took a wadded bandana out of his pocket, honked into it, and replaced it. He stood and staggered toward the rest of our group. Finn took his arm and led him along.

I stood, and my vision filled with black dots. The hag's memories played in my subconscious as I absorbed it. The dizziness faded, but I needed sleep. I hurried toward Tubby's car.

My eyes fell on a still figure. One of the dead. I took a closer look. The Mystical Johann. Poor son of a bitch. The man lay on his stomach. From his back protruded several long, skinny lengths of rebar.

Queenie's reading came back. *The Tower. Death. The Ten of Swords.*

This had been the big upheaval. And I'd either die or be changed forever by beating it.

6

———

We raced around trying to figure out how to best make use of the few working vehicles we had left.

Cecil and Shelly commandeered Kenny's monster four-door truck, which had somehow escaped damage. Dillon and Zora crowded with them. Brad, with more resourcefulness than I'd credited him, drove up in an old Suburban. Its owner was probably dead. Finn climbed in with them, Zander on his lap. They all hightailed it out of the RV park.

Hannah didn't want to leave her expensive motorhome. She stood in front of it, arms hugging herself, and looked like she might want to cry. Tubby marched over to her and put his arm around her.

"It's a thing. Let it go." He turned and walked toward the Cutlass.

A few seconds later, Hannah followed him. I was already

in the backseat, so she had to sit in the passenger seat. She sat gingerly, as though Tubby might do something inappropriate any second.

He started the Cutlass and said, "I'll cut off your fingers if you fuck with my radio."

He turned the Latino rap back on and drove. On the way out, I forced myself not to look back.

We stopped at a twenty-four hour discount store and bought what we needed to get through the next days. Hannah complained mightily that all the jeans were made for short people. That's when I knew she'd make it.

Back in the car, Tubby turned to me. "Papaw said he gave you GPS coordinates for where we're headed."

Tubby's calling Cecil Papaw, as the rest of us did, stopped me. It was usually reserved for members of Sanctuary. But Tubby had saved Cecil's life. Maybe that helped him make the cut. For now.

I handed Tubby my phone and called out the passcode. He programmed the mapping function to give us directions to our destination.

"That's in the middle of nowhere," Hannah said. "Is Papaw sure there's somewhere to stay?"

"If he says there is, there is." I trusted that much to be true.

Tubby started driving. I lay on the back seat of Tubby's Cutlass and tried to relax. Hannah and Tubby talked quietly in the front seat. The dashboard lights played over their faces. Watching them interact, exchanging insults, laughing at each other, somehow helped my mind unspool. I drifted somewhere between waking and sleeping.

The rough buzz of the motorcycles became part of my half-dreaming state. My imagination put Wade on one of the motorcycles, leaned way back, the muscles of his forearms taut under their jungle of tattoos. Thinking of Wade no longer woke up feelings of love lost. I only wished my old friend well, hoped he could avoid Corman and stay alive. Once I ended this mess with Oscar, Corman needed to go away permanently. Few people deserved it more.

Then I remembered the ghost version of the Six Gun Revolutionaries Motorcycle Club. My eyes snapped open, and I sat bolt upright and stared out the back window. Motorcycle headlights burned in the dark night, right on the Cutlass's bumper. The rumbling engines shook the car. I squinted at the darkness, searching for the horsemen. But clouds covered the moon, and a murky fog rose from the highway.

"Oscar's back already?" Queasy terror bubbled in my stomach. Tubby, Hannah, and I couldn't fight off that horde of murderers alone. We'd die out here on this lonely road.

Hannah turned enough so I could see the anger creasing her face.

"No. It's not Oscar. These are real motorcycles, driven by

living people. But if they don't watch out, they're gonna be ghost riders." She raised her hand enough for me to see the pistol clutched in it.

Oh boy. Tension wound the muscles in the back of my neck. My headache throbbed harder. I stared into the night and counted three motorcycle headlights. Either we'd kill them, or they'd kill us. I reached for my magical energy. A weak pulse answered me. The black opal echoed it. I was too tired for this fight.

Before I even had time to consider how tired I was, one of the motorcycles cut in front of us.

"What the fuck, dude?" Tubby yelled and slammed on the brakes.

The car's tires screamed. The force nearly flung me over the seat and out the windshield. I pushed myself backward and landed on the backseat.

"Oh no, no, no," Hannah muttered.

"What is it?" I pushed myself back to a sitting position.

"Hold on," Tubby yelled.

The car bumped hard, jarring me off the seat and into the filthy floorboard. My elbows ground against the dirty carpet as I tried to raise myself. The car's wheels rattled over gravel.

"Stop," Hannah screamed.

"What do you think I'm doing? Pulling my damn pud?" Tubby yelled back.

We slammed into something. I banged my head on the padded back of the driver's seat. I struggled to get myself off the floor. My depleted energy made it feel as though I was swimming through semi-set Jell-O.

"Why did you do that?" Hannah yelled.

"They was motorcycles parked across the road." Tubby's words came between pants.

"You should have just plowed into them. That was Corman Tolliver. Didn't you see him?" Hannah sounded more disgusted than scared now that the whole thing was over.

"Woman, don't you think I know that?" Tubby turned to glare at her.

Hannah glared back and stuck out her tongue. Tubby grabbed for her face, and she dodged out of his way.

I tuned out their antics, one word echoing in my mind: Corman.

"You actually saw Corman?" I asked Hannah. *Please let her say no.*

Hannah quit arguing with Tubby long enough to address me. "Yes, I saw him. He was sitting in the middle of the stupid road on his dumb motorcycle."

My stomach plummeted. How had Corman found us? The answer was easy enough. King's ghost could have told him if Corman was receptive to contact from the dead. It would have been easy work for Corman to track us from the RV park that Oscar and his band of spectral thugs had destroyed.

The knowledge burned at my already singed nerves. If Corman was this serious, he'd stop at nothing to have his revenge on Wade.

Hannah cut into my silence.

"Rather than running Corman's sorry ass over, Tubby ran off the road. After that, we hit a tree." Hannah pointed at it.

"You don't have to say it like that, like I did it being stupid." Tubby thumbed the seatbelt release and slung the belt off him so he could face Hannah.

"I'd have hit them. I'd have run right over them and squashed them flat." She closed her fist and made a grinding motion.

"Bullshit. You'd have done the same damn thing." Tubby had twisted around so he could sit on one skinny hip and argue with Hannah.

I ignored them and maneuvered myself to look out the back window. The cloudy night blocked out the moon. The night was so dark it looked like black soup. My eyes slowly adjusted to the murky light. Three figures crept toward us.

"Shut up," I whispered.

Tubby and Hannah kept right on debating the correct handling of a blocked road. I shoved Hannah in the shoulder. She turned her snarl on me.

I hissed, "Somebody's coming."

Without a pause, she said, "I'm ready." She lifted the handgun. "I've been waiting for this chance."

Tubby spoke in a near whisper. "Y'all duck down."

The first crack of gunfire cut the silence. Bullets punched into the car with hollow sounding *thunks*. I held my breath, waiting for one of us to cry out. Nobody did.

Tubby started the car and slammed it into reverse. The bumper let go of the tree with an ugly screech. We flew toward the figures. Gunfire punched into the car. Tubby hit the embankment we'd flown down on our way to hitting the tree. The impact knocked me into the front seats again.

Tubby put the car in drive and floored it. I rose in time to see a black jacketed figure running in front of the car.

"Hit him, hit him, hit him," Hannah chanted, leaning forward as though this was a particularly good sporting event.

The figure ran for his life. I couldn't even tell if it was Corman. Tubby gave the car one last blast of gas, and overtook the runner. He disappeared under the car like magic, and we bumped over him. Tubby reversed over our victim and went forward again.

He lowered his window, the old mechanism grinding, and yelled into the darkness, "Who's next?"

Gunfire answered. The flashes came from the woods on Hannah's side of the car.

Hannah slammed open the door, braced her pistol on the top, and fired off several rounds in the direction of the muzzle flash. Nothing answered. She sat back down in the car and lowered her window.

"I think I hit one of 'em. Maybe killed him." She said it like she'd just won the lotto.

But she was wrong. A figure ran out of the darkness, pistols in both hands, firing. Hannah propped her arm on the open window and returned fire. This time, the guy did fall.

I sat in the back, heart pounding so hard it jarred my vision. Everything had happened so fast. And now we'd run over one person—several times—and shot another one.

Gunfire exploded again. This time, it came from Tubby's side of the car. We all hunched down.

Tubby stared through the space between the seats. "There's a shotgun and a box of shells underneath the back seat." He held out one skinny hand for it.

I dug and found a beat-up shotgun and a box of birdshot.

This was it? We were going to die out here. I gave him the weapon.

"What am I supposed to use?" I asked.

Hannah, a pistol in each hand, gave me no more than a quick glance. "You suck at shooting. Hit them with something worse."

"Something worse? What do you think I am? A magic dispensary?" I shot question after question as though it might change the fact that we were being shot at, and one stray bullet could kill any of us.

Nobody answered.

"You ready?" Tubby asked Hannah.

She nodded, eyes fixed and hard. "On three?"

Tubby nodded. They counted off together. On three, they slammed open their doors and began shooting, Hannah over the hood of the car, Tubby crouching behind his door.

The cloudy night was impenetrable except for the muzzle flashes.

"I'm out of bullets," Hannah hissed at Tubby. She squatted and began reloading.

A few more gunshots came, and Tubby answered.

Tubby reloaded his shotgun. "I can't hit anything at this range. Need a deer rifle or something."

"Peri Jean Mace," Corman screamed.

My insides shrank in on themselves. I hunched deeper in the seat, no longer worrying about who Tubby had run over.

"Peri Jean Mace," Corman screamed again.

"Answer him," Tubby muttered.

"No," I hissed.

"Do it," Tubby bared his teeth at me.

"What?" I yelled.

"My father's dead because of you, you nasty bitch." Corman choked on the last word.

"I hope that asshole's burning down in hell," Hannah screamed back.

Corman shot once.

"He's running out of bullets," Hannah whispered to Tubby.

"So are we," Tubby whispered back.

Something deep inside me turned over. A feeling, one I recognized from when the hag and I shared my body, flowed through me. The pure, black-hole emotional destruction the hag delivered twitched at my fingertips, asking to get out.

Something similar had happened when I ate Loretta Nell Grimes's soul back in Devil's Rest, Texas. For a few days, I'd felt flashes of her murderous rage inside me. Now I had a measure of the hag's ugly gift. Could I use it against Corman? I thought so.

"Let's talk about it. Negotiate." I shouted out the broken back window.

Tubby sneered at me. "Whaaaat? You can't negotiate with doo-doo. It just gets on you, and then you're all shitty."

"We're never going to get him by shooting at him." I reached forward, touched Tubby and gave him a light shock of magic.

He grunted from the pain. "Girl, you better know what you're doing."

I hoped I did.

"Get out of the car," Corman yelled back.

"We all getting out," Tubby answered him. "If you hurt one of us, the other two is gonna kill you."

"I'm going to kill him anyway," Hannah whispered.

Nobody bothered to answer her. We all got out of the car and met near the front bumper, huddled together.

"Show yourself," I called into the darkness.

Corman stepped out from between some trees, only a few feet from us, a chunky semi-automatic pistol pointed in our general direction. Even in the darkness, the hollow-ness beneath his eyes and under his cheekbones was obvi-ous. He'd also had his nose broken, badly.

"I spent three fucking months in jail because of your sorry ass." The hand not holding a gun reached up to touch his nose. "Your stupid cop boyfriend did this."

"Dean's not my boyfriend. Hasn't been for over a year." I barely paid attention to the conversation. The dark power moving inside me took up all my attention. It yearned toward Corman, ripe with expectation.

"Tell me where Wade Hill is, and I'll let you all go." Corman rested the sights of his gun on me.

"Wade walked out of my life. Dunno where he is." This wasn't true at all. I had Wade's sister's address and could find him with no problem whatsoever.

"Liar," Corman yelled as though he could read my thoughts.

Before I knew what I was doing, I stepped out from between Hannah and Tubby and stalked toward Corman. Power sang through my body and lighted my vision as though we were standing underneath a streetlight.

He raised the gun and took a step backward. "Stop. Stay the hell away from me."

Power sang to me from the trees and the ground. Even the sound of the night frogs seemed just for me. I closed the distance between me and Corman. The darkness Corman carried so deep that he wasn't even aware of where it began or ended called to me. I wanted to eat it.

Corman pointed the gun at my face, pleasure flickering

behind his eyes. His finger tightened. The gun bucked in his hand. The world slowed down to a crawl.

The bullet crept out of the barrel. An eternity seemed to go by before the muzzle flashed. I focused on the bullet, on the killing energy inside it, and sucked it into me. The bullet dropped to the ground halfway between Corman and me.

Still in slow motion, Corman's mouth fell open. He aimed the gun again. I used the energy I'd stolen from the bullet to set fire to the gun. It turned red in Corman's hands before he realized what was happening. He screamed and slung it at me.

From behind me, Hannah laughed.

Corman backed away from me, eyes wide, hand out, warding me away.

"Devil, devil, devil," he chanted.

"That's no way to talk." I took the last steps running, grabbed his jacket in my fists, and pulled him close. Touching Corman made my stomach roll in queasy waves, but my need overpowered my revulsion.

I jammed my lips down on his with the vague notion that I could draw from him psychically. Corman's hands pushed at me. I ignored them and inhaled all that made Corman evil, most of it learned at his awful father's knee. What was left of the hag's spirit lapped it up.

The world took on color I hadn't known existed. Even in

the dark of this night, the leaves on the evergreen trees were greener than green. The night air smelled sweet, perfumed with dry grass and Corman's fear. Euphoria filled me to bursting. I sucked deeper. Corman's evil tasted so very good. I took one last deep sip of his darkest heart and let him fall to the ground.

Shoulders hunched, head hung low, Corman tried to crawl away from me, whimpering like a hurt animal. I watched him the same way a frog watched a moth getting a little too close.

Hannah walked past me, gun arm out. She was going to kill Corman. That was fine with me. He deserved it.

A woman's voice came several yards away. "Oh my god. What are you people doing?"

Hannah ignored her and advanced on Corman. She'd take the head shot. Put him down clean and fast.

"Stop right there, ma'am," came a man's voice. "Put the gun down. We've called the police."

Tubby, Hannah, and I spun around. Two dark shapes headed toward us, one of them shining a flashlight. This was Texas. They could be armed to the teeth just like us, but I stomped toward them anyway.

When I got close enough to see the whites of their eyes I growled, "Get out of here or I'm going to eat you alive."

The guy shone his flashlight in my face, and the woman screamed. They nearly tripped over each other getting turned around. Then the man fell down trying to climb the embankment. The woman left him where he was and scrambled away.

Thunder clapped in the sky. Underneath it, I heard those shouts, the ones of Oscar's band of murderers. The frenzy from feeding off Corman and using his evil to replenish my energy faded in a flash.

"They're coming back," I said to nobody in particular.

"Fine," Hannah said. "Let me go kill Corman, and we'll go."

"He's gone," Tubby mumbled. "He run off while Peri Jean was making them folks piss their pants. Let's just go."

He stomped toward the car. I followed.

"I sucked out his energy. Maybe he'll go off somewhere and kill himself," I told her.

She snorted. "Oh, I hope he does."

Tubby got in the car and gave the ignition key a vicious twist. The car fired to life.

"Get in." He pounded the car outside of the door with open hand to make his point.

Neither Hannah nor I made fun of him. We just did what he said.

I would replay the moment I decided to let Corman slip

into the darkness that night many times over the years to come. But right then, I didn't know any better.

———

We sped down the highway, lightning flashing behind us. I sat on my knees, watching the show through the back window. Each lightning flash silhouetted the mad band of killers in the clouds. Every clap of thunder echoed their merry shouts. The ghostly headlights of the motorcycles flickered at the cloud's edges. The insectile buzz of their engines drilled at the edge of my sanity. The wind from the open front windows whipped at me, bringing the smell of wet dog, horse sweat, and gasoline.

The storm picked up speed. Gusts of wind shook Tubby's Cutlass. The clouds dipped so low they seemed to touch the road. They'd be here soon. How would the three of us alone survive their kind of attack?

"Give me that shotgun," Hannah poked me in the back.

I patted the floorboard where Tubby had thrown it. My fingertips connected with it just as the ghostly motorcycles roared up behind Tubby's Cutlass. It might have been my imagination, but I thought I could see King Tolliver's big teeth, stained red by the glow of the Cutlass's taillights. It was time to do all the damage I could. I yanked the shotgun off the floor and pushed it at Hannah.

Hannah got to her knees, leaned out the passenger window, and began firing at them. The bullets passed right through the ghostly motorcycle riders. They weren't quite alive enough for bullets to matter.

"No," Hannah and I wailed together.

One of the motorcycles roared closer. King. It wouldn't seem possible for a skull to grin, but King's did. A big, cheesy-toothed leer. A chill crept over my skin. We had no way to hurt him. He'd keep coming until he killed us.

Or maybe not. My gift allowed me to reach out and touch the spirit world. It would take some doing, but draining away Corman's resolve had given me a second wind.

I opened my third eye and viewed King and his motorcycle in the realm of spirit. In that dimension, his energy glowed sickly green, velvety black at the edges. He'd chosen to manifest just as he had in life—a dickless despot riding a motorcycle. It made sense. That identity had ruled his life. Time to see if I could blow it up.

I narrowed my focus on the motorcycle, gathered my energy, and imagined the gasoline inside the tank burning. The gas tank exploded in a shower of sparks. It was nothing more than an illusion, but King's eyes widened. His mouth opened in a scream. He lost his grip on the energy holding his persona together. The illusion dissolved in a shower of green and blacker-than-black sparks. His image of who and what he'd been in life had burned him in the end.

It would have been more satisfying had I not known King would be back. Ghosts always came back.

The horses took the place of the motorcycles, the dogs running right along with them. Hannah raised the shotgun.

"Don't bother." I pulled on both our energy. Hannah squeaked when my power hit her but didn't protest. I molded the combined energy and opened up blossoms of red-hot flame in the midst of our pursuers. Both inside and outside my head, dogs yelped. A horse screamed in pain. It hurt my heart to harm animals, but they were spirit. They'd be back.

No matter how many times my energy hit its target, the horde simply regenerated and returned. The roar of the motorcycles rose over the thunder of pounding horse hooves. Hannah let out a scream of fury at the sound. But I was too scared to make a peep.

I had already used most of my energy and Hannah's. There was no way I could keep fighting them. Frustration sat down hard on my shoulders. Soon I'd run out of energy, and that would be that. There was no way to win.

The engine howled as Tubby held down the gas pedal as far is it would go. It was a good effort, but not good enough. These monsters could come at us all night. Soon we'd run out of gas. Then what?

I had to switch tactics and fast. Back at the campground, Oscar had run when I hurt him. He was the one I needed to focus on stopping.

I concentrated on finding Oscar. Though he'd achieved a

kind of living-dead status, he was still half-dead. He'd never be able to hide from me. His nasty, hateful spirit bobbed behind his warriors. Of course. *The boss isn't going to risk himself.*

I latched onto his life force with no problem. Oscar never even felt my presence. He was enjoying terrorizing me too much. I gave his energy a hard pull.

All my aches and pains went away. I drank in the energy like the finest of gourmet meals. It was ironic. Oscar himself taught me this trick.

Oscar, on the other end, slowed. He had a hard time holding onto his horse. He began to slide off the back of his saddle. He realized what I'd done at the last second.

"You cheating little coward," he bellowed as he crashed to the ground.

Oscar rolled onto his back, so furious his spirit seemed a red ball of hate. With the last of the magic holding him together, he drew a hollowed out cow horn from his belt, held it to his lipless mouth, and exhaled into it. The instrument emitted a long, eardrum-shattering blast.

I jerked in shock at the eardrum rattling noise and popped back into my own consciousness. Oscar's warriors dropped away from the car like magic. As abruptly as they'd come, our pursuers were gone, leaving behind only a few disagreeable grumbles of thunder. I broke my connection with Oscar, and hung on in the back seat, panting. Tubby sped into the night.

The energy I'd gained from the Hag, Corman, and Oscar congealed in me like a greasy meal, their evil nauseating me. The fatigue rolled back worse than ever. I slumped onto the seat.

Hannah peeked around the side of her bucket seat. "What can I do for you?"

"Leave me be," I groaned.

Hannah reached out to touch me but drew back. She turned around and began arguing with Tubby. I lay on the back seat sweating and shivering as my magic tried to process three doses of pure evil. Hannah's and Tubby's argument turned to conversation. The rise and fall of their voices felt warm and comfortable. I quit paying attention.

———

I must have dozed. The next thing I knew, the car slowed and gravel cracked under the wheels. I sat up, rubbed my eyes, and took my first look at Cecil's bug-out plan.

My stomach sank. I had expected to see a middle-of-nowhere motel. Maybe a house. But darkness reigned supreme in this place. Tubby's headlights splashed over two darkened buildings. He turned in front of one and let the car roll to a stop.

The weak glow from the headlights illuminated a dilapidated wooden building. Judging by the unreadable sign above the boarded over front door, it had been a business at some point. Now it seemed empty. Both its dark windows and its empty parking lot indicated disuse.

"Damn. I think we got the wrong place, y'all. This don't look like nothing." Tubby glanced back at me. My tough, tough friend's face pinched with worry.

I didn't know what to say. Had Cecil given us the wrong coordinates?

My great-uncle had been sick, very sick, since a bad episode with his heart a couple of months earlier. But he hadn't been forgetful. He'd seemed distracted more than anything.

A figure came around the side of the building, face in shadow. Tubby flashed one skinny arm back, grabbed the shotgun, and was out of the car with it before I could move.

"This is Thomas Tubman," he yelled. "I'm looking for Cecil Gregg...or Gregson...aw shit, I don't know. He's an old dude..."

The figure put its hands up. Cecil said, a smile in his voice, "I'm Cecil Gregory today. But I might be Cecil Gregg tomorrow."

Cecil loved playing with variations of the name Gregg and had fake IDs in just about every version imaginable. Now I realized the name dated way, way back in our family. Back to the Gregorius Witch. Cecil came closer and leaned into the car, eyes finding mine. He nodded, satisfied, and stood up straight.

"Pull the car around back of this next building. Get it out of sight." Cecil waved his arm in the direction he wanted Tubby to go.

Tubby got back into the car. Hannah and I climbed out, laden with sacks of cheap clothes and toiletries. Cecil hurried to me and grabbed me in a tight hug. He drew back and kissed first one cheek and then the other. He did the same to Hannah.

"What happened to you kids? We've been worried." He took my arm and led me away.

"What didn't happen?" Hannah muttered.

"Remember Corman Tolliver from Gaslight City?" I pulled out my cigarettes and lit one.

Cecil pulled it out of my hand and dragged on it. "That little asshole you should have killed and didn't?"

My face heated. I was glad nobody could see it. "He forced us off the road, made Tubby hit a tree. We ended up having a shoot-out with them."

"Kill him this time?" Cecil handed back the cigarette.

"Nope. All I had a chance to do was drain his energy." I trudged along, waiting for my scolding.

Cecil gave me a sideways glance but said nothing. Thank fate for small favors.

"Then those assholes from the RV park attacked us again," Hannah said.

Cecil stopped in his tracks. "And you're still in one piece?"

"I did something bad to Oscar. Took his energy, made him fall off his horse. He blew his horn, and they left." Fatigue ached in my back.

Cecil led us around the side of the building that I guessed had once been a business. He opened a door and motioned us through.

The interior of the building was a far cry from the run down exterior. The door opened on a large, well-lit kitchen. The cabinets, stove, and refrigerator had seen better days, but looked in working order. The windows had been blacked out.

Every set of eyes turned to us. Zora and Zander, the only children to survive the attack, ran to us, both of them hugging our legs. Hannah and I greeted them with as much enthusiasm as we could muster.

Brad came to me next. He pulled me into a tight hug and held on for a beat longer than was necessary. Poor guy. He'd probably just realized what he married into. Brad let me go and slumped back to Jadine, who had an array of candy, soft drinks, and cigarettes spread out before her. She even had one of those candy necklaces around her neck. At least Brad loved his wife enough to stop at a convenience store as they ran for their lives and buy her junk food.

Shelly came over to rummage through the bags in my arms. "Did you buy the underwear I requested?"

I put down the bag, fished out the ones in Shelly's size, and handed them to her.

She pursed her lips at the package. "Discount Dilettante brand, I see."

"Puleeze. This is Bargain Babes brand." It had taken time to catch onto Shelly's humor, but the effort had been worth it. She filled a maternal role I had missed.

Shelly dug through the sacks until she had toothbrush, toothpaste, soap, and a towel. "Let me give you the grand tour now. I'm going down for the count as soon as I get clean."

I grabbed the sack of things Hannah and I had picked out for ourselves and followed Shelly out of the kitchen. The next room, large and open, contained stacks of sealed, unlabeled boxes. A few months ago, I'd have wanted to know what they contained. Now I knew not to ask.

The wall behind the boxes, which should have faced the street, had been covered with plywood, blocking the windows. No wonder it appeared dark from the road.

Shelly motioned us through the mess, speaking over her shoulder. "Welcome to the Snake Creek Hotel."

She led the way up the stairs, which opened into a long hallway lined with closed doors on each side.

"Snake Creek?" Hannah made a face.

"Yep." Shelly motioned us along. "The hotel was established in 1898, when the town of Snake Creek got its post office. The town dried up during World War II."

Shelly opened the door to a long, narrow bathroom. "The Snake Creek Hotel dates back to the days when travelers expected to share a bathroom. This is the only one."

She left the door standing open and led us three doors down and across the hall. She used a key to unlock it. "This room is for you girls."

Hannah pushed open the door, revealing a room empty except for two cots. Neither had sheets or a pillow. Hannah arranged her face into her old almost-famous, over-bright smile.

"You up for a slumber party?" She waggled her eyebrows. We giggled.

"Papaw and I don't know what to do about Tubman." Shelly said. "We hate to ask him to leave. We hate to ask him to stay downstairs with the boxes. That's a lackey's job. Tubby's...almost one of us." She shrugged.

"You mind if he stays with us?" I asked Hannah and hastened to add, "He'll behave if we're firm."

"I know how to handle Tubby Tubman." Hannah's casual statement spoke volumes about months of her life I didn't want to contemplate. She walked into the room and pulled another cot, this one still folded, away from the wall. I hadn't even seen it. I helped her open it. Shelly watched from the door.

"If you're set, I'm going to shower. I recommend you two do the same before the men nasty up the restroom." Shelly hurried down the hall, went into the bathroom, and closed the door.

Hannah shut the door separating our room from the hallway. I opened the sack holding our toiletries and discount clothes, and we began splitting up what we had. Someone knocked. I got up to answer the door. Tubby, struggling with my witch trunk and backpack, stood outside the door.

"Looks like I'm bunking with you two. We gonna have a threesome?" He grinned.

Hannah giggled. I stared at her in surprise. She used to loathe that kind of humor from men. She shook her head at me and shrugged. She had a point. It was best just to take Tubby as he came. I helped Tubby get my witching supplies into the room. We put them on the dusty floor underneath the blacked out window.

Tubby faced me and sighed. "I take it you ain't tried at all to get in touch with Tanner Letts?"

I shook my head, too tired to answer.

Tubby sat down on his cot and stared at his filthy, worn out sneakers. "Tanner and me ain't made friends, but you need to call him."

I glanced at Hannah. She shrugged.

"Tanner's a bad son of a bitch when he goes to war, and we need help." She gave me an apologetic smile.

Outside our door, footsteps approached. Someone rapped three times, and Shelly's voice came through the old wood.

"Peri Jean, I'm done with the restroom. Take your turn if you're going to." Shelly's footsteps receded.

I grabbed a few toiletries and hurried out of the room. It was easier than explaining to two of the toughest people I knew that I was afraid to call Tanner. He might tell me to get bent.

7

In the restroom, alone, I put the lid down on the toilet and sat. I took out my phone and stared at Tanner's contact information. I ached to speak with him. He had said to call if I needed him. If this didn't qualify, I don't know what did. But, boy, it hurt my pride. Before I could change my mind, I tapped his name and then "call."

On the other end, the phone rang once and cut off before that ring could finish. A message came on telling me that number was unavailable and invited me to leave a message. I listened, stunned, and did something I never would have believed I'd do.

"Tanner, it's me. Oscar Rivera is back and worse than ever. I...need you." I hung up before I could say more and took my shower.

I scrubbed my body with shaking hands, adrenaline still pumping. Calling in reinforcements didn't bug me. But

Tanner telling me to call if I needed him and then not answering got under my skin.

My oversized pride stung and twisted. I could just imagine Tanner listening to the message and rolling his gorgeous eyes. Maybe even making fun of me to Dave and Neecie. But then he'd help. Tanner was too decent to refuse to help.

I listened for the phone's ring and even cut short my shower because I thought I heard it. Soon as my hands were dry, I picked up my phone and checked it for missed calls. Nothing. I emerged from the bathroom rubbing my hair with a stiff discount store towel.

Cecil leaned against the opposite wall, smoking a cigarette.

"Call Mysti Whitebyrd. Tell her we need her help and will pay." He turned and walked away without waiting for my answer.

I didn't want to call Mysti. My mentor had risked herself to help me so many times. It embarrassed me to keep asking. She probably thought I was the world's slowest learner.

But I had no other ideas about what to do next. As things stood, Oscar would keep attacking until he wore us down. I didn't have the magical umph to kill him outright.

Cecil's willingness to pay Mysti testified to the urgency of our situation. My uncle kept a tight fist on his wallet and avoided paying whenever he could. He wouldn't tell me to call Mysti if he saw another option. Cecil, who met life's twists and turns with stoic defiance, was afraid. Terror tightened my chest, closed my throat.

I took out my phone. My hand shook so hard I dropped it. I let the shakes take me. The panic subsided as quickly as it came. I picked up my phone off the floor and called Mysti's number. She answered, breathless. "Peri Jean? Oscar just attacked us. He might be heading your way…"

I cut her off. "He's already gotten me twice tonight. Destroyed everything I had." I rubbed at the headache throbbing in the back of my neck. "What happened on your end?"

"We're on a job in San Antonio. Or were. They tore the roof off our hotel. Killed our client." A car door clunked in the background.

"How'd you make them leave?" I asked.

She was silent several beats. When she spoke, her voice had lost most of its strength. "We escaped while they killed our client."

The Mysti I knew liked to win. Running must have hurt her pride something terrible. I hurt for my friend, sad I had called to ask for more help.

"Cecil wants you to come here and help us. He said he'd pay." I went into my room to find Tubby lying on his bunk, feet crossed, playing with his phone. Hannah had her back to him, legs tucked under her. Probably asleep. Or ignoring him so he wouldn't drive her crazy.

Mysti sighed on the other end of the line. Also unlike her. Most of the time, she was eager to help.

"But you don't have to," I said quickly.

"No. We're coming. But after what just happened, I wonder how much help we'll be." Her voice changed to her usual brisk tone. "There'll be no fee since we're fighting together. Where are you?"

I texted her the GPS coordinates. "When you get here, drive around to the back of the building next to the hotel. There's a place to hide your vehicle."

"Under deep cover, are we?" Mysti laughed. Despite everything I'd seen and experienced, I joined her. When she stopped laughing, Mysti said, "How are things with Tanner?"

"He left yesterday for California. Supposedly on business. But I think we're done." The memory of the way Tanner's phone went straight to voicemail floated to the forefront of my mind, and something new occurred to me. Usually it would ring several times before it rolled to voicemail. He'd deliberately ignored my call.

"Really? He seemed so into you." Mysti's voice rose in surprise.

"Win some, lose some. Right?" I tried to sound cheerful, but my voice wavered on the last word.

Mysti changed the subject. "We're going to find somewhere

to rest tonight, but we'll be there first thing in the morning."

"There's cots but no sheets and one bathroom for everybody." I laid down on my cot, which shrieked in protest.

"Understood." Mysti hung up.

Tubby put down his phone and turned to me. "What if I come over there with you? Help you make that cot squeak."

As Hannah had done, I turned my back to him and tucked my legs under. It was the only defense. Tubby talked to my back a little, the suggestions more and more pornographic until he began to snore softly.

I lay staring at the wall, thoughts buzzing. Every once in a while, one of them swooped down and stung me.

Oscar and his soldiers blazing out of the sky like gods on a rampage. I replayed those horrific seconds of watching people I'd cared about die. I examined every detail of the attack. The wild screams and victorious shouts. The galloping horses with their red eyes. The wild dogs ripping and tearing people to shreds. The ghostly motorcycles roaring around. All those people who hated my guts.

Oscar rode through my head on his gray horse, sword brandished. I picked apart every detail. The headdress. The way Oscar himself seemed to be made of bone and metal with no flesh. The way they all died but then got up to fight again.

My stomach clenched in dread. They'd be back. That was the worst part. Because there was no way to beat Oscar. I didn't have the power or the knowledge.

Priscilla could talk all she wanted about shedding the scar tissue spell and gaining my destiny. I didn't see it happening in time. Not after all I'd tried. Everything I did thinned it, but nothing made it completely go away. What else was there for me to try?

The Wanderer. Both Cecil and Queenie acted as though he was the answer. But I'd seen Queenie's tarot reading first-hand, watched her tap that Death card and say the Wanderer wouldn't intercede until I died and was ready for rebirth. Those baptisms of fire would likely kill me. Then Oscar would take my magical core, kill what remained of my loved ones, and summon hell on earth.

I don't know when I slept, but I woke to an empty room. Both Hannah and Tubby had risen and left me to sleep. I climbed out of the cot and did a few aching toe touches. My bones cracked. I shed last night's cheap pajamas and put on jeans and a plain black T-shirt. I fished in the pockets of yesterday's filthy clothes for my smokes, my roll of antacids, and the odd little hag's heart. Shoving them into the pockets of my stiff, new jeans, I went looking for human life.

Cecil and Shelly sat at a long folding table in the kitchen, picking at eggs and bacon. An empty coffee carafe sat between them. I grabbed it on the way past, filled it at the sink, and began coffee. Once it was brewing, I sat down at the table and acknowledged them with a nod.

"Queenie called from Mexico City to see how things were going. When I told her, she appealed to the Wanderer to see you. He still refuses." Cecil's words blew away some of my pre-coffee haze.

It was almost as though he'd been watching my dreams. For a man whose only talent was spirit medium, just like me, he was pretty damn good at guessing what I was thinking. I couldn't manage more than a grunt in response.

"Have you heard from Tanner?" Shelly pushed her half-eaten breakfast away.

I shook my head.

"Have you left him a message apologizing for whatever you did?" Cecil lit a cigarette.

Shelly gasped. "Peri Jean does not owe that man, or any other, an apology."

Cecil gave his wife the finger.

I shook my head again but understood something new. Neither Shelly nor Cecil believed I could fight off Oscar. Between Mysti, Tanner, or the Wanderer, they thought the answer to survival lay with someone other than me. The coffee maker finished. I got up, poured a cup, and went to the door, cigarettes in hand.

"Chilly out there. Fall's coming." Cecil took off his flannel shirt and held it up.

I set my stuff down, took the shirt from Cecil, and put it on. Then I kissed his cheek. He patted my back. I lit a cigarette and went outside. The cool, humid air cut through my clothes, calling for chill bumps on my arms.

Hannah sat on the hood of a junked car. Tubby stood nearby, pinwheeling his arms and talking in a loud voice. Hannah giggled at whatever he said. She saw me coming and turned her attention away from Tubby.

He stopped what he was doing and hurried to me. "You sleep good?"

I shrugged. The real answer was no. My head swam from lack of sleep and whatever poison still lurked in my body.

A black SUV crept down the road in front of the hotel. The window rolled down, and Griff leaned out, squinting at the Snake Creek Hotel. I ran out so he could see me, waving and pointing where he needed to park.

Griff pulled off the road and drove around the side of the second building. I followed, relief surging through me. Griff and Mysti would know what to do. They always did.

But when my friends got out of their vehicle, they looked more beaten than I did. Mysti had a bruise forming on one cheek, and scratches covered her arms. Griff moved stiffly, as though he'd suffered some injury his clothes covered.

Closer inspection revealed dots of blood soaking through his shirt.

"Are you okay?" I pointed at the blood.

"Damn dogs clawed me. Every time I move around, the cuts open again." Sad lines bracketed his mouth. "They killed the people we'd come to help,"

There was nothing worse for Griff. He may have worked in the supernatural world, but he took helping people seriously.

"It's because of me. I'm so very sorry." Shame took a heavy seat on my shoulders.

Both Griff and Mysti shrugged, as though this was the way things went, the risks people like us took on. Maybe it was.

"There's coffee inside. Shelly and Cecil had eggs and bacon." My stomach rumbled at the thought of food. I hadn't had anything since before Oscar's attack.

"Sis!" Brad yelled from behind me. He shoved me out of the way and grabbed Mysti in a hug. He squeezed his eyes shut, and I realized how much he must have missed the safety of his big sister. Growing up orphans, Mysti had been his rock all his life.

Jadine trailed behind Brad, aluminum cane in one hand, sightless eyes set at a point in the distance. Griff approached and spoke to her. She smiled and hugged him.

Thunder rumbled in the distance. We all watched the sky

as though Oscar and his murderers might come down right now.

Mysti went to the SUV and got out her laptop. "Let's go inside. We need to talk about what I think we're dealing with here."

A few minutes later, Shelly and Jadine stood at the stove frying more bacon. Mysti and Griff listened as I told them everything I'd experienced from eating the hag's magical core to finding out about the Gregorius Witch and my ultimate destiny.

Griff took a sip of coffee. "I'm surprised eating that little monster's magic didn't kill you."

"I think it came close." I didn't go into that awful smelling funk water Priscilla Herrera made me drink. Mysti would want me to guess what had been in it. Instead I dug in my pocket and came out with the hag's heart in my fist. I dropped it on the table. "I kept a souvenir."

A hush fell over the room. The hard little heart rocked back and forth, ruby crystals glinting in the harsh overhead lights. Coolness crept over my skin. It was the kind of chill felt in places that poked the primitive part of the brain and told it to hit the road.

"What are you going to do with it?" Griff's lips turned down as he studied the thing.

I shrugged. "Sell it. Trade it. Use it to make a potion."

Mysti, using a ballpoint pen, moved the heart where she could get a better look.

"Even dead, it's powerful." She pushed it toward me, my signal to put the thing up. "Use it well."

Mysti winked and changed the subject.

"So the combined power of the Gregorius Witch, plus every witch in your line, will be yours if you can shed the scar tissue. Correct?" A smile hovered on her lips, and a manic brightness gleamed in her eyes. Mysti had encouraged me to accept my destiny at every turn.

I bit my lip to keep from reminding her how spectacularly I could fail at all this.

She squinted her eyes and leaned close. "Don't be afraid. You got this. Now, think back to Oscar's attacks, both of them. Did you see anything else of note?"

I lowered my head and thought carefully. This was Mysti's information gathering phase. She liked to hear even the smallest detail. As I sifted through my awful memories, one flashed to the surface. Something big that I had almost forgotten.

"They were eating souls and magical cores." My words rushed out.

Mysti raised one eyebrow in question.

"Oscar's huntsmen," I said to her unasked question. "They'd lean over their kills and sort of inhale. The magical core—or soul, whatever the person had—would come right out." I stopped for a breath. "It was making Oscar's warriors stronger."

Mysti closed her eyes and groaned.

"What is it?" I knew it was bad, but Mysti rarely reacted with such pessimism. She always knew the next right thing to do.

Mysti and Griff exchanged a meaningful look. He shrugged.

"We saw them do it too," Mysti said.

Griff took over the story. "We went to San Antonio to help a young woman whose house was infested with malicious spirits. It was so bad, we checked her into a motel in San Antonio. When Oscar and those others ripped the roof off the motel, those hounds came in first. They clawed the girl to death."

Mysti tapped the table. "But listen to this. Once she was dead, those horsemen leaned over her and breathed in her soul. They got bigger and more solid. More real."

Stomach churning, I remembered what I'd seen back at the RV park. My mother killing Anita came back in stark detail. This time, I could see her mane of long dark hair thickening. The same had happened when Joey Holze killed Lorrie the face painter. Her soul had nourished him, made him more than just bone and metal. And when King Tolliver killed Early Ramey, his gross teeth had seemed to get bigger. I wanted to scream at the endlessness of it.

"They're doing the same thing I did to Loretta Nell and the hag. And they're gaining power and getting stronger with each one." I accepted the plate Shelly held out and began wolfing down bacon and eggs, so hungry my stomach growled as I ate.

"Is that how they're coming back to life then?" Cecil, still smoking, rubbed his stubble.

Shelly strolled by and plucked the cigarette out of his fingers. "You're not supposed to be smoking."

"Hey," Cecil said to her back. Shelly kept walking, ignoring him.

I touched his arm to get his attention. "I think that's some of it. But there's also something else. After I ate the hag's magical core, I saw Oscar through the hag's eyes. He was saying that he and his army were neither dead nor alive. That's why they can't be killed."

Mysti opened her laptop. "Are you ready to hear a theory on what we're dealing with?"

"I don't want to hear it, but I guess I need to." I ate the last bite of egg, lit a cigarette, and leaned back in my chair.

Cecil snapped his fingers at me and pointed at the pack of smokes. I slid it across the table. He lit one with relish. Shelly might have won a skirmish, but the war was far from over.

"Let's hear it, Ms. Whitebyrd." Puffs of smoke accompanied each word out of Cecil's mouth. Mysti smiled at him and sat a bit straighter. She loved having the answers.

"I think Oscar has managed to raise the Wild Hunt. Do you know that term?" She glanced around the table.

"I do," Griff said.

"Not you." Mysti turned her laptop around so Cecil and I could see.

A piece of artwork covered the screen. Wild horseman raged through midair, seemingly chasing something.

"That's Johann Wilhelm Cordes's *Wilde Jagd*." Mysti tapped a key, and the image changed. "This is *Wodan's Wild Hunt* by Friedrich Wilhelm Heine. This second image is important because it leads to the next thing we need to talk about." Mysti was in full teacher mode. She even had a pen pointed at the hunt's leader. "In German mythology, the Wild Hunt was storied to have been led by Odin or Krampus. Perhaps Berchtold or Holle. But here's the cool thing about the Wild Hunt."

"Depending on what you consider cool," Griff cut in.

Mysti ignored him. "The Wild Hunt can be found in many cultures. In Italy, it's called *Estantiga*, which translates to 'the old army.' In England, it was called by many names—Cain's Hunt, Herod's Hunt. In Cornwall, they called it the Devil's Dandy Dogs."

I jumped at that, remembering the way the dogs had

ripped into people I knew, biting chunks out of them while they screamed for mercy that never came.

Griff spoke, lending a voiceover to the horrific images in my head. "The huntsmen are described as specters, demons, sometimes the fae. It is generally agreed they are not humans but creatures from another dimension. Which could mean they are neither alive nor dead." Griff stared at me as he repeated my words from a few minutes earlier.

"In some tellings, the hunt is associated with Yule." Mysti glanced up from her screen and met my eyes. "But it can also be associated with Samhain."

Samhain was in a few days' time. The veil between our dimension and the next would be at its thinnest. Oscar would be at his most powerful. Worry gelled in my stomach, turning the coffee and food into a flaming acid. I got out my antacids and crunched three between my teeth.

"He chose this time of year because he has the best chance of beating me. He's planned this down to the last detail." I stared at Mysti, wanting reassurance.

"You're right." The excitement from teaching fell off her face. "And there's no way to reverse your status as the target of the Hunt."

I frowned, puzzled.

"I did a little spirit work this morning. My spirit contact from the dark outposts says being named as the hunt's target is sure doom." Mysti plucked at the beads on her top with trembling fingers. "The hunt will ride until its target is annihilated, down to the last friend and the last drop of shared blood."

I tried to digest all the bad news, but one piece wouldn't quite go down.

"How did Oscar know to call the hunt? How did he wield such power?" I muttered the question almost to myself, not really expecting an answer.

Mysti, lips turned down, shook her head. She didn't know. Maybe it didn't matter. We were in grave danger either way.

Tubby burst into the kitchen, Hannah on his heels.

"Storm's coming." His face had gone white enough to make his freckles stand out.

From outside came a rolling clap of thunder. Underneath was the rumble of horse hooves beating a non-existent ground. Motorcycles roared behind, competing with the baying of hounds.

They'd found us already.

———

The thunder went from a rumble to a cacophony of hoof-beats, shouts, and barking dogs. The drone of the motorcycles chased behind them. The noise, both in and outside my head, became all I heard or knew.

Every nerve in my body drew wire tight. My heart quivered in my chest, like the breath of a trapped animal. They were coming. I still wasn't ready.

I drew on the mantle, still trapped behind the thin wall of scar tissue. The previous night's rest had done me good. My magic throbbed to life. Warmth spread throughout me, tingling at the surface of my skin.

Orev cawed behind me. The rustle of his wings came closer until his feet closed on my shoulder. Power hummed between us. The tiny, fine hairs on my arm stood on end and prickled on the back of my neck.

Something slammed into the door separating the kitchen from outside. The building shook. Several people screamed. The sound of running footsteps came through the roofing and wood. The beams creaked. More screams.

Hannah came to stand next to me. In one hand, she carried a rusty tire iron. "I don't have enough bullets left to fight."

I only nodded. Drawing power took all my focus. Throwing out both arms, I pulled magic from the naturally occurring components of everything around us.

Something slammed against the door. Breaking glass tinkled. The smell of gasoline had time to reach my nose before a whoosh rattled the door in its frame. Fire licked around it. Wisps of smoke drifted from the dry wood.

"Gonna burn you out, you fucking witch," Joey Holze yelled, voice both inside and outside my head.

"Burn her out!" Barbie's hoarse scream cut off so she could guffaw.

Something heavy hit the roof. The old wood popped and groaned. A motorcycle engine buzzed as one of the ghostly iron horses rolled over it.

"They's pouring gasoline on the roof," Kenny yelled from the big open room with all the boxes.

Brad ran into the room. "Everybody come on. We have to get out."

People streamed out of the kitchen. I followed them. Smoke drifted from the ceiling like errant ghosts. The wood popped as the fire ate it. Soon the flames would take over the building. Anybody left inside would die.

Someone had pushed all the boxes to one side and ripped the plywood off the building's old front door. My family and friends hurried to it, so afraid of the fire they weren't thinking. The huntsmen would be out there, waiting to slaughter them.

"No," I screamed at the top of my lungs, the force of it scalding the inside of my throat.

Everybody stopped and stared at me.

"They're waiting to kill you," I said, already doubting my decision to stop them.

What else could they do? The choices were to leave and be killed or stay and burn to death. Fire licked the ceiling above, sending down little cinders to remind us time was running out. I glanced at the stairs. My witch pack and trunk were up there. But a thick cloud of smoke belched down the stairs. I'd die if I tried to retrieve them.

Anger and grief stopped my thought processes. I was about to lose all the witching supplies I'd so carefully chosen. Including Priscilla Herrera's spell book.

"We've got to get out of here. Now." Dillon had one kid on each hip. Finn hurried along behind carrying a bag of baby supplies.

"I think I know what to do." Griff appeared with his sleeves rolled up. In one hand, he held a metal can with the word flammable on it.

"Fight fire with fire." Finn dropped the bag.

"That's our baby's diapers," Dillon snapped.

"You want to fight instead of me?" her husband said to her.

He shouldn't have asked. Dillon handed both kids to her husband and hurried away with Griff.

Over her shoulder she said, "Don't forget the damn diapers, Finn."

Trying to hold onto his two kids, Finn grabbed for the bag. Brad handed it to him and took Zander in one arm. With the other, he held onto Jadine.

"All right," Brad said in a low voice. "Let them go out first with whatever they're making. The rest of us'll run for the cars."

Kenny came over and stood next to me, hairy arms crossed over his chest. Over the course of the evening, his cheeks had hollowed, and his mouth had turned down.

Griff, Dillon, and Mysti came from the kitchen, all holding torches. With red cinders raining down around them, they looked like fire nymphs. Cecil and Shelly brought up the rear, both holding their own torches.

I channeled the power I had managed to gather. It burned in the center of my chest. The over-tight indigestion from eating the hag came back. Sweat popped out over my body, sliming my skin. I fought for control. I had to have it together for this.

The ceiling gave a loud crack. Red sparks rained down, stinging my arms. Several screams filled the room. This was it.

"Go!" Mysti yelled.

Griff kicked open the door. He held up a can of aerosol spray and depressed it against the torch. Flame shot out. A horse screamed, and so did my mother's voice. Good.

I crowded behind the torchbearers and twisted to speak to my family. "Run for your lives. Don't wait for anybody. Don't help anybody. Just go."

I burst into the hazy light, throwing up my left hand. Fire

formed in a beautiful orange and red ball. The colors undulated and sent up tiny sparks. I focused on Nash Redmond a few feet away and threw the fireball. It hit him in the chest and knocked him off his horse. Mayhem broke out.

The people behind me scooted past and ran to the building next door for their cars. The battle raged in front of me. Griff and Dillon used aerosol cans and torches to set horses and horsemen on fire.

Dogs surrounded Mysti, saliva flying from their mouths, red-tipped ears glowing. She lifted a bottle of clear liquid to her mouth and blew fire into their faces. They ran away yelping, their white fur turning black.

One of the dogs, the one who'd gotten the biggest blast of fire spit, fell on its side and stilled. Its eyes glazed in death. Then the black soot faded from its white fur in a fast sweep. The dog got back up, shook itself, and snarled.

Sorrow melted my resolve. We couldn't beat them. We'd die fighting, and Oscar would have my power once and for all.

A lump formed in my throat as I watched my friends fight for their lives. It was useless. Griff's dark SUV blasted from behind the second building, Brad at the wheel, his face set and fierce. I pointed at where Griff and Mysti were back to back surrounded by dogs but still trying to fight.

Brad plowed toward them. He ran over dogs. The phantom animals yelped, went through their death throes, and then got back up to fight again. Brad ran over Michael Gage, the SUV pushing the bone and metal his body was fashioned from under the SUV's wheels and crushing it. He pulled up beside Griff and Mysti. Finn opened the back door.

"Get in," he screamed.

Griff and Mysti blew fire at their attackers and leapt into the SUV. Brad took off, but Finn yelled something, and he slammed on his brakes. Horsemen and dogs closed in on them, a couple going around to circle them.

I watched in disbelief. Why weren't they leaving? Everybody in the SUV was watching a fight several yards away. Then I understood. Dillon.

My cousin-by-marriage, the only woman in camp skinnier than me, stood back to back with Hannah. Dillon used her aerosol can to spray fire to keep back the dogs. Hannah had made her tire iron into a torch, which she stabbed at anything that got close. She already had a bleeding wound on her cheek.

Oscar sat nearby on his gray horse, watching the dogs and other huntsmen wear down the two women. His sides heaved with mirth, and he pointed one gloved finger. Of course he was enjoying this, laughing at it. He was too evil for anything else.

Fury built in me and mixed with my magic. I held out my left hand. Another fireball glowed to life. I let it fly at Oscar. The fireball hit him in the knot of bone and sinew that served as his neck. Its force knocked him off his mount. I ran toward him, channeling more magic. The beginnings of fatigue ached deep in my bones.

When I got near enough, I reached into the raging mass of Oscar's consciousness and pressed on it. He was already dead, so I couldn't make him stroke out, but I could scramble his thoughts, maybe interrupt whatever magic he was using to manifest on both the living and the dead plane.

But I didn't stop to think I had already played a version of this little trick on Oscar when I drained his energy back on the highway. He was waiting for me.

Oscar's consciousness rose around mine like a cage of red thread and ensnared me. I tried to pull away, but it was like trying to get away from melted cheese. It just stretched with me, creating new strings to connect us. The more I wiggled and tried to escape, the more thoroughly it coated me. Oscar had me.

I staggered to the side. Shelly and Cecil came out of nowhere to stand on either side, both sending fire out to Oscar. The fire didn't faze him. He batted it away with one chain-mail gloved hand. He narrowed his focus on me and siphoned off my power. My brain fuzzed. I couldn't fight. I couldn't do anything but let it happen.

Brad sped over in the SUV, headed straight for Oscar. He slammed into him. Oscar fell, and the wheels bumped over him. As soon as the SUV cleared, he stood again, glittering eyes fixed on me, cinching his mind tighter around mine.

Brad staggered out, brandishing a hunting knife. He buried it to the hilt in Oscar's back, closed his eyes, and began moving his lips. Brad, an energy witch who specialized in calling circles, began to tremble with effort. Though I had no way of knowing his intent, I could only guess he might try to bind Oscar's magic.

Lights flashed in the eye sockets of Oscar's skull. He pinwheeled his arms, reaching for the knife and Brad. Brad pushed the knife in deeper, face knotted with concentration, and kept moving his lips. Oscar's armor chinked. His body seemed to settle in on itself.

It was working. If Brad could keep up this effort, I'd be able to free myself from Oscar. I saw movement in my fading peripheral vision.

My mother appeared, sword raised and riding fast toward Brad. No. I couldn't let Mysti's brother be killed. Not like this.

"Brad, get in the car and go," I yelled.

Orev flew at my mother, landed on her face. A mass of blackbirds joined him. Crows, ravens, magpies, and buzzards. Their heads pecked, and black ichor that might have blood flew.

Barbie screamed. The horse, a beautiful white stallion

with bunching muscles, bucked off my mother and the mass of birds covering her and ran.

Oscar used the distraction to sling Brad off him. To his credit, Brad ran for his life. That left me lurching around, head aching like a rotten tooth. Oscar tightened his grip on my mind. I convulsed once with the pressure of it.

Cecil redoubled his efforts of keeping the huntsmen and the dogs away. Fatigue bent his shoulders forward, and his hands trembled. He wouldn't last much longer.

Kenny sped up in his huge heavy-duty truck. He pushed the passenger door open. "Y'all get in. Now!"

I took a couple of steps toward the truck. Oscar's mind whipped tighter around mine, strands of him invading me with red, vengeful hate.

Shelly and Cecil ignored Kenny and kept fighting as I staggered around, hands holding my head. It felt as though it might explode any second. I got control of myself enough to connect with Orev. Together, we pushed against Oscar.

Hannah and Dillon, somehow having slipped their attackers, ran up behind us. Dillon grabbed my arm and dragged me toward Kenny's truck. I shook her off.

"Shelly and Cecil." I pointed desperately at my elderly great-aunt and uncle.

Dillon's face fell, but she did as I asked, ignoring Shelly's and Cecil's attempts to fight her off. Hannah came to help her, shooting fearful glances at me. Just as they'd gotten the two to the truck, she dropped Cecil's arm.

Her mouth opened in a perfect *O*, and her eyes rounded to the point it scared me. She screamed one word. "Nooooooo...." It seemed to go on forever.

Fire blossomed in my lower abdomen, turning my bowels into liquid. I glanced down to see what had happened. A sword stuck out of me. Vision graying, I raised my head to see who'd killed me.

Oscar grinned at me from the other end of the sword. "This is it, you vapid little bitch. I'll have what I deserve."

A black mass of feathers dove at Oscar's head and landed squarely on the headdress. Orev. Thank goodness. The rest of the birds joined my raven familiar.

Instead of clawing out Oscar's eyes, which was what they should have done, they covered his headdress. Made of leather with deer antlers and jewels attached, it was obvious why birds would gravitate to that. But it wouldn't hurt Oscar. Clawing out his eyes would hurt him. Even if they grew right back.

Oscar, however, had a different reaction. He screamed and let go of the sword. The weapon slid out of my middle and thumped to the dirt.

A stream of my blood followed it to splat on the ground. I slapped one hand over my lower abdomen as though hiding the wound would fix it. Shock held the pain at bay for the moment, but I had only seconds before it took me. I tried again to shake Oscar's hold off my mind. He was still too strong.

The birds' wild caws blotted out all other sound. They flapped and clawed, battling Oscar for the headdress. He went down, holding onto the thing with both hands. His panic beat at me. The more hysterical he got, the more his hold slipped.

His mind unwrapped from mine a bit at a time. At the last I jerked away. But it was too late.

Blood leaked out of my abdomen in a steady stream. The shock had gone, taking with it any merciful unawareness of the pain. My insides ached. Cold spread inch by inch through my body. Gray fogged the edges of my vision.

The birds quit squawking. I glanced over at Oscar to see they'd flown away, except my Orev. Poor Orev staggered around, disoriented, sharing my injury. He was too sick to control them anymore.

I grabbed for the mantle, only to find its shine had dulled. Its power felt more like a light push than its usual electric pop. The world around me faded a bit more.

No. This couldn't be it. I wouldn't let this be it.

The ghostly Six Guns and the horsemen stopped to watch my end. Barbie stood right out front. Skin had grown over some of her bones, and one eye shone out of a socket.

Enough hate radiated from that one eye to burn a hole through my heart.

Oscar joined them, picking up his sword off the ground. "Time to die, Peri Jean Mace. I would say you fought a good fight, but it was really a shitty effort."

I groaned in pain and frustration. Vision fading, I fell to my knees, hands laced over my stomach, still horribly aware of all that was going on.

Cecil screamed and bawled from inside Kenny's truck. Shelly held him back from coming to me, her dark eyes leaking tears.

"Go," I croaked at them. They didn't need to see me die. I curled my knees to my chest.

An engine screamed up behind me, and a door slammed. A ball of flame hit Oscar in the chest. The gas can carrying the flame fell to the ground, gave a polite cough, and spewed fire up his legs. Oscar danced around.

"Help me." His armor clinked as he beat at himself.

In my mental fog, he reminded me of a kid doing the pee-pee dance. I giggled and tasted blood at the back of my throat.

Skinny hands closed around me, and Tubby Tubman scooped me into his arms. I screamed from the pain of being moved.

"It's okay. It's okay," he chanted, his voice choked. He was crying. Tubby Tubman, the toughest person I knew, was crying.

Veronica Spinelli and Trench Coat put Oscar out by rolling him on the ground. He lay still a few seconds and bounded to his feet, holding his sword up.

"Get them, you morons. Kill them." Oscar led them toward us.

They'd kill both Tubby and me, and they'd have what they came for. I tried to plan, but I was in too much pain and too weak.

Kenny appeared in front of us, holding a torch and Mysti's bottle of clear liquid. "Get Peri Jean in your car and go. I'll stay."

"You can't. They'll kill you," I slurred at Kenny.

"Anita's dead," he choked. "This is the end of my road. Safe and long travels. Both of you." He turned from us, shoulders square and brave. His sacrifice touched me. Even assholes could be heroes.

"Kenny, wait." Saying the words hurt every inch of my body.

He came back.

I gripped his arm with bloody hand. "You were one of us. A Gregg, if not by blood, then spirit. Godspeed."

Kenny picked up my hand and kissed it. Then he marched toward the assembled huntsmen and his death.

Tubby carried me to his car. Each step jostled and hurt worse than the one before. Just as Tubby shoved me into the back seat, Kenny let out an agonized scream. I raised my head to find him, to honor him by watching his last moments. Tubby slammed the door in my face. I twisted around on the back seat and leaned my face against the window.

Kenny had somehow managed to set all the horses and their riders on fire. He bled from more wounds than I could count. He dropped to the ground and rolled over on his back to stare at the sky while he died.

Cecil raced Kenny's truck through the horsemen and their riders, tearing them apart, dispersing them for the moment. He swerved to miss Kenny's lifeless body and peeled out of the dirt parking lot.

Tubby took off. I hurt too bad to turn my body to see more. The pain clutched at me, pulling me under. I wanted to hear Tanner's rough voice speaking words of comfort.

I pulled out my phone, surprised I hadn't lost it in the scuffle, and unlocked the screen. My finger smeared blood all over it. I dialed Tanner's number.

A recording picked up, and an impersonal voice said, "This is no longer a working number."

Grief stabbed through my fading emotions. Tanner had turned off his phone. I'd truly lost him. With a sob, I let the phone drop into the floorboard, wishing I could tell him how much he'd meant to me.

The world turned around, as though someone had flipped it. I found myself on a airplane full of people. The white noise from the engines filled the cabin. How had I gone from dying on the backseat of Tubby's car to the inside of a plane?

I glanced down at my hands. Tawny skin with a sprinkling of dark hair. I knew those hands. Tanner. I had somehow found my way into Tanner's body. Was I here to say goodbye?

Before I could figure out what to do, or how to do it, a familiar voice spoke from beside me.

"I'm thinking we'll call up our old contacts, and..." Dave moved forward and into my field of vision. He waved a hand in front of my face. "Tanner? What's wrong, buddy?"

"I thought I heard Peri Jean's voice. Calling for me," came Tanner's raspy purr.

Dave gave a nervous laugh.

"It's not funny, David." Tanner's voice had gone sharp, each word clipped off precisely. "Something's wrong. Bad wrong. I need to get in touch with her soon as we land."

Neecie's voice came from the other side. "Don't worry about her. You're doing the right thing. Let those people get back to their lives."

"Those people? Their lives?" Tanner's voice raised. "What is that supposed to mean?"

"Calm down," Neecie whispered. "You didn't belong there. Think of this as a course correction. Leave her behind."

Tanner let out an angry growl. "I've had enough of your barbs about Peri Jean and the Greggs. I love her, and they're family to me. If she needs me, I'm going back."

The world turned again, and I was back in Tubby's car, jouncing painfully with every bump. It really seemed I had been with Tanner for just that one second. But that was impossible. I was a psychic medium. Not a telepath.

The whole thing had probably just been the fevered dream of a dying woman. Brought on by a last wish to tell Tanner just how deep my feelings had gone. That he had been the right one. But now it was too late. Now I'd have to face whatever lay on the other side of life.

The thought trailed off. The world faded, first gray with black dots, and then white. I let my consciousness slip away, hoping Tubby wouldn't get too upset about me dying in his car.

8

Tubby's shouts gave me a rude push back into consciousness.

"No, I don't see any damn gate. It's dark out here." Tubby brayed a few sobs. "She's dying. Oh shit, can't you do something?"

My consciousness crept back in little by little. A clammy chill coated my skin. I wanted to shiver, but I was too tired. A red ball of pain pulsed at my center. My jeans clung wetly to my skin. Had I pissed my pants? What a great way to end things.

Tubby cried some more, but then shut it off like the flip of a switch. "No. You're right. I'll calm down." He paused. "I see the sign. There's the gate. The code's 55632?"

The car door opened, and the car shifted as Tubby got out. The sound of coyotes yowling in the distance drifted through the open door. They were singing me home, to whatever waited in the great beyond. Tubby got back into the car and slammed the door, sobbing again. The tires thumped over a cattle guard.

"Fight," said a voice next to my head. A freezing hand pressed against my forehead, the cold of it seeping in my head like an ice cream headache.

My eyes flew open at the pain. Priscilla Herrera leaned over me, this time as her young, tattooed specter.

"You can't die. You have to pass on the power." She patted me with cold hands.

The death wound woke up. Its intense pain spread through me. I wished for sleep, the kind I'd never wake from, just to end the misery. I accepted my own death. A peace I had never expected slipped over me. With it came a revelation.

"You don't need me to pass on the mantle. Mysti White-byrd took on Petunia LeBlanc's mantle, and they weren't even related," I told Priscilla and relaxed, eyes drifting closed.

"The Gregorius mantle can only be passed daughter to daughter. That was the bargain made thousands of years ago." She stroked my forehead and pressed cool lips to it. "You, my sweet, have a long and fruitful road ahead. You are the next generation of our line. Don't give up."

An image flashed into my mind. In it, a very pregnant me sat on the scarred wood floor of a room with the softest yellow walls, putting together a crib. Tanner spoke to me from the doorway. We smiled at each other. Just as quickly as it came, the image faded, leaving me to wonder if it had been a real vision of the future or just wishful thinking. I looked for Priscilla, so I could ask, but she was gone.

Tubby's sobs and curses came from the front seat. The electric window hummed as he rolled it down.

"This ain't a house. Why didn't you tell me to look for a damn storage building?" he yelled.

Another male voice rumbled a sharp answer. I knew that voice.

"Don't matter anyway. I think she's done dead. She was back there talking to people who ain't here." Tubby began to cry again.

Pain gripped me again. I yelled, barely recognizing my own weak voice.

"She's not dead," the familiar voice said. "Let's get her out of the car and carry her in the house."

Tubby got out of the driver's seat and pushed it forward so he could get to me. The sharp smell of his sweat enveloped me. He pushed his skinny arms between the seat and me and lifted.

The movement poked the pain, hard. Like hornets swarming from their nest, it came, seeping over me, becoming all that I was.

"Just leave me here," I managed to whisper.

"You'll die," Tubby grunted. His steps crunched over dead, dry vegetation. Each one provoked the agony in my gut a little more.

"Leave me. Let me go." I gasped from the pain and coughed. The salty taste of blood filled my mouth. I tried to spit but didn't have the strength.

"I got the door," the familiar voice rumbled. "Hurry. She doesn't have long."

A door opened, and light shone in my eyes. I winced and tried to turn my head away. My muscles didn't work. We brushed past another person. The scent of sunshine and gasoline filled my senses. It hit me whose house this was. Wade. Tubby had brought me to Wade's.

"Put her on the couch." Wade's voice followed us through the too-bright room.

"I'll get blood on it," I whispered.

Tubby let out a whinny of laughter. He lowered me onto something soft. I moaned with relief.

"Please make her better." He curled his fingers around mine. I couldn't squeeze back, but I wanted to tell him how much I'd liked knowing him.

A blast of cold touched my skin. Priscilla had come back.

"You're not going to die." She didn't sound so sure. In fact, she sounded pretty scared.

I opened my eyes, wanting to see what fear looked like on her, but they didn't work. I saw nothing but bright light with two figures silhouetted over me. A third figure joined them, this one not quite solid. Priscilla.

"Tell the healer I am here and will lend power through you." Her voice shook in my head.

I tried to repeat her words but only got out two. "She's here."

"What is it?" Wade leaned so close I smelled soap and shaving cream. Did he shave now? I tried to touch his face, but Tubby had hold of my hand.

"Priscilla. Here. Power." I listened to myself not make sense but couldn't help it. It was too late.

"It is not too late," Priscilla yelled. The lights blinked on and off.

"You see that?" Tubby's voice went from sad to scared in an instant.

"No, what?" Wade rose from me. He drew in a sharp breath. "Okay. It's Peri Jean's spirit guide. She just wants to help." He knelt beside the couch and put both hands on my stomach. He let out a moan.

"Don't stop," Tubby yelled.

"I'm not, you jumping jackass." Wade took a deep breath, then another. The room quieted except for the hum of electricity.

Pinpricks of magic rushed over my abdomen where his hands rested and approached the burning wall of pain inside me. The magic probed at the pain. I screamed.

Wade began to speak. *"Father over the heavens and the underground, the sea and the land, the night and the day, let me heal this woman, Peri Jean Mace."*

My black opal heated first, radiating power throughout my body. The heat spread to my internal injuries. The warmth became fire, and the fire became agony. I clenched my teeth against it. The whine of a wounded animal escaped from between them.

Priscilla Herrera's cold hand covered my forehead. The energy she possessed as a spirit raced through me. My back arched. Wade cried out but only tightened his grip on me.

He began to chant in a cadence as old as mankind. *"When thou wast in need, I found thee. I knew thee by thy real name, Peri Jean Mace. I laid the hands of heaven above upon thee."*

More power flooded into me, the sweet pressure filling me. I cracked my eyes open to see Wade wreathed in a bright nimbus, sweat dripping from his flushed face, his eyes squeezed shut.

He said, *"By faith, I healed thy wounds. The old gods have blessed me and will bless thee. My blessing is yours. Heal her wounds."* He paused, gasping. "Say it with me, Tubman."

Tubby's nasally twang joined Wade's deep rumble. They

spoke the words again and again. Fire filled my body, especially the spot below my navel where Oscar's sword had stabbed into me. The pain spread through every inch of muscle and skin. My back bowed, body tight and quivering.

Wade began to speak his incantation again, his voice more forceful than ever. His sweat dripped onto me, cool against my feverish skin.

"It's closing. The wound's closing." Tubby's excitement made him sound like a little boy.

I cracked open my eyes and watched him, damp hair plastered to his face, sweat rings under his arms. He reached out and cupped my cheek with one hand.

"You gonna live, baby." A tear slipped out of the corner of one eye.

"One last time," Wade panted. "We need to make sure the internal wounds are closed."

I searched for my magic again. This time I found the mantle pulsing behind the living gauze of the scar tissue spell. I pulled on it and lent it to Wade's power. He grunted when this new surge of energy hit him, but kept right on chanting. The heat built in my body as more healing took place.

Wade's words cut off. He fell away from me. His running footsteps shook the house. The noise of him being sick came from nearby.

"Gross," Tubby whispered.

"He has to get rid of it somehow," I mumbled.

"You talked. You talked." He gave me a sweaty hug.

To my surprise, I was able to lift my arms and put them around him. He was right. Wade had saved me.

A short distance away, a toilet flushed. Water splashed in a sink. Wade's footsteps shook the house again. Cabinets slammed. More water ran. Wade stood over us holding a glass of water.

"Let me kneel down beside her." He kicked at Tubby. The smaller man gave him a glare but did what he said. Wade knelt beside him. "Now get her head up." Wade pressed a glass of water to my lips. "Drink it. Now."

I took a few sips but sputtered them out.

"Try again." He held the glass to my lips.

That time, I took a few sips. Wade put the glass of water on a whitewashed coffee table. Someone had gone to a lot of trouble to paint a fern design on it.

Wade used his shirt to wipe sweat off his face. He slapped Tubby on the back, smiling. "We did it, you nasty little turd. We saved her."

Tubby sat on the floor, which I now saw was plain wood plank, and leaned back on his hands. "You're just as nasty as me."

I tried to get up.

"No, no, no." Wade got back to his knees. "Just settle down."

"I'm getting blood on the couch." My voice came in a weak gasp, but it was better than before. I pushed Wade's hand off my chest.

"All right. All right." Wade stood and took my arm. "What do you want to do?"

"I want to be clean." My legs folded like overcooked spaghetti. If it hadn't been for Wade holding me up, I'd have hit his pretty coffee table.

He sighed. "All right. Tubman, you passed my sister's house on the way in."

"I didn't see it," Tubby said.

"Well, you drove right past it." Voice tight with impatience, Wade sounded like he was getting ready to start shouting. "Unlock the front door with the key from underneath the flowerpot. My niece's bedroom is the first one to the left off the living room. Find sweatpants or tights and a clean shirt. Bring them back here."

Tubby turned to go.

Wade grabbed his arm. "Do not get into anything. Do not take anything. You hear me?"

Tubby tried to pull away. "What kinda man you think I am?"

"You really want me to answer?" Wade let go of Tubby with a shove.

Tubby stumped off muttering under his breath. I caught the words "Godzilla" and "cocksucker."

"Come back here and say that," Wade called, my arm still gripped in one huge hand.

Tubby slammed the door. His footsteps rang on steps, and then he was gone.

Wade and I were all alone.

———

Wade twisted me where he could look me in the face, and I got my first look at him.

The scar on his head from where he'd been shot several months ago was now white and looked very old, like it had happened when he was a child. His beard covered only his upper lip and chin and had been trimmed close to the skin. The skin on his cheeks was smooth shaven. That's where the smell of shaving cream had come from.

He licked full lips that I'd never noticed back when he had his Rasputin motorcycle man beard. "You want to clean yourself off, right?"

Almost frozen with shock at the transformation of Wade from wild man to regular guy, I managed to nod. He hauled me past a bed and into a tiny bathroom with only a shower, toilet, and sink.

"Hopefully it doesn't smell like vomit in here." He flipped on the lights, looked at me, and winced. "You'll need to take off your clothes. Do you want to wait until Tubman gets back?"

I shook my head and began to pull off my shirt. Wade pushed me to sit on the toilet and took off my shoes. I still had on Cecil's flannel shirt with the black T-shirt underneath. Wade pulled them over my head. Then I sat there wearing nothing but a bra and blue jeans, chest smeared pink with blood.

I raised both arms. "Hold me up, and I'll pull down my jeans."

He did as I asked, his face an inch from mine, one black eye boring into mine. I got my jeans unbuttoned and unzipped, and Wade sat me back on the toilet and pulled them the rest of the way off.

We both looked at my wound. It was so small, it could have been a cat scratch.

"Thank you for saving me." My voice came out weak and too soft.

Wade flushed. "I got a washer and dryer in here. Let me put these in to wash."

He turned away, clothes bundled into his arms, and hurried out of the bathroom.

I leaned back against the cool porcelain of the toilet, wishing I'd told him to take my underwear but not wanting to be that naked in front of him. The thing Wade and I had always had, that odd connection, had come roaring back. I didn't want those feelings to bloom into something we had to acknowledge. Wade was the wrong man. I knew that now.

Tanner Letts had stolen my heart. Despite the disconnected phone, some part of me still hoped for another chance with him. If what I saw of him on the plane with Dave and Neecie was real, he'd been thinking of me. Then there'd been that other vision, the one of me in the sunny room with its soft buttery walls, pregnant and assembling a crib. I wanted that with Tanner.

Before he'd left, I'd known I was in love with him. I didn't want to let that go without fighting for it. The connection I felt with Wade was real, but the one I had with Tanner was more solid. Maybe because we'd actually acted on the attraction and worked to build a relationship.

Wade came back with a big plastic bowl. "Your bra and panties are disgusting. They're going to stink in the morning."

Our eyes locked. Before I knew what I was doing, I disrobed the rest of the way. Wade turned away and kept his eyes averted. He took the bra and panties from me and put them in the bowl. He filled it with water and left the room again.

His heavy footsteps approached, and I covered my breasts with one arm, skin crawling in something almost like embarrassment. But not quite.

He ran the water in the sink until it was warm, soaped up a washcloth, and began washing me, face set and businesslike. The front door opened.

"Bathroom, Tubman," Wade yelled.

Tubby's quick steps approached, and he gasped upon seeing me naked. I turned my face away but felt his eyes crawling over me. Wade washed the rest of me with brisk, almost rough movements, rinsed the cloth, and wiped me down.

It was almost funny. Less than a year ago, I'd wanted Wade with all my heart and soul. Now Tanner dominated my thoughts. He'd be upset to know Wade not only saw me naked but touched my skin. Wade pressed a soft towel to my fingers.

"Dry off." He stepped away from me, threw Tubby a glance, and rolled his eyes. I followed his gaze.

Tubby stood frozen in the doorway, a ball of clothes clutched to his chest, looking at me.

Wade snatched the clothes from him. "Pull her up off the toilet so we can get these clothes on her."

Tubby approached and did what Wade asked. Unlike Wade, his eyes roamed my body, lingering on some of the tattoos. He saw me watching and reddened but didn't glance away.

"Sorry," he muttered.

I'd have expected no less from Tubby, but I didn't bother to tell him that.

Wade wrangled me into a too-big T-shirt and yoga pants and scooped me into his arms. He took me to the bed and nodded to Tubby. He pulled down a pretty quilt made of floral patterned fabric. It didn't seem Wade's taste at all. Wade laid me on clean white sheets.

"She's got to rest, at least tonight. Call whoever you need to, tell them she's gonna live." Wade dug in an armoire that looked to have once been a TV cabinet. He got out a light blanket and spread it over the couch. "I'm so tired I'm almost sick. I get the couch. You can either have the floor or go sleep on my sister's couch. I'll send her a text message that you might be there."

Wade tapped on his phone and then pulled his boots off. I watched in a fog, noting vaguely that he'd lost the engineer boots and now wore the kind of boots a factory worker might.

He caught me watching and smiled. "Steel toed, darlin'. Don't mess with me."

I laughed as much as my beat-up body would let me. Laughing with me, he padded over to a light switch and flicked it off. He turned on the light over the stove and came back to the couch in its dim glow. Wade took off his shirt, revealing familiar tattoos and chest heavier with muscle than when we'd been roommates. He lay down on the couch. It groaned in protest of his bulk.

"Just rest," he said.

I drifted then, in a fog halfway between sleep and waking. My dreams were fragmented and frightening. Tanner walked through them. I followed, making promises, and begging him to come back.

Shelly and I talked about the future of Sanctuary next to a grave. I realized with a shock the tombstone had Cecil's name on it.

Finn stood at the front of a church, wearing a cheap suit, waving a Bible, and screaming. Zora sat behind him on a bench swinging her legs and smiling.

My dreams skipped track, and I lay in bed with Tanner, his hands running over my body. With one thumb, he caressed my nipple until it stood stiff. I arched my back toward him. He dipped one hand between my legs, lips brushing mine in rhythm with the movement of his hand. I rocked my hips against his fingers. He groaned.

Wait a second. That groan sounded wrong.

My eyes flew open. In the half-light Wade leaned over me, naked. He had one hand down the front of the yoga pants I'd worn to bed. The too big T-shirt had been pushed up to my collarbone.

His dark eyes searched mine. "Is this okay?"

His fingers teased, featherlight, sliding back and forth in the slickness between my legs. I gasped, too turned on to think about an answer. I couldn't concentrate on anything but the movement of his hand between my legs and his breath tickling my lips.

Wade had been my fantasy for a long time. He'd flirted, teased, shunned, and went back to do it all again. His exit from my life had been abrupt, had left things unfinished. Now I had a chance to finish it.

Tanner and guilt hovered at the corner of my mind. But I remembered that disconnected phone number message. Those seconds of being with him on the plane to California and the wishful dream I'd had of the sunny room and the baby crib might not even be real. For all I knew, Tanner and I were done.

I let my body take over because old desires always die hard.

Wade's hand found the best spot of all, the one that blotted out all rational thought. I undulated my hips against his fingers. He watched, a smile twitching at his lips.

"Say yes." His tongue teased the corner of my mouth.

"Yes." I spread my legs wide and let my fingers trail over the ridges of stomach muscle to drift over the slick tip of his shaft. I curled my fingers around him and slid my hand over his length.

He groaned, eyes fluttering almost closed, but he snapped them open and fastened them back on mine.

"You sure?" His hand kept moving between my legs, as though to ensure my answer.

I nodded and kept stroking, maybe for the same reason.

We'd wanted each other so long and so badly, nothing else seemed to matter other than the heat of his skin against mine and his smell in my nose. I wanted this experience, even if it was just one time. Something, some fact, nagged at the back of my brain. But it drifted away before I could latch onto it.

Wade fastened his lips over mine, tongue fluttering against mine to match the almost-not-there motion of his fingers. He broke the kiss and pulled away from me.

Had he changed his mind? Some still rational part of me insisted that might be best. Before the thought could take root and blossom, Wade crouched over me and pulled off the yoga pants. The rasp of the material over my skin brought chill bumps. I yanked off the t- shirt. Wade grabbed my ankles, hoisted them onto his shoulders and pulled me to him.

"I wanna watch you," he whispered. He pushed the tip of his cock down to tease my over-sensitized skin.

I drew in a sharp breath and whimpered, "Please, oh please."

Eyes on mine, he lifted my hips. "Anything you want, baby."

I let out a little scream and dug my fingernails into his wrists as he pushed his thick length all the way into me. The sensation of being stretched to my limit made every movement, even the tiniest one, intense.

Wade moved gently at first, my fingers still squeezing his wrists. His eyes devoured mine, roamed over my body, and came back up again. The bed squeaked out the beat of our lovemaking.

A low rumble filled the room. At first I thought it was thunder, but then realized it was Wade's moans. The sound of them drove my frenzy. I rolled my hips, pressing down against his hardness. I wanted to feel all of him I could.

Wade pulled his wrists out of my hands and moved my ankles off his shoulders. He wrapped my legs around his waist and braced his hands on either side of my head, fists clutching handfuls of sheet, dark, fierce eyes locked on mine. His hips bucked against me.

The bed's cries grew louder. So did mine. He stiffened, and we both screamed our pleasure.

Then he was beside me, sweaty body pressed against mine. He kissed my lips, one hand caressing my cheek. I stared into his eyes. They'd softened, and the light of his good humor shone in them.

"That was amazing. I always knew it would be," he whispered against my lips.

He was right. It had been. I murmured my agreement and kissed him. Somewhere in the back of my mind, some detail begged to cut in and ruin the moment, but I was too tired and too sated to give it notice.

Wade turned me on my side so my naked back pressed against his chest. His arm rested over me, protecting me from the whole world. I sighed, as content as I'd ever been.

9

I woke with a sharp inhale. I'd been dreaming I'd died and was at my own funeral as a ghost. Tanner had been there, crying, and I hadn't been able to let him know I still existed. I shook off the dream and rubbed my face. I patted the bed next to me. Empty.

"Good morning," Wade said.

I raised my head to find him sitting at a round table with a cute little red checkered tablecloth.

Who had decorated this place? Not Wade. I'd lived with him. His idea of decorating was a calendar with a nude woman on it thumbtacked to the wall. His sister must have done all this. She had a real flair for decorating. I loved this cute little space.

"Mmmph." I pointed my toes and raised my arms over my head to stretch. My body screamed, especially the area below my navel where Oscar had stabbed me. I let out a squeak.

"That's gonna hurt for a while." Wade got out of his chair and lumbered to the kitchen counter. He spooned coffee grounds into the spotless, stainless steel coffee maker, poured in some water, and started it.

I picked my way out from under the sheets and quilt mounded on me and sat on the edge of the bed. I put one foot on the floor and tried to stand. Just that effort sent a stab of agony through my middle that doubled me over.

Wade watched me, head tilted to one side, dark brows raised. I glanced down at my body. Naked. The night before came back in vivid detail. My skin heated.

The fact that had nagged at the edge of my mind the night before jumped into full view. Wade's sister, Desiree, had predicted he'd die if he ever hooked up with me. That had been the detail I'd kept shying away from. That was why Wade walked out of my life. If Desiree was right, I'd just helped Wade sign his death warrant.

I drew in a sharp gasp. Oh, no. What had I done? Traded sex for someone's life, that's what. And not just anybody. This was Wade. A man who'd risked himself to save me more than once. A man who'd been my friend when I desperately needed one.

Iron bands of guilt squeezed my heart. Bile crawled up my throat, stinging all the way. The reality of what I'd done spread over me like poison ivy. It burned with a fire nothing could soothe. I'd done the wrong thing. Again.

The worst part? I regretted what Wade and I had done. He was no longer my heart's desire. Tanner was. Wade held the key to a long lurking, unsatisfied question. After Tanner's rejection, I couldn't pass up the chance to answer that question.

But things were always clearer in the rearview mirror. I should have used some restraint. Wade's sister had asked me to stay out of his life because doing so might save it. Now look what I'd done.

The guilt put on weight, growing fat on my self-pity. It pressed against my heart hard enough to make it ache. A sob built in my throat. I gave it a savage push back. No crying. A bunch of weak, girlish tears wouldn't change a damn thing. I cut a guilty glance at the table to find Wade smiling at me.

"I dried your clothes this morning." He pointed to a neatly folded pile of clothes on the floor next to my side of the bed. The hag's heart lay next to them on a strip of paper towel. Hopefully being washed and dried hadn't ruin any value it might have.

I nodded my thanks and snatched my panties off the top of the pile. I jerked them on, relishing the rough feel of the material against my skin. I didn't deserve for the material to feel soft. Not after what I'd done. By the time I got to my jeans, I had to stop and pant from the pain. I embraced that too, welcomed it as a sick little penance. Wade got up and walked to the shining white stove.

"Breakfast? I got bacon and eggs." He held up a black cast iron skillet.

Who had time to think about breakfast? I was busy beating myself up. When would I ever get my shit together and do things right?

I glanced out the window at Wade's tree-covered yard. A narrow driveway cut through the trees. The Cutlass was gone, but Tubby had to be somewhere out there. He wouldn't just leave me. Would he? I hoped not. He was my way out of this situation. I might not have deserved to run away, but I wanted to.

"Where's Tubby?" I directed the question to Wade's broad back.

"Up at my sister's," he answered without turning around.

I nodded, glad Wade couldn't see how much I wanted out of here. Soon as I could, I'd find Tubby and get him to take me back to my family. I didn't even know if they were okay.

A white 1970s Cadillac, its distinctive boxy headlights dim, eased down the narrow lane through the trees. It stopped in front of Wade's house. The door opened, and a woman with big boobs, long legs, and a bush of blonde hair got out.

"Who's that?" I yanked on Cecil's ruined flannel shirt. The

bloodstains had seasoned to an ugly chocolate milk color, but it at least smelled clean. Wade let the cast iron skillet clatter to the stove.

"Shit. I forgot she was coming. Stay away from the windows." Wade bolted out the door, closing it securely behind him.

I stepped out of direct sight of the window and watched Wade jog up to the woman. They kissed. She curled her hands in his hair and hooked one leg over his hip. She broke the kiss and stared into his eyes.

Wade, face creased into a charming smile, put both hands on the woman's cheeks and began talking. Judging by his posture, he was apologizing for something.

That was when I let myself see Wade's one-room house through clearer eyes. The carefully painted fern on the whitewashed coffee table. The floral quilt on the bed. The clean kitchen. The gingham tablecloth. His sister didn't do all that. The woman who shared his bed did.

And this one looked like an actual girlfriend. One who cared enough to put little Día De Los Muertos painted skulls in his kitchen window for Samhain. The guilt came roaring back, more intense than ever. How much worse could this get?

Chest tight, I glanced out the window. The long-legged woman smiled and shook her finger at Wade. She grabbed his shirt in both hands and pulled him in for another kiss. He obliged, hands roaming over her body, and squeezing her shapely butt. She got back into her car, did a quick turnaround in the yard, and was gone.

Shame radiated through my entire body until sweat popped out on the back of my neck. That little exchange made it obvious Wade had a girlfriend he liked, and here I was, the ultimate white elephant. Wade came back in, cheeks flushed, and let out a deep breath.

"That was Aspen. I was supposed to go garage sale-ing with her this morning. She buys furniture, refinishes it, and sells it. It pays for her... Why am I telling you this?" He made a face.

I could barely look at him. "Wade, I am sorry for everything. Tubby shouldn't have brought me here."

He approached me and gripped my upper arms. "Shut the hell up and look at me."

Face flaming, I couldn't imagine doing any such thing. He put a finger under my chin and forced me to raise my head.

"If Tubby hadn't brought you here, you'd be dead right now. No hospital could have fixed that. As it was, Tubby barely got you here in time." He stared into my eyes, eyebrows raised.

"We did the wrong thing." I stepped away, sat on the bed, and pulled on my boots. Every movement hurt.

He came to stand next to me and plucked at my blood-stained flannel shirt. "Take off that disgusting thing. It looks like death."

He pulled the shirt off my shoulders, tossed it in the garbage can, and brought me one of his. It hung to my knees and smelled like sunshine and gasoline. Like Wade. A tear spilled out of my eye. I'd probably never smell Tanner's earthy musk again.

I peeled off the shirt and held it out to him. "I can't."

"Yes, you can. Come here. Let's talk." He took my hand, led me to the table, and motioned for me to sit down. I did with an audible grunt. The coffee was ready. Wade got us both cups and sat down. "Two spoons of fake creamer, right?"

I took a sip. It chased away a little gloom, but not much. "We shouldn't have done what we did last night. That woman likes you. A lot."

Wade chuckled into his coffee and took a long drink. "They all do, baby." He lit a cigarette and passed it to me. "Here. This'll make it better."

I took the cigarette and smoked, staring out at the gray morning because I couldn't stand to look at the man across from me.

"Do I have to ask you to look at me again?" He put his hand over my wrist. I drew away. He laughed this time, loud and long, throwing his head back to stare at the ceiling.

"Damn. I never expected this from you," he said almost to himself. "You don't have anything to feel guilty over. I knew what I was going to do the second Tubby dragged you in here half-dead. It's my fault."

I stared at him across the table. The wide, straight smile. The fan of wrinkles at the corner of each eye. And those black eyes. They sparkled like magic. He wasn't sorry. Not a bit.

As though to prove it, he said, "I figured the timing was perfect. One night, you know?"

A new emotion had come to stand next to the shame. I wasn't sure what to call it yet, but it made my stomach hurt. Nausea ripped through me.

Wade continued, completely oblivious. "I mean, you've got your thing with Mr. Rockabilly...what's his name? Tyson?" He snapped his fingers, still grinning ear to ear. "Tristen?"

"Tanner." My voice sounded dead. A chill spread through me.

"I knew it was something with a T and an N. But something hip. Not Tyrone." Wade snickered.

"Tanner," I muttered again because my mind was frozen. Wade had done this, thinking I was still with Tanner, which was okay because he was with Aspen and it was just one night of his life.

The smile fell off Wade's face. He sat back in his chair. "This is not the first time I've been unfaithful to Aspen. It certainly won't be the last. I'm working my ass off to pay for that stupid damn Cadillac she insisted on. I wanted to have some fun, so I did."

He stared across the table, eyes flat and stubborn, edging toward pissed. More than ever, I wanted away from him. I wished I could have kept my memories of him the way they were. I pushed back my chair.

"Wait a minute. What are you so mad about? You sure weren't mad last night." His voice had that sharp edge to it, the one I knew to stay away from.

I raised my head and locked eyes with him. "I'm mad that you don't even have enough respect for that woman out there, who obviously likes you, to not sleep with other people."

His eyes went flat black. "No. I'm not faithful to Aspen, but let me tell you something, sweetie. I wouldn't have been faithful to you either." He waited a beat for that to sink in.

It sank in with the kind of sting I never wanted to feel again.

Wade leveled that flat, dangerous gaze on me. "The reason I walked away from you wasn't fear that I'd get killed hanging around with you. It was that I didn't want you looking at me like you're looking at me right now. And eventually you would have."

He took out his cigarettes and popped the pack on the

table, even though he held a burning cigarette between his first and second fingers. It was time for me to go.

I pushed out of my chair, stood, and patted my pockets. No phone. I walked to where my clothes had been. Each step felt wobbly and insubstantial. Like I might float off at any second. I searched on the floor and under the bed. Still no phone.

I turned back to Wade. "Where's my phone?"

He stood, towering over the table, and stubbed his cigarette out in the ashtray. "Don't go yet. I want to tell you something. Last night was what I've wanted since the first time I saw you. Did I ever tell you about that?"

"Does Tubby have my phone?" I stared at the door, longing to go through it and leave this awful scene.

Wade hurried to me and grabbed my arm. "The first time I saw you, I'd just moved to Gaslight City and joined the Six Gun Revolutionaries. You were telling off Chase Fischer." Wade turned me so I was facing him, but I wouldn't look at him. "Chase had apparently stood you up, and you'd gone to find him. He was standing in front of you glassy-eyed stoned, and you were screaming at him in the street. I said to myself, 'I've got to have that girl.'" His voice trailed off on the last word, and he let go of me, shoulders rounded.

"But you'd have never been faithful to me." The revelation, though it didn't matter now, shook me to the core. I'd completely misjudged Wade. What else had I misjudged?

"Sex doesn't mean anything," he yelled at the top of his lungs.

I backed away from him. He could kill me with one hit.

He stormed toward me and grabbed me. "I left because I loved you too much for it to end like this."

I was too scared to speak. Wade had never come close to losing his temper with me, but I was afraid he might now. He took in the look on my face and slowly released me.

He whispered, "I'm sorry."

"I want Tubby." My voice shook. I couldn't stand this anymore.

"He took his car up to my sister's and slept there." Wade's voice trembled.

I walked toward the door. My hand was shaking so hard, I had trouble getting hold of the doorknob. Then I had a hard time turning it. Finally I got the door open.

"Peri Jean," Wade said from behind me. "I did love you. Still do. I wish I was a different kind of man…"

I stepped outside and shut the door on his words. The truth had been there. Wade had been a shark where women were concerned the whole time I'd known him. But I had refused to see that the same rules would apply to me.

I had idealized him, tried to make him into what I wanted. If I had never come to this place, I could have kept telling myself that story. But now I knew the truth. It stung like a million red ant bites, hurting the kind of deep feelings I never told anybody about.

Head down, tears of shame flooding down my face, I ran right into somebody. At first, I thought it was Tubby. Good. I'd tell him to get me the hell out of here. But women's perfume flooded my senses. Nothing cheap, but nothing expensive either.

Aspen. She'd seen me through the window and come back to beat the religion out of me. I deserved it. Bracing myself for the first punch, I raised my head.

Desiree stood in front of me, face set in a snarl. I gasped. She grabbed my arm, squeezing too hard and digging in her fingernails. It hurt, but I said nothing. I deserved this. Desiree began dragging me away from Wade's cabin.

———

Face set in fury, Desiree towed me through the trees. I wanted to be mad at her. I wanted to call her a bitch and give her a bloody nose. Everything I'd managed to learn about survival required me to fight. But learning who Wade Hill really was had taken all the fight out of me.

Wade's and my night of passion had so many consequences, none of them good. Wade might not care that he had cheated on Aspen with me, but I cared. I wouldn't want to be treated that way.

Worse than the betrayal, being with me put Wade in danger. Desiree's long-ago card reading predicted he'd die if we became lovers. Mad as I was at Wade for using me to betray his girlfriend, I didn't want him dead. I'd once loved him, wanted to spend my life with him. I still wanted him to find whatever made him happy.

Desiree got me out of sight of Wade's house and shoved me down in the leaves. My elbows took the weight of the fall, jarring my injured abdominal muscles. I let out a little scream.

Desiree reared back one of her sexy boots, gave me a kick in the thigh, and screamed, "Don't cry!"

I cut off my cry and stared at her, waiting for more. Maybe a beating would help me feel better. My one night of stupidity with Wade had the potential to create a world of hurt.

Desiree leaned toward me, teeth bared like a vicious animal. "How dare you come on my property? I begged you to stay away from my brother. Don't you care about anybody but yourself?"

The tears rose up then. I pulled my knees up to my chest, put my hands over my face, and cried. The guilt worked its way through the swell of bitter grief and overtook it. Crying was nothing but a silly little girl's ploy. I dropped my hands.

"Go ahead, kick me. Kick me to death." I met Desiree's furious gaze. "I deserve it."

Desiree reared back her sexy boot again and kicked me in the hip.

I did nothing to block the blow but couldn't stop the tears rolling down my face. "Go on. I deserve this. Wade doesn't even care. He thinks it's stupid."

Desiree, who'd balled up both fists and was drawing one back, stopped short and let her arm fall to her side. A dark cloud of grief passed over her face.

She snorted. "So you finally met the real Wade Hill. The one who gets off on being a walking cloud of destruction. Heartbreaking, isn't it?"

I didn't answer. The two kicks she'd delivered throbbed. If she didn't kill me in these woods, they'd be the color of eggplants soon.

Desiree jammed her hands onto her hips and stared at the sky. "To hell with this. He chose what he did with you. I can love him with all my heart, but I can't save him." Her face crumpled for a second. By some force of will, she pulled it straight and held out her hand. "Get up. Let's go to my house for coffee."

I peered at her through my tears. "You're not going to kill me? You should."

"Nope. You've hurt yourself worse than I ever could." She put her hand in my face. I took it and let her pull me to my feet. Pain ripped through me. My vision wavered. I rocked on my feet, gasping.

Desiree took my arm and held me steady, a far cry from her fury a few moments earlier. "All right?"

I nodded.

"No, you're not all right. Tubman said you like to have died. I figured he was full of shit." She gripped my arm with both hands and practically carried me down the path away from Wade's house.

Every step sent a shot of agony through my injured pelvis. Soon sweat ran down my face and dripped into my eyes. By the time we reached the steps to her wraparound porch, nausea rocked my stomach and my bowels were hot and loose. I grabbed onto the porch step's railing and hung there.

"Tubman," Desiree yelled at the house.

Tubby came to the door holding a cup of coffee. As soon as he saw me, he set down his coffee and rushed at me.

"Oh, baby. I'm so glad you're alive." Tubby grabbed me in a hug.

I let out a pained bleat.

Desiree pushed Tubby off me. "Carry her inside and put her on the couch."

He picked me up more gently than I'd have imagined him capable and mounted the steps. Ceramic dogs painted flat black with a white skeleton pattern lined the path to the front door. Hay bales scattered the porch, watched over by a scarecrow with a cloth sack head and cutout eyes. Desiree caught me looking at it and gave me a wink.

"Samhain's my favorite holiday of the year." She swatted at Tubby. "You better have made enough coffee for me to drink, son."

"I did." His voice went up several octaves. He sounded like a little boy defending himself to his mother. If I hadn't been hurting so bad, I'd have laughed. Tubby carried me across the threshold of Desiree's house the way a groom carries his bride.

"Right here." Desiree pointed at a worn sectional sofa.

Tubby set me on it.

Desiree spoke to Tubby in a brisk tone. "Get us coffee and get bacon started."

Tubby hurried through the room. Desiree had it tricked out for Halloween with black and orange ceramic cats everywhere. A ceramic pumpkin's eye cutouts flickered with the light of a burning candle inside. A gourd painted to look like an owl spilled fresh orange mums. Tubby stopped to sniff the flowers.

"Wait a minute," Desiree said in her smoky voice.

Tubby stopped in his tracks but didn't turn around.

"There's French vanilla creamer in the fridge. Put some in my coffee." She sat next to me and began taking off her boots. When Tubby was out of earshot, she turned to me and whispered, "Damn, he's cute."

I didn't know what to say to that. Tubby saved me from having to comment by bringing in our coffee. He carefully set a cup in front of each of us.

He said to me, "Yours just has powdered creamer in it. I know what you like."

I nodded my thanks and forced a weak smile.

Desiree took a sip of her coffee and glared at Tubby. "Did you start the bacon?"

"No, but I'm fixing to." He marched back to the kitchen.

Desiree spoke to me in a low voice, "That little skinny butt reminds me of my first husband, God rest his sorry soul."

An ashtray in the shape of skull sat on the coffee table. At least Desiree smoked in the house. She lit a cigarette and offered me one.

Once I had a little nicotine coursing through me, I said, "I'm sorry. I've done the wrong thing most of my life, but this is the worst. Your card reading is one step closer to coming true."

She stared out the window at the hills in the distance. The seconds ticked by, so many that I began to worry she was getting ready to change her mind about beating me to a pulp.

"Fate is almost always chance mixed with choice," she

finally said. "My brother is a grown-assed man. I realized back there in the woods that I just have to accept what he's chosen. That's why I didn't finish kicking your ass."

I watched her, waiting for hysterical tears, fierce anger, or some show of emotion. None of that came.

"My brother knew the consequences of being with you," she said in her smoke-fogged voice. "He always claimed to love you. Maybe one night of passion was worth whatever it cost."

Cold fingers worked their way down my back. I didn't want to be the reason Wade didn't get to grow old. There was nothing all that special about me. I wasn't worth it. I caught Desiree watching me, a sardonic smile curving the full lips she shared with Wade.

"You don't believe a man like Wade would make a choice like that? You ain't lived much yet." She let out a rough laugh, lines spreading outward from her smile.

"Would you make a choice like that?" I asked her.

In this light, the gray roots of Desiree's blonde hair showed. So did the crevice of wrinkles between the boobs her low-cut shirt showed off. But her long legs, encased in tight jeans, still looked better than many women young enough to be her daughter.

"Naw, girl. But I'm a woman. We deal in superglue, coupons, and shitty diapers. Life beats the romance out of us a lot faster than it does men." She took a pull on her cigarette, the cracks in her lips like crazing on porcelain, and tipped me a wink.

I thought about what she'd said. Wade had seduced me last night knowing it would be the only time. He'd even said he didn't care if his connection with me killed him. Did he do it out of some romantic notion of true love? Or because he didn't want to do the work and risk the heartbreak of a real relationship? Either way, he was cheating himself. He was a great man with so much to offer the right woman.

My mind circled back to Tanner. This time Hannah's voice played over the memory of leaving him on that street in Austin with his California friends. She'd said I didn't love myself enough. The first time I'd heard those words, I had denied them with all my might. Now I wasn't so sure. Best I could see, Wade and I both ran around trying to destroy our own lives.

Desiree sat up and stubbed out her cigarette in the ashtray. "Let me take a look at that wound."

I reached for my shirt.

"Let me do it. It might hurt a little less." She raised my shirt and pushed my jeans where she could see. She hissed through her teeth. "You'd be dead now if Tubman hadn't brought you."

She let go of me and stared out the window at the hills. Her lips moved. "For everything there is a purpose…"

"What?" I almost hated to ask. The answer might reawaken her wrath.

She cut her eyes at me. "It's from the Holy Bible. 'To everything there is a season, and a time to every purpose under the heaven.' To that, I'll add that the fighting we do against the universe's plans for us often takes us where we were supposed to end up in the first place."

The smell of bacon drifted from the kitchen. Tubby came out, took one look at us sitting on the couch, and left the room again.

Desiree sat a few minutes longer. Finally she seemed to come to herself. "How about I get you something for your pain?"

Without waiting for my answer, she left the room. I sat in the stillness alone, pondering her words.

I had spent a lifetime trying to escape my fate. But it seemed every step I took forced me to accept a little more of my true nature. Desiree had expended force and energy trying to keep Wade from his fate. Yet fate, in the form of Tubby Tubman, had brought me back to Wade's door. And he'd made a choice that doomed him so I could live to fight Oscar again.

Right then, my life pressed on my shoulders, heavy enough to crush. It seemed a labyrinth of lost highways, one hairpin curve after another. I kept searching for the last exit to normal. More and more, I suspected it didn't exist. This was it for me.

Desiree bustled back into the room wearing latex gloves and holding a little aluminum tub. She sat back down and motioned me to get my clothes out of the way. Once I did, she slathered a cloudy ointment over the exposed skin.

"This'll sort of numb you. Let the muscles rest so they'll keep on healing." Finished, she capped the container and handed it to me. "This is poisonous. Don't eat it, and wash your hands after you apply it."

"Thank you." I slipped the tub in my pocket. Wonderful, sweet numbness had already begun to spread through my sore body. My vision sharpened at the edges. Whatever was in this ointment was some potent shit. I leaned back and breathed a sigh of relief.

"No need for thanks. I think me helping you is part of what's supposed to happen." Her eyes clouded over again, and her brow creased with thought.

I sank deeper into the couch. As the mystery ointment relaxed me, I started telling Desiree about my battles with fate, about the scar tissue, and finally about Oscar and the Wild Hunt.

Tubby brought out a plate of bacon, a loaf of bread, and three plates. He made his sandwich and listened quietly. A couple of times, I caught Desiree watching him, a small smile on her face.

When I stopped talking, she said, "That's a lot to process in such a short time. I do understand why you've struggled." She made herself a bacon sandwich and took a bite before she spoke again. "You will have to eventually make peace with your fate. You likely won't shed the scar tissue until you've truly done that."

"But I don't know how." I made my own bacon sandwich, even though I didn't really want it.

Desiree chewed. "It has to do with accepting what you are."

"But I do." The words felt true, but I knew they must not be.

Desiree shook her head. "You might think you have, but you haven't yet. Even I can see that, and I barely know you. But if the Wild Hunt is after you, it might not matter anyway."

"Why not?" I set down my sandwich.

"I don't know much about the Wild Hunt. Just stories I heard growing up. In my opinion, here's what you need to think about. Oscar Rivera has named you as the target of the hunt. The question you need to ask yourself is how to kill Oscar. That would put an end to the whole thing." Desiree popped the last bite of her sandwich into her mouth.

Oscar no longer had a body. He was spirit. He could possess a body, and that body could be killed, but Oscar would still survive. He could survive because his soul still lived.

"His soul," I muttered, picturing the way Oscar's army was eating the souls of the people they killed for extra power.

Desiree nodded and lit another cigarette. "Wade told me that Oscar hid his soul somewhere as part of an immortality deal. That right?"

I nodded, remembering the vision where I'd seen Oscar sacrifice a baby to seal the deal.

"Okay then. You need to find the soul and destroy it." Desiree squinted at me through her haze of cigarette smoke.

But Desiree didn't understand. I had already, accidentally, found where Oscar hid his soul. The hole where I threw the runes away. I'd given him everything he needed to beat me, all wrapped up in a nice package.

Tubby, who understood the problem, said, "No, his soul probably ain't there no more, but he's just hid it somewheres else. There's a rhyme or reason to where he hid it. We'll find it."

Tubby pulled a phone out of his pocket and glanced at the screen. "We probably need to be heading on down the road."

"That's my phone," I yelled.

Tubby dropped it next to me and began helping me off the couch. Desiree's ointment must have done its job because I got up a lot easier than I'd gone down.

Desiree stood and held open the door for us. "I would say come back again, but...fate has a way of making you end up where it wants you." She and I exchanged a wry smile. She turned her attention to Tubby. "Bye, honey."

Tubby slipped her a wink, and she shut the door. The sound of the deadbolt engaging came through the door.

10

Tubby tried to help me into his now trashed Cutlass, but Desiree's poisonous ointment had me feeling better by the second. I pushed his hands away.

"I got it. Thanks." I buckled my seatbelt with only a twinge of pain through my middle.

Scrolling through my phone, I saw where Tubby had been answering my text messages from Hannah to Cecil and everybody in between. The messages, riddled with misspelled and non-words, had put my family in an uproar.

One message from Cecil read, "Tubman, if you're lying to me, I'll have Finn scoop out your eyeballs with a sharpened spoon."

I began sending messages to everybody telling them that Wade had managed to heal me and Tubby and I were leaving now.

Cecil sent a message back with more GPS coordinates and "Don't come in here like the peckerwood mafia. This is a tourist place for nice folks."

I answered, "Yes, sir," but wondered where we'd landed and what exactly Cecil was thinking. We didn't need to be around a crowd of people right now.

Tubby got into the car and started it.

I lit into him. "Why were you answering my text messages? They knew it wasn't me."

Tubby turned to me, blue eyes cold as winter clouds. "Because you were fucking your brains out with Goliath back there. You want everybody to know about that?"

"No," I muttered. "I'd like to pretend that never happened."

Tubby jerked the car into reverse, did a hard turnaround, and sped off Desiree's property. He stared straight ahead as he drove, jaw clenched.

I sat back in my seat, muscles tense with apprehension. Was this Tubby's version of jealousy? I hoped not.

Tubby and I had shared a brief, yet passionate, romance in our twenties. I had said goodbye to it with a sigh of relief. Years passed. Out of the blue a few months earlier, Tubby had tried to get me to go out with him. I'd refused and said I just wanted friendship. My feelings hadn't changed. I let the radio do the talking for the next several miles.

Tubby held his silence until we got off Ranch to Market

Road 187 at Medina. He pulled into the parking lot of a convenience store and twisted to glare at me.

"What're you gonna tell Tanner about fucking Wade?" He narrowed his eyes at me. He'd know a lie if I dared tell one.

"Tanner's gone. I don't owe him any kind of explanation." I propped my elbow on the window and put my face in my hand.

Tubby rolled his eyes. "That's so weak."

I dropped my hand and glared at him. "I'm grateful you did what it took to save my life, but it doesn't give you a front row seat to my fucked-up shit. Okay?"

So fast I didn't have time to react, Tubby unbuckled his seatbelt, jammed his knee in the seat, and came at me. I pressed myself against the car door, still unable to comprehend what was happening. Tubby wrapped both arms around me and pressed his lips to mine.

Heart hammering, I put both hands on his chest and pushed as hard as I could. But it was no use. He was stronger and not recovering from a life-threatening injury. I pressed my lips together and tried to get my knees between us, but the seatbelt hampered my movements.

Tubby drew back as though stung. "So Wade's good enough, but I'm not?"

Of all the times for this crap. Couldn't Tubby wait until a time when I hadn't almost died and had my heart broken twice in two days? Obviously not.

My first impulse was to put my arms around Tubby, to hug him and comfort him. He was one of my oldest friends. Despite how ridiculous he came off, he was an intelligent, complex man. He just sucked at actual relationships. But I didn't dare touch him, not right in the middle of his play for me.

I said as gently as I could, "You and I tried this, remember?"

"I've grown up since then." He hovered over me, face pleading. "I want you back in my life."

"We can't." There were a thousand reasons, all of them good.

"At least let me kiss you. If there's nothing..." He shrugged, bow-shaped lips crimping into a smile.

I shook my head. There'd be something. I didn't have to let him kiss me to know that. Tubby and I had had enough chemistry to blow the world into an unrecognizable mess.

"If you let me do this, I'll never ask again." He ran one finger slowly over the chill bumps on my arm.

I thought about Tubby never asking again, never hinting again, never flirting with me again. His attention had made me feel good at the worst times in my life. A lightbulb went on in my head. I had used Tubby to feel better about my disappointments in life. It was time for me to let him go.

Could I do this? Show Tubby he didn't want me but still

keep him as my friend? Probably not both. But he deserved more than he'd ever have with me.

I unbuckled my seatbelt, pushed myself off the seat, and straddled Tubby, staring into his blue eyes. I put my mouth over his but made it about as sexy as using tissue to blot off lipstick. Tubby, never one to give up, put his hand behind my neck and deepened the kiss.

He stopped abruptly, laughed in my face, and gave me a light shove. "Get off me."

I did what he said and sat on my side of the car, hand on the door handle in case he lost his mind again. Tubby wiped his mouth with the back of his hand and threw his head back to let out a string of mad cackles. He glanced at me and laughed some more.

"That was awful," he yelled.

I started to laugh too, mostly out of relief. Now he could let this go.

He came toward me, smiling and normal, and wrapped his arms around me.

"I love you, friend," he whispered in my ear.

"I love you too." I squeezed him tighter.

Tubby let go, scooted into the driver's seat, and started the car. He got us back on the road.

"You seriously wish it hadn't happened with Wade?" He turned off the radio.

I relaxed then, let out the breath I'd been holding. "Seriously. I'm in love with Tanner. He probably won't ever come back. But if he does, he'll see it as a betrayal."

"Baby, I hate to say it, but if he cut off his phone, he ain't coming back." He cut a guilty glance at me, one that told me he'd tried to call Tanner to let him know I was hurt bad and learned the same thing I had last night.

"It'll be whatever it's going to be." My voice trembled.

Tubby put his hand on my leg and squeezed, probably the only comfort he could offer. "I had an idea for finding Oscar's soul."

He was changing the subject. Thank goodness. My romantic life sucked. I wanted to quit thinking about it.

"Tell me." I took out my cigarettes, lit two, and pressed one between Tubby's lips.

"Find out about Oscar's history. He might've hidden it in one of his old haunts." He dragged on the cigarette and exhaled through his nose in twin jets of blue smoke.

"Not a bad idea." I thought back. "The first time I met Oscar, last February, I found an entry about him in a book. It didn't say much other than... Hold on. I've got it here in my phone."

"What would we do without those things?" Tubby laughed.

I took out my phone and searched through the notes I'd

kept when I worked more often for Griffin Reed and Mysti Whitebyrd. "Here it is."

I read aloud from my phone's screen. "'A more interesting case of obsession is that of Oscar E. Rivera, a native of Houston, Texas. Rivera enjoyed success leading séances for the Houston rich but became obsessed with an ancient immortality rite he discovered. Rivera took on the name Lord of Babylon and left Houston in 1870 seeking an underground river he believed would connect him to the underworld. He never returned.'"

Tubby nodded, eyes fixed on the road. He cracked his window and let the wind take his cigarette butt.

"There's several things there." He glanced at me. "You've got the underground river leading to the underworld. You've got the Lord of Babylon thing."

"He also committed at least one murder in Austin," I said. "She was the first person he killed after making the immorality pact. Her bone made the first rune."

Tubby shuddered. "Ewww. And just think. You touched those runes."

I ignored him. "Oscar was also a native of Houston. He may have hidden his soul somewhere there."

The idea of poking around Houston filled me with dread. For one thing, it was a good five-hour drive north and east from our current location. For another thing, the traffic was insane. Too many people, all in a big hurry.

Tubby nodded but said, "Yeah, but Houston is a big, big city."

No shit. Another lightbulb flashed behind my eyes. "How far are we from Austin?" I loved Texas's Hill Country, but the open country made things seem farther away than they really were.

"'Bout two hours, but Cecil's coordinates are taking us that way anyway." Tubby glanced at the map on his phone. "You got an idea?"

"Maybe. Let me make a phone call." I got into my contacts and called someone I'd met under pretty bad circumstances, hoping he'd answer the phone.

Linus Bramwell, author on the occult, answered on the first ring. "If it isn't my favorite troublemaker. What's shaking?"

"I'm looking for information about Oscar E. Rivera. He's the subject of an urban legend in which he's called the Coachman. He's also used the name Lord of Babylon." I paused to let Linus take in what I was saying.

"Sounds familiar." The sound of him clicking computer keys came over the line. He went silent as he read whatever he'd found. "Oh, I've heard about this guy. Why do you want to know about him?"

I blurted out my sordid history with Oscar Rivera. I told him about the way Oscar had hidden his soul and bargained for immortality. About the way he'd sent Miss

Ugly to kill me and recruited my ex-husband to help him. Then I told him about Oscar calling the Wild Hunt to kill me and what he'd do with my magic if he succeeded.

Linus sucked in his breath at that point. "What are you going to do?"

"I think I can get rid of him forever if I destroy his soul." The magnitude of it chilled me.

"Fairy tale justice. It might work," Linus muttered, still clicking. "How can I help you?"

"Oscar may have hidden his soul somewhere from his past, but I don't know enough about him to figure out where that would be." My cheeks heated asking this man for another favor. He'd helped me before just because I'd asked. Now I was asking again.

Linus said nothing for several long minutes. "I have some resources, but I don't want to become a target of the Wild Hunt." Fear hushed his voice to a near whisper. "Why don't you start by telling me what you know of Oscar's history? That will give me a starting point."

I read him the same passage I'd read Tubby and included the name of the book it had come from and the author.

Linus's only answer was the clicking of keys on a keyboard.

"We're two hours away from you. Is that enough time?" I was already sending Cecil a text message explaining where I was going and that I'd be later than expected.

Linus came back with, "That's fine. I'll leave yours and Tanner's names at the gate."

"I'm with Thomas Tubman today." Anxiety bloomed in my gut at having to give Linus some explanation for Tanner's absence.

But Linus simply barked a dry laugh and said, "Understood."

Tubby and I sped toward Austin, only stopping to buy cheap hamburgers at a fast food restaurant, which we ate on the way.

———

Tubby gawked at at the entrance of Linus's subdivision. "Damn thing's twice as fancy as the one where Rainey lives."

Tubby was right. Though Rainey lived in the nicest subdivision in Gaslight City, this place far outclassed it. The guard shack alone made hers look like a kid's lemonade stand.

We followed a flagstone drive of variegated colors to the guard shack. A steel arm that could have easily finished killing Tubby's Cutlass barred the road into the community of expensive houses. Stone walls at least twelve feet high, emblazoned with the subdivision's name, protected the development.

The guard's eyes widened at Tubby's beat-down car, but he

quickly rearranged his expression into a poker face and took Tubby's and my driver's licenses. He came back less than minute later. "Mr. Bramwell is waiting to see you."

We cruised through the subdivision's narrow streets. When Tanner and I had come here a couple of months ago, it had been early morning with barely anybody stirring. Now, at midday, people were everywhere, despite the gray day.

Eyes widened, fingers pointed. A few clapped phones to ears, probably calling the guard shack to ask about the nasty car invading their pristine corner of paradise. A small part of me didn't blame them. Tubby and I looked like what we were: white trash.

"This one." I pointed to Linus's Spanish-style house with its tile roof.

Tubby parked at the curb and leaned across the car to stare at the house. "Who is this guy?"

"He writes occult fiction." I worked the door latch and got out. Tubby hurried to follow. We approached the door, and I rang the bell.

Linus opened so quickly, he must have been standing on the other side.

"Well, if it isn't Peri Jean Mace." He held open his arms, and I gave him a hug. He turned to Tubby, hand out, smiling. "Linus Bramwell."

"Tubby Tubman." Tubby wiped his hand on his pants and

shook Linus's hand, craning to peek inside the fancy house.

Linus held open the door. "Come in."

We went inside, Tubby goggling at the made-to-look-old features of the obviously new home.

"This's a nice place," he muttered to me.

I nodded, remembering the way Tanner had looked around. It had been as though he knew about places like this, wished himself back in one of them instead of slumming with me. Probably at least some of the reason he'd gone back to California.

Instead of leading us to his spacious kitchen, which looked out on his luxurious pool, Linus lead us through a living room with exposed beams, warm terracotta-colored tile, and rustic furnishings that probably cost a small fortune.

"Let's go into my office." Linus held open a heavy door made of rough wood.

Tubby stared at it as we passed. "Where do you get a door like this?"

"It's reclaimed from an old house in France, Mr. Tubman." Linus's shoes tapped softly on the floors until he crossed onto a faded Persian rug. He went behind his desk, also made of rough wood, sat down, and motioned for Tubby and me to take the red leather-covered wingchairs in front of the desk.

We sat, Tubby still staring at all the details.

"I managed to dig up a little on Oscar." Linus's grim face gave me a bad feeling.

"I appreciate your effort." I leaned forward, trying to ignore Tubby's gawking.

Linus smiled in acknowledgement, clicked a few keys on a silver keyboard, and stared at his monitor.

Tubby half rose from his chair to peer at an expensively framed print of Hieronymus Bosch's *Garden of Earthly Delights.*

"What the fuck?" he muttered.

I reached over, popped him on the leg, and hissed, "Straighten up."

He gave me the finger. Linus looked up about that time. I swatted Tubby's finger away and tried to act dignified.

Linus acted as though he'd seen nothing. "Oscar was an occultist in Houston, Texas, which you already knew. In the census for 1870, he listed 'professor' as his occupation." Linus tapped a few more keys. "I suspect Oscar considered himself a professor in spiritualism. He was quite popular among the wealthy, which plays in our favor. Those people had time to write letters to each other, and those letters were preserved."

I had a hard time imagining Oscar behaving himself well enough to fit in with the well-heeled. But he'd been handsome and had a commanding presence. He must have figured out a way.

Linus leaned close to his screen and squinted. "In one of these letters, a society woman writes that Oscar told her he'd been orphaned after his parents died of influenza. He claimed to have spent the rest of his childhood in a tiny German farming community where he was raised by a German witch. Whatever the truth was, this socialite notes that Oscar spoke fluent German with a cousin of hers."

I perked up. This could give us a big clue about where Oscar hid his soul. "Does it give the name of the town?"

"Unfortunately, no." Linus went back to reading from his computer screen. "But this might interest you. From everything I've found, Oscar Rivera was a phony."

"W-what? How?" This went against all I knew about Oscar. Even as a spirit, he had powerful magic.

"Séances are easy to fake. There was stuff like tapping and automatic writing." Linus sounded like he was winding up for a lecture, one on the wrong topic. I'd have to cut him off.

"Of course, but I was more curious about you calling Oscar a phony. He's a lot of things, but not that." I told Linus some of the things I'd seen Oscar do in visions of the past.

"It seems he changed after something very bad happened to him." Linus spun his monitor and showed us a badly scanned picture of a young Oscar Rivera and a woman with two young boys. Like all the pictures of the time, the subjects looked as though they were about to be led to the guillotine. Linus turned the monitor to face him again.

"The woman in the picture was Olive Allen. She married Oscar Rivera in 1860. Over the following years, she gave birth to the two boys in the picture." Linus's eyes scanned over the screen. "This part of Oscar's life is only well documented because it's so tragic. Even so, information is limited. Oscar lived in Houston right after the Civil War. It was a rather lawless period in which some shameful tragedies occurred. If you think people are intolerant now, imagine how they were back then."

The idea chilled me. Some people who'd known me all my life had tried to kill me because they thought I was satanic. They'd been willing to kill Rainey Bruce and Wade Hill right along with me just because they were in the wrong place at the wrong time. I nodded my understanding.

Linus watched me, both sympathy and curiosity evident in his gaze. "The most detailed account I found says that Olive, Oscar, and their sons were dragged from their home and lynched right in their front yard."

"For being Satanists, I assume." I muttered the words.

Linus rolled his eyes and nodded. "Oscar somehow survived. He claimed not to know who hurt his family."

"What happened after that?" Tubby lost interest in the expensive furnishings enough to speak. "I mean, what did Oscar do?"

"Impossible to know for sure. But after I got some ideas of his social circle, I was able to find a few clues." Linus tapped a few keys. "Rumor claimed Oscar summoned a demon to help him carry out revenge. The men suspected of lynching Olive and the children were found ripped apart, as though animals had attacked them. After that, Oscar became a known spell caster, one who had no problem with the darker side of things."

My cheeks tingled. Though this gave me no hints where Oscar might have hidden his soul this go-around, it did give me a sense of this man, who he might have been and what might have driven him.

I'd never know for sure, but I suspected Oscar's near-death experience gave him a little something extra. I'd seen it before. A man like Oscar, one who'd been unable to protect his wife and children, would have grabbed onto that extra power.

Linus talked about Oscar summoning a demon. It probably murdered the people who hurt Oscar's wife and children. I'd have done the same. Did that make me like Oscar? I shied away from the thought and forced my mind back on track.

The demon Oscar had called forth had surely wanted some form of repayment. I'd dealt with their kind too and knew something of their ways. Mysti called them chthonic beings. Tanner called them boogers. Priscilla Herrera called them dark beings. I called them trouble.

Once a booger had a human in its snare, it handed out favors like a politician. But one day, all those favors would come due. At that point, most humans found themselves up crap creek in a sinking boat.

But Oscar had sought immortality. He had let himself get pulled even deeper than simply having revenge on his family's murderers. What had driven him?

All my experiences with Oscar had centered on revenge and power. Could anybody be that boring and shallow?

Linus's soft, scholarly voice cut into my thoughts. "When you called, you read to me an entry from a book about spiritualists."

"Sure." I dug out my phone. "I've got a picture of it right here. I can send it to you."

"Not necessary. I found it online." Linus's eyes crinkled into a smile. "I was able to find out a bit about the immortality rite referenced."

I raised my eyebrows.

"It supposedly came from a book found in an abandoned monastery. Oscar bought it from an explorer known only as Black Silas." Linus stopped reading to stare at me. "Are you all right, dear?"

I croaked a non-answer at him. It was all my airless lungs would let me do. Black Silas. We'd met because of my adventure in Devil's Rest, Texas. He'd helped me auction off a book that drove people into a murderous rage. He scared me witless.

Linus watched me, intelligent eyes sharp and probing. "What is it?"

I chewed my lip and brainstormed possible answers. Black Silas was dangerous. I'd sensed that much about him. He'd been pleased to meet me, but he might be less than pleased if I gossiped about him. Careless words might put Linus in danger.

I shook my head at my friend. "I can't say anything."

Linus sat back in his seat, eyes suddenly dull and angry. "That's not fair. I've helped you more than once. This is of interest to me."

"Can I say I've met Black Silas and be done with it?" My heart trembled giving even this much detail.

"That's impossible. This man would be well over a hundred and fifty years old..." Linus paled.

"Black Silas is not human, and he's not anybody you need to know about." I hardened my voice into the one I used when necessary on underlings.

A warm wind began to blow in Linus's office, making papers flutter off his desk. Horror stole into my veins. What on earth was this? The answer came without much thought. Injured and scared, my tenuous control on my power was even looser than normal.

Magic crackled at my fingertips, and the smell of ozone filled the room. Whispers teased at the edge of my mind. I tried to pull back the power. But getting it back in was a lot harder than letting it out. A low hum came from the wood floor.

Linus's face turned gray. He grabbed for his desk and stood, chest rising and falling. The wind whipped around him.

"Oh, boy," Tubby muttered.

I strained to control the magic seeping from me, shaking with the effort. If a little force had done this, how did I ever expect to be an accomplished witch? I sucked in a hard breath and pulled at the magic so hard the pain returned to my newly healed injury.

The wind died. The papers lay still on Linus's desk. The poor man still stood behind it breathing hard.

"I'm sorry," I whispered. "It's over now. But you can't know Black Silas. You're my friend, and I'm afraid of what he might do to you."

Linus licked his lips and nodded, nostrils flaring. He sat carefully behind his desk. "We may revisit the issue at another time. For now I'll accept your answer. The last historical mention I found of Oscar was of him consulting a geologist about underground rivers. He disappeared after that."

I had vague ideas of Oscar's further adventures. He'd gone

out to Central Texas, where there were caverns and pools of water underground. He'd sought out the hole where I'd thrown the runes and somehow got himself down there without falling and killing his own stupid self.

Linus began clicking keys on his computer. "You came here on a theory that Oscar hid his soul somewhere in his past. As I pulled together all the information I just shared, my heart sank on your behalf. I don't think your theory is going to pan out."

My head snapped up.

"Houston is a city of progress. It's not like, say, New Orleans where you can go to a carefully preserved historic area." Linus still looked a little green from his fright, but he was too curious to throw us out. "Houston doesn't have an abundance of structures that would date back to the 1860s. The likelihood of one of those few being linked to Oscar is slim."

I fell back in my chair. Oscar had been raised in a German-speaking community in Texas's Hill Country. Maybe he'd hidden his soul there. "And there's no further mention of where Oscar was raised?"

"I found nothing more." Linus gave me a sad shake of his head.

I put my forehead in my hand. We'd gone out of our way to come here, but Linus hadn't had the magic answer. What now?

A voice that sounded suspiciously like Memaw spoke up in my head. *The first thing you need to do is thank this nice man for his time.* A smile spread over my face. Memaw had been all about good manners. I raised my head.

"Linus, thank you for taking time out of your busy day for us." I stood and held out my hand.

He didn't take it. Instead he gave me a crafty smile. "We're not finished. Sit back down."

I did, heart speeding up, body tensing.

"After I figured out my research wasn't going to help you, I called a contact of mine." Linus smiled. "You're not the only one who has non-human affiliations. They agreed for you to come see them."

Tubby leaned forward in his seat, gaze steady on Linus. "What's the catch?"

"They'll want payment," Linus said.

"Do you know what they'll want?" Paying them worried me. These beings asked for things that would keep someone connected to them. I didn't want that.

Linus flushed. "In the past, I've traded them peyote buttons and high grade marijuana. Or methamphetamine."

"What kinda stuff do you ask them in exchange for the dope?" Tubby still stared at Linus, almost menacing in his seriousness.

Linus let out a sigh. "Nothing as big as what you're about to ask."

Tubby turned to me. "I say no. Let's do our own thing."

We had no time for that. Oscar would be back. It was just a question of when.

I met Linus's gaze. "I'll do it. When do we leave?"

"Now." The older man stood from behind the desk, went to a closet, and took out a thin jacket. "Ride together or you two follow me?"

"We'll follow you." Tubby stood.

Linus saw us out the front door and disappeared back inside the house to get his car out of the garage. I followed Tubby out to the Cutlass.

"He's gonna get us into trouble," he said over his shoulder.

"Then you don't have to go with me. Linus will take me. You can either go back to Gaslight City or to where Cecil and my family are." I stopped a few feet from Tubby's car.

Tubby swung around and rushed into my face, shaking one bony finger. "The fuck you think this is, girl? Date night with Sheriff Dean? I ain't just walking off and leaving you to whatever monsters this Linus feller has lined up." He leaned so close our noses brushed. "We friends. I stay until it's over."

A lump rose in my throat. Tubby wasn't perfect, but there wasn't another one like him.

I nodded my understanding and tried to explain. "We have to do this. Oscar will be back. The next attack might kill us."

Tubby stilled for several seconds. "You're right."

He got into the car and started it. The door to the garage began to rise. My RV could have fit inside it twice. Linus backed a deep green Lexus onto the street and led the way out of his fancy subdivision. The guard had a look of relief on his face as we passed his shack.

11

———

We left the city and drove west, into the great wide empty. Linus Bramwell drove like the old man he was, but that didn't bother me. After living and riding with Tanner for several months, not riding with someone who drove like he was racing for a checkered flag was a nice break.

I spent the time on the phone, first with Cecil, then with Hannah.

"This place is weird," she hissed. "Everybody's huddled up and whispering, but nobody will tell me what's up. Where are you and Tub?"

Hannah was calling him Tub now? When had that happened?

"Somewhere Linus Bramwell knows. He said these people deal in information, and they aren't human." I hoped this didn't turn into a shit show but sort of knew it would.

Hannah made a worried humming sound. "You know how those beings are. They all want something."

"I don't have much to take. Not even my dignity." My night of passion with Wade had dampened that part of me I'd worked so hard to build up, took me right back to tramping around for a night of carnal satisfaction that left me feeling empty and lonelier the next day.

"What are you not telling me?" Hannah's voice dropped to a near whisper. "Did something happen with Wade?"

Everything. But I couldn't talk about it with Tubby next to me. My tryst with Wade had made Tubby feel like a pile of monkey poop. He was a true friend and didn't deserve that.

"I'll take that silence as a yes. I'll also take it to mean it's over now." She muttered something under her breath.

"What'd you say?" I wanted to get angry, to let that hissing wildcat that had controlled so much of my life out to play.

"I said, 'I'm not too surprised.' Wade Hill has a big heart, but lives under a cloud of self-destruction." Her voice had the flat tone it always took on when she remembered her tenure as a Six Gun Revolutionaries groupie.

Not for the first time, I tried to imagine what she'd seen Wade do, what he'd said to her. Just to know him from an outside point of view. I swallowed the questions. Hannah might say stuff I didn't want to hear.

The trauma she'd suffered had changed her, had taken away the lighthearted kindness she'd given away the way some people drop pennies into the tray next to a gas station cash register. This new Hannah told the truth, even the hurtful truth.

Tubby's voice cut into my thoughts. "That Hannah? We're going right past where she is. She wanna join us?"

I thought it over before I said anything. Asking Hannah to come would put her in whatever danger Tubby and I were walking into, but this new fierceness she possessed might help us get out. That made up my mind.

"Tubby says we're going right past where you are. Want us to pick you up?" I glanced at Tubby to find him grinning. *Interesting.*

Hannah's lighter scraped as she lit a cigarette, and she inhaled. "Yeah. There's a farm road about a mile from here. I'll meet you there." She rattled off the road number.

I called Linus to let him know what we were doing. Ten minutes later, we picked up Hannah. True to her word, she stood on the roadside, purse slung over her shoulder, red hair blowing in blustery wind. Tubby swung to the roadside, got out, and held the front seat down for her. She took his hand as she climbed in. *Even more interesting.*

"Smells like blood and death in here." She tossed her purse on the seat next to her and rifled for her smokes.

"What did my family say about you leaving?" I twisted in the seat, earning a howl of pain from my still tender midsection.

Hannah watched with interest but didn't ask how I was. She wasn't that woman any longer. You either lived, or you didn't.

"I didn't tell 'em. They're now having a big powwow about the Wanderer." The hard lines around her mouth deepened with her words. "Anybody who doesn't have Gregg blood is out."

"What do they think they can do?" Nobody could talk chthonic beings into doing things they didn't want to do. You either bargained or accepted their decision. Were they bargaining? Surely not. None of them were that foolish.

"They're just scared..." Hannah trailed off and leaned forward, her brows rumpling, and pointed.

Linus had pulled into a driveway with a closed gate. Lined up on the fence posts were animal skulls. Somehow I just knew we were in the right place.

A very white-skinned man with a crop of ginger hair on his chest strolled out, opened the gate, and motioned us through. This guy looked like a bad album cover from the 1970s. He wore his hair short on the top and sides but long in the back. His jeans hung almost to his pubic bone and belled around his ankles.

"Dear God," Hannah whispered as we passed.

I looked to see what she meant. Ginger Chest Hair wore a big smile, showing off a mouth overcrowded with pointed teeth. *Oh dear.*

We passed through some of the fragrant juniper trees native to the Texas Hill Country, rolling slowly down the rough rock and dirt driveway.

"Peri Jean, look back." Hannah's voice carried a note of urgency.

Ginger Chest Hair jogged behind our two-car caravan, still smiling that creepy smile. The hair on the back of my neck rustled and stiffened. What had Linus gotten us into?

Tubby tilted his head to watch the man in the rearview mirror. "Got my .45 and bullets, it goes bad."

"I've got my Walther PPK," Hannah said, never taking her eyes off our pursuer.

Great. We were going down like Butch Cassidy and the Sundance Kid.

The trees ended abruptly and opened up to a line of three houses. All three of the houses made Wade's converted storage shed look fancy, with their uneven porches, peeling paint, and sagging roofs.

A thick woman wearing too-tight pants came out holding a rifle of some sort. Her dirty blonde hair spread down her waist in greasy clumps. She walked toward our car, muffin top jiggling over her pants.

Linus got out of his car and said something to her.

She smiled, showing a mouthful of the same jagged teeth as the man who opened the gate, the one who now stood a short distance behind our cars, grinning. The two must have been family of some form or fashion.

Another man, also shirtless, with dark, swarthy skin and greasy brown hair came out of the center cabin. Right behind him followed a woman who would have been normal looking if she hadn't been wearing tight jeans and nothing else but a pink bra. They crowded around Linus.

Linus motioned us to get out of the car. Tubby, Hannah, and I glanced at each other.

Tubby said, "We here. Ain't much else to do."

That got me to open the door and climb out. I halfway expected the weirdos to run over like a pack of ignorant yard dogs, excited to see someone different. To my relief, they just stared.

Linus motioned me to stand next to him. "This is the young lady I told you about."

The swarthy guy, who'd been playing with a pair of black lacquered sticks, which I now saw were pieces of a fishing rod, came over to greet me.

I held out one hand, but he crowded into my space, sniffing my neck. Tubby let out a menacing growl and put one hand on the butt of the pistol tucked into his pants.

The guy drew back and spoke to the others. "She's what Bramwell said. Witch. Maybe more, just like Pappy."

It was then I saw his teeth for what they were. A scream

built in my chest, but I knew better than to let it out. The man who'd sniffed me had two rows of teeth, all jagged with pointed ends, just like shark teeth. I held as still as I could. Hannah crowded close, one hand shoved in her purse, fingers probably wrapped around her pistol.

Linus said, "Peri Jean is having trouble with..."

"Oscar Rivera." The thick woman moved closer, rifle still propped on her shoulder like a soldier getting ready to march.

"We done heard." The guy with the ginger chest hair had crept up on us without a sound and now brushed past, his skin warm and rough against mine.

"What you want from us?" The thick woman came forward. She shifted the rifle to lay flat across her shoulders and propped her arms on it. She hadn't shaved her armpits.

"Oscar separated his soul from his body in an immortality bargain..." I began.

"We know about that too," the skinny woman with the pink bra cut in.

"Yep. He left it at the final gateway. Near the last river." Ginger Chest Hair came close for another sniff of me. It took everything I had not to flinch away.

"Not anymore," I said. "I made a mistake and gave him power to move it. Now it's somewhere else."

Ginger Chest Hair cocked his head, more curious than shocked.

"And you need to know where that soul now is," said the swarthy man.

I nodded.

"We can probably…" Ginger Chest Hair began.

"Oh no, you don't," the thick woman cut him off. "You're not giving away our services just because she's pretty and you want to impress her. Only way these women would touch you with a ten-foot pole is if you forced 'em. Then they'd scream the whole time."

Hannah stood a little straighter, the arm inside her purse tense. She'd go out fighting. I would too.

"We can pay." Linus leaned over and dug in his car. "I have more peyote buttons and some medical grade marijuana."

Pink Bra came forward to stare into Linus's car, as though checking to see what else he had. She sniffed the air, nose wrinkling. Just when I thought she'd agree, she said, "That ain't enough. We want more'n that."

"Yep. This is big shit." Thick Woman hadn't moved from her spot.

It was big shit all right. Big enough that these people might decide to turn us away. Now that I saw them—and smelled them—I wouldn't protest too much. Maybe it would be better just to get in our cars and get out of here. If it wasn't too late.

"Linus, we might be asking too much of these nice people," I said from my position of safety between Hannah and Tubby.

"Didn't say we couldn't find out." Pink Bra made her way toward me, double rows of teeth flashing as she spoke. "Just saying it's worth more'n some dope."

"What do you want?" It might not be worth it.

"Wanna know who you are, is one thing." She lunged forward to sniff at my neck, her cold nose rubbing against my skin.

I jumped away, heart hammering and adrenaline pumping. "Who I am?"

"You smell like the other side." Pink Bra sniffed near my armpits.

I backed away, muscles jumping with revulsion and fear. "Let's get out of here."

They surrounded Tubby, Hannah, and me before we could take even a step toward the Cutlass. Ginger Chest Hair leapt forward, grabbed me, and dragged me away from Tubby and Hannah. Hannah stormed after me, gun already drawn.

"I'll kill you, I swear." She jacked the slide and chambered a bullet.

"You kill him, and I'll kill you." Thick Woman pointed her rifle at Hannah.

Swarthy rushed forward and put a small, sharp-looking knife to Tubby's throat. My old friend went still but showed no other sign of fear. Linus, both hands up, scooted away from the fight.

"Stop it, all of you." My voice had more than a little Priscilla Herrera in it.

They all froze and turned to stare at me. Tubby took the opportunity to elbow Swarthy in the stomach. Swarthy, caught by surprise, lowered the knife for an instant. It was all Tubby needed. He hurried to me, hand on the butt of his pistol. I held up both hands.

"Tell me what you want in exchange for the information. If I can pay it, I will." These people—or whatever they were —could save us some time.

"Like my sister said, we wanna know who you are and what you are." Thick Woman still had her rifle pointed at Hannah.

"I'm a spirit medium and a witch. I'm descended from the Gregorius Witch." A little pride tingled in my chest when I said those words, as did some curiosity.

The two men, Swarthy and Ginger Chest Hair, stared with open desire. Pink Bra and Thick Woman watched them, anger growing on their faces.

"You know what? I can't stand girls like you." Thick Woman set down her rifle and took slow steps toward me.

I backed away.

"You're the kind all the men want. The kind they'll walk away from a woman like me just to have a chance with." Her eyes heated with hate. "And you run around acting like it ain't a thing."

I kept backing up, testing my strength with each step. "So what do you want to do? Cut off my face?"

She snorted like a pig and rolled her eyes. "I wanna see what you got other than that pretty skin and that face."

No way. She outweighed me by at least fifty pounds. Hurt as I was, she'd beat me like a dirty rug.

"Not with your fists, idiot, with magic." She pulled a crooked wand from her back pocket, polished it with her hand, and pointed it at me.

I stood there, both hands up, feeling like the world's biggest idiot. I had no idea how to fight like this. Did we shoot spells at each other? I didn't have any prepared. My witching supplies had burned up in the Snake Creek Hotel. Lost forever.

"You want to know where your enemy's soul is so you can beat him?" Ginger Chest Hair spoke up. "This is the only way."

My stomach woke up then, crackling with electric fear. The muscles still ached and trembled from my healing injury. I wasn't in shape for this. But I was out of options. I had to fight Thick Woman with magic if I wanted to get the jump on Oscar. I tried to agree to the duel. Nothing came out but a weak croak.

Thick Woman snickered. That pissed me off. Anger was better than fear any day and twice as good on Sundays.

I cleared my throat and spat. "What do we do? How does it work?"

"We magic each other until one of us hollers for mercy." Her wand dangled from one hand. Magic radiated off it. What kind of damage could she do with that thing?

I nodded. "Fine. Let's do it."

———

Fear of losing took over my mind. I tried to plan, tried to center myself to call a circle.

Priscilla's voice spoke up in my head. *You don't need spells. You're descended from* the *Gregorius Witch. You have a raven familiar.*

Before her words even faded, a fluttering heat moved in my chest. My consciousness moved backward until I was staring inside myself. The mantle glowed red from behind the scar tissue spell. The sphere of magic pulsed, expanding and contracting the now-thin membrane separating me from the full measure of my power.

Wisps of it leaked out of the scar tissue. They connected with the slam of an electric shock. The black opal heated against my chest, magnifying the magic. Each pulse jolted my entire body.

Thick Woman raised her wand like a pistol, one she obviously knew the ins and outs of using as well as she knew her name, and said, "Burn her down, baby."

The fire started at my feet, not more than a prickle of discomfort. Thick Woman stretched out her wand arm and bared her rows of teeth, straining to push as much of her power at me as she could. Blackness slipped over her eyes, making her look more inhuman than ever.

"Burn her," she rasped.

In an instant, the prickle in my feet turned to unbearable, invisible flame. I jumped and screamed. The fire went out.

Thick Woman dropped her wand, giggling. Pink Bra joined her. Ginger Chest Hair and Swarthy cawed out screechy laughter. They danced a quick hoedown. Swarthy actually leapt up and clicked his heels together.

"You shut up," Tubby yelled at them, pulling his gun.

Hannah gave me a puzzled glance. Of course she didn't understand what had happened. Thick Woman had burned me from the inside out. Made me jump around and squeal like an idiot.

Humiliation raced to take the place of the pain. Anger

chased behind it, snapping and snarling. The pulse of the mantle evened out into one long throb.

"It's okay," I told Tubby and Hannah. "I know what to do now."

The spot I knew as my third eye tingled. I let it slide open and saw the creatures before me for what they were. Human, yes, but not by much. Flat black eyes stared back at me. They all had gray skin, almost the color of the clouds littering the sky. Ginger Chest Hair and Pink Bra had slits on the sides of their necks like gills.

Thick Woman raised her arm for another blast. A word I didn't understand slipped from her lips. My vision blurred, and the light from my third eye winked out. My eyes burned like I'd gotten soap or some other corrosive substance in them. I stumbled, turning my back to Thick Woman, rubbing at my face.

"Tell me how to help." Hannah tugged at me. I couldn't answer. The stinging in my eyes took all my focus.

Thick Woman didn't give us a chance to regroup. She whispered the word again. This time I heard it, but not with my ears. The word registered in some deep, dark part of me I didn't yet have access to.

Thick Woman had said, "*Trepidatio.*"

"Look at her. She don't know what to do." Ginger Chest Hair giggled.

"She's gonna figure out how to die," Thick Woman yelled.

Wait a minute. We hadn't agreed to fight to the death, had we? I'd thought this was more of a playground scuffle. Whatever it was, I was losing. I needed to get my shit together.

"That's what you think," Tubby shot back. Words barely out of his mouth, he drew in a whistling breath. "No. Not that."

Hannah echoed Tubby's panicked inhale. "Get 'em off her."

I gave my eyes another rub and forced them open. A scream lodged itself in my throat but wouldn't come out.

Snakes roped around my feet. A copperhead, tongue flicking from its thick, triangle-shaped head crawled up my leg, diamond-pupiled eyes empty of anything other than ruthlessness. I stilled.

He won't bite if I don't move. He thinks I can't see him. He'll go away if I stand still enough. The thoughts ran together in a jumble. Hysteria sparked and then roared as though doused with gasoline.

The copperhead inched its way up my leg, tongue still flicking the air. A coral snake, its red and yellow bands on prominent display, slipped over my boot. From somewhere behind me came the chitter of a rattlesnake's warning.

The panic, now a roaring fire, seized my heart in a burning vise. It begged me to brush off the copperhead, to kick the other snakes away from my feet, to run fast and far.

But the snakes had me beat in terms of speed. I'd been bitten by two snakes, both of the supernatural persuasion. I occasionally had nightmares about the speed at which they'd moved.

"We can't shoot them. We'll hit you. Use your magic." Hannah said from behind me.

I found the spark that made me different from most people and latched onto it. Just that small action broke Thick Woman's spell. The copperhead flashed transparent a couple of times. Then its woodsy pattern faded back into existence. But now I knew it wasn't real.

I raised my head to snarl at Thick Woman. "That all you got?"

I forced my third eye open again. Those soulless black doll eyes made gooseflesh shiver over my skin.

Thick Woman chuckled. "Had Red kept her big mouth shut, you'd 'a never knowed. But that's all right. I can take care of 'er." She flicked the wand in Hannah's direction.

Hannah let out a scream, but it was muffled as though she was screaming behind her hand.

Going against my instincts not to turn my back on Thick Woman, I spun to see what was the matter. Hannah's lips appeared to have disappeared altogether. From the nose down was one rough stretch of skin. She grabbed her chin, still screaming through her nose, and tried to pull it apart.

I took a step toward her. Fire stabbed into my back. My vision flashed the same way a bolt of lightning does. The shockwave raced through my brain. My knees softened and folded. I hit the ground hard. I lay staring at the gray sky like it was the most interesting thing since streaming TV.

"Now wait a minute," Tubby shouted, his voice far away.

"Take him," Thick Woman yelled.

Tubby let out a girlish scream. He staggered into my vision, Pink Bra fastened to his back like a particularly ugly jockey. Tubby ran out of my field of vision, still bleating that pitiful high-pitched scream.

I searched for Linus. Swarthy had him by the arms. Linus fought, but he was an old, soft human man. He didn't stand a chance.

Tubby ran past, trying unsuccessfully to shake Pink Bra.

"Help me, Hannah." He slapped at Pink Bra's legs. "Don't matter if you can talk. They taking me down like lionesses on the savannah."

Thick Woman tackled Tubby and dragged him to the ground. Both women crawled over him, arms and legs everywhere.

Ginger Chest Hair stepped into my field of vision, rows of teeth bared in a menacing grin. "My sister's been wanting a man."

Someone, maybe Swarthy, let out a scream. "Fucker bit me."

I swung my head in time to see Linus elbow Swarthy and make a run for his car. He opened the door of his Lexus. Was he going to abandon us? Before the thought even had time to ripen, Linus reached into the car and made the horn blow.

Linus let off the horn and yelled, "Twila, you and Demeritus get off Mr. Tubman. Right now."

Both girls screamed laughter. Thick Woman popped her wand at Linus. He fell into his car as though pushed by a huge, invisible hand. The door shut, and the locks engaged. He tried to start the car. All the engine did was go *urrrur-urrrur-urrrur.* Linus pounded the wheel, face contorted with anger and more than a little terror.

Tubby screamed, this time in real pain. I tried to roll over and found that I could. Whatever Thick Woman did to me must have been wearing off.

What I saw infuriated me. Both Thick Woman and Pink Bra straddled Tubby. He was bleeding from one arm. The wound looked like a bite. What the hell were they trying to do to him?

I got my knees under me and crouched, panting and clutching my sore stomach. Pink Bra and Thick Woman were trying to pull poor Tubby's clothes off. He pushed at their hands, bleating like a trapped animal. His eyes rolled over to me.

The panic in them tripped a switch inside me. Unfortunately for this family of weirdos, that switch was right next to where I hid all my magic. I got to my feet and walked on unsteady legs to Hannah.

She'd started crying and clogged her nose with snot. Now she staggered around, trying to draw oxygen. I imagined myself knocking the magic right off her and clapped her on the back. She fell forward, sucking air in large whooping breaths. I grabbed onto the branches of a tree and used my other hand to steady her. The effort pulled at my sore muscles, and my vision swam. Hannah got hold of herself and faced me, red-faced and angry. There is nothing scarier than a pissed-off redhead.

"Get them," she gritted through her teeth.

Still staggering, I approached Pink Bra and Thick Woman. One of them had raked scratches over Tubby's face. I didn't have the strength to get them off Tubby, but Orev might.

I raised my arms as though wings were attached, gathering my power and making contact with my raven familiar. His caws echoed through my head.

The gray sky darkened with the silhouettes of many birds. Their wings beat a malevolent thunder. A hawk swooped in and clawed Pink Bra's back with lethal looking feet. He pecked her cheek, drawing blood. A piece of flesh flapped open. Pink Bra shrilled, rolled off Tubby, and ran for one of the dilapidated houses.

I imagined myself as a bird, diving for Thick Woman. The

birds flocked to her. They flogged and pecked at her. Unlike Pink Bra, she didn't scream. She waved one arm, and the birds swept back, driven by some invisible force. The birds scattered into the sky, angry squawks the only thing to prove they'd been there. She got off Tubby and faced me.

I held out both hands, this time in a challenge. "Finish it."

Anger beat at my temple and neck. Thick Woman had hurt me and my friends. Now we'd dance.

I limped toward Thick Woman, abdomen aching so badly I could barely lift my feet. This injury had taught me that every nerve in the human body had some connection to those muscles below the navel. For the first time, I thought about my broken fertility. Had Oscar's sword killed it forever? The thought made me see red. Unfortunately, the only enemy in front of me was Thick Woman. Too bad for her.

I drew magic from the humidity, the dirt at my feet, even from Thick Woman herself. The mantle grew like an extra lung, one filled with magic.

Control yourself. Don't kill her. The possibility of causing her to stroke out was very real. I had done that to Michael Gage.

Thick Woman had electrocuted me, caused me to hallucinate, trapped Linus in his car, tried to rape Tubby, and sewed Hannah's lips shut. But no permanent harm had been done. Other than the bite marks and scratches on Tubby.

I glanced at him. He stood staring at the bite mark on his arm, a sick expression on his face. A flash of anger threatened to undo my control. A few deep breaths, and I had it again. What could I do to Thick Woman that would scare the smartass out of her but not do permanent damage?

Burn her clothes? Blow up her gun? No. Both had the potential to get out of hand. My memory flashed on Thick Woman's snake trick. It had scared me, but it also said a lot about her. People hurt others in ways they fear being hurt themselves.

I focused my magic on Thick Woman. It slipped into her brain through the corner of her eye. She screamed and clapped her hand to the eye. She raised her wand.

Hurriedly, I planted seeds of the images I wanted her to see, but I did it gently. By the time I finished, sweat rolled down my sides and slimed the back of my neck. Controlling the magic was harder work than just letting it go.

Thick Woman coughed. The cough wracked her body, and she bent over with it. She tried to clear her throat. That turned into her gagging.

She bent at the waist, straining and gagging at the dirt. It sounded as though she had something caught in her throat. She dropped to her hands and knees, back arching with the force of trying to dislodge whatever it was. Her nostrils flared with her panicked breaths.

I gave what I'd lodged there a gentle push that cost me way more energy than an all-out shove would have been.

A huge snake head, complete with flickering tongue, pushed its way out of her mouth. I bit back a smug smile. It had worked.

"What the hell?" Ginger Chest Hair ran to Linus's fancy car and jumped on the hood, denting it.

Thick Woman's eyes crossed, trying to see what was coming out of her. I gave the snake a gentle nudge forward so she could see its shiny head.

Her eyes widened to the point that it wouldn't have surprised me if they had popped out. Thick Woman screamed around her mouthful of snake.

I grabbed my knees, panting with effort, and continued to seep gentle magic into the snake.

Thick Woman fell on her back, legs kicking, still shrieking through her nose. She slapped the ground next to her, signaling her surrender.

I let go of the magic powering the snake. It disappeared, and Thick Woman relaxed. She lay on the dirt, sobbing and breathing hard. After a few minutes, she began to catch her breath. She rolled to her knees and grabbed her wand off the ground where she'd dropped it.

"Now, Twila, you done lost fair and square." Swarthy came forward.

"I didn't holler uncle." She got to her feet and held out the wand.

"If you do anything else, I'm going to kill you." My tired voice barely rose above a whisper, but Twila—aka Thick Woman—must have seen the truth in my eyes. She stuck the wand back into her pocket.

"Fine. You want the location of a damned soul? Only person can give that to you is Pappy." She pointed at a nearby hill. "He's at the top of that hill."

I stared at Twila, throat clogged not with phantom snake but incredulity. She could have sent me to that hill before we started this whole pissing match.

"Why'd we just do what we did?" I managed to ask.

She turned to me, smiling, those awful rows of teeth on full display. "I done told you. I hate chicks like you. You get all the men, and you ain't nothing but a little slip of a girl who don't know how to give 'em proper use."

She spun on her heel and marched toward the house Pink Bra had disappeared into. Over her shoulder, she said, "Don't be here when I come back out."

She went inside and slammed the door hard enough to rattle the windows. Swarthy approached and stood picking at his fingernails a short distance way. He might have thought it was too far for me to hurt him. He'd have been wrong, but I wouldn't prove it.

He pointed at the spot where the yard ended in cactus and

wild brush. "Path back there. Take you right to Pappy's hill."

I stared hard at the hill but still saw no house. All I saw was a big, gnarled oak tree, limbs stretching far and wide. If Pappy lived on this hill, where did he live? And what was he? I had a feeling I wouldn't like finding out.

12

The three ramshackle houses of Freakazoid Ranch sat on the edge of a hill. The path Swarthy mentioned, a well-traveled white dirt lane, was between the second and third house. Muscles aching with tension, I made my way to it.

Behind the houses stretched out a valley spotted with patches of vegetation. The death throes of summer had burned most of it to a crisp, but a few dots of color here and there attested to the resilience of nature. The sky, even full of clouds as it was today, spread out vast and endless like an artist's canvas. The path to Pappy's, bright and sandy, traveled up the nearest tall hill, right to that huge tree with its long, crooked limbs.

I stepped onto the path and took one last glance over my shoulder at my friends. Hannah, Tubby, and Linus had congregated near Linus's car. Hannah waved to me.

None of them had offered to accompany me on this little

errand. I didn't blame them. This whole experience was the stuff of nightmares. If Pappy turned out to be as much of a dead end as those freaks behind me, the better part of a day would be lost. And Oscar would surely be back tonight.

Thick Woman and Pink Bra sneered at me through the window of the house they'd fled into when I'd started to really hurt them. The memory of their glee as they attacked Tubby slithered behind my eyes. Their behavior had been frightful and ugly. Anger sloshed inside me, ready to spill over and spread some crazy. One sneer from any of us would start the fight all over again.

If Tanner had been here, he'd have given me some bullshit lecture about letting it go and being the bigger person. But I knew better. The simple truth was that people who hated other people on sight usually had a few empty drawers in the old mental toolbox.

Even so, I'd have just about eaten a turd to have Tanner with me. The image of his earnest face and those green, green eyes haunted my memories. Loss stabbed deep into my heart. The night with Wade pretty much guaranteed Tanner and I were quits even if he came back. I'd have to tell him what happened. Then he'd never speak to me again.

I gave my head a hard shake. Now wasn't the time to mourn Tanner. I needed to be thinking about what lay ahead.

"That might serve you better." Priscilla appeared next to me, swinging tattooed arms like a suburbanite on a power walk. Only this walker was transparent and wore an ankle-length dress topped with a sleeveless chemise.

"What do you think's at the end of this trail?" I pointed at the tree. Something hung from one of its branches. Maybe a swing. We were too far away for me to tell for sure.

"Whatever it is, you'll find a way to use it to your advantage." She marched along beside me, feet hovering several inches over the tops of the cacti.

"What happened to me being a coward and a loser?" I almost missed the constant criticisms. This new, nicer Priscilla scared me a little. Maybe something awful was coming, and she didn't have the heart to tell me.

"I still think those things of you." She shrugged. "But you're changing. Becoming something more. Our time together is almost over."

"What do you mean?" My voice echoed in the wide expanse of empty before us.

"Once you absorb the mantle, I'll no longer be separate from you. Just as the Gregorius Witches before me became part of me, I'll become part of you." She delivered this piece of information with another mysterious smile.

I trudged along, thinking that over. Would I gain Priscilla's cold ruthlessness?

"You've already got it." She stopped and faced me. "What is it you really fear? Why not just say it?"

I stopped on the trail. Anything I said would start an argument, and Priscilla would win. She had answers I'd never even thought of the questions for.

She crossed her arms over her chest, the primitive tattoos rippling with her movement. "Speak."

"I fear not being me anymore." And that wasn't all. I feared something else, something I couldn't quite articulate, but it loomed big, stitched so deeply into the scar tissue spell that I couldn't even see it enough to identify it.

"You'll be more you than you ever were. You'll be part of something immortal." Her dark eyes bored into my face, their chill creeping deep.

But how much of Peri Jean Mace would be left? I wanted to still love my friends and family.

Priscilla shook her head and took off walking again. I followed at a safe distance. We closed in on the hill. There was no dwelling up there. Only that tree and whatever swung from it. The object swinging from the tree gave me a bad feeling. I turned to say something to Priscilla, but she was gone. Of course. Just when I might need her.

I climbed a little more of the hill. The use of my climbing muscles woke up the pain in my gut. My stomach let loose a blinding blast of agony. I stopped, put my hands on my knees, and tried to catch my breath. There was no way I'd be able to fight anybody like this.

"You don't need your physical muscles for the fight." Priscilla's voice seemed to come from nowhere.

I turned a slow circle, holding one hand over my aching middle.

Orev perched on a small tree nearby.

"Use your head, or you'll never make it through this." Priscilla's voice came from his beak.

My raven took flight to the top of the hill. His caws drifted back to me.

Come on. Come on, they seemed to say.

Both Orev and Priscilla were right. It was time for me to face what was up there. I walked the last few yards, sweat snaking down my back and sides. The top of the tree became visible at first, its lower limbs coming into sight with each step I took. A corpse swung from one of the low branches. Orev cawed a greeting.

"Pappy?" I asked the bird.

He cawed.

The wind kicked up, and the dead man swayed, noose creaking. His tattered clothes fluttered around what was left of his body. Pappy had been dead a while. Most of the muscle and skin from his bones was gone, probably eaten by predators. A wide black stain had spread on the dirt underneath the hanged man.

Communicating with a spirit didn't faze me the way it would have only a couple of years ago, but my instincts held me back. Something was wrong here.

For one thing, the well-decayed corpse hung from a new rope. Bits of old, rotten rope scattered the dark stain below the corpse's skeletal feet. A coil of new rope lay against the tree. I couldn't make sense of it.

I opened my third eye and took a better look at the corpse. Magic pulsed from the dirt through my feet. The mantle flipped over and pressed at the scar tissue, too cramped to really stretch. The black opal heated on my chest.

The corpse slowly raised its head to stare at me. The empty eye sockets filled in with black eyeballs just like the ones I'd seen back at Freakazoid Ranch. The mouth opened, displaying rows of sharp teeth. A hiss came from a not-there throat.

A voice spoke in my head. *Why do you come?*

"I'm looking for the soul of Oscar E. Rivera, also known as the Coachman and Lord of Babylon." I spoke in a firm, clear voice. I called it my spirit-dealings voice. They tended to get unruly if I wasn't clear about what I wanted.

I know where that is. One skeletal hand went up and pulled at the noose. *Let me down, and I'll tell you.*

The wind on the hill picked up, whispering against my

skin. The hanged man swayed with it, rope creaking, waiting for his answer.

Let me down. He yanked at the rope around his crooked neck.

My heart picked up speed. I could control a ghost, but Pappy wasn't a ghost. Though decayed, the thing in front of me lived.

As if to prove my point, Pappy gave his noose a harder yank, his long, yellowed fingernails digging into the rope's rough fabric and making it creak.

Please. I'll tell you everything about Oscar Rivera. I'll tell you everything you ever wanted to know. Just let me down. His voice sounded reasonable, nicer than anybody back at Freakazoid Ranch.

I looked around for Priscilla. She'd know what to do. My great-great-great-grandmother's ghost crouched in the tree, watching me like a big animal ready to pounce.

"What do I do?" Standing well clear of Pappy, I tilted up my head to address her.

"If you had full control of the Gregorius Witch mantle, you'd know." She gave me another Mona Lisa smile, eyes glinting with equal measures of malice and amusement. She shook the branch, making it rain bark and leaves into my face.

Young witch, you have nothing to fear from me. Pappy locked his bony fingers in a pleading gesture. *Let me down.*

Light fingers danced in my head. He was reading my mind. Straining so hard my head ached, I slammed down my defenses.

I can tell you how to gain the full measure of your power. You want Tanner Letts back? I can tell you how to get in touch with him. Pappy had started to sway in his excitement.

Priscilla chuckled from somewhere above. She was enjoying this little shit show.

Just let me down... The light fingers moved around in my head again. *...Peri Jean Mace. Let me down, and I'll tell you when your first child will be born and the sex.*

I glanced again at Priscilla, silently begging for help.

She shook her head. "You don't want my knowledge to be part of you. Let's see how you do without it."

I'm the only way you'll find Oscar's soul in time, Pappy babbled in my head. *If you don't defeat him before the Samhain, he'll be too strong.*

That did it. "How can I get you down?"

He pointed one bony finger at the ground. *Underneath the rope is a knife. Hand it to me, and I'll cut myself down.*

Sounded easy enough. I did what Pappy said, standing on tiptoes to get the knife into his hand. His smell filled my senses, dusty, like dried flowers in an antique shop, mixed with maybe rosemary. Pappy snatched the knife. I backed away.

Legs kicking, Pappy cut the noose. The desiccated corpse landed on his feet in front of me. His knees bent to catch the fall's impact. His power brushed against my skin, far greater than it had been while he hung from the tree.

Fear seized my heart and squeezed. I backed away, realizing too late that I'd messed up and wondering how long it would take for my mistake to bite me in the ass. Turned out, it wasn't long at all.

The corpse threw his hands over his head and stretched. His bones made cracking sounds. He turned to me, black eyes assessing. My pulse pounded harder.

Pappy bowed at the waist. "Thank you, thank you, thank you. It's been far too long since I've had a break."

My mouth went dry. Wrongness beat at my temples. But it was too late for that now. Pappy came closer, reaching for me. I backed away.

He stopped. "You said you want to know where to find Oscar Rivera's soul. Is that not true?"

I forced myself to nod. There was no choice but to play this out.

Pappy took another step toward me. "I have to touch you to put the images in your head. They don't make sense to me."

I focused on a piece of tendon dangling from one brown, skeletal hand. My skin crawled. Maybe it wasn't too late to say no. But maybe it was. Pappy hadn't put down the knife he'd used to cut himself out of the noose.

He watched me assess him. "Either you want the information, or you don't."

At last, I took a step toward him, indicating willingness. Pappy closed the distance between us faster than I'd have thought a skeleton could move. He put one hand on each cheek, bones pressing into my skin.

"No," I whimpered. Another bad move. I really knew how to screw up.

As soon as my mouth opened, so did Pappy's. His black, shark eyes locked on mine. A sound like a dozen devils screaming all at once came from Pappy's mostly fleshless skull. It shot into my mouth before I could get control enough of myself to snap it shut.

Nighttime. The thunder of horse hooves. Oscar and his huntsmen ride through flat, moonlit country, the inky sky a blanket of stars. The hounds run alongside them, their bounding strides eating up distance much faster than the horses.

The huntsmen's shouts and laughter echo over the plains. The hounds bay in answer. Night predators run into the darkness, hackles raised. These things are greater, more evil, than any simple night predator. Even the ones with big teeth.

The troupe passes by my line of sight. For the first time, I see them not as fleshless creatures, fashioned from bone and metal, but as they'd been while alive.

Oscar Rivera comes first, his sloe eyes and thick lips as arrogant as ever. My mother rides next to him, swaying with her horse's movement, her spine arched. Of course. Good old Barbie never settled for anything less than the boss man. The moonlight plays over her beautiful again face. Even as a ghost, she's still far prettier than I'll ever be.

Joseph Holze, a man who tormented me most of my life, finishing with the flourish of attempted murder, comes next. Joey is healthier than I ever remember him, his broad face and slightly protruding eyes set into a grimace of disgust.

Tim McSwain, my ex-husband and tormentor, rides behind Joey Holze. In death, he is restored to his glory as a bearded hippie messiah. But now I see the cruelty shining from his eyes, cruelty I should have noticed the first time he smiled at me.

Michael Gage comes next, his dark, handsome features filled with vicious pleasure. A far cry from the night I forced the blood vessels in his brain to explode.

Nash Redmond follows close behind his father. Now that I know, I see the resemblance. The leading man's square jaw. The dimples. The two exchange smiles.

On the backs of the next two horses are two faces I'd hoped to never see again. Camden DeVoss, finally free of Nazareth, Texas, in death, throws his head back to howl like a coyote. The real coyotes don't dare make a peep. Camden turns to Colton

Starr, easily the most handsome man I'd ever met in person, and smiles at him. Colton pretends not to see.

What had happened to Colton? I'd watched him taken away by police for the murder of Shayne Turgeau and for trying to kill Dean Turgeau's ex-wife and me. Prison must not have agreed with him.

Veronica Spinelli brings up the rear. Gone is the road whore I watched Dean Turgeau shoot to death. She's a golden goddess on horseback, eyes alert and searching the landscape.

The troupe comes to a small grouping of darkened, disintegrating buildings. The horses slow to walking speed, and they pass through a gate.

I follow, pushing my spirit self as fast as it'll go. A cemetery. They've passed into a cemetery. I strain to make out the words on the archway over the gate. They're in German. I don't know German.

But I do remember Linus's discovery of Oscar's early life, his being raised by a German witch in a German-speaking settlement. Linus had dismissed the information, but it had been the one useful thing we'd discussed. Of course.

I break off my thoughts and hurry after the specters. They ride to the center of the cemetery. Next to it hulks the tattered shape of a deserted church, its crooked steeple stabbing at the night sky.

Oscar dismounts next to a tombstone shaped like an obelisk and kneels next to it. He speaks, his voice pitched too low to hear. His shoulders shake. He's weeping for someone from his growing up years. Something almost like pity tightens my throat. I push it aside. I do not want to feel sorry for something as evil as Oscar.

Oscar stands and extracts something from his cloak. It sparkles in the moonlight.

Even though I can't see it clearly, I know it's his soul. I creep forward. This is what I need to see.

Oscar wheels around. "Who's there?"

His statesman's voice echoes over the tombstones. I hold my breath, even though I am only spirit right now, and pray he doesn't see me. Seconds crawl past.

"Gage!" Oscar calls. "See what's out there."

A horse wheels around and gallops in my direction.

Bony hands yank me from the vision.

I came back to myself on the hill with Pappy's skeletal hands still cupping my face. I took a step away from him.

His hands tightened. "You've not paid for my service."

Priscilla chuckled from above. My face heated. She was right. I didn't think to negotiate. I was too busy worrying about Tanner Letts, my aching guts, and not wanting to lose myself to the Gregorius Witch mantle.

Panic seized my throat. I fought for control. This was no big deal. I might have been at Pappy's mercy, but I could still negotiate.

"What do you want?" I managed to choke out.

"A taste of your blood." The warmth left his voice. Now it sounded cold and amused.

"No. If I do that..." I didn't really know what would happen. I just knew it was a big deal, not to be taken lightly.

"I'll know all about you, all your secrets. Secrets are my trade." Pappy's black eyes stared into mine, his consciousness rifling freely through mine.

I reached out for Priscilla, now desperate enough to beg for her help.

Her voice came from within my head. *You aren't willing to take on all I have to offer? You can't have any of it.* Our connection broke with a pop.

Pappy let go of my face and seized my left hand. I tried to yank away from him, but it was no use. He twisted my arm at a painful angle, forcing me to my knees. I barked a wimpy cry for help. Priscilla's cruel laughter answered.

Pappy stabbed the dirty tip of his knife into one of my fingers. A blackened, withered tongue crept from his mouth and scraped across my fingertip like sandpaper. Revulsion shivered through my heart.

Pink, healthy flesh began to fill in Pappy's cheeks. He opened his mouth and lunged for my hand, as though to take a big bite. I jerked away from him.

Pappy, now a young man with waves of long, dark hair cascading down his back, widened his stance, knife held loosely in one hand. He laughed, rows of shark teeth flashing white.

I glanced down at the hand he'd licked. The tip of my finger was black and withered. Black veins formed under the skin and crawled up my forearm. The rot spread over my hand.

"Get him hanging again. Or die. Your choice." Priscilla's voice came from next to me. A puff of wind and the rustle of her long dress marked her leaving me to my fate. Screw her. I'd figure it out.

Pappy and I circled each other. He hissed laughter, every so often feinting at me with the knife. I dodged away. Each effort sent a tear of pain through my midsection. I backed away, holding my stomach like the guts might fall out.

I had to face facts. There was no way I could physically fight Pappy. My body was still healing. Magic was the only answer.

I should have guessed that in the first place. Priscilla was a wise old spirit. She knew exactly when I'd need her help and when to withdraw from me. When it would count.

Pappy feinted at me again. I dodged away, tripped over my own feet, and hit the ground. My teeth clicked together. Agony shot through my stomach. Pappy hurried in for the kill.

The mantle jerked to life, instinctively sensing a threat. Heat rushed to the surface of my skin. Magic tingled at my fingertips. Golden sparkles filled my vision.

Pappy raised the knife to stab me.

An invisible force yanked me into the sky. My organs reacted to the change in force with a sinking sensation. My ears popped. Then I realized what had happened. I was levitating.

Pappy ran underneath me, realized he'd missed, and raised his head. Those flat, emotionless eyes latched onto mine.

My energy ebbed, and I dropped gently to the ground. Pappy ran at me again. This time, a blast of fire hit him in the chest. It knocked him onto his back. His shirt flamed for a second, releasing the odor of burning garbage. He got back up. I hadn't hurt him a bit.

The static of fear filled my mind. I fought against it. If fear took over, I wouldn't be able to think. If I couldn't think, Pappy would eventually outsmart me.

I brushed away the thoughts. The frenetic lines of illogic, all incomplete and unusable, died down. What weapons could I use against Pappy?

As a spirit medium, I had experience binding and banishing spirits. Though Pappy didn't qualify as such, binding still might work. But how? I didn't have supplies to draw a circle. I didn't have incense.

Priscilla Herrera chuckled in my head. I ignored her.

I pushed my consciousness against the mantle, stoking its fire, and concentrated on binding Pappy. A stick caught my eye. I grabbed it and an overgrown strand of grass. I poured magic into both until the air around them wavered.

I held up the stick. "*I name this stick Pappy.*"

Pappy, who'd been trying to sneak up on me, halted, face still.

"*Pappy, I bind you from hurting others.*" I wrapped the blade of grass around the stick.

Grass pulled itself from the ground, roots dangling, wove together, and circled Pappy. He slapped at the green rope, but it looped over his arms and pulled them to his sides.

"*Pappy, I bind you from doing evil.*" I made another loop around the stick.

More grass wove together and joined the green rope already squeezing at Pappy's arms. He strained against it, cords standing out in his neck, long, black hair whipping side to side. The muscles in his neck bulged as he strained against his binding. The grass rope held him fast.

I went to the coil of rope next to the tree. Rough fibers of the rope chafing my fingers, I fashioned it into a noose. Now all I had to do was put the noose over Pappy's head. Easy as herding armadillos.

I approached Pappy, feet light on the grass. His head rose.

His black eyes stared into mine, full of depth and mysteries. I couldn't look away. The light fingers tapped against my brain again.

"*Dimittis me,*" he whispered.

My bowels went loose and hot. My vision wavered and darkened at the edges.

"*Dimittis me,*" he whispered again.

It meant release me. The mantle knew. The command took root in my mind, spreading roots. My hand rose on its own. My index finger, the one turning black and necrotic, pointed at the grass rope. I watched stupefied, no more in control than a kid watching a movie. My index finger curled in a come-along motion, and the grass rope separated and dropped to the ground.

Pappy's knife arm rose. He lunged at me, screaming another word I didn't quite catch.

The mantle lashed inside me. My paralysis broke with a snap. I clambered out of Pappy's way, a scream pounding in my throat. He ran a few feet and spun with an enraged roar.

I backed away, heart leaping. Why couldn't I just carry a gun like Hannah? I could have shot Pappy and run. Oh, wait. I didn't carry a gun because I had magic. But it hadn't worked on Pappy.

Spit forming at the corners of his mouth, Pappy stalked toward me.

This was it. Everything I'd gone through, and I was going to end up dead on this hill, killed by a monster with ugly teeth. I didn't even know what he was.

"You don't have to." Priscilla's voice came from all around me. Her freezing finger pressed against my breastbone.

The mantle worked its way out of a thin spot in the scar tissue and spread. My ribcage ached with the pressure. Hot, vibrant energy burned through my veins and snaked into my brain.

I focused on the rope coiled at the base of the tree. Pumping power into it, I said, "*Come.*"

The rope slithered toward Pappy's feet. He watched it come with the same stupid surprise he'd shown at my attempt to bind him.

"*Take him.*" I gave the two words power. My voice trembled with it.

The rope wrapped itself around the branch Pappy had been hanging from, the fibers whispering against each other. The noose slithered after Pappy. He tried to run. The rope lunged and crawled up his leg, traveling up his body too fast for my eyes to track. The noose slipped over his head. Pappy let out a howl that shook the earth beneath my feet.

"*Hang him,*" I grated out.

The rope whipped over a high branch and hoisted Pappy into the air. His legs pinwheeled and pedaled. He tried to saw at the rope, but only managed to stab himself in the neck. Blood ran down in a hot gout.

I reached with my left hand. "*The knife.*"

The knife flew from his fingers and into mine. I set it at the base of the tree where I'd found it.

Pappy continued to kick and flail as his blood rained onto the earth. After what seemed forever, his movements slowed. His skin turned gray, then brown and shiny. Pieces of him flaked off and fell around my feet.

Priscilla's voice came from beside me. "Do you see now? Your magic just saved you. You won't survive unless you accept your destiny."

Without answering, I turned and walked down the hill. Embarrassment beat at me with each step.

13

On the walk back to Freakazoid Ranch, I swung my arms and forced myself to hum. Priscilla had to be watching and listening. I'd show her this was a walk in the park for me. The humming and arm swinging got old and sounded stupid even to my own ears pretty fast. I shut up and thought back to Pappy hanging from that tree.

His survival baffled me. Was it an animation spell? An immortality bargain like the one Oscar had taken? Aside from going back to ask Pappy, there was no way to find out. Unless I asked one of my new friends at Freakazoid Ranch.

Little chance of that. Those people—or whatever they were—had no limits. Their disgusting behavior made me wonder what Pappy had done to end up hanged and exiled from the rest of the family.

My family had rules. No crybabies topped the list. What

you saw in Sanctuary stayed there. No calling authorities into our business. Unflinching loyalty.

Kenny, dead now in an act of sacrifice for Sanctuary, had acted as a traitor. Cecil probably would have killed him. But he'd left the choice to me. I had robbed Kenny of his status within the community, assigning him the lowliest jobs, but let him live. He had repaid me with his life. At the end, he'd been one of us.

Did the members of Freakazoid Ranch protect each other by hanging Pappy on top of that hill? My instincts said yes. They must have had a sad life with him among them, even sadder than what they had now.

Nearing the small grouping of houses, I slowed my pace. Thick Woman and Pink Bra stood at the mouth of the trail. *Just great.* I couldn't fight them again. Dealing with Pappy had drained me both magically and physically. Tubby and Hannah would help me fight. Linus would too. But could we beat them without magic? I just couldn't imagine moving any more energy right then. Every inch of my body hurt. Even my hair follicles ached.

"You chicken out?" Thick Woman flashed her rows of teeth.

I held out my hand to show them where Pappy had pricked the finger. The black rot had faded, but the wound was red and throbbed with each beat of my heart.

"Nuh-uh." Pink Bra crowded close, giving me a sour whiff of body odor.

"She's lying. She did that herself." Thick Woman leaned close. Her hair gave off a stale, unwashed smell.

Anger flashed in my brain. I formulated a retort but stopped short of saying it. Why bother with these two?

I brushed past them, yelling, "Hannah!"

Hannah hurried toward me, already reaching into her belt for her gun.

"It's fine." Getting shot sounded like the least fun way to end this day.

For one thing, I didn't want another up close and personal encounter with Wade Hill. Desiree might not let me live through it.

Linus hurried to me. "Thank goodness. I'm sorry I didn't warn you. After everything..."

He had known what waited for me on that hill and didn't bother to give me any kind of heads-up? I simmered more anger but refused to act on it.

"What is that thing?" I kept my voice low and even, but Linus's eyes widened all the same. Some of the color drained out of his face.

"Pappy is a half-god." He came a little closer and dropped his voice to a whisper. "The child of a human and one of the Old Ones."

A half-god. More specifically, an insane half-god. Priscilla had told me most weren't viable mentally or physically.

She'd also said I'd have the power of a half-god if I took on the mantle. Would I be like Pappy?

Another memory came. "I thought half-gods could be killed."

"Sure. But they don't want him dead." Some of Linus's color returned. The role of scholar must've been a comfortable one for him. "They keep Pappy alive because he knows things, and they deal in knowledge."

I asked my last question. "Why did they hang him?"

Linus dropped his voice to a near whisper. "The children hanged Pappy for raping his daughters and killing the offspring."

A wave of cold washed over me. All of a sudden, I wanted more than anything to get out of this place and never see these people again. I glanced back toward the houses to see the whole crew—Pink Bra, Thick Woman, Swarthy, and Ginger Chest Hair watching us. Yes. We needed to go. We could figure out where the cemetery with the German writing on the gate was after we got elsewhere.

"Let's get out of here." I turned toward Tubby's trashed Cutlass.

Linus stopped me with one hand on my arm. "Were you at least able to find out where Oscar hid his soul?"

I told him what I'd seen.

He listened, frowning. "So the bit about Oscar being an

orphan was true. And I know that place. Damn it. I wish I hadn't gotten so old. It's right on the tip of my tongue."

By this time, Hannah and Tubby had joined us. He watched Linus think for several seconds before he spoke.

"What's special about it? Maybe that'll help you remember." Tubby lit cigarettes for himself, Hannah, and me. I noticed his fingers touched her lips. And she smiled at him.

"Oh, I know exactly what's special about it." Linus's voice rose in irritation. "I used the place in one of my books. A witch is buried there. People visit the grave to petition her protection."

That was the grave Oscar had visited and cried over. The witch must've been someone special to him.

Linus paced around, lips moving. Finally he raised his head. The look on his face dashed my hopes.

"It's in my notes back at the house. Follow me back there. Spend the night even." He pulled his keys out of his pocket, smiling.

Hannah and I exchanged a glance. I didn't want to go back to Linus's house. Though he'd no doubt prove an excellent host, I wanted the comfort of my family. They equaled safety and home. Especially when I was hurting.

Linus's smile faded.

"It's not that we don't appreciate the offer, but I got hurt last night and don't feel so good." I took a couple of steps toward Linus and pushed aside my clothes to show him my wound.

"This asshole stabbed her with a sword," Tubby said. "She like to have died."

"Who healed you?" Linus's eyes went bright with interest.

"Can't say. He'd be angry." I took a step back from his avid interest.

He recoiled from my refusal with a quick nod. "Very well. I'll call you once I get home and look through my notes."

It didn't take genius level intelligence to know he'd conveniently forget since I wasn't willing to tell him Wade's name. I'd refused to play ball regarding Black Silas and was refusing again with Wade. I seemed like nothing but a well of need to Linus. The truth smarted, but I took it in stride. *You can't have everything.*

"Thank you for helping me today." I stuck out my hand.

Linus gave it an unenthusiastic shake. "Of course. Anytime."

He didn't mean it, and that was okay. I strongly suspected I could reopen communications by offering something else that interested him. For now, I needed to find out the name of that cemetery. I knew two people who dealt in that kind of thing. Mysti and Griff.

Linus walked to his car. I led the way to Tubby's Cutlass and tried to get into the front seat.

Hannah blocked my way. "Shotgun."

"You're kidding," I whined but climbed into the back seat without further protest.

Hannah took the front seat without answering and started fiddling with the radio as soon as Tubby cranked the engine. The two of them exchanged a smile. Tubby followed Linus back to the main road but didn't turn back toward Austin.

"We headed to where Cecil and the others are?" Tubby had to yell to be heard over the radio.

I took out my phone. "Let me call Mysti."

Mysti answered on the first ring and began babbling. "Where are you? Tubman said you're okay, but you know how he *lies*. If you don't tell me where you are right now, I'm going to hex you. No, I don't mean that. But where are you?"

I told Mysti about the people we'd just met and what they'd showed me. "Linus said the graveyard is well-known because a witch is buried there. The area around her grave is supposed to offer protection."

I fell quiet, praying to whatever ruled the universe that Mysti had heard of this place. If she hadn't, I was going to have to kiss Linus's ass. Maybe even give up Wade's name to get what I wanted. I still wasn't willing to put Linus in the path of Black Silas.

But Mysti didn't let me down. "I do know that place. Well, Griffin does. Hold on." Mysti patched Griff into the call, words running together as she explained what we needed.

Griff was silent for several long moments. Long enough for fear to take root and bloom next to my heart.

Finally, he spoke. "Just a minute. I'm seeing if I have the location recorded on my phone. Otherwise, it's going to be an expedition." A few seconds later, he said, "Shit. But I remember the road. Is Tubman chauffeuring you and Hannah?"

"He is," I said.

"Give him the phone." Griff had switched from concerned friend back to boss.

Without thinking much about it, I handed Tubby my phone. He and Griff had a short discussion. He handed my phone back to me and started driving.

I scrolled through my phone to Tanner's contact info and dialed him again. I got the same message I had when I was dying. The number had been disconnected.

It made sense. Tanner had first joined Sanctuary dead broke. We got together, and I'd wanted him to have nice things. I'd paid for his phone service. But Tanner's pride wouldn't let him continue to use a phone paid for by a woman he was no longer in a relationship with.

That told me a lot about what to expect from him in the future. I leaned back against the seat, tears burning my eyes. Tubby reached out to change the radio station. Hannah slapped his hand away. He pulled her hair. They were flirting. The realization opened a pit of the deepest sadness and loneliness in my heart. I couldn't even send them a mental well-wish.

After long enough for me to want to crack their heads together, Tubby turned off the little two-lane highway onto a cracked one-lane asphalt road. I peered out the windows at the landscape, willing myself to recognize something from my vision. But the overgrown trees and roadways mostly looked the same.

The asphalt road ended, and we crept along a dirt road. I didn't recognize any of this. My gut clenched at the possibility we were going to the wrong place. Then a little clump of weathered buildings came into view. My heart jumped.

"This is it," I muttered.

Hannah turned back to me, flushed and grinning.

I pushed down my misery at having lost Tanner and smiled back. She likely wouldn't find lasting happiness with Tubby, but at least he didn't have a wife stashed out of state. He might kill people in front of her, but he would never hit or abuse her. He might not be able to love her, but he'd treat her well.

The sign with the German words on it came into view. In

daylight, I could see it stood over a brick entrance to a gated cemetery. Griff and Mysti's SUV was parked on the side of the road, which I could see ended a few feet beyond the cemetery. Griff slid out of the driver's side and waved unnecessarily.

Tubby parked nose to nose with the SUV and shut off the Cutlass. He started to say something, but then cut it off. "Holy hell."

Mysti, colorful clothes flying, ran toward the Cutlass, her face pinched in determination.

"Better let me out," I said. "Otherwise, she might tear the car apart."

———

Hannah leapt out of the car and pushed forward the back seat just as Mysti reached it. I began the painful process of pulling myself out. Mysti, with more strength than I'd given her credit for, yanked me from the car. She threw her arms around me and squeezed until I yelped.

She startled and let go of me, gaze running over my unstained clothes. "Wade healed you."

I nodded. The rest of it didn't deserve a mention. Wade's and my tryst had hurt my heart. I didn't want to talk about it anymore.

Her eyes, not as dark brown as mine but with a little more

honey in them, flicked over my face. Her lips pursed. She knew something wasn't quite right with me.

"May I see?" She gestured at my midsection to let me know what she meant.

I pulled away my shirt and lowered my jeans. This was getting to be a habit. Maybe I should pursue a career in exotic dance if the witch thing went south. Griff hurried over. The three of us examined the still livid, though fading, mark together.

"Not bad," Griff whispered.

Mysti frowned. "What's the shiny stuff smeared on it?"

"An ointment Desiree had. She said it's poisonous to ingest." I took the tub out of my pocket and showed it to Mysti.

She took it from me, unscrewed the lid, and sniffed. She made a face and raised her eyebrows. "I don't know what that is."

"Me either." I held out my hand for the ointment.

After a second's hesitation, Mysti handed it over. She'd have probably kept and studied it had I not demanded it back. Not for the first time, I wondered at the shift of power between us.

Mysti had started out as my teacher. She still advised me when I needed it. But she now treated me more as a contemporary. Someone who performed just as effective magic as she could.

"Daylight's fading. Shall we?" She gestured at the cemetery, eyes crinkling in a smile.

We walked below the arched gate into the quiet world of the cemetery. Mysti took my arm and hurried my step away from our friends. She hustled me a short distance away, stopped walking, and faced me.

"I can tell something's wrong. Spill it." Her sharp, probing gaze clashed with her wrinkled peasant blouse and tiered, ankle-length skirt.

I didn't want to tell her. I'd made a mistake. But she'd asked because she cared. I motioned her closer.

"I slept with Wade," I whispered.

She drew back and stared into my face. Her lips turned down. "And you finally saw him. Really saw him. I'm so sorry."

The pain of what I'd done throbbed to life.

Mysti pulled me close and spoke into my ear, her breath hot on my face. "Life is full of lessons. The only shame is when you don't learn from them."

"But Tanner..." I choked off the words.

"Tanner left. Your world didn't stop the second he walked out the door." She held me tight. "If he can't accept that, he's not worth a second's worry."

The others caught up. Mysti and I let go of each other.

Hannah pointed. "Is that the obelisk?"

I swallowed a big gulp of dread and nodded. We trudged through the huge, old oaks standing guard over the graves. The monument seemed bigger with every foot of ground we covered. Waves of energy emanated from the huge stone. They found my energy and tapped at it, testing it. Yes, the person buried here had power even in death.

"This damn place is creepy," Tubby whined behind me.

"It's warning you not to play with things you can't handle." Mysti ducked under a low hanging branch as thick as her body.

"As you can see, most people ignore it." I gestured at the prayer candles crowding the base of the obelisk and leaned in to see the name. It was blank. I drew back, confused.

"Other side. It faces west," Griff called.

We had to walk around the obelisk to read the inscription.

Herta Schüler

Born in Hamburg 1800

Died in Texas 1898

She was the right age to have been a foster mother to Oscar Rivera.

In addition to the candles, visitors had drawn upside-down

crosses, pentagrams, and some *X*s on the smooth, gray stone. Dead flowers of all kinds littered the ground.

Where could Oscar have buried his soul? In the vision, I saw him take it out of his cloak and saw it glint in the moonlight, but I'd gotten pulled out of the vision before he did anything with it.

Griff held out a spade. "I guess we just start digging?"

Tubby crowded in, grabbing for the tool. His blue eyes shifted around the enclosed space, and chill bumps made the blond hair on his arms stand at attention.

"Come on," he muttered. "Let's get this over with and get the hell out of here."

I elbowed him away. "Wait a minute. Oscar's going to know the second we have his soul. He's going to come for us. We've got to have a plan, or this is a waste of time and energy."

"Good point." Griff moved the spade out of Tubby's reach.

Tubby frowned at me. "What's the plan then, boss lady?"

My shoulders rounded. "The only thing I've ever done to get rid of souls is eat them. And I'm not eating Oscar's soul. The hag almost killed me." I cringed at the memory of the pain.

Mysti's nose crinkled. "You're lucky it didn't. The hag was a higher being. Don't try that again until you have full use of your power."

I gave a tough shrug. Deep down, I agreed.

Griff spoke in my silence. "There are weapons that will kill anything—spirit, chthonic being, you name it. Unfortunately…"

"Tanner would be the one to know about that, and he's lost to us." My face heated.

Mysti gave me a fierce frown. I interpreted it as "Not your fault."

"Wait a minute." Tubby wouldn't stay quiet, even when the topic went far beyond his area of expertise. "Aren't spirits just made of energy?"

Nobody answered, and Tubby rolled his eyes. "Energy can't be killed, right? So how do special weapons or eating souls kill them?"

I saw where he was going and hoped we could reason it out. We were, after all, nothing more than a couple of witches, a nosy grave dowser, a former B-list celebrity, and a redneck crime kingpin.

I began talking, thinking as I spoke. "When I ate Loretta Nell Grimes's spirit and the hag's magical core, I absorbed them. The energy didn't die. It changed. Both what Loretta Nell and the hag had been personally faded away. I gained the energy for my own use." I pushed myself to see a solution and didn't.

"So how do you change Oscar's energy without eating it and without one of these weapons?" Tubby asked.

We all stood thinking.

"You did fine with Loretta Nell, but not the hag." Mysti spoke barely above a whisper, face tight with the pressure to think of a solution.

It hit me. The solution had been there all along. I spoke in a rush.

"Loretta Nell worked out fine because I had more magic than her." I remembered Mohawk calling me the Gregorius Witch. That had been the first time I'd heard that name. But now I understood all that it meant. "But the hag was a being greater than me. So it almost killed me." I shook my finger at Mysti, heart hammering. "Oscar's spirit is *more* than me right now."

Mysti stood up straight, a hard light burning behind her eyes. "He is. So we need something greater to kill him."

Or to contain him. I rummaged through my list of contacts. Sol and Bub had refused to help me when Oscar had sent a supernatural assassin after me. They had, instead, taken bets and had fun seeing how things worked out for me. I couldn't depend on them. But I did know one person who dealt in supernatural oddities, someone for whom Oscar's soul might have value. I shivered at the memory of him.

"I know someone who might help. But that still doesn't take into account Oscar coming for us. And he will once we have the soul." I glanced around my friends.

A voice came from all around me. "You'd have to distract Oscar, of course. But why would I let you have his soul?"

Fear landed with a jolt in the pit of my stomach. I spun around to face a very elderly woman's ghost. Had to be Herta.

Wrinkled flaking skin. White eyes. Dark lips. Her coldness seeped into my skin, making my sore muscles ache. Whispers scrabbled at the back of my mind. A querulous old voice rose above them.

"Get away from here. This ground is protected." She flicked her fingers at me.

I flew backward, right into Hannah. We fell in a heap. Tubby rushed to help Hannah. Mysti held out one hand to help me up. I took it and got to my feet.

She whispered, "Herta wouldn't have mentioned distracting Oscar so we could get away with his soul if she weren't willing to help."

I nodded. It was time to make a deal with Herta. I hated this part.

Aloud, Mysti said, "Help me clean the marks off Herta's tombstone. She wasn't this kind of witch and wouldn't have liked these things."

We spent the next few minutes rubbing the marks off the tombstone. Mysti left the flowers, but took the prayer candles covered with Xs to the cemetery's fence and left them. She motioned to Griff, and he brought over her witch pack. She set out old china bowls. In one, she poured water. In the other, she placed a crust of bread.

She put her arm around me and spoke in a whisper. "Summon Herta. Explain your need. I can feel her magic. She was a good person. Maybe once she understands the evil Oscar intends, she will help us despite her personal relationship with him."

I reached inside, searching for my ability to summon a ghost. My power sprang forth, willing and overly excited.

"Herta Schüler, please talk to me." I meant to whisper the words, but I boomed them out, sounding like Priscilla Herrera.

Herta's form flashed in front of the grave. Both eyes were black pits, not an uncommon sight in the spirit world. The water in the bowl dissipated in seconds. The bread in the other bowl began to smoke. It blackened into ash.

Herta's power, frightfully strong for one so long dead, radiated off her. It brushed against my power. Static blared in my head.

"You're here to steal from my son." She had a strong German accent, spoken with sharp, clipped sibilants. It was almost as threatening as her magic.

There was no point in lying to her. "Yes. But Oscar intends to kill me and to wage war on the living with my power."

Her form flickered, eyes filling in to a faded blue. "I know the boy I raised grew in *einen Teufel.* But he is still *mein Sohn.*"

I caught onto *mein Sohn* because of the context. But *einen Teufel* had me puzzled.

Herta let out an impatient snort. "A devil. My son is a devil."

I nodded my understanding. "If you know Oscar grew into a devil, then you know he must be stopped. Let us dig up his soul and rid the world of him." I still held the spade in one hand, ready to finish this errand.

The breeze moving through the ancient trees turned icy.

"I won't betray my son. Even if I would, he'll come as soon as you tamper with his soul. Someone would have to stall him for you to get away." This was the second time she'd mentioned distracting Oscar. Though her refusal sounded final, she was giving me a solution.

We needed to negotiate. What might Herta want that I could grant? I glanced at the prayer candles and other crap we'd piled by the fence and at the smudges where we'd rubbed the Xs and pentagrams off her grave.

"I can clean your grave. Make it look nice again. If this is where you're choosing to spend eternity, I can make it nice." Even as I said the words, I couldn't believe Herta would want to stay here. What a lonely place.

"I don't want to be here. I'm trapped." Herta stopped her

advance and hovered over the ground, white hair blowing in the wind. Anger began to radiate off her.

"Then I'll help you get out of this cemetery and on to whatever's next for you." Even better. Something I could understand her wanting.

"Nobody can help me." The air turned even colder. "Father Weber trapped me here for eternity."

This was Herta's price. She wanted out of this place. Herta moved toward me. She wanted to touch me.

I stiffened, skin crawling, but stood still. Her freezing hand connected with my forehead. There was a snap, both inside and outside my body. Blue light flared.

Wind filtered through the trees, rattling the leaves, blowing hard enough to send a flurry of them dancing to the ground. My brain ached with what felt like an ice cream headache, and the smell of decay filled my senses.

Something passed between us. On my end, it felt like a hard pull on my magical energy. Herta Schüler's story seeped into my mind, fragmented and mundane, detailed and horrific.

Herta Schüler had been a natural witch like Mysti and me. She'd used her power to make healing potions and to bless this little settlement with prosperity. She'd been a childless widow with money. She had taken in children in need of a home and loved them.

Flashes of Oscar as her adopted son played behind my

eyes. He started as a skinny boy, eyes dark and full of fear. He carried water and hoed in the garden. He grew. The fear left his eyes. Herta taught him reading and writing. The final image of him showed him packing a small wagon attached to a horse. Herta saw him off smiling but then went into her house, sat at her table, and cried.

Further flashes showed her surrounded by other adopted children and later their children. She went through the same ritual as she had Oscar of seeing them off to greater fortunes.

Then came Father Weber. Flashes came of this short, bald-headed, buck-toothed asshole turning Herta away from the doors of the church, making a warding-off-evil gesture with one hand.

Father Weber had Herta's tombstone turned the wrong way. At Herta's burial, he had buried a piece of iron over her casket and, by doing so, trapped Herta's spirit on this plane.

The fury started in my belly, liquid fire and intoxicant of the self-righteous. People who abused their power pushed my buttons. The victims, little people like me, often had nobody to help them. My anger grew.

I wanted to personally piss on the grave of the man who did this. But such actions fueled no purpose. Best to focus on how I could help Herta.

"What if I dig up the iron so you can leave here? Maybe turn your headstone around. Would you show me where to find Oscar's soul then? Tell me how to stall him?" Shivering from worry and the cold Herta emanated, I waited for her answer.

Herta's brow creased. Oscar had been a son she loved. Giving him up presented a moral dilemma.

I felt sorry both for Herta and Oscar. He had been a sweet boy, and they'd loved each other. But life had knocked him around. Killed his wife and children. Oscar came up fighting, but he took the dark path and lost himself along the way. It could happen to anybody, even me. As much sympathy as I had, Oscar would be a danger until he left this plane forever.

"Yes or no?" I licked my lips. If Herta said no, I'd have to fight her. It would drain my energy to dangerous levels, and I still might lose.

"Oscar was my son. It goes against my nature as a mother to betray him." Herta hung her head.

My stomach sank. All that for nothing. She had changed her mind.

"But..." She put her freezing hand on me. "It is my fault Oscar is doing this. It is I who told him the legend of the *Wilde Jagd*. It is I who taught him how to contact *die dunklen Wesen* and make deals. So this is *meine Strafe*." She shook her head at the confusion on my face. "The Wild Hunt. Demons. Punishment."

I let out the breath I'd been holding. "Show me where the iron's buried. Let's get it off you."

She flickered out of existence and reappeared a few feet away.

We went to work digging. Griff kept the spade for himself, and the rest of us used knives, keys, whatever we had. Herta had been in the ground a long time. It took many minutes for us to hit the iron. Once we did, our movements reached a feverish pitch. Griff finally pulled out a short section of iron decorated with curlicues.

"My house," Herta whispered next to me.

I stiffened. Father Weber had defaced Herta's home so that he could trap her spirit forever in this cemetery. Rage flashed hard enough to make my vision waver.

"The tombstone," she whispered. "You promised to fix my tombstone."

Griff glanced at the spade in his hand and made a pained face.

"It'll have to be done with magic." I came closer to the huge monument. It probably weighed hundreds of pounds. Mysti came near.

"We could combine our power to move it." She regarded the huge stone with an expression of dread.

I held out my hand. Mysti clasped her fingers over it. Her power hit mine and almost knocked me staggering. She'd claimed not to be as powerful as me, but this blast of pure energy was like nothing I had inside me. My power was connected to the element of fire. Mysti's power dealt more in air. How we'd do this came to me in an instant.

I called on the shining light of the mantle and let the fire join forces with Mysti's air. Together, we sent out our magic, pushed it toward the monument. The energy wrapped itself around the stone.

"Now push," Mysti ordered.

Bending my knees as though lifting a heavy weight, I gave it everything I had. The tombstone began to turn. It was like watching a turtle cross the road. My magical muscles began to throb with the strain. Next to me, Mysti began to shake with effort. Sweat popped out on her face and made streaks through her makeup.

The tombstone shifted a tiny bit at a time. After what seemed like forever, the inscription finally faced perpendicular to Herta's final resting place.

"Just a little more," Mysti gritted out.

I nodded and redoubled my efforts. Sweat rolled down my forehead and burned my eyes. A low whine came from my throat. Just when I thought I could stand it no longer, the tombstone moved the last few inches.

Mysti and I both fell backward. She pulled her knees up to her chest and wrapped her arms around them, sides heaving. I lay on my back and turned my head to watch her. After a few seconds, she gave me a smile.

"You did great. I knew you could do it." Still panting, her words came out uneven.

I shook my head at her. "Why do you keep that hidden?"

Mysti tinkled laugher, stood, and held out one hand. She'd say no more. I let her help me up.

"Are you free now?" I asked Herta.

Herta answered by flitting around the edges of the graveyard. She even left the fenced area and made bright revolutions around the church. A seed of worry sprouted in the fertile soil of my mind. What if Herta didn't keep her end of the bargain? It might take us hours of digging around Herta's tombstone to find Oscar's soul. And she'd promised to help me distract Oscar when he came to stop me. I still needed her to do those things.

"Don't go yet," I called.

Griff shook his head and began digging with the spade.

Herta zipped back to her grave, wind of her passage rattling the leaves.

She pointed at the church. "Don't waste time digging. The soul is in the church. Under the pulpit. Hurry."

14

———

The church wasn't too many yards away, but even the short distance made my abdomen ache. Hannah caught up with me, huffing and puffing.

"I need to talk to you about something." Hannah pulled her fingers a few times.

It didn't take a genius to guess what she was about to say. The glances between her and Tubby told an obvious story. It woke up the ache of losing Tanner, but I had no regrets about taking a pass on a do-over romance with Tubby. Too much risk of losing the bond we had. If Hannah wanted to see where a flirtation with Tubby led, she should. Before I could tell her that, she spoke again.

"Normally I'd stay away from Tubby because the two of you had a thing." She pulled her index finger hard enough to make the joint pop and flinched.

I cringed on her behalf. Did she really think I'd get angry?

Or was she afraid of Tubby? Sometimes the men who instilled a little spark of fear did so because they were the right one. A memory of dancing with Tanner flashed in my mind. Deep, hollow sadness filled my chest and ached at the base of my throat. He'd been the right one. I'd never deny Hannah the chance to see if Tubby was the right one for her.

"You don't have to ask my blessing, but you have it. Take a chance." My voice wavered on the last couple of words. Tears flooded my eyes. Not wanting Hannah to see, I quickened my pace and hurried up the church's crumbling brick steps.

When I reached for the door of the rickety old building, an invisible force rose up and knocked me backward. I flew up several feet before I dropped and landed hard. Pain flared in my midsection. I put my arms over it and whimpered.

Hannah dropped to her knees beside me. "Are you all right?"

"I'll live." Trying to catch my breath, I opened my second sight. Something supernatural had shoved me away from the door. What?

Over the door of the church hung several horseshoes. Not those. I handled them all the time. Hoisting myself to my feet, I stared at the bricks. Nothing unusual there. The only other thing that caught my attention were two decorative posts with geometric flower shapes burned into them.

Footsteps crunched toward us. I twisted, knowing it was Mysti and Griff.

She kept her distance. "Father Weber covered all the bases, didn't he? Horseshoes, witch marks burned onto the posts. Why, I bet at one time there were even witch balls."

"But I handle horseshoes all the time," I protested.

"Haven't I told you that it's all about intent?" She winked.

Cringing with embarrassment, I crawled to my feet. Mysti had made note of all this before she even climbed onto the bricks. I hadn't seen them until I looked for them. Then I'd had no idea what I was seeing or why it could hurt me.

"How did Oscar get in if this place is protected?" The depth of my ignorance terrified me. How was I going to survive?

"Oscar can bypass this ward because he is neither living nor dead. Being in-between grants immunity." Mysti rattled off the answer without an ounce of reproach, but my cheeks grew even hotter.

"Then what do we do?" My pride made the words almost too big for my mouth. But I managed.

"Remove them, Tubby." Mysti snapped her fingers at him.

Tubby hurried on to the church entry with his bolt cutters. There was finally a use for them. He swung at the decorative post. It only took him a few hits to dislodge it. He kicked it off the porch and moved on to the next one. Griff yanked on the post between each hit. This one took fewer blows. Tubby jumped to pull the horseshoes off the doorframe. He pitched them into the church's overgrown yard.

I glanced at Mysti. "Shall we?"

She slipped her arm through mine. "We shall."

We hadn't taken two steps before the shape of a short, ugly man appeared before us. Father Weber in spirit form. He stood with his stubby legs apart, rabbit teeth clenched in a snarl. *No witches*, his awful, grating voice exploded in my head.

"How is that awful man keeping us out?" I yelled at Mysti.

Mysti walked back to where her witch pack was and came back with a handful of something. She tossed a couple of Mercury dimes on the brick. They turned black and began to smoke. Her shoulders rounded, and she made a face.

"He's put a witch bottle, probably full of his fingernails and urine, underneath this brick porch. It's meant to ward off evil." She kept her distance from the church door. "Before you ask, Oscar's in-between status let him pass on through."

"Fine, but I'm not evil," I snapped. A lifetime of hearing that made me a little sensitive.

Mysti gave her head an impatient shake. "No. Nor am I. But Father Weber empowered the bottle to keep people he considered evil out. We are those people."

"Do we dig it up?" The suggestion made my body hurt. We had neither the equipment nor the time.

Mysti twisted to face me, one eyebrow raised. "Are you saying that sorry little man is stronger than us?"

I scrambled to my feet. Memories of the way this man had treated Herta pulsed in my veins. "No."

I marched back up the brick steps. The wall of energy Father Weber had put in place rose up to meet me. I took one second to gather myself. The shining power of the mantle raced through me, both hot and cold at the same time. I threw up one hand and pushed at Father Weber's wall of energy.

Father Weber's ghost materialized in front of me. "Stay out, devil."

Energy from his force field blasted into my chest. I tumbled down the brick steps and landed hard on my tailbone. A pitiful scream escaped me.

Tubby hauled me to my feet. "I can probably pass. I'm evil, but I ain't got no magic."

Sadly, he was right. Father Weber would have considered my murdering friend a non-devil. But I wouldn't let Tubby take care of this. My anger at Father Weber had risen up like a fire-breathing monster. It demanded blood, or something like it. I pulled my arm from Tubby's.

"If he kills me, dig up his bones and piss on them." I stomped back up the steps.

"Want some help?" Mysti asked as I went by.

I held up one hand as a no. At the threshold of the church, Father Weber waited, translucent arms crossed over his chest.

"Let me in," I growled. My voice didn't even sound human.

Father Weber made the sign of the cross.

"God won't stop me. I'm one of his children too." I gathered my energy and made Father Weber's ghost my central focus. Body shaking with the effort, I grabbed the ghost by the scruff of his neck and pulled as hard as I could.

His feet left the bricks and wood of the old threshold. The ghost's howl of fury made my back teeth ache until they seemed ready to explode. The bricks hiding Father Weber's witch bottle cracked open. Noxious smoke danced up lazily. I adjusted my grip on Father Weber's ghost.

Without planning, the words came from me, almost as though someone else spoke them.

"I call the element of air

Send this weak little man's spirit

So far away, nothing else will ever come near it.

Imprison him alone in wickedness

Where he may enjoy his own perniciousness."

I threw Father Weber's spirit into the great beyond. It flew like a huge dark bird, its shadow cold and malicious. As it faded from sight, so did his shout of rage.

"Good riddance," I muttered and marched into the church.

The old building's floorboards bowed and popped with each step. Finally one broke. I danced away as the board tumbled to the dark crawlspace below. I took more careful steps after that.

The pulpit leaned to one side, rusty nails exposed where it had been yanked off its base.

"Sloppy job, Oscar." I took mincing steps around and knelt in front of it.

Oscar's soul radiated evil and hate. It felt the same as listening to a speech by a politician not worth voting for. I pushed the pulpit slightly, not wanting to reach underneath it blind.

The chittering hiss of a rattlesnake's warning answered me.

Heart thudding heavily, I scrambled to my feet and took a few steps away from the pulpit. Oscar had enlisted a deadly sentry to guard his treasure.

Had my magic supplies not been lost when Oscar and his merry band of assholes burned down the hotel, I might have had a way to draw the snake away from the soul keeper. But my stuff was gone, burned up. Even Priscilla Herrera's spell book. That left me few choices.

The rattlesnake would only get angrier if I tried to scare him away. I could kill him, but I didn't have the heart. The snake was just doing what snakes did.

My mind flashed on a figure swinging from a tree. Pappy. Why on earth was I thinking of that nasty thing now?

Dimittis me. Pappy's words came with a blast of foul-smelling air.

An idea formed. I focused on Oscar's vileness and whispered, "*Dimittis me.*"

The snake's rattling increased in speed, and his head popped against something.

I said the word again. "*Dimittis me.*"

Something scraped underneath the pulpit. Oscar's soul box. It must be moving. The sound of the snake striking at the moving object came through the boards. After several seconds, the gold edge of something peeked out from under the pulpit.

One more time. "*Dimittis me.*"

A shining, tiny golden box scraped toward me. I bent my knees and held out my hand the way I would for a dog to lick. The box slid right into it.

A bolt of fire flashed in my head. I staggered to the side, reaching for something to steady me. I slammed into a wall, hearing the crack of the dry rotted wood, but unable to control myself enough to put less pressure on it.

Fire flashed again. The forgotten church faded away. Wood smoke stung my nose. A crackling fire with some animal roasting over it filled my field of vision.

"She's got my soul, you incompetent morons," Oscar's melodious voice thundered.

I jerked away from his consciousness, even though I knew it was too late. Pushing myself off the old church wall, I staggered across the floor, black motes dancing in my vision. Arms grabbed me. The scent of Mysti's rosemary sachet replaced the fire smell. She dragged me out of the church.

"He's coming," I rasped at my friends. "We've got to run now."

Herta appeared off to the side. "If you want me to stall him, you must do one thing more."

I tried to walk toward her, but fatigue jellied my knees. Griff got me by one arm and Mysti the other. They dragged me along behind Herta.

She stopped at the foot of a huge cedar tree, which hulked over a crumbling chimney. Her emotions seeped into me, telling me better than she ever could that this had been the site of her home.

"Underneath the bricks of this chimney. That's where I hid it when I knew I was dying." She pointed.

"Let me go," I muttered.

Griff and Mysti did as I asked. I found my feet easier than I'd expected. Whatever connecting with Oscar had done to me was already fading. My strength and stamina increased with each trial. I pointed.

"Dig here."

Tubby, who now had the spade, hurried forward and did what I asked. It didn't take him long to unearth a porcelain box. I took it from him and set it in front of Herta.

"Open it," she said.

I did as asked. A tarnished locket lay inside. I took it out and tried to give it to her.

"See what's inside." She wouldn't take it.

I opened the locket and stared into the faces of Oscar's wife and children.

He wanted me to help him avenge them, and I wouldn't do it. Herta's voice filled my head. *He left angry and forgot this. I should have helped him. He'd never have become what he did.*

Maybe. Maybe not. It wasn't worth arguing now. I held out the locket to Herta.

This time she took it. *Go now. I'll stall him.*

I turned away from Herta, wishing I could have done more for her. Thunder shook the sky. Underneath was the faintest baying of hounds. Oscar was on his way.

———

"What are we doing with that?" Mysti pointed at the tiny gold box holding Oscar's soul.

I turned the thing over, examining it for the first time. With bird's wings carved into the top, it resembled a woman's jewelry box more than protection for something as delicate as a soul. But then, if Oscar's soul was anywhere near as heinous as its owner, maybe it wasn't so fragile.

"I expected a piece of jewelry." I ran my finger over the delicate design.

In a long ago vision, where I'd watched Oscar separate his body from his soul, I had seen a glint of gold from the soul keeper, but this was the closest I'd ever been to it. It emanated Oscar's essence. Evil. Selfish. Stubborn. Crafty. Now that essence tried to crawl into my skin. I fought against it.

Thunder cracked again. A cool wind rustled through the lost settlement.

"We need to go, girl." Tubby stared at the fast-moving clouds.

"What are you going to do?" Mysti pressed.

"Something I probably shouldn't." My voice shook, and my hands trembled as I unlocked my phone's home screen and scrolled through pictures of Tanner and me. Each one pierced my heart. Finally I found the one I wanted. It was a picture of a business card. Solid black with the name Black Silas and a ten-digit phone number. I showed it to Mysti.

She shrugged and held up her hands. "You know they're liars. Every last one of them. And you know they have plans on top of plans."

"Who are you calling?" Griff pressed closer, face creased in concern.

"Black Silas." I squeaked out the name like a little girl and hit dial. The rings burred in my ear. One. Two. Three.

A click and a familiar voice. "Peri Jean Gregg. I was just speaking of you with an old friend."

Gooseflesh formed on my forearms, and a shiver worked its way through me. Black Silas bothered me on a level I couldn't quite explain. It dug right underneath my skin and hovered in a dark cloud at the edge of my brain. It pricked at a secret, invisible place, one that knew danger by its old name and understood the consequences went much further than death.

"Hello? You didn't butt dial me, did you?" He let out a hearty laugh.

"No, Mr. Silas." The short sentence left me breathless.

"Is this about the box emblazoned with the mythical phoenix? The one you're holding in your beautiful hand right now?" Amusement filled his voice. It wasn't hard to picture the handsome, if a bit old-fashioned, Black Silas smiling.

"Yes," I whispered, chill bumps racing over me.

"And you want me to…let's see…help you get rid of Oscar E. Rivera because you're not big enough or strong enough to do it yourself." *The devil always knows exactly what one needs.*

My heart thudded faster. "Yes."

"Let's be clear. You're asking for my assistance in this matter?" He'd let me hang myself. It was the only way.

"Yes." The word sounded like the final nail pounding a coffin closed. "What does it cost?"

"Cost?" He did laugh then. "We'll discuss that when I see you."

I shook my head. There was no way I'd agree to owe Black Silas without knowing what. "Wait a second."

"I'm sorry, dear. Too late to renege. Arrangements have already been set in motion." He sounded almost sympathetic, even though I doubted him capable of sympathy.

"But…" I trailed off after the one word. I didn't know what to offer.

Black Silas cut off anything I might have said. "Bring Oscar Rivera's soul to the crossroads near where your family is staying. Do it right after dark. We'll settle up then."

"No, wait. Please." My voice came out high and breathy. A sharp wind cut through the cemetery, cooling the sweat on my face.

He hung up.

Heart throbbing, I turned to my friends. "I just screwed up so bad."

Griff leaned in. "What did you give him? There are ways to break deals with these things."

"I don't know. He just said it was too late for me to change my mind." My cheeks tingled, and a cool lightness tingled in my head.

Griff's and Mysti's eyes locked. He tipped his head at me. She shook hers. He frowned at her.

"There's something you need to know." He threw Mysti a guilty glance.

"Griff, no. Cecil said not to..." Mysti looked at me and shrugged. "Go on. There's no need trying to hide it now."

Hannah sidled closer to me, breathing so hard her nostrils flared. Her warm eyes had a wild edge.

"Cecil had a spell with his heart after you got injured. He's not in great shape." Griff could barely look at me. That alone told me how bad off my uncle was.

My stomach went weak and woozy even though the news was no shock. Cecil's heart had been bothering him since I met him. He'd had surgeries. He took a lot of medicine.

Seeing me take what should have been a killing blow had been too much for him. Every time something like that put a strain on his heart, it could kill him. The fear I usually felt at the prospect of losing Cecil jumped up, ready to play. I sidestepped it. We could dance later.

Something more important had my attention. Why hadn't anybody told me?

Mysti read my face. "Cecil insisted you not be told. He threatened me with death, Hannah with exile. He offered to have Griff framed for murder."

I almost wanted to laugh at Cecil's threats. Each one was deadly serious. But his ability to come up with them so quickly and be so resolute about them still impressed me. He knew more about exerting influence over others than I ever would. I both understood the fear of Cecil's threats and wished somebody had told me Cecil was sick. I kept my mouth shut. Nothing would be solved by recriminations at this point.

"Why isn't he in the hospital?" I spoke to Hannah.

"The man who owns the place where they're staying is some kind of retired doctor." She rolled her eyes. "Cecil said he'd have to be good enough."

"We need to get there now," I said to nobody in particular.

"I'll message Tubman directions." Griff tapped on his phone. A few seconds later, Tubby's phone dinged.

Tubby glanced at the directions and ambled toward his car. Hannah joined him, leaning close to speak. He nodded and winked at her. I turned away, not wanting to watch them flirt anymore.

"Is it okay if I ride with you and Griff?" I asked Mysti.

Thunder rumbled hard enough to shake the ground at our feet. This time, the shouts of men followed. Instead of answering my question, Mysti took off running. I followed close on her heels. Griff ran with us, thumb jabbing at the remote unlocking device clutched in his hand.

The SUV's lights flashed. The doors unlocked with a clunk. We all scrambled into the vehicle. I barely got my door shut before the SUV's engine roared to life.

"Seatbelts buckled," Griff yelled and sped away from the crumbling old settlement. From the window, I got one last glimpse of Herta's ghost. She held the locket with the pictures of Oscar's family in one hand as she waited to confront the boy she'd loved and raised. I should have felt pity for her plight, but I was too busy hoping she kept her promise to buy me some time. When the decaying remnants of the lost town faded, I turned to find Mysti watching me.

"Black Silas said you couldn't change your mind about involving him because things had already been set in motion. Am I getting it right?" She chewed the corner of her lip.

My face heated, but I nodded. I knew I'd done the wrong thing.

She let out a breath. "Something has been going on with your family since we got to Ghost Town."

"Ghost Town?" I raised both my voice and my eyebrows.

"Yep. Ghost Town." Griff's eyes met mine in the rearview mirror. "This retired doctor friend of Cecil's owns it. It's a tourist attraction. Some old buildings. A cavern."

I processed the information. This sounded exactly like the kind of place Cecil avoided. He must have needed a doctor mighty damn bad to go there. My skin tingled with the knowledge. "Tell me what you saw."

Mysti shrugged. "Your Uncle asked everybody who wasn't a Gregg by birth or marriage to please get the hell out."

This didn't surprise me. Hannah had already said as much.

"I got to hear a little more than you did," Griff said. "Cecil said something about contacting the Wanderer in the cavern. Then Finn saw me lurking in the bathroom and kicked me out."

Pieces of information fell into place. Cecil was back on his crusade to get me an audience with the Wanderer. The Wanderer who had already said he'd only meet with me when I got to the Death card. The Wanderer wouldn't change his mind. He'd simply give us a way for me to fulfill the prophecy of the Death card. The idea of facing whatever that was made me want to puke.

I needed to put a stop to whatever Cecil had in mind. If Black Silas came through, no matter what he demanded in return, Oscar would be dead forever. I could put off dealing with the Wanderer for now.

"I need to stop Cecil from doing whatever he's planning." I said aloud.

Griff nodded and pressed his foot harder on the accelerator. We said little else as we sped through the deepening dusk. I leaned my head back on the seat and stared off into the cliffs and valleys of my life. The last few days flashed behind my eyes in a series of depressing images I had no idea how to process. Black Silas's cold voice played on repeat. *Too late to renege. Arrangements have already been set in motion.*

Cecil might have already made a deal with the Wanderer. One that involved me in something I couldn't begin to imagine. What awful thing could he have agreed to? I fidgeted.

After what seemed like an eternity, we drove underneath a sign that spelled out "Boone's Ghost Town" in ghostly neon green and rattled down a rutted dirt road. I heard the music before I saw the lighted sign reading "Ghost Town Dance Hall."

The dance hall, shaped like barn, had a wide sliding door across the front. Light poured out of it. Dozens of people milled around. I frowned. Worse than I thought. This place was full of townies.

Cecil usually didn't put himself in situations where outsiders might see or hear things that were none of their business. Were we really that desperate? My inner realist provided an immediate answer. *Yes. This shit is dire.*

Griff shot past, Tubby close on his bumper, and parked in front of a long one-story building. Griff shut off the engine.

"What is this?" I looked around for signage and saw none.

"Buckaroo Bunkhouse," Mysti said drily. "For cowboys who have too much fun to drive home. We've got the whole thing to ourselves."

I shucked off my seatbelt and reached for the door handle, trying to prepare myself for whatever waited inside Buckaroo Bunkhouse. But the last twenty-four hours had taken its toll. I was in no shape to make life or death decisions, and I knew it.

The bad part? I had a feeling this was a done deal, that I was traveling a one-way road with no exits. My last exit had passed long ago. I had no choice but to tough it out and hope I had what it took. I sucked in a deep breath and trudged toward the bunkhouse.

15

———

Shelly slammed out of the bunkhouse and stalked toward me. "You should have been here hours ago. What happened?"

"It took a little effort to get Oscar's soul." I showed her the tiny phoenix box.

She recoiled from it. "Get inside. Your uncle's waiting."

I hurried into the bunkhouse. It turned out to be a long room lined on each side with ten bunk beds. Twenty beds. Plenty for thirteen people. But only if those people liked each other an awful lot.

"Here comes that mean little woman." Cecil's voice came from a bottom bunk. A skinny bare foot stuck out from under one side of the sheet. His face was pasty, his olive skin faded to the color of chicken broth.

"What happened to you, old man?" I sat down on the little chest beside the bed.

This was my joke with Cecil. I'd call him an old man, and he'd call me a mean little woman. Stuff like that made this bad turn of health hurt all the worse. He'd be gone too soon. His loss would be like Memaw's. There'd be nobody who could ever take his place.

He rolled his eyes. We wouldn't discuss it. "Did you find the madman's soul?"

I took the soul box out of my pocket and held it out to Cecil.

He cringed. "Get it away."

I stuffed it back in my pocket, ignoring the brush of evil against my skin. Cecil lifted a shaking hand, two fingers extended. *Give me a cigarette.* Hating myself, knowing Shelly would black my eye if she saw, I did what he wanted.

He lit his cigarette. "What's your plan?"

"We have to destroy Oscar's soul. Eating the hag's magical core almost killed me. I don't have a weapon strong enough to kill a soul. So I called someone who is strong enough—Black Silas." I leaned my head back against the wall, suddenly aware of the ache of fatigue in my bones, of the coldness in my skin.

Cecil gave a resigned nod. "Not a bad plan."

I studied his face. "Now you talk to me. Mysti and Griff told me you were trying to contact the Wanderer. What are you up to?"

"Doing the best I can with a shit situation. Same as you." He stared at the bottom of the bunk bed over him.

"The Wanderer isn't going to see me." I couldn't bring up that Death card. Not now, not without screaming.

"You, my sweet, are in the winter of your naivety about this world. My heart aches for you." He put his hand over mine, the clammy skin chilling me even more.

I pulled back my hand. "What is that supposed to mean? You just said contacting Black Silas wasn't a bad plan, didn't you?"

"It's not a bad plan. You just didn't consider everything." Cecil tried to inhale his cigarette, choked on it, and let out a string of ugly coughs.

I shot off the chest and fluttered around him. He shook his head, coughs still wracking his body, and motioned me to sit again. I obeyed, scared to upset him more. Cecil's coughs slowed. He took a few deep breaths, then pulled on his cigarette. The smoke jetted from his nose in a bluish plume.

"What are you going to do *if* Black Silas actually destroys Oscar's soul?" He waved away the cloud of smoke between us and peered into my face.

I shrugged. "If Black Silas gets rid of Oscar, that's it. I win."

Cecil shook his head. The expression on his face was one I knew well. It said, *You should know better.* But I didn't. Too much had happened in the last few hours. My mind was scrambled. The only two things I knew for sure were that I missed Tanner and that I was scared of the bad thing I sensed coming. I hung my head and shook it.

"Don't be ashamed. Queenie's the one who told me when I called to ask her advice on contacting the Wanderer." He gripped my arm in one cold hand. "Think. Who are Oscar's huntsmen? Name them for me."

I took a deep, shaking breath. "Joey Holze, Michael Gage, Nash Redmond, Veronica Spinelli, my own damn mother..." I trailed off, trying to think of more, and finally said, "Ghosts of people who hate me."

Cecil spoke my thoughts. "These spirits are your sworn enemies. So even if Black Silas kills Oscar for you, they're still going to exist. What are you going to do?"

I slumped and shook my head, more ashamed than ever. There was so much I hadn't thought of.

Cecil let out an impatient breath but stopped short of saying anything. He put his cold hand back on me. "Sweetheart, listen to Papaw now. Even if Black Silas destroys Oscar forever, you're going to have to call the hunt against the remaining huntsmen."

But I didn't know how to call the hunt. I didn't even have a clear understanding what it was. Dimly, I remembered we'd originally been talking about the Wanderer. Cecil had managed to change the subject. Why had he done that? The cords in my neck began to throb from tension.

Cecil dropped his cigarette butt in an empty soda can on the floor. It hissed as the fire died.

"You're going to have to wield a great deal of power to call your own hunt. How will you get that power?" He didn't have to say more. We were still talking about the Wanderer. Just from a different angle.

"I'll have to absorb the mantle completely." The news came as no surprise. Just another shovel of shit on a growing pile. Worse, I had no clear answer how to fix it.

I owed a chthonic being named Sol an unspecified favor for eating a hole in the scar tissue. That hadn't done the job all the way. Letting go of my own baggage thinned the scar tissue spell a little here and there. I could probably let go of the rest over time, but this transformation needed to happen now. Cecil was right. I needed the Wanderer's help. And he'd done what it took to secure that.

Cecil's voice, brittle with years and rough with experience, was so soft I had to strain to hear him answer my unspoken thoughts. "Now you see why I contacted the Wanderer. I managed to secure a meeting for you. The meeting will take place in the cavern on this property."

"Why the cavern?" I didn't want to go down there. Some people came out to the Hill Country just to tour caverns. But they gave me the creeps. So damp and dank. And dark. Very, very dark.

Cecil tapped me to get my attention. His eyes bored into mine. "I expect you to do whatever it takes to keep this meeting."

I closed my eyes. Black Silas's words suddenly made sense. Arrangements had already been set in motion. My deal with him over Oscar's soul was just one facet. Outside, the sky rumbled with thunder. Herta had given me a little time, but Oscar was on his way. Soon I'd face both him and Black Silas.

"Oscar's coming. How am I going to get rid of him and meet the Wanderer?" The words spiked worry though my heart. No telling what the Wanderer would do to give me control of the mantle.

Cecil shook his head. "Things will work out. I've made arrangements. Once my end of the deal is complete, someone will tell you what to do next."

I tensed. Why not Cecil? He was the one who'd made the arrangements with the Wanderer. I had such a bad feeling about all this. My whole world was swirling around a toilet bowl, and I had no way to stop it.

Cecil hoisted himself out of the bunk bed and grabbed for his white button-down shirt. "When is Black Silas meeting us?"

"After dark." I helped him get one skinny, tattooed arm into the sleeve and then made him sit back down.

"Then we need to go." He kept struggling into his shirt.

"You stay here and rest." I tried to pull the shirt away from him. He yanked it from my grasp.

"Help me get ready. Now." Cecil's dark eyes gleamed with authority.

Heart pounding from his rebuke, I helped Cecil pull the shirt over his shoulders.

"Where is the meeting?" He barely glanced at me.

"Black Silas mentioned a crossroads near here." I shivered against the cold premonition something bad was about to happen, something that couldn't be fixed.

"Of course. It would be there." Cecil snatched his socks off the top of his boots and tugged them on. He scowled. "Help me. Now."

I did what he said. Soon we walked out of the bunkhouse, me holding Cecil up by one arm. Shelly hurried over.

"What are you doing?" Rather than speak to Cecil, she spoke to me.

Tired of all the arguing, I shrugged.

Cecil pointed at Kenny's huge truck and spoke to me, ignoring Shelly. "Help me into the truck. Then tell the others we're all going to the crossroads. They need to bring weapons."

Shelly helped Cecil while I faced what remained of Sanctuary. Shelly, Brad, Jadine. Hannah with Tubby as her plus-one. Dillon, Finn, and their kids. Griff and Mysti, stuck by circumstance. They all stared back, faces filled with varying degrees of fear and defiance.

"Get your vehicles loaded and ready. Bring weapons." My voice competed with the country music coming from the dance hall.

A rustle of uncertainty went through what remained of my friends and family.

"Do it now." I lowered my voice just the way Cecil would have, lowering my chin and glaring at them.

They broke apart, doing as I'd said, throwing me odd glances.

I went to Dillon and stopped her from crowding her kids into the truck she and Finn had procured from somewhere. "Except you. Take your kids somewhere safe and hide with them."

She bared her teeth at me. "Fuck that. I'm coming to help you."

"Who's going to raise your kids if you get killed?" The words rolled off my tongue, cold as well water in winter. I sounded just like Cecil at his meanest.

Dillon flinched and slumped away from me. She grabbed one kid by each hand and marched for the bunkhouse. My heart ached as I watched my best warrior leave my side. But what else could I do?

A hazy night had fallen by the time I climbed into the late

Kenny's monster truck with Shelly and Cecil. Brad and Jadine took one look at the three of us, turned on their heels, and got into Finn's truck. Griff, Mysti, Hannah, and Tubby rode in Griff's SUV.

The tension hung between Cecil, Shelly, and me, heavy enough to be an extra person. Cecil drove the mile from Boone's Ghost Town to the crossroads in silence. I stared out the window at the thick clouds, waiting for a peal of thunder holding the shouts of men and the bay of hounds.

By unspoken agreement, we parked in a line half on and half off the dirt road.

Cecil stared at me in the rearview mirror. "Get out. I want to talk to my wife."

Shelly, staring straight ahead, made no reaction. Not even a glance.

I slid out of the truck, sour acid pooling in my gut. Something bad was about to happen. Cecil knew what it was and wouldn't tell me no matter what. My ignorance ached like an infected wound. The options before me looked like a choice of rotten fruit. No matter which I picked, I'd get something I didn't really want.

I stood still and took deep breaths. It did nothing to calm me. The magic of the season crackled in the air and popped against my skin. The date was October thirtieth, one day before Samhain. Tomorrow night, the veil between the living and dead would be at its thinnest. Oscar would be even stronger. If my plan with Black Silas didn't work, if the Wanderer refused to help me again, I'd be knee-deep in shit creek.

Mysti and Griff hovered around me but didn't talk. Finn stood next to me, arms crossed over his skinny chest. He had my back. Brad and Jadine stood off to the side. Jadine had hold of Brad's arm as though he might run if she let go. Tubby and Hannah stood close together. Hannah had a hand on his arm.

A truck with only one headlight approached. We all stiffened. Tubby and Hannah hurried to my side, both reaching for guns. The truck, blaring jukebox country, slowed. The driver, his face a dim blur in the murky darkness, turned to stare at us. He gunned the accelerator and hurried past, taillights fading within seconds.

Thunder rumbled the sky. The shout of Oscar and his huntsman vibrated faintly underneath. They were on the way to stop me from handing over Oscar's soul to Black Silas to destroy. And Black Silas was on the way, supposedly to help me.

Cecil and Shelly finally got out of the truck. Tears streaked Shelly's face. Cecil lit a cigarette, the flame creating ghastly shadows on his gaunt face. Shelly watched, lips turned down, but said nothing. The worry I almost had under control came roaring back, flaming higher than ever.

Cecil tugged my sleeve. "Walk over here. Let's talk."

I followed him a short distance away from the others. He stopped and faced me.

"I need you to make me a promise." Cecil blew a cloud of poisonous smoke into the night.

"Let's hear it." I swallowed hard against the panic crowding my throat.

"Never run from your destiny again." He gripped my arm with more strength than I would have imagined such a sick man could have.

I blinked twice. "What do you mean?"

He leaned into my face, breath reeking of cigarettes. "Who you are is enough. Be who you are."

"Is this about the Wanderer?" I couldn't understand why he'd tell me this.

"It's about everything going forward." Cecil turned away from me.

I followed, ready to demand answers.

Finn stepped in front of me. "This might be Black Silas."

Two round headlights drifted toward us, flickering weakly. It took me several seconds to understand why Finn had known this was Black Silas. But it came with a rush. There was no sound of an engine running. The headlights came silently, as though they were the ghost of a car.

Headlights blinding us, the car pulled to the intersection of the four roads and stopped. It was too dark for me to see the car's color, but I could make out enough to see that it was an old model car. Like the one Bonnie Parker and Clyde Barrow died in.

The door creaked open, and the huge revenant I'd met at Black Silas's auction house in China Grove, Texas stepped out. He left the headlights beaming. Without acknowledging us in any way, he opened the car's back door and stepped aside.

Black Silas stepped onto the road and nodded at Cecil. "The deal is done, old friend."

Cecil stiffened but returned the monster's nod.

Fear pricked its way up my back. Some secret, back-door deal had passed. Now bad things would happen, and I couldn't do a damn thing to stop them. A darker cloud than before covered the moon.

———

Black Silas walked toward us, the headlights creating a nimbus of white fire around him. Darkness pooled over his face.

He beelined for Cecil and held out his hand. "It's been too many years."

Cecil took Black Silas's hand. He jerked when they touched. Remembering Black Silas's too-hot touch, my skin crawled.

"Funny coincidence that this is where we've ended up."

Black Silas gestured at the crossroads. Another story I'd never know.

Cecil barely nodded. Black Silas shifted position, and the headlights beamed on Cecil's face. It shone with sweat. He gripped one of my arms too tight and pulled me forward.

"Show Mr. Silas what you have." He tightened his hand around my arm.

Wrongness crawled over my skin like the sticky gossamer of a spider web, the kind that stays no matter how hard you try to brush it off.

Cecil stepped closer and whispered, "It's going to be okay." He kissed my cheek.

I dug the phoenix box out of my pocket, careful not to pull out the hag's heart with it. Some instinct told me to keep that to myself for now. I held the box out to Black Silas. He drew in a sharp breath at the sight and took the box. He raised his eyes to mine. His teeth gleamed in the darkness. With the bright beam of the headlights silhouetting him, he looked like a film negative.

"Oh, what this would bring at auction." He waved one long-fingered hand over the box.

With the wave of that hand, the icy heat of Oscar Rivera's inherent evil pushed at my skin, testing my barriers. I strained against it.

"Can you kill the soul?" This was the only question that mattered.

Black Silas bounced the box in his hand. "You asked my assistance, and I intend to give it."

Not an answer. Acid heated my stomach. I patted my pocket for my roll of antacids, but they weren't there. I'd lost them along the way. Just like Tanner. Just like my witching supplies. I pressed one hand to my mouth, winced against my burning insides, and tried to decide what to do next.

Thunder clapped, nearer than ever. Right behind it came the shouts of Oscar and his huntsmen, the neighs of their horses, and the hoarse barks of the red-eared dogs. The thunder of motorcycles faded in for a second.

"What are you waiting for?" We had to get this done before Oscar came. Something told me that once he got here, it would be too late.

"I said I'd help. I just didn't say what I'd do." Black Silas made the gold box containing Oscar's soul disappear and turned his back on me.

"Now wait just a damn minute," I yelled and grabbed for Black Silas.

Cecil pulled me away. I fought my uncle with all I had. This was our only chance. If Oscar came again, he'd have another chance to kill me. I couldn't allow that. Cecil gripped both my wrists with more strength than I expected, holding me away from Black Silas. The monster never acknowledged us. To him, we could have been ants fighting.

I jerked one arm away from Cecil. My great-uncle, a man I loved and trusted, motioned to Finn. My cousin hurried over and reached for me.

"Don't you dare," I snarled at him, used to being in charge.

At Cecil's signal, Finn put both arms around me, picked me up, and dragged me away from Black Silas. Cecil followed, hand on his chest, nostrils flaring. I struggled so hard against Finn that he kicked my legs out from under me and forced me to the ground.

Cecil knelt next to me. He spoke through clenched teeth. "Stop it. It's done."

I had more fight left, but the fierceness in Cecil's eyes stopped me.

"You finished?" He spoke to me like a child who'd been showing his ass.

Breath whistling through my nose, I nodded.

Cecil signaled to Finn to let me up. He helped me to my feet, eyes averted. I faced Cecil, embarrassment blazing over my skin.

Cecil put one arm around me and pulled me close. "No matter what happens, know that you didn't fuck up. You used the resources you had."

"But I failed, didn't I?" The question was barely worth asking.

Cecil let me see the barest of nods. "There is only one way, and you don't have it yet."

The mantle. The center of the Gregg family's power. My inheritance. My destiny. My curse. I flinched away from Cecil, wishing for the millionth time I was normal.

"Someone's coming." Finn pointed.

This crossroads rippled with magic. Deep, old magic. I hadn't felt it when we first got here, but now it whipped around me, combing through my hair, trying to figure me out. A sharp, metallic smell filled my nose. It reminded me of blood. I pressed against Cecil, and he slipped an arm around me.

"This has to happen," he said in a low, trembling voice.

"What?" I asked, but a clap of thunder covered the word.

Underneath the thunder, shouts of men rose and fell. So did the drumming of hoofbeats and the howls of dogs. The Wild Hunt. They were here. It was too late.

Bile shot up my throat. My eyes stung. I swallowed hard, heart already matching the hoofbeats in speed and force. I jerked away from Cecil, slipped Finn's grasping hands, and ran to Black Silas. I reached for the box.

"Give it to me." My words grated in my throat.

He shook his head. "I'm sorry, Miss Gregg. I cannot interfere."

The hoofbeats and shouts grew louder still, rumbling the

earth like a passing freight train, filling my head so full of chaos I couldn't think. The mantle's hackles burred out, like a dog sensing an intruder. It stretched the scar tissue to its limit. My chest ached with the strain. I struggled to breathe.

A shadowy figure approached from the left fork of the crossroads. The burning headlights of Black Silas's car picked up the spikes of horns pointing at the sky. The goat's gray fur came into focus next. He trotted toward us, bell around his neck clanging.

Thunder clapped again. Lightning jagged across the sky, turning everything too bright for just a second. The sounds of the hunt echoed in the night.

I ran back to Cecil and grabbed his arm, ready to drag him out of here. "Come on, Papaw. We've got to go."

He spun, face contorted in anger. "We can't. We have to see this through. You can't just run away like a scared kid." He caught himself then. His face stilled, and he took a deep breath. "Listen to me. I love you, and I'm proud of you. But you must endure this."

Cecil turned me to face the goat. It was now only a few feet away. Its otherworldliness joined the crossroads magic brushing against my skin. Dread ached between my shoulders.

The goat clopped merrily toward us. He might have even been smiling. I knew one supernatural being who liked to pose as a goat, but this wasn't Bub. Bub would have come to us wearing the garb of clergy. Maybe even carrying an ancient Bible. It was his schtick. He'd have also greeted me by now. We weren't friends, but we tolerated each other.

When the goat came within touching distance, its front hoofs left the ground. Its bones made wet thunking sounds as they shifted under the skin. The face rearranged into something almost human but kept the horns.

Now I knew this goat. It was the one Oscar had made his immortality pact with. I began to shiver. Cecil gripped my hand.

"You have something of mine." The goat had a whiny, cold voice.

Something of his? I didn't know what he meant. Right then, I barely knew my name. A gibbering sound came from my mouth.

"I have it, Your Lordship." Black Silas stepped forward, holding out the phoenix box, and kneeled before the goat.

The goat reached out one spindly-fingered hand and snatched the golden box. He held it up to the glare created by the headlights and studied it.

Then he turned to me. "Usurp Oscar's position as master of the hunt, and this soul is yours to kill. My covenant. But you must win that honor on your own."

The thunder grumbled again, shaking the ground. The wild shouts of men having fun, chasing something smaller and weaker, but still good quarry, came out of the clouds.

A bolt of lightning zigzagged across the sky. The bay of one lone hound spoke to it. The goat man raised both arms like someone taken by the spirit in an apostolic church.

"Come now." His whiny voice clapped loud as thunder.

The bay of many hounds answered.

"No," I whispered and glanced at my friends and family.

Finn stepped in front of me, brandishing a shotgun. Shelly came closer, clothes blowing on her slight body. She held a high-power deer rifle in front of her. I groaned. Those weren't going to do anything. Hannah's bullets had done nothing to harm Oscar and his marauders.

I tapped Finn. "Don't bother. Bullets don't hurt them."

Without turning, he said, "These are special bullets, made with iron. It'll hurt 'em all right."

Hannah and Tubby came to stand on the other side of me. Between them, they had four pistols, one for each hand. Both had their eyes slitted. Not afraid, not angry. Just two modern-day gunslingers ready for high noon and whatever carnage it brought. Maybe they were right for each other.

Mysti and Griff stood off to the side, stuck in this, but not really a part of it. Like the others, Griff held a pistol in each hand. Mysti held only her wand, energy crackling on the end of it. Our eyes met. She gave me a slight nod.

I didn't have to speak to her to know the message. *You can do this.*

I loved Mysti, but I feared she was wrong. There was no way I could beat Oscar. I'd given away his soul, the one bargaining chip I had. Without full control of the mantle, there was no way I'd be able to usurp him as master of the hunt. This fight would go just like the others. I'd hurt Oscar a little. He'd hurt us more. Maybe I'd be able to run him off before he killed anybody, but he'd be back.

The mantle, still expanding inside me, nipped at the edge of my consciousness. It would lend a little power. I relaxed and let it in. The magic flowed through my brain, iron hot, making explosions of light flash behind my eyes. The black opal heated on my chest and reached out.

Orevorevorevorev.

Orev, who usually slept at night, answered. His voice came from everywhere and echoed inside my head.

Hoofbeats approached, now louder than the thunder that had preceded them. The shapes of horses and deadly riders emerged from the billowing clouds. Behind it buzzed the sound of motorcycles. Their ghostly headlights came into view first, hovering just above the road. The first huntsman, Michael Gage, raced alongside them, whipping his horse to run faster.

Tubby fired the first shot. The rest took up their arms and joined in. I aimed energy at the gas tank of King Tolliver's motorcycle and let it fly. The gas tank exploded in a bright flash, flames licking over King's body and face, their roar covering his screams. The iron bullets punched into Michael Gage's horse. It fell with a scream, trapping Michael.

I watched, fascinated. Finn had been right. These bullets did their job.

Oscar's antler headdress danced in Black Silas's headlights as his horse touched down from the sky. He charged toward Cecil and me, raising his sword. The metal caught Black Silas's light and seemed to glow.

I stepped in front of Cecil. He tried to push me away, but I roared a word at him, one I didn't even know when I was my regular self. My poor old uncle cowered from me.

I lowered my head and focused on Oscar's sword, pouring all my concentration into it. My body jittered. I ground my back teeth and pushed harder. Fire flashed from the sword and began to climb up Oscar's arm.

His shriek rattled my eardrums. The horse ran a few more steps. Its pained screams hurt my heart. But survival was survival. I pushed more energy into the fire, urged it higher. The horse staggered and fell. Oscar went down with it.

The flaming sword clumped to the dirt. The fire whipped in the wind. My magical core pulled me toward the sword. I took one step in its direction. The sword's flame roared brighter, its magic reaching out. The two magics touched.

The sword went out and lay blackened on the road. It was over. I'd defeated Oscar.

I turned to the goat man, hand already out for the soul box.

He shook his head and pointed. I turned back.

Oscar got up and shook off the ash. His armor glowed good as new. Still smoking, Oscar picked up his sword and sheathed it. He helped his horse to its feet and climbed on its back. The charred duo shook themselves like wet dogs. The black ashes dropped from them.

"No," I said to the goat man. "I killed them. I won."

"Until you take his position as master of the hunt, he cannot die." The goat man turned his attention to Oscar and said, "Finish what you came here to do, and you can have your soul back."

Oscar adjusted his headdress, fixed his gaze on me, and raised his sword. I felt, rather than saw, Oscar's smile. He had me.

"No," I muttered. "This isn't fair." My breath tore in and out of my already dry mouth.

"Life isn't fair," Cecil said in my ear.

Oscar cued up to take another run at me. I drew on my power, but setting him on fire had taken most of it.

Oscar raced toward me. He held the sword aloft. Cecil

stepped in front of me. He pushed me backward with one hand.

"No." I ducked around Cecil.

Cecil and I struggled to get in front of each other, arms flailing like two teenage girls. I could only give our tussle half my attention. The other half went to my magic. I needed enough to fight Oscar. One eye on Cecil, I tracked Oscar's movement. Cecil gave me a hard shove away from him and planted his feet.

Before I could regroup, Cecil slammed his fist into the side of my head. My brain short-circuited as it sloshed against my skull. I went down on one knee. Cecil reared back one of his pointy-toed boots and kicked me in the side.

"Stay down." Dark eyes blazed out of a mask of fury I'd never seen on my uncle, who'd been nothing but sweet to me.

Cecil stepped in front of Oscar, drew a revolver from his pants, and began firing. Oscar jolted each time one of the six shots hit him but kept coming. Cecil didn't even have his pistol loaded with iron bullets. What was he thinking?

I called for Orev. Our minds connected. Something winged and huge brushed past my face in a rustle of feathers and headed straight for Oscar. It hit him at the same time that several other birds did.

Pecking and flogging, they knocked Oscar's horse off course. It turned a confused circle less than a foot from

Cecil and me. But it got right back on course and came again, Oscar leaning forward. They reached us. A long howl filled the night. It came from me.

Oscar's sword arced through the darkness, right toward Cecil. I struggled to get my feet under me, grabbing at Cecil's legs. He kicked me away just as the sword swiped across his chest at an angle. He staggered backward and fell. I grabbed Cecil and clutched him to me, my body hunched over his.

Thoughts scattered, heart jittering, I accessed every drop of power I could and transferred it to the birds in the form of instructions. *Kill. Kill. Kill.* The birds converged on Oscar's face and head. Their squawks and calls took over the night.

So many birds covered Oscar I couldn't see him. They latched onto his headdress with their feet and flapped their wings as though trying to pull it off. Oscar quit trying to defend himself and focused on keeping it on his head. Some knowledge teased at the edge of my brain, but Cecil let out a pained moan and I lost it.

I glanced down at him. The fight around me faded in importance. All I saw was Cecil, shirt soaked with blood, gasping in my arms. Suddenly, I understood the deal Cecil had made. How he'd bought me a ticket to see the Wanderer. Sometimes the Death Card was spiritual. But this time it had been literal.

A knot of emotions twisted in my chest, as painful as the

nervous acid had been earlier. My failure to shed the scar tissue and gain full control of the mantle had led to this.

"No," Cecil gasped. "Don't think that."

He took a few more rough breaths and said something else. It was hard to hear him over the birds, so I leaned close enough to see blood bubbling from the corner of his mouth.

"Tell me again." My words ached in my throat and sounded all thick. That was when I realized I was crying, loud, braying sobs.

"I said, I know I'm dying because I can read minds again. Just like when I was a little, little boy." He stroked my face, leaving trails of wetness. "You're the only one I ever met whose gifts stayed the same, didn't fade. That's why you're the right one. That's why..." He coughed.

I strained to raise him, a muscle in my back pulling the wrong way. Cecil turned and spat a wad of blood and phlegm on the ground. He stared into the distance, lips moving.

"I'll tell her," he said.

"Tell me what?" I bawled.

"Now listen. Your memaw is over there." He wiped blood off his mouth.

My head snapped up. Memaw. I'd not seen her since the night she died and her ghost walked off with my grandfather's, both of them young again. I squinted at the night, using all my power. Nothing was there. Was Cecil hallucinating?

"Your memaw says to tell you to get both Oscar's headdress and his sword. Once they're yours, you are master of the hunt." He coughed again, more blood dribbling from his mouth.

Shelly ran over and dropped to her knees next to Cecil, her usually cool face knotted with tears. She gripped her husband. He put one bloody hand on her back but held me with his eyes.

I focused my attention on Oscar. The birds still swarmed around his head, flogging him. *Bring Oscar's headdress to me.* Just that little connection drained so much energy. My vision wavered, and I rocked on my knees.

Cecil started to cough again, this time worse. Blood ran from his mouth in thin strings.

"Help me." Shelly could barely say the words. She was crying too hard now.

Shelly and I got Cecil's head up enough for him to spit out the blood. Our eyes locked. Hers blazed anger. I'd stolen her husband from her. I nodded my understanding. We'd settle it later.

Cecil's fingers gripped my wrist, smearing blood on my skin. It glowed in the dark night. "Leticia and I are both so proud..."

Cecil's body began to seize. Shelly and I both gripped him, neither of us with any knowledge of what to do for him. He was probably bleeding internally. How could I fix that? I racked my brain and came up with no solutions.

Cecil's convulsions seemed to go on forever, even though it couldn't have been more than seconds. Each one tore at me. When his body stiffened with the final one, Shelly and I both clutched at him. He let out one last rattling breath as his life left him.

I eased my uncle to the ground and wept tears of regret and loss. Cecil had been flawed, but I'd loved him. He'd always known what to do, what to say, who to be. He'd loved me when I needed it.

"Oh, Papaw." I stroked his hair back and drew in a quivering breath, the loss so deep and painful it seemed to consume me. "Those bastards will think the devil is a nice guy by the time I get through with them. That's a promise."

With that, I pulled together my resolve. Kill now, mourn later. I glanced at the birds. They'd converged on Oscar's head, pulling at the headdress, wings flapping with the effort. It was as good an attack as any. Body aching, I looked for energy to push into them and had none. I let out a frustrated growl. Of all the times to be low on energy.

The huntsmen came to Oscar's aid. They all bore the wounds of this battle. Part of Joey Holze's head had been shot off. King Tolliver's face had several bullet holes in it, and his arms were burned black. My mother, missing one arm, rode up on her red-eyed horse. Despite their injuries, they all lived. Unlike Cecil. Veronica Spinelli swung her sword back.

A flash of anger filled me. No way I'd sacrifice these birds to her.

Go, I shouted mentally.

The birds flew away before Veronica's stupid sword even arced through the air. I held out one hand, not sure what I wanted. Someone put a pistol in it. The iron bullets would fix Oscar. Hurt him good. I walked toward Oscar with it pointed.

"Stop." The goat man that Black Silas had called master stepped from the shadows.

"Eat shit," I growled and kept coming.

He waved one crooked hand at me.

He was waving me off? *Oh, hell no.* I pointed the gun at him. Or tried to. My arm wouldn't move. I tried to take a step. My feet seemed frozen to the ground. Straining with all my might did nothing but make me grunt.

Behind me, Mysti yelled, "Help me. I can't move."

"Let me go," came Hannah's fury choked voice.

I tried to answer them and couldn't even move my tongue. The goat man produced the box holding Oscar's soul. In his other hand, something white flashed. I was too far away to see exactly what.

"Oscar Rivera, you must take possession of your own soul. This is a battle that must be fought to the death. I can no longer protect you." The goat man clapped the soul box and the white object together.

The white object began to grow arms and legs. It expanded until it was about a foot tall. It looked just like a man, only one whose neck ended in a stringy clump instead of a head. The texture of the thing's skin reminded me of a carrot. Only a glowing white one. What the hell was this thing? A root of some kind maybe.

The goat man laid the ugly little object on the road. He tapped it three times. The man-shaped root got to its feet. Oscar's evil emanated from it. Somehow, the goat man had put Oscar's soul in this little root.

Horror crept over me, cold and sneaky. The sight of that hideous, inhuman object taking on human form made my skin crawl. A scream filled my throat. But frozen like I was, there was no way to let it out.

The goat man gave the root holding Oscar's soul a little shove. It ran for Oscar, scrambled up his horse's legs, and disappeared into the suit of armor he wore. Armor clanked. Oscar went rigid, his body shaking. His posture tightened. A high whine came from him. I entertained a fantasy that he was dying. But then he relaxed into himself again.

He nudged his horse toward me and adjusted his grip on his sword. The goat man held up his hand in my direction.

Energy surged through my limbs, flowing through my body until my teeth vibrated with it. The mantle plumped up and pushed against the scar tissue. The goat man dropped his hands. I tripped forward as he released me.

I snatched the pistol off the ground and ran at Oscar, firing. I'm pretty sure none of my shots hit the mark because Oscar didn't react at all. The flapping of hundreds of birds wings came from within my head and around me. I opened my mouth, and a raven's growling battle cry came from it.

A jolt of energy came from behind me. In my heightened, restored state, I could see Mysti's signature on it. It dislodged Oscar from his horse.

I ran harder and leapt for Oscar. With one hand I grabbed onto the horns on his headdress. With the other, I grabbed the hilt of his sword. Oscar blasted an agonizing jolt of magic into me and threw me off him.

I called all the energy I had and sent a stream of it into him, hoping to shock him enough that I could get the sword and the headdress away from him.

Shelly appeared beside me. "For Cecil!"

Together we lunged at Oscar. I grabbed for the headdress, Shelly the sword. Gunfire began as Oscar's huntsmen came to his aid. The headdress slipped. Some of its magic seeped into my fingers. A blood-thirsty rage filled me.

"It's coming off." I gave the headdress another yank.

"Retreat. Retreat." Oscar's voice echoed in the night.

The horn blew. Its force threw both Shelly and me backward. Oscar wheeled his horse around and ran for his life. Before the horn's echo faded, Oscar and his horse blended into the night. The huntsmen followed, their hoofbeats mingling with the rolling thunder.

The headdress gone, my rage faded back to its normal low simmer. I picked myself up off the ground and looked around for the goat man and Black Silas. They could kill me, sure, but I was going to say what I had to say. Both seemed to be gone. Cowards.

I stomped back to Cecil's body. Each step felt like a mile, and my chest ached as though I'd been kicked. My family surrounded me. We stood over our lost elder like crows do over one of their dead.

Black Silas appeared next to me. "Come with me."

"My uncle's dead. Fuck off, please." I gave him a shove.

Suddenly, he was in my face, eyes blazing with something worse than fury, something more powerful than my paltry magic.

"Oh no, you don't. I liked Cecil Gregg. He was a smart man. You'll not disrespect his sacrifice out of silly human pride." He gripped my arm with fingers like iron and dragged me away from my family. I pounded him with one fist, which he ignored. They seemed not to even see our struggle.

With a voice that stank of the grave, Black Silas spoke into my ear. "Cecil sacrificed himself so the Wanderer would grant you audience. I'm to explain the particulars of this meeting to you as a final favor to Cecil." Black Silas gave me a hard shake.

I stopped hitting him and glared at him, my teeth bared. If I had even sort of believed I could kill Black Silas, I'd have tried. Cecil was gone. I wanted to spread the hurt.

Black Silas glared back. He was scarier than I'd ever be. "Are you ready to act like a woman of your station instead of a spoiled child?"

Heat rushed over my body and collected in my cheeks. I dropped my eyes from Black Silas's and nodded.

"There's a cavern at the place you're staying," he said. "Meet the Wanderer there at the devil's hour. He'll give you two items. Do not lose either. Your life depends on it."

I hung my head and let the tears drip from my chin. Black Silas grabbed my chin and forced me to look at him.

"Do whatever the Wanderer says, or all is lost." With a breath of hot wind, Black Silas was gone. Engine revving, his old car backed up, and went back the way it had come, leaving me alone with my mourning family at the crossroads.

16

We put Cecil's body in the bed of Kenny's truck. It felt like an insult to a man I had considered great. Shelly, crying too hard to talk, climbed into the driver's seat and motioned for me to ride with her. Shelly drove my dead great-uncle, one of the finest, kindest men I'd ever known, back to Boone's Ghost Town the same way we would have a load of groceries.

The green neon still glowed on the sign leading into the attraction. Lights still shone from the dance hall. Music still blasted. People dressed like cowboys partied on. It was just another night to them, but everything had changed for my family and me.

Shelly steered the truck on past the dance hall, her face set and shiny with tear streaks. The three vehicles behind us, full of friends and family, made it seem like some kind of funeral procession.

"He deserves better than this." She parked in front of Buckaroo Bunkhouse.

I nodded but otherwise couldn't move. Regret stiffened my muscles and sat heavier on my shoulders than any weight I'd ever carried. Cecil was dead because of me. My mentor. My elder. My friend. I'd barely spoken to him over the past few days.

Cecil had taught me so much about embracing who I was. About what I could do if I wanted to. He'd accepted me when I needed someone to do that. Now he was gone. My life would never be the same.

If I'd understood Black Silas correctly, Cecil had sacrificed himself so the Wanderer would see me. Then he'd told me to do whatever the Wanderer said. This set up all kinds of freaky scenarios. What kind of being took life sacrifices in exchange for appointments?

Shelly's voice, raw from crying, cut into my thoughts. "This was the last thing Papaw could do for you, and he was proud to do it." She sobbed a few times but got control enough to speak again. "Papaw has known he was dying since the last hospital visit. They told him he had six months...maybe."

That didn't help my feelings. Cecil might have had only a few months left to live, but he'd died tonight because of me. I choked back my grief. Shelly pulled me into her arms. We clung to each other, sobbing. She hitched out the rest of what she wanted to say.

"He wanted to die a hero. On his own terms. Not in some damn hospital with tubes running out of him." She took a shuddering breath, exhaled with a low moan, and let go of me.

"That what he told you before it all happened?" I took out my cigarettes and lit one, the smoke sour in my mouth. I deserved all things sour.

"He didn't have to. We lived together almost as many years as you've been alive, honey." She twisted to face me, dark eyes bleak and hard. "You want to know what he told me after he made you get out of the truck?"

I didn't. Not really. Because it would make me feel even worse. But Shelly would tell me because she'd just lost her partner and needed to mourn.

"To take care of you. To make sure you fulfilled your destiny." She unbuckled her seatbelt and sat staring at me.

The tears welled up, stinging my sinuses, and overflowed my eyes. They left cold trails down my cheeks and neck.

She took out her phone and checked the time. "You've only got a few hours until you meet the Wanderer. Before you do that, I'd like to..." She glanced toward the bed of the truck where Cecil's mortal remains lay.

Bury Cecil. The unspoken words hung in the air. I wouldn't have been able to say them either. Shelly was right, though. We'd have to get Cecil out of the bed of this truck and bury him. That would take some arranging, and it would be up to me to smooth the way. Shelly seemed to read my thoughts.

"You're our leader now, so get yourself together, come inside, and help us plan. Meanwhile, I'll go comfort Cecil's and my daughter." Shelly opened the door and slid from the truck.

Jadine's sobs drifted in. Shelly went to her daughter and held her. Dillon ran out of the bunkhouse. Shelly and Jadine showed her what was in the bed of the truck. Dillon began crying too.

"No, Papaw, no," she said between sobs.

She and Jadine embraced and wept together. Both saw Cecil as I did, a father-figure, the world's best coach on how to be an outlaw and never get caught. Shelly ushered them into Buckaroo Bunkhouse. I sat alone in the truck, smoking and letting the tears run their course. The door on my side opened.

I turned, expecting to see Finn. It was Hannah.

"You're out of time. Shelly needs you." Her eyes were wet. She'd been crying for Cecil too.

I hopped out of the truck and caught up with Hannah, putting one hand on her back. "You did good back there. Kept them off us."

"Papaw died anyway." She walked with her head down.

"The worst part of it all is that he planned it. He traded

what life he had left so the Wanderer would see me." I grabbed Hannah's arm, needing her sympathy.

Hannah stopped and faced me. "That's some serious baggage to carry."

"Think how awful it'll be if I fuck it all up." I swiped tears off my cheeks.

She grabbed me in a fierce hug, but didn't assure me things would turn out okay. They didn't. Not in the real world. I hugged her back.

Shelly's voice rose inside the bunkhouse. "Don't you say no to me, you little pin-headed turd."

Uh oh. She'd gone full-on angry Yankee. I let go of Hannah. Both of us took off running.

I reached the bunkhouse first, slammed inside, the bright lights burning my eyes. My eyes adjusted just in time to see Brad pull Shelly out of an unfamiliar man's face. The man and Shelly continued snarling at each other.

The man looked to be around sixty and had a wiry build with visible muscles in his arms. I had a bad feeling this was the man who owned this property. And now that Cecil was dead, whatever charity he'd felt he owed us had run out.

Brad stood between the man and Shelly. He saw me, and relief flooded his face. Poor guy. Brad and Mysti had both grown up in foster care, but Mysti was the tough one. Now he'd married into a family of outlaws.

I walked right up to Brad and stepped between him and the unfamiliar man. He and I stared each other down. Hadn't someone told me this guy was a doctor? Griff and Mysti, yes. They'd told me Cecil got out of going to a hospital by bringing this guy into our troubles.

The man sure didn't look like any doctor I'd ever seen. Unless we were talking about the kind who sold prescriptions out of a ratty mobile home. Hard, cold eyes gleamed back at me. The tattoos on his arms were punch tattoos, so old the ink had faded to a bluish green. They had the look of jailhouse tattoos. Old ones, from the days before prisoners started making tattoo guns out of old cassette players.

"What's the problem?" I hoped I sounded like Cecil. He'd always asked questions like he could listen to the answer or shoot somebody dead.

"You can't bring a dead body on my property." The doctor's spittle hit my face. It took everything I had to hold still.

"It's already done. Let's work on the solution." I took my eyes off the doctor's for a second and found Finn. I motioned for him.

My cousin, now my right-hand man, pushed his way forward and stood next to me. He crossed skinny arms over his equally bony chest. He wasn't much tougher than me, but he talked a good game. Tanner, on the other hand, would have twisted this guy's arm behind his back until he begged us to do whatever we wanted. But Tanner wasn't here. I'd lost him, and now I had to do the best I could.

"Shelly, what are you and..." I didn't know the guy's name, so I just gestured at him.

"Daniel Boone. *Doctor* Daniel Boone," the guy said, straight-faced. I tamped down my laughter.

"Shelly, what are y'all arguing about?" I stared at the doctor as I spoke, daring him to make a peep.

Shelly shoved Brad off her and stood next to me. "I want to bury Papaw in that graveyard right as you first enter Ghost Town property."

"And I still say hell no." Doctor Daniel Boone shook his head. "Some of those graves date back to the 1800s. Now I loved Cecil. But I need you people to get his carcass..."

I didn't give him a chance to say anything else. I brought one knee squarely and swiftly into his nuts. It wasn't a hard hit, but in my experience any direct hit worked. Sure enough, Doc clutched his balls and bent his knees, face reddening.

I took slow breaths, the way I'd seen Cecil do in situations like this, and spoke in an even voice. "Don't call Cecil a carcass. Okay?"

The doctor grunted and continued his junk-cupping squat.

Finn gripped the doctor under his arm and raised him.

"My cousin asked you a question. Answer it, yes or no. Nodding is fine."

The doctor nodded his head. Finn let him drop. We surrounded him and waited for him to catch his breath.

When he did, he glared at us. "That's a historic cemetery. I don't want you putting an unmarked grave in there."

I squatted down in front of him. "The farther away from this place we go with Cecil, the more chance the po-po's going to catch us. If we say we were here...and we will be forced to do just that..."

I threw a pointed glance at the tattoos. The doctor flushed. Exactly the reaction I'd hoped for. He didn't want a close encounter with law enforcement any more than we did.

Shelly spoke into my ear. "Cecil loved the Texas Hill Country. Being buried in a place like this, one with history, is exactly what he'd have wanted."

The doctor muttered again about an unmarked grave. I reared back my foot and raised my eyebrows. He waved one hand to let me know he understood.

I smiled. "I think the best solution is for us to bury Cecil in your cemetery here. It's what he'd have wanted. You'll need to go close your juke joint..."

"Now wait a minute." The doctor pulled himself to a standing position. "I started out helping an old, sick friend. Now you're closing down my business. That's how I make money."

I felt for the guy. I really did. But we couldn't take Cecil to a mortuary. They had to make reports, and we didn't need questions from law enforcement. Cecil's death would be too hard to explain.

"This is going to happen." I took a step forward. The doctor flinched. I bit back a smile, ashamed of myself. "You can consider this your final favor to an old friend, or you can make us beat the Jesus out of you."

The doctor's shoulders rounded. A darkness spread through me. This was the first thing I'd done as my family's new leader, and it made me feel dirty inside. Had Cecil ever felt this way? I wished we'd talked more about situations like this. *Too late now.*

Doctor Daniel Boone held out one hand for me to help him up. I nodded for Finn to do it. The good doctor brushed himself off.

"There's an equipment shed across the property. Shovels and shit in there." The doctor spoke in a breathless voice. His nuts must have still hurt. *Good.*

"Fine. Brad can drive..." I didn't want to say Cecil's body. "Brad can drive the truck over to the cemetery." I tossed him the keys.

We left the bunkhouse and walked to the equipment shed. The doctor went inside and flipped on the light. He pointed at a row of shovels hung on the wall. "This is all the shovels I've got."

A farm tractor sat at the back of the shed. I pointed at it. "Got any attachments that'll dig a grave, Doctor Boone?"

The doctor turned around and studied me. I hoped he didn't decide he wanted to fight.

"I insist that people who coerce me into digging an illegal grave call me Dr. Danny. Nice to meet you." He stuck his hand out for me to shake.

"Peri Jean Mace." I shook with him.

"I know. Cecil spent all day bragging about you." He climbed up in the tractor's seat. "Now let's bury that stubborn old bastard."

Things went fast after that. Dr. Danny got the tractor out of the equipment shed and hooked it up to a small backhoe. A few of us grabbed shovels and followed the tractor to the cemetery. Dr. Danny drove the tractor inside and directed Brad to pull the truck over to a grassy, vacant area near the back fence. We closed the gates again and stood in the darkness.

Dr. Danny took out his phone. "I guess I've put it off as long as possible."

He made a call and said, "Helene, I need you to shut things down." A pause. "I don't care if it is Halloween Eve." A longer pause. "I don't care if we're making more than we did all summer. Shut it down, and shut it down now." He hung up on her talking and put the phone in his pocket.

Helene must have been good at following orders. Within

ten minutes, a female voice came over the loudspeaker system. "I'm sorry to break up the party, folks, but we just discovered a safety issue."

A rumble went up. Helene waited until they quieted.

"No cause for alarm. No danger right now. But we do need to vacate the premises for your safety." Her cheerful voice had an angry edge. "Please come back and see us another time. We'll have this fixed by tomorrow night." Then she muttered, "I hope."

Car and truck engines started. Backup lights flashed. Pretty soon, a convoy of headlights rolled out of Boone's Ghost Town. They drove right past the darkened cemetery, unaware of our presence. Dr. Danny watched them go with a sick expression on his face.

I got a little closer and lowered my voice. "While we wait for them to get gone, maybe we could have a little wake for Cecil. Why don't you start, Dr. Danny? Tell me how you knew Cecil."

It hurt my soul that a group of outlaws standing in a darkened cemetery was as close to a wake as my wild and wonderful uncle would get. He deserved more, and I wished I could provide it. But things were too desperate right now.

Dr. Danny nodded his head. "I suppose I could."

The low murmur of my cousins talking among themselves stopped. They formed a tighter circle around Dr. Danny.

Dr. Danny shrugged. "In prison. But you probably guessed that. I was a doctor with a drug problem. Led to me doing all kinds of shit. Which led to me losing my license and serving a few years in the federal pen. Cecil was serving out a sentence for tax evasion. I was mad at the world and pissed off the wrong guy. Cecil kept me from getting killed."

It didn't surprise me. Cecil had had a habit of helping people remove thorns from their lives. He'd had a talent for picking people who'd benefit him on down the road. *The life and times of a con man.*

Shelly stepped forward, dropped her cigarette on the dirt, and carefully mashed it under her shoe. She intended to speak next.

"Cecil knew my husband," Shelly said in her Yankee accent. Her voice trembled on the last word. She cleared her throat and stood straighter. "They did business together sometimes. I thought Cecil was cute, even though he was at least twenty years older."

She smiled, that same faraway smile I'd seen her give Cecil over the months. Her smile told the story of many years spent together, of the kind of bond you found once a life-time. The ache of Tanner's desertion tightened my chest. I drew in a shuddering breath. Shelly picked up her story in a sad, soft voice.

"I'd been out of love with my husband for quite some time. We had our kids, and that was about all we had in common. Cecil and I started having an affair. My husband knew I was cheating on him but couldn't figure out with whom. It boiled over the night before my husband and some other men were going to rob a bank. We argued all night, and I said I was leaving." She glanced around the group, maybe gauging reactions. "My husband beat me up, tied me to a chair in the kitchen, and left to rob the bank. Said he'd deal with me when he came back."

Shelly touched a spot high on her cheekbone. In the dark, the mark was invisible. But I'd seen the divot in her skin and wondered about it often enough to know what she was touching. Now I knew how she'd gotten it.

She began speaking again, a smile growing on her face. "Next thing I knew, Cecil came in the back door and untied me. We got in his car and left. He made an anonymous call to the police. They interrupted the robbery. My husband, who bragged to everybody he ever met that he'd never spend a day in jail, started shooting. The cops killed him."

Jadine cleared her throat. "I don't remember this because I was just a baby, but Cecil and Shelly found me in some woods in a box crying. They treated me like I was really theirs. They always encouraged me to be just who I was."

I nodded, unable to speak. Cecil had been a con man, a murderer, and who knew what else. But he'd also been a good friend, a good husband, and a good father.

Life rarely painted people in black and white. Shades of gray colored them, made them a mix of good and evil. My vision blurred with tears. When I wiped them away, several people stared at me. It was my turn to speak.

"Cecil accepted me at a time in my life when I wasn't sure where I belonged. He helped me find myself. He tutored me. He loved me." My voice shook on the last word, and I could say no more.

The parking lot was empty by then.

Brad turned on the truck's lights so we could see what we were doing. Dr. Danny dug a hole, and we buried my uncle, who'd been nothing but good to me, in an unmarked grave in a graveyard full of strangers. The ugliest truth of life is that it just stops. The ends we come to are neither glamorous nor beautiful. Then everybody left figures out a way to go on.

As though reading my thoughts, Dillon said, "I guess we'd best go back to the bunkhouse. Maybe start packing."

She threw a long glance at Dr. Danny. He ducked his head. He wouldn't ask us to leave. We'd hurt his nuts too bad for him to dare. But people like us, life's travelers, knew when to go. I gave her a nod. My family began milling back to the bunkhouse.

I checked the clock on my phone and saw that I had less than half an hour until my appointment with the Wanderer. In the nice, dark, shadowy cavern. My favorite place.

"I need in your cavern," I told Dr. Danny. People who used

the caverns as tourist attractions kept them locked, either to keep out freebie seekers or for insurance purposes. I'd never know which and didn't really care.

He exhaled a long breath through his nose and squeezed his eyes shut. This night probably felt as though it could never end soon enough for him. I knew how he felt. "Meet me back at the storage shed. Once I put this up, I'll give you access." He started his tractor and drove away without waiting for my acknowledgment.

I trailed behind, rubbing my aching stomach, steps heavy with grief for Cecil and worry about the next mountain of feces I'd have to climb.

———

Hannah walked with me to the equipment shed, head hanging, wringing her hands. We stood a short distance away and smoked while Danny unhooked the backhoe and put everything away. Hannah stole glances at me out of the corner of her eye.

She tossed her cigarette away half-smoked. "Where to next? Now that Cecil's gone, you're the one who says."

I kept smoking, staring into the dark night, trying to prepare myself to meet the Wanderer. My nerves ground painfully. Deciding where to go was the last thing I wanted. I tried to channel my uncle's wisdom but knew I didn't have it. Then I remembered the date. Today was Samhain.

"I'm going to end this whole crap-fest tonight."

She raised her wet eyes to mine. "Tonight?"

"Yep. It's October thirty-first." I held up my phone and showed her. "The Samhain is tonight. The veil between us and the spirit world is thinner than ever. If Oscar wants to use my power to rip a permanent hole, tonight's his best chance."

"What if the Wanderer won't help you?" Hannah's shoulders drew up.

"I don't know." The words came out in a near whisper.

Dr. Danny came out of the equipment shed and locked it. "You ready?"

I nodded and gave Hannah a quick wave. She trudged away, head hung low. Danny walked fast across the property. I had to jog to keep pace.

We stopped at a light-colored stone building with a gate across its front. Dr. Danny unlocked the gate, reached in, and flipped a switch. The whole thing lit up like Saturday night. If I hadn't been scared out of my wits, I'd have thought it pretty, even if it was a cavern. Dr. Danny took a step back.

He motioned for me to go inside. "Steps take you straight down. There's lights all along the way." He chewed his lower lip.

"Say it. I'm not going to whip your ass." It was no lie.

Without Finn to help me, there was no way I'd be able to beat up Dr. Danny.

"Tours of this cavern start at ten in the morning. That's just about seven hours from now." He stared, as though waiting for an answer.

My patience with Dr. Danny grew a little thinner. "If I'm not out by then, something has gone wrong, and there was nothing I could do to help it."

I walked away from Dr. Danny to keep from biting him. The building turned out to be nothing more than an open room with a stone floor. At the far end of the room was a wide set of stone steps.

Now that I was here, all the worries came back. The Wanderer, despite whatever bargain Cecil had made with him, might still refuse to help me. Cecil forcing the coming of the Death Card might not be enough. Queenie had indicated the Wanderer thought me not ready for his kind of help.

Exactly what is his kind of help? whispered a sinister voice from the dark of my mind.

I made myself walk to the steps. The lights lining the way emitted a maddening buzz. It didn't matter what kind of help the Wanderer offered. He was my last hope. I gathered my courage and took the first step into the unknown.

A layer of dampness from the humidity slicked the stone steps. I held tight to the metal bannister, also wet with condensation, and forced myself to take step after step. The staircase ended in a dimly lit room with high ceilings showing off the rock formations, which looked to me like dripping lava. The room was empty.

"H-h-hello?" Despite my pounding heart and singing nerves, I wouldn't call him Mr. Wanderer or another silly name.

A scraping sound echoed in the huge room. I jumped and clapped my hand to my chest. The gesture reminded me of Cecil. Ashamed, I dropped my hand. I checked the clock on my phone just in time to watch the time change from 3:00 a.m. to 3:01. The Wanderer was late.

The sound came again. My heart leapt, a caged animal flinging itself against its bars in a futile attempt at escape.

"Is anybody here?" I licked my lips.

A dark blob appeared on a nearby wall. I took a couple of steps backward. The shape morphed until human shoulders, and a head became visible. A man stepped out of the wall.

Tall with long, graying strawberry blond hair and a red beard, I put him in late middle age. Creases cut the skin next to his eyes and on the part of his cheeks not hidden by beard. He took purposeful strides toward me on long, muscular legs encased in rough leather pants. Items tied to rawhide patted against his legs. If I'd imagined a frontiersman from the eighteenth century, the Wanderer would have come to mind.

He stopped a few feet from me. "You're Peri Jean, the next Gregorius Witch."

His words echoed in my head. *The next Gregorius Witch.* A clammy sweat broke out over my body. If I understood Priscilla Herrera right, taking on the full measure of the mantle would give me the power of a demigoddess. Forever.

My pulse fluttered. Though I'd said goodbye to normal a lot of times, this one was the real deal. There'd be no take backs. Whatever becoming the Gregorius Witch did to me would be the new me.

I might hate it. I might suck at it. I might spend the rest of my life a freak and a pariah.

The Wanderer cocked his head. "Are you the next Gregorius Witch or not?"

Oh boy. He expected an answer. I gulped and nodded.

The Wanderer held out one hand covered in crisp reddish hair. At first, I thought he meant for me to shake it, but instead he gestured to a natural bench set into the stone wall.

"Dr. Danny won't mind if we sit here while we talk." The Wanderer had a slight accent, somewhat like Herta's. He continued holding out his hand. Finally I understood he meant for me to go first.

I walked past him. "How do you know Dr. Danny won't mind?"

He smiled, folding the creases of his face even deeper. His eyes, blue as the winter sky on a pretty day, twinkled with good humor. The Wanderer wore the skin of a very sexy man, middle aged or not.

A flush worked its way over my face and body. The Wanderer was desirable in a way none of the other chthonic beings had been. I didn't know what to think about that, so I sat on the cold stone.

"My uncle Cecil died so you'd see me." I said it in the same way I'd have told the pizza guy I had a coupon.

"He did." The Wanderer hitched up his pants and sat down next to me, his arm brushing mine. The smell of leather hung between us. Neither of us said anything. It reminded me of a red-faced first date. That irritated me.

"Do you know what I need?" At best, we'd get this show on the road. At worst, the Wanderer would tell me to rot in hell and leave. I didn't care which at that point.

"Queenie has informed me." The Wanderer glanced at me, no longer smiling, but eyes still dancing with humor. "Let me ask you a question. What do you think holds this scar tissue spell, as you call it, in place?"

Few questions would have been harder to answer. I searched for a way to explain that didn't involve telling my life story.

"It's all my emotional baggage, stuff I can't let go of." I couldn't make it much simpler.

"Have you noticed that you only try to rectify this issue when your life or someone else's is at stake?" The Wanderer stared at me until I squirmed. He nodded. "Would you believe me if I suggested your baggage is rooted in one simple thing?"

I didn't believe him. The scar tissue was made up of many layers, all bad things that had happened to me or because of me.

He nodded at whatever he saw on my face. "Of course you don't. The root of this scar tissue, the thing that holds it together, is something so old and so ingrained, you think it's who you are."

The Wanderer grabbed one of his rawhide strings and showed me a piece of amber with some kind of bug suspended in it.

"You think you're trapped by it. That to let go of this thing, you'll lose who you are, all that you believe." He let the amber bug drop.

He was wrong. I had already lost everything because of who and what I was.

"Have you ever thought that by losing all, you can start to rebuild?" He waved one hand. The tarot cards Queenie had drawn appeared on the wall in front of us.

The Tower. Death. Ten of Swords.

"The man with the swords in his back. Isn't that how you feel most of the time?" The Wanderer smiled at me. "But if you let it all break apart and die, like the Tower, you can be reborn." He paused. "But only if you understand what to give up."

I slumped. Circles and riddles. That's what this whole conversation was turning into. I didn't have enough mental energy left for that kind of thing. "What do I need to do?"

"I cannot tell you. Only you can discover it." The Wanderer let out a sigh. "This was why I told Queenie you weren't yet ready."

"But I need to shed the scar tissue to fight Oscar." My voice rose with my frustration.

"But if you get rid of the spell before you're ready, you'll either go mad, die, or both." The Wanderer's voice rose too, much more forceful than mine.

"But if I don't, I'm going to die anyway. And so are a lot of other people." This time I shouted. My voice echoed in the chamber, magnified and disembodied.

He drummed his fingers on his leg, thick brows furrowed. Without warning, he turned to me and cupped my cheeks in his hands. His eyes closed. Was he going to kiss me? No. I didn't want that. I struggled, kicking uselessly at this man who probably outweighed me by a hundred pounds.

The Wanderer tightened his grip, fingers digging into my cheeks to force my mouth open. My teeth ground against the tender skin, the pain growing more and more intense until I lost control. My mouth popped open. The Wanderer opened his mouth and inhaled deeply.

Deep inside, I felt a tug. The Wanderer inhaled again. The tug turned into a pinch. Something inside me let loose and passed between the Wanderer and me.

My heart pounded in my throat and began to slow. Light flashed behind my eyes and faded. The Wanderer eased me onto my back. He stood and stretched out my legs.

I tried to speak, but my voice was frozen in my throat. My slowing mind registered the Wanderer leaning over me.

"You'll need two tokens. One for the trip there. One for the trip back. Don't lose them." He closed something cold in my hand and then placed both hands on my chest. He brushed a kiss on my forehead and whispered, "Just let go."

The Wanderer straightened to his full height and walked away. He faded back into the rocks and was gone.

My heart slowed to a beat every once in a while. The Wanderer had taken my breath just like in an old fairy tale. I was dying. The thought scared me, elated me, and pissed me off all at the same time. The Wanderer had cheated Cecil. He'd come with no intention of helping me. He'd simply killed me and left me in this cavern.

As I raged inwardly, my vision filled with growing black dots. They expanded until there was nothing but a tiny pinpoint of light. After a while, it winked out too.

Tanner's face loomed large in what consciousness I had left. How I hated not to see him again in this life. Deep down, I had believed I could win him back. If not that, then make it where he crossed the street when he saw me coming.

And my family. Finn would step into the leadership position. I loved my cousin, but some of his decisions made less sense than tamales served with ranch dip. Hopefully Hannah and Tubby would get out before Finn got them killed.

The thoughts raced. They went faster and louder with each revolution until I thought they'd drive me mad. Then they slowed. One realization remained.

There was nothing I could do. No matter how much I hated it. The darkness deepened, took on textures I didn't know it could have. It was happening. I was moving to the next plane.

Fear took over. I worried about what lay in wait for me on the other side. I'd made a lot of people and things angry. This recent war with Oscar proved as much.

The sound of water dripping somewhere in the cave seemed overly loud. It became my whole world. But then it faded too.

The dampness from the stone seeped through my clothes, cold against my skin. Little by little, the cold mattered less until it no longer felt like anything.

I tried to draw a breath and couldn't. Was I dead? No. I still thought. Or was this what it was like to be a ghost? Floating with no body and no senses, just a ball of thought.

The Wanderer had been right. I wasn't ready to take on the mantle. I wasn't ready to be the Gregorius Witch. Need and preparedness were not the same.

The Wanderer had said one little root held the scar tissue together. That one thing stood between the mantle and my magical core. What was it?

I searched my mind until I wanted to scream. It wasn't there.

No, but it will be. When the time is right, it will be.

The voice wasn't Priscilla Herrera, but it wasn't me either.

Not yet. But it will be.

The voice was right. I'd been on this path since that day a lifetime ago when I'd called my power to keep my mother from killing me. This path had taken me on a tour of hell, but I was closer to finding my place in the universe than ever.

I was the next Gregorius Witch. It was my destiny and had been since the day I was born.

The only thing left was to let go so I could take the next step on this journey.

So I did.

17

Water lapped nearby. Its fishy, humid smell filled my senses. Something splashed, and wood creaked beneath me. I snapped awake.

A dusky sky hung above me. I stared at it as the memory of how I'd gotten here flashed. The Wanderer had stolen my breath.

I sucked in a deep breath just to prove I could and whipped my head side to side. I wiggled my foot. At least I could move again.

My hands lay clasped on my chest the way funeral directors arranged corpses in coffins. I moved one of them, and something rolled down my side and bounced on a hard surface.

The coins the Wanderer put in my hand after he stole my breath. My breath caught. He'd said I'd need them both. So had Black Silas. Two warnings about the same thing. That was serious business.

My body jerked into action. Gripping the coin I still held, I and rolled over on my side. My other arm snaked out to snatch the escaping coin. It rolled across damp wood planks and teetered on the edge of one of the cracks.

Blood pounding in my ears, my free hand slapped the boards. But my motor skills were still sluggish. I couldn't quite catch it. Panic rocked my brain. Underneath was water. If it fell, I'd never get it back.

It paused on the edge of the board, rocking back and forth. I forced myself to sit up. My head swam, and my still sore stomach muscles let out a pained screech.

Magic tingled on my skin, reminding me of something important. I was a witch. Without me telling it to, something reached out of my mind and tapped the coin. It tipped backward onto the plank and lay still. I snatched it and closed my trembling fingers over it.

How had that happened? I closed my eyes and turned inward, looking for the shining light of magic. It was there, no different than usual. Then how had my mind reached out like an extra finger and kept the coin from rolling into the water?

You're almost ready to become. That voice again, the one that didn't sound like me at first. But this place made me hear it a new way. The voice sounded a lot like my voice when I whispered. Chill bumps formed on my arms. I shivered.

The splash came again. I searched the dark water. A shadowy figure standing on a boat floated toward me. The coins twitched in my hand.

I opened my fingers and studied the coins. Shiny gold, blank except for the raised image of a bee or a wasp. I ran my finger over the metal and found an indention in the coin's back. Some poor bug had been covered in molten gold to make these.

Why were they so important? In fact, what was this place? My mind shied away from the answers. It didn't matter now. All that mattered was taking care of the business I had here.

The boat bumped against the pier. The coins twitched again. I rolled onto my knees and stood on shaky legs. Steps unsure, I walked to the end of the pier, footsteps ringing hollowly on the boards.

The figure standing in the boat held a long pole half submerged in water. A dark hooded robe hung to its ankles, swaying with the breeze. The mist coming off the water and the hood hid any telling details of his appearance. We stared at each other.

"I'm Peri Jean Mace." My voice echoed over the water. "Are you here for me?"

Instead of answering, the figure held out a hand, wrapped in dirty strips of fabric, palm up. One skeletal finger poked out of the fabric. The fingernail on the end had been filed to a sharp point.

Fear jumped in my chest, tried to run. But I didn't have time for its nonsense right now. Carefully, so as not to drop it, I placed one coin in the outstretched palm. The fingers closed over it.

A hand pressed to my back, and Priscilla Herrera's voice spoke up inside my head. *Get in.*

I climbed into the boat. It rocked back and forth, sloshing in the water. I dropped into a crouch and grabbed the edge, fear unspooling in my stomach.

The figure, who I suspected was an animated skeleton similar to Pappy of the Shark Teeth Rednecks, dug the pole into the water and gave it a shove. The boat began to move.

Black water lapped at the sides. We passed a set of huge eyes staring out of the darkness. The eyes sat above the long flat snout I associated with an alligator or other modern-day dinosaur. It ducked under the water.

Humidity rising off the water settled on my face in a cold dew. The damp air filled my senses, reminding me of days I'd spent on the open water, fishing or watching someone else fish.

The tall figure stood at the bow of the boat, digging the pole into the water and pushing on it to propel us.

"Where are we going?" I asked its back.

The figure gave no sign it had heard.

I opened my second sight and searched for Priscilla Herrera. She'd been with me before I got on the boat, but now her dark, cold presence was nowhere near.

Orev. Maybe he could come to me. I reached out to him. The rustle of flapping wings came across the water. Orev landed on the boat's edge.

He cawed at me. The meaning came. *Be careful here. This is the land of the dead.*

My stomach lurched and plummeted. The land of the dead. Of course. No Samhain was complete without a trip to the land of dead. Especially when it was my Samhain.

Was this my new home? I glanced at the other coin the Wanderer had given me. No. This coin would pay my way back to the land of the living. But first I had to withstand whatever waited at the other end of this boat ride.

Back in the cavern, the Wanderer had mentioned finding the root of the scar tissue spell. The thing that held it together. How would I find that here?

Fear stretched out the seconds of the trip. Orev had warned me to be careful. Of what? I sent out the question to Orev. A picture came back of a bottle on a chain. Before I could ask for more information, we bumped against something.

The ferryman stepped aside for me to get off the boat. I scrambled past him and used a post to pull myself onto a pier exactly like the one where he'd picked me up. I turned back to ask him what to do now. The water in front of the pier was empty, as though he'd never been there.

Pulled by a force I couldn't have named, I crossed the pier. It ended on a sandy beach bordered by thick woods.

Orev appeared in front of me, cawed at me, and flew into the woods.

Mouth sour with worry, I followed my familiar. Closer to the woods, a wide path led into the brush. Orev called from a tree near the mouth. I stepped into the woods and breathed deep the scent of cool, damp pine.

A young man wearing a calf-length black fur cloak stepped out of the shadows. A huge dog's head rested on top of the young man's head. The rest of the dog's pelt covered his back, tail dragging the ground. The smell from the hide hit me. Bile filled my mouth. What a gross getup.

I took a step back, grabbing for my magic. The air around me crackled as it came to life.

The young man held up both hands. "I'm not going to attack. I just wanted to tell you that's the forest of the dead. Sure you want to go?"

"I have to." I kept a hold on my magic in case I had to blast this freak.

But he stepped back into the shadows without another word and disappeared before my eyes.

Orev squawked at me. *Come on.*

I gathered my resolve and stepped into the forest. Brush hugged the bases of the trees like an unkempt beard. It made seeing more than a few feet ahead impossible. I crept along with my shoulders hunched. How would I find anything in this thicket? A few yards along the path, the undergrowth thinned. Someone—or something—had cleared it away so it seemed the trees went on forever. The shape of a structure winked in the distance. I didn't need Orev to tell me this was the right way to go.

I trudged along the path, still tense, imagining everything that could possibly go wrong. Any journey that required a boat ride with a skeleton through the land of the dead would host more horrors than good times.

Orev cawed at me from a tree. A message came with the caw. *Just go forward.*

He was right. There was nothing to do but follow the road I was on and do the best I could.

The house, which had seemed a distance away, now appeared right through the trees. Apprehension and the need to see what awaited convinced me to take the first step off the path.

The world darkened, the trees crowding closer. Whispers and giggles reached my ears. A nude figure with skin so white it seemed to shine in the darkness darted behind a tree and disappeared. Death radiated from the creature. Cold hands squeezed my heart.

A branch snapped behind me. I spun, hands up to fight,

but saw only another milky white figure darting just out of sight. Another branch popped. I turned on my heel as fast as I could. This time, the figure brushed against me. The contact sent a shock of cold through my body.

Get your ass to that house, girl. My inner self had a damn good idea. I raced toward the structure, fairy tales about errant children who strayed from the path filling my mind. Something—*a hand, oh fucking shit, it's a hand, one of those dead white hands*—grabbed at my shirt. I yanked out of its grasp and ran harder.

Footsteps crashed behind me. The creature's breath rasped in and out, not in exertion but chuckles.

Fear tripping my senses, flashing lights behind my eyes, I sprinted for the cabin. The front door cracked open.

A woman about my age with a baby propped on her hip appeared. "Come on before they catch you. We won't be able to help you then."

I reeled toward her. My ankle twisted on a branch. The whispering chuckles behind me grew to a full-blown giggle. Fingers snatched at my back again. I leapt for the door.

The woman stepped aside so I could gain entry and slammed the door, but not before I saw the face of the thing that had been after me. Nose-less with a round hole of mouth, lined with a corona of teeth. Long, skinny white body. Hands with long fingers, tipped in sharp points.

Shuddering, I twisted to see if it had scratched my back, pulling at my shirt.

"You're okay." The woman bounced her baby on her hip and kissed its downy hair. The baby, eyes closed as though sleeping, didn't react.

I put my hands on my knees and gasped. Even in the land of the dead, my lungs still felt like two charred pieces of meat.

———

I dragged breath after breath into my lungs. My heart slowed enough for me to take in my surroundings.

From the outside, the cabin had seemed tiny. Inside was a different story. Shelves full of bottles and jars lined the walls nearest me. A black cat peered at me from atop a table, tail swishing back and forth.

"So you're the next Gregorius Witch?" the woman with the baby asked.

I stood straight before I answered, "I am."

The woman with the baby nodded. "Are you ready to go forward now?"

I wasn't sure. The way forward could be worse than what lay behind me. I stood frozen at the precipice of my future, whatever it held.

"Come forth," hissed a voice from deeper inside the cabin.

Wood smoke from a roaring fire obscured the back wall of the cabin, which seemed way farther away than it should have been. Whoever had called to me hid behind that smoke. I didn't want to go back there.

"Come now." The voice sharpened with impatience.

I glanced at the woman with the baby. She nodded her head, dark curls bouncing on her shoulders, and shifted the baby. "You must. Or this trip was all for nothing."

I didn't want that. Cecil had died for me to be here. I had let the Wanderer steal my breath and had come to the land of the dead. What's more, if I didn't do this, I'd never beat Oscar. He'd kill me and use my magic to bring about some cataclysmic event.

I ducked into the smoke. My eyes stung and teared up. A few seconds later, my sinuses throbbed.

The cabin took many steps to cross. I walked with my hands out, stumbling over furniture I could barely see in the smoky haze. I followed the dancing light of the fire until I stood before its wavering warmth.

Fingers closed over my arm and turned me. I stared into the face of an ancient woman. Wrinkles obscured both homeliness and beauty, her lips a dark, shapeless pucker. Gray hair hung past her shoulders in thick waves. Around her neck hung a small bottle on a chain.

I groaned. Almost exactly the image Orev had shown me. I'd led myself to danger.

"We're no danger." The gray-haired woman's lips stretched into a kind smile. It transformed her into a person, rather than a visage of extreme age. In her face, I saw the woman who'd answered the door. The two must have been related —grandmother and granddaughter. Or maybe even more generations separated them.

"The danger you face is in what we'll sell you." A clear voice came from my other side.

I jumped and gasped. The woman on my other side couldn't have been more than eighteen, if that. Her dark hair hung to her waist, twisting into curls.

Her smooth, unlined eyes crinkled, and she let out a dainty, crystalline giggle. The older woman laughed too, her laugh hoarse and uninhibited. The woman with the baby stepped through the smoke, her confident laugh joining the other two. The three women laughed as one, making the same gestures, bending their knees and throwing back their heads the same way.

The ball of fear I carried everywhere uncoiled and slithered smoothly through me. Orev cawed from outside, warning me to stay calm. These creatures could turn ugly if things didn't go their way. Unable to calm myself, I tightened my control. It would have to be enough.

"The Wanderer sent me here. I have this spell that blocks me from accessing my true..." I trailed off, feeling more foolish than ever.

The women cut off their laughter at once. They all spoke together. "We know who sent you and why you're here."

The older woman broke away from the other two. She went to the hearth and stirred something in a big pot. The woman with the baby leaned over a wooden crib and laid her baby carefully inside. The older woman rose from the hearth and nodded at the other two women.

Before I had a chance to think about what the nod could mean, the two younger women leapt on me. I struggled, throwing punches, but quickly realized I was no match for them.

The younger woman grabbed my hair in a hand stronger than most men and forced me off balance. They dragged me toward the hearth. I locked my legs, but they lifted me as though I weighed no more than a pile of laundry.

The old woman smiled as the other two set me down next to her. I tried to run, and she hooked a finger over the waist of my jeans, holding me in place with no effort whatsoever. The three women closed their eyes and began to chant in another language. To my surprise, I picked out a few words.

"Elixir of life

Elixir of death

Born by fire

Death by the same..."

It was enough to make me wish I'd heard nothing.

The chant ended as abruptly as it began. The mother lifted a dagger with a jeweled handle. The young girl gripped one of my fingers, pulled it over the steaming pot, and held it fast while the other woman stabbed her dagger into the tip. She milked out three drops of blood. At once, all three women let go of me.

I backed away, heart filling my throat, wounded hand held to my chest. The wild desire to run beat at me. I stilled my feet. The mother had been right when I first got here. If I ran, this horror of a trip would be wasted.

The women hunched over the hearth, all three chanting that language. Now I couldn't understand a word of it. They had to be making a potion for me. If they'd wanted to cook some part of my body, I'd be in the pot right now. A sulfuric odor filled the room. I put my hand over my nose.

The older woman tapped the pot three times with a crooked, nubby wand. Light flashed from the boiling brew. The fire dampened beneath the pot. She turned and crooked one finger at me. "Come."

I did as told, resigned to whatever fate had in store for me. With the fire now little more than glowing coals, the steam issuing from the pot had died down. Whatever was inside stank to high heaven.

The youngest woman slipped a sparkling glass vial into my hand. "You must draw your own draught."

I nodded and reached over the pot. The heat from the liquid inside moved the fine hairs on my arm.

A voice, one I recognized as Priscilla's, tickled against my ear. "If you don't want it to burn you, don't let it."

A deeper than deep part of me understood she was right. I turned my mind inward and found the mantle straining behind the scar tissue. Sensing me, its efforts became frantic. I drew on a little of its vast power and whispered, "Fire don't reach me."

I stuck my hand in the pot. The liquid felt no hotter than good bathwater. I held the dram underneath and let it fill. I drew it out dripping. The older woman popped a cork in the tiny bottle. She fitted a metal cap over the dram's top and threaded a chain of the brightest silver through it.

"The matter of our payment is at hand." The mother retrieved her baby from the crib and rocked the still-sleeping child.

"What do you want?" I assessed what I had of value and came up with nothing.

The three women crowded around, studying me. They touched my hands, ran their thumbs over my fingernails. My body tightened at the thought of what it might feel like to let them remove one. They fingered the raven tattoo.

Orev cawed from outside the cabin. He'd come, even though the closed door kept us from each other. The women quit touching me.

"We'll take the necklace." The youngest women lifted my black opal pendant and studied the setting.

Panic surged. No. They couldn't have that. The black opal had been with me since right after my life had started changing. It helped me, made me stronger. I might not be able to beat Oscar without it.

The women tinkled laughter as one.

The eldest one stopped first and fixed me with kind eyes. "If this bit of magic works, you'll be able to beat anything lower than us. And this creature you fight? Even with the power of the dead, he's barely your master."

"If this bit of magic doesn't work, you'll die." The youngest one gave me the same kind smile.

"And you won't need the black opal anyway if that happens." The mother slipped the black opal off my neck and put it on her sleeping baby.

A pit opened somewhere deep in my emotions, bottomless and black. It took a second to recognize it as grief. It wasn't just losing the extra magical umph. It was grief over letting go of a piece of my past. It was sadness that the black opal, which had chosen me, had now let me go.

Then I remembered where I'd gotten the black opal— Dean's mother. That time in my life, and my romance with Dean, seemed like somebody else's life. I had learned and changed since then, become almost a new person. Maybe it was fitting for me to let the black opal go.

A tiny pop sounded in my head as the connection between me and the black opal severed. Unshed tears stung my sinuses. I pushed them down.

The elder women unfastened the chain attached to the dram and nodded. I was to put my head through it. I bent and let her slip it over my head. The clasp clinked as she fastened it. A bolt of magic shot through me, straining the scar tissue spell and rattling the mantle behind it.

"Choose the time to take this magic into you very carefully. You'll not survive if you choose wrong." The old woman stared into my eyes as she spoke.

Something flashed in my mind, a quick flare of light, but then it was gone.

The mother walked to the door and held it open. "Now you must go."

I edged toward the open door, dreading another confrontation with the white things. She gave me a light shove out of the cabin and shut the door. The cabin faded and was gone. It was just Orev and me. And the creatures who'd chased me.

It took them less than a minute to find us. Flashes of white came through the trees, branches snapping with their passage. They'd be on me in seconds. Then I remembered. They'd left me alone while I walked the trail. I'd be safe if I found my way back to it. I crashed through the branches and pine needles littering the forest floor, but the trail was nowhere to be seen. I waited for the first set of cold, white hands to close on my shoulders.

Orev cawed from a tree right next to me. When I glanced up to see what he wanted, he gave the ground at my feet a pointed look and ruffled his feathers. I was on the trail. Orev took flight, leading me out of the woods.

I trudged along behind him, full of questions. The potion would kill me if it didn't work. I had to pick the right moment to take it, but when was that?

Before I knew it, I'd followed the path back to its beginning. I quickened my steps, ready to be out of these woods. A shadow stepped in front of me.

"You can't go." It was the man wearing the dog skin. The head of the dog still rested right on top of his head, its empty eyes creepy and dark.

"I have business across the veil. Let me pass." I took a step toward him, gathering my energy. It'd give this weirdo a blast that would singe the hair off his ass.

The man seemed to grow wider and his nose broader. The tail of his dog cloak twitched. "No spirits who come in can leave."

Orev gave me a warning caw from a tree a few feet away. I couldn't interpret the exact meaning, so I went on instinct.

"I'm not a spirit. I'm the next Gregorius Witch." I stood a little straighter, fully expecting him to step aside. The statement had carried so much weight with others. Dog Boy didn't seem to care.

"You entered the forest of the dead. Nobody leaves." His voice deepened into a growl on the last words.

The hairs on the back of my neck rustled. Orev cawed again. Another warning. But of what? I didn't see how I could reverse this situation.

———

Dog Boy and I glared at each other. The only way around him would be to go off the path and face those hideous creatures that had chased me to the cabin. Even if I did that, there was nothing to stop Dog Boy following me. Then I'd have to fight both him and those disgusting, giggling creatures.

"Get outta my way." I clenched my fists to let Dog Boy know I meant business.

The dude growled, and damned if he didn't sound just like a dog. He even had the sharp canines of a dog. Holy taco meat. When did that happen?

I threw up my hand and let the ball of energy I'd been gathering fly. It hit Dog Boy square in the chest and blew him backward. He fell with a yelp and rolled to his feet. As he rolled, the dog pelt on his back melted into his skin. His torso changed shape, and his hands seemed to shrink and ball up. His nose became a snout. In mere seconds, a dog the size of a pony stood in front of me.

The dog bared his teeth, a deep growl bubbling in his chest. The coarse, matted hair on its sides vibrated with each growl. Huge muscles bunched in the thing's hindquarters as it tensed to lunge, tail slowly waving back and forth.

Fear prickled at my nerve endings, begging me to scream and run. But dogs chased things that ran. This one was so big, it would be over in seconds if we played that game.

Dog Boy's growls increased in intensity. A line of saliva dripped from his sharp, ivory teeth, stretching and snapping back. He feinted at me. I gasped and jumped back from him. It was all he needed.

Dog Boy lunged and caught me in the chest. I screamed and fell backward, arms up to keep him off my face. The hard-packed ground slammed into my back. The air belched out of my lungs. My arms faltered. The dog's snarling snout came even closer. Panic seizing my heart, I got control of myself and shoved the dog upward just as he snapped in my face. Saliva dotted against my skin. My shoulders began to ache from the strain of holding the dog off me. I couldn't do this forever.

Orev swooped down from the canopy of trees and landed on the dog's back, digging in with his feet and squawking for all he was worth. The dog took his attention off me and twisted to snap at Orev. The bird rose, a blur of flapping wings, and dove into the dog's face. The dog winced away. The movement gave me enough leverage to throw him off me. The effort caused a sharp ripping sensation in one of my shoulder muscles. I ignored it and struggled to my feet.

Dog Boy, already back on all fours, launched himself at me again. His mouth yawned open as he came, slobber spraying from it. I raised one arm to neck level. In the next instant, his powerful jaws clamped down on it. I howled in horror and used the other arm to push at him. It was no use. He dug his teeth in deeper and gave my arm an agonizing yank. I squealed like a trapped animal, which I suppose I was.

Orev swooped in, talons digging at the dog's eyes. The dog screamed, dropped his hold on my arm, and clambered backward. Orev followed. His furious caws filled my ears. The dog's snarls and yips joined Orev's anger.

This was my chance. I could dart around Dog Boy and Orev and get out of this forest. Make a run for the dock and hope my skeletal tour guide was waiting for me. Orev and Dog Boy blocked the path going out, but I could cut around them. Those faceless, naked men who lurked off the path would come for me. But maybe I could slip them. I had to take a chance.

I raced at the brawling pair. My injured shoulder throbbed with each footfall. I gritted my teeth against the pain, took a deep breath, and jumped off the path.

They were waiting for me. A half dozen fish-belly-white

hands reached for me, their hissing laughs taking the place of Orev and Dog Boy's brawl. I backpedaled away and burst back onto the path in time to see Orev swoop at Dog Boy. The dog snapped at my bird, and a cloud of feathers rose.

Oh, hell no. I ran at the dog and hit him with my injured shoulder. It knocked him back several paces. A bolt of pain shot through my shoulder and climbed up one side of my neck. The creature rebounded as though I'd done no more than tap him. Orev swooped in before he could bite, herding him back a few paces.

I called my magic. It throbbed through my injured shoulder and down that arm. My hand twitched, but no magic came. Instead the memory of plucking the hag's sparkling, hard heart from its chest flashed. My jeans pocket, where I'd stowed the heart, heated. The magic left in this nasty last piece of the hag sent pinpricks through my body.

"What do I do?" I muttered to myself.

Think, came Priscilla Herrera's voice from inside my head. *You can come up with the solution yourself.*

I pulled the hag's heart out of my pocket and stared at it, racking my brain for ideas. The ruby crystals encrusted on the organ sparkled in the weak light filtering through the trees.

Orev flew to me, his exhaustion traveling through our connection, and landed on my shoulder. He cawed at the dog but made no move to go back to fighting it. He was too tired.

Turning the hard, sparkling hag's heart over and over in my hand, an idea came to me. Orev and I might not be able to outfight Dog Boy, but what if we distracted him with a treat? Surely a dog would love eating the heart of another beast.

I held up the hag's heart where the dog could see it. Dog Boy's wild, mad eyes tracked it.

"Yum yum." I sniffed the heart and immediately wished I hadn't. It might have been hard as a rock, but it smelled of old blood.

Dog Boy, however, raised his ears and cocked his head.

Shaking the heart in the air where the dog could see it, I tossed it behind me. It hit the ground and rolled. The dog shot past me, thick tail moving in a circle as he bounded after the treat. I spun and ran for the light at the end of the path.

The dog's running footsteps stopped. There was a pause, during which he must have eaten the heart. Then he came after me, grunting and panting. He hit my back. The ground rushed up to meet my face. This was it. Now I would die.

But instead of biting me, Dog Boy let out an ugly, dry cough. I twisted in time to watch him arch his back and gag. Nothing came up. Dog Boy began the series of coughs that led up to retching again. He seemed to have forgotten all about me.

I shoved out from under him, clawed my way to my feet, and took off running. Behind me Dog Boy gagged. He tried to bark but just started coughing again. I raced for the end of the path and didn't stop running until I hit the pier.

"Come on, come on," I whined at the foggy mist covering the water, dancing foot to foot. Soon Dog Boy would dislodge that piece of nastiness from his throat and come after me. A particularly loud barf sound came from the forest. Any time now, Dog Boy would come charging out to drag me back.

The boat came out of the mist, and the skeleton held opened its hand. I put my final coin in the hand and climbed aboard. It rocked no less, and it scared me just as much. We went back the way we came, many sets of eyes watching us across the black water.

Something fluttered against my face. I brushed it away, wondering what kind of flying creatures this realm of the dead housed. It came again. This time as a sharp pop.

"Peri Jean, wake up." The voice came from all around me. The pops on my cheeks started again.

My eyes flew open, and I sucked in a sharp breath. Oxygen filled my lungs, replenishing the way cool water does on a hot day.

Hannah rose and spoke to someone nearby. "See? I told you she wasn't really dead."

Taking deep, gulping breaths, I glanced around the room to see my entire family, faces set in various degrees of distress. Mysti and Griff stood off to the side, eyes wide, hands clutched. Mysti gave me a weak smile.

Had I dreamed that whole episode—the women, the woods, the weird boat ride? I took deep breaths until I could move and sat up. Something unfamiliar and cold banged against my breastbone. My fingers found the dram of potion the three women had sold me in the land of the dead.

Nope. No dream. All I needed to do was figure out a way to take this without killing myself. My eyes found Mysti's, and I pointed the dram.

"Help?" I mouthed.

She nodded.

I climbed to my feet and made my way toward her. Mysti would know what to do, what it all meant. Things would be okay. I hoped.

———

Mysti met me halfway. I explained about the Wanderer and the three women. Her eyes grew wide. What remained of my family and friends crowded around to listen.

"You gave them your black opal necklace?" Tubby wrinkled his nose.

"They said I only needed this to beat Oscar." I pointed to the little bottle hanging from my neck.

Mysti leaned close and squinted at it. "Take it off, please."

I hooked my fingers under the chain and pulled. Nothing happened. I tried again. The chain wasn't stuck to my neck. It didn't pull at my skin. It was like trying to lift a car. No matter how hard I pulled, it didn't budge.

Mysti tried. Hannah did too. Even Finn and Dillon took a turn. Mysti backed away to talk to Griff. They spoke with their heads together, faces pinched in worry. Seeing me watching, they motioned me over.

"Tell me again what the three women said about this potion." Mysti leaned in to look at it again.

"To choose when I took it carefully, or it would kill me." Curious about Mysti's curiosity, I took out my phone, turned on the camera, and reversed it to see the dram.

The potion looked like melted silver. Iridescence shimmered through it. The molten silver went through the full spectrum of the rainbow, all the way to black, and then silver again. I watched it the same way I'd have watched a kaleidoscope.

Griff's voice broke into my reverie. "The Wanderer mentioned the scar tissue spell having a root, yes?"

I nodded, still fascinated by the color moving through the dram.

He tugged my arm to get my attention. "The root of the scar tissue, whatever that is, and the warning about when you should take the potion are connected."

I snapped to attention. Griff was right. The conversation with the Wanderer seemed eons away after fighting the monsters in the forest of the dead. But I needed to examine it further. The Wanderer had said the scar tissue was connected to a root. A place where it began. This one thing held the scar tissue spell together.

"The root has to be gone for the potion to work," I muttered, still trying to put it together.

"I disagree." Mysti glanced at Griff.

He nodded his agreement. "Think about the words they chanted...born in fire, death by same. Your magic often comes out as fire. Perhaps this potion will allow you to burn away the root of the scar tissue, thus destroying the whole spell."

"If you can identify the root." Mysti still stared at the dram, her eyes moving with the shifting color.

The root of my scar tissue. Of course it would all boil down to that one thing. I had no idea where to begin finding it. Was it a memory? The Wanderer had said it was something I'd learned so early that it had become deeply ingrained in my psyche. He had also said I wasn't really ready to find it and that was why he hadn't jumped to my aid in the first place.

Dr. Danny came down the steps into the cavern. "I want you folks off the property in fifteen minutes. Please."

"Gee, thanks." Shelly gave him a withering smirk.

"No. Don't start that crap. I'm done. Any favors I owed Cecil ran out when I buried his body in a historic cemetery. I depend on this place for my income." He crossed his arms over his chest.

I could tell Finn and Tubby to beat his ass, and they'd do it. But I saw no reason. There was something to be said for treating people the way I hoped they'd treat me. Even if they ended up shitting all over me.

"He's right." I raised my voice, surprised it didn't hurt the muscles in my lower stomach and the shoulder muscles I'd injured fighting Dog Boy. Something about being in that other place and then leaving it had made those muscles feel a hundred percent better. I flexed, looking for hurties, and found none. Everyone stared at me.

I straightened and said, "Let's get our things and go."

Dr. Danny gave me a grateful smile. "I've already lost the fares for the cavern today. If I don't open the dance hall in an hour, the whole day's a loss."

Huh? I cocked my head at him and then glanced around at my friends and family.

Only Dillon met my gaze. "You laid in here all day. Dead."

"She wasn't dead." Shelly swatted her arm.

"Was too." Dillon ducked away from Shelly and spoke to me. "They all sat around crying, trying to decide what to do. Dr. Danny wouldn't let us bury you next to Cecil." She shrugged. "I guess that's a good thing now."

"Wait a minute...are you saying it's night?" When I'd looked at my phone earlier, I was positive the time hadn't even been eight. I checked it. It was before eight. Eight p.m.

I groaned and slouched. "We're cooked."

"What is it?" Finn crept closer but didn't touch me. It was as though he was afraid I'd explode.

"Oscar will be here any time. It's the night of the Samhain. The veil is thinnest tonight. He'll be at his most powerful. This is his best chance to kill me." I slumped toward the stairs.

Shelly hurried after me. "We knew he'd come. We've been preparing all day. Or I have. The rest of them cried a lot."

I took in Shelly's red eyes. She'd been crying too. Maybe for Cecil, maybe for me. Today had been an upsetting day for all of them. I reached for her hand, and she let me take it. We walked up the steps together, our progress slow.

If Shelly had spent the day preparing for our final battle with Oscar, I needed a report of what had been done. Then I'd decide what still needed to be done.

It all felt pretty dire. We had no master plan to beat Oscar. No access to a weapon that would put him down and keep him down. No magic that would fry him forever. The dram hanging from my neck was our only ace in the hole. And I knew in my heart I wasn't yet ready to drink it.

Shelly and I stepped outside the cavern's outer building and into the deepening darkness. Another cloudy night with no moon. Maybe my last one.

"Shelly, I need…" I began.

"Hey, skinny," a familiar voice rumbled.

I spun at the sound of it, wondering for just a second if I'd lost my mind entirely.

Wade leaned against the sedan I'd seen parked in front of Desiree's house. Over his shoulder, he'd slung the kind of axe nerds carried at medieval reenactments. I saw Wade with new eyes. A warrior. A highwayman. A gambler. The kind of man no woman would ever catch because he was too busy fighting the war of life. The kind of man you wanted on your side when you went into battle.

Desiree sat on the hood of the car, long legs swinging. In her lap was a spear with a knife affixed to the end. Amazon goddess. The kind of woman who'd leap out of a tree to cut her enemy's throat. Our eyes locked, and she gave me a slight nod.

I glanced back at Wade to find him watching me expectantly. Not too long ago, I'd have run for him, thrown my arms around him. But not now. Whatever passion that had lurked between us had crashed and died a fiery death. My eyes ran over the owl tattoo sleeve on his arm. We'd come so far and lost so much since the night we met. I swallowed against a Texas-sized lump in my throat.

Wade blinked several times. He set his axe on the hood of the car and came to me, his steps hesitant. He pulled me into his arms. Into my ear, he whispered, "I may not be the kind of man you wanted, but maybe I can be the kind of friend you need."

I put my arms around his waist and hugged him back, the ache of disappointment in what could never be welling in my chest and then fading.

He let go and stared into my face. "You look pretty good for a dead woman. Or was that screaming, crying call I got from Hannah a joke?"

"I wasn't crying," Hannah yelled from behind me.

Wade snorted. "What are we doing here?"

"Oscar will be here soon to fight to the death. Go for his headdress and his sword. I can't take over the hunt without those two things." I glanced at Desiree and nodded, silently thanking her for coming.

"What about killing his soul like I suggested?" Her eyes flicked over me, sharp with challenge. I gulped. Now I'd have to tell her how I both succeeded and failed.

"I found the soul, but I didn't have enough power to kill it.

I called in help and got betrayed. Oscar's got it now in this root-like thing." My cheeks heated at how stupid I'd been.

"It was a mandrake root," Mysti said from nearby. "Some folklore names it as a vessel for spirits."

Desiree studied her as though she just might tell her to piss off. Mysti gave her a forty-yard stare right back. Power crackled off both women. Both used to being the wise one, the one everybody looked to for answers, they saw each other as competition.

Desiree turned her attention on me. "So we're going to take the headdress and sword. Once we do, you're going to have to call the hunt. That takes a lot of magic. I'm assuming you still don't have the full measure of your power."

I showed her the dram and explained my dilemma. She shook her head as though she was dealing with a tedious bank teller instead of facing death at Oscar's hands. She lit a cigarette as though she had all the time in the world and squinted one eye at me.

"So what we have here is a lot of ifs. If you drink the magic potion. If we get the headdress and sword." She blew smoke in my face. "Here's the problem. The Wild Hunt isn't made up of humans. It's spirit."

Mysti bristled. "Not necessarily. Other legends have the hunters as gods, like Woden. Sometimes the hunters are the fae."

The corner of Desiree's mouth twitched. Whether out of anger or a desire to laugh, I couldn't tell. "And we're neither gods nor fae."

Mysti pressed her lips together in concentration. I'd come to know Mysti well. She liked being the expert. Desiree came off as a combination of femme warrior, full of confidence and easy knowledge. This must have challenged Mysti. She would want to one-up Desiree. I didn't see a point. Oscar would come. We'd fight him. Then we'd live or die. Who cared who was right? Finally Mysti turned to me, eyes bright. Eureka. She'd found what she knew that Desiree didn't.

"If Peri Jean successfully sheds the scar tissue spell and absorbs the mantle, she'll be the Gregorius Witch." She gripped my arm. "You'll call the hunt as an Old One. That's how this will work. We will be swept up as your chosen court and hunt as such." She gave Desiree a chilly smile. "Now you let me ask you a question."

Desiree's lip twitched again. This time, she let it become a smile. "Go ahead."

"If you think we won't win, why be here?" Mysti asked the question as though she might consider telling Desiree and Wade to hit the road.

Desiree jabbed one thumb at her brother. "This is what he's chosen. I'll stand with him."

Mysti drew back. She understood that. She was loyal to her brother too.

Shelly, who'd been watching the exchange from a short distance away, came over and gripped my arm. "Let's go to the crossroads. Let Oscar find us there."

I nodded. "Good point. We don't want him tearing up Dr. Danny's Ghost Town."

"I don't give a shit about that," Shelly snapped.

Desiree cut in. "We go to the crossroads because on this night, the veil is thin. It's even thinner there." She then addressed Shelly. "I take it you've called in reinforcements other than us?"

Shelly nodded.

"Who?" As leader, I needed to know.

"The vengeful dead," Mysti said. "Brad and I contacted them." Brad watched from nearby.

I raised my eyebrows at him. He raised his eyebrows and gave me one of his surly smirks.

"We don't have your talent, but we can do it," His words carried a dignity that did not match his scraggly goatee and new tattoos.

I nodded my thanks. "Good job."

Tubby joined us. "I made some phone calls."

His meth army. I forced a smile and patted his back. Had I been consulted, I'd have told him not to bring them in. But it was done. No point in arguing now.

Finn approached. "Dr. Danny's getting antsy. We need to go."

"I'll ride with you." Without waiting for a response, I turned and began walking.

Finn followed me to his beat-up truck. He walked with his head down, his hands jammed in his pockets. We got to the truck, and Finn stood in front of the passenger door.

"What is it?" I wanted to push him out of the way and just get inside. Any more drama, and I was going to start crying and not be able to stop.

"Dillon's upset, afraid of losing your respect for running with the kids." He shuffled his feet in the dirt.

I gripped his skinny arm. "She'd lose my respect if she didn't take those kids and Jadine somewhere safe."

If I lost, I could only hope Oscar wouldn't go looking for them. At one time, he'd coveted Zora's gift of raising the dead. Though that gift seemed to fade more with each passing month, as Cecil had warned it would, Zora was still a powerful little girl.

"Listen to me." I stepped into Finn's personal space. "If I fall, get in your truck and go. Don't look back. Just meet up with your family and run."

He stared at me with sad eyes. "If Oscar kills you tonight, we're all dead eventually. He'll find us. Might take a week, might take years. But he'll find us."

I knew. But I'd hoped Finn hadn't realized it. Finn held open the door for me. I climbed in. Feeling someone's stare on my back, I turned. Wade pointed at the car he and Desiree had come in. I smiled and shook my head.

Nope. Never again. Not with a man who openly told me I'd never be enough. Even though I'd always love him in some small way.

Finn drove us away from Boone's Ghost Town as his wife drove his kids in another direction. I glanced back at the place and sent Dr. Danny a silent well-wish.

18

Finn parked on the steeply slanted shoulder of the cross-roads. I got out of the truck and stared at the inky sky. Just like the first night we went there, both roads were deserted and still. No noise from animals of the night. No whisper of wind through the squatty trees. A full moon beamed down from a clear, starlit sky. But in the distance, thunder rumbled. The hunt was coming.

Our rag-tag group got out of their cars and wandered over to me. We huddled in a circle. Brad stood next to Mysti and Griff. I was glad he had convinced Jadine to run the other way with Dillon and the kids. What a relief.

Shelly and Finn stood together, arms around each other, both hollow-eyed and sad. Tubby and Hannah, heads close together, talked in low voices. Wade and Desiree, both tall and strong with fierce eyes, stood so close together they nearly touched. Though Wade had black hair and Desiree colored hers blonde, the family resemblance was hard to miss.

They all waited for my orders. It was time for us to talk strategy. We had none. Until I gained full control of the mantle, we couldn't actually beat Oscar.

But I had the magic potion, as Desiree called it. I could just drink it right now. See if it killed me or fixed me. I tugged at it but couldn't move it.

A sadness so deep and sure it almost felt like peace spread through me. We were stuck. We couldn't win. We couldn't run. All we could do was try to go out with honor. Honor needed purpose.

I climbed up on a rock so everybody could hear. Before I could speak, the sound of car engines drifted to the crossroads. A freezing wind whipped through, so strong it peppered dust against my skin. Something was coming. I tensed, hoping I hadn't run out of time.

Two sets of headlights appeared, coming toward us. They flickered out but then reappeared stronger than ever.

Brad came to stand beside me. "It's Cecil."

My respect for him went up several notches. Right then, I let go of my worry that Brad would never make it as a Gregg. He was going to do just fine.

The car, a 1950s four-door Chevy with cat-eye fins, drew abreast of us and shut off. Cecil got out. He wasn't the Cecil I had known. This Cecil had a full head of black hair and a layer of muscle. He looked like somebody you crossed the street to avoid. He also floated several inches off the ground.

His dark eyes settled on me. "You ready to fight, girl?"

I came close to Cecil, ignoring the cold radiating off him and pointed at the dram. "I still haven't done it. The Wanderer said I had to find the root of the scar tissue. I can't drink this until I do."

Cecil, still my mentor and elder even as a ghost, said, "Don't give up until you're dead. I brought you an army. They'll buy you the time you need." He gestured at the ghost car he'd come in.

A moon-faced man with slicked-back black hair got out of the passenger side of Cecil's car. This was Samuel Herrera, the fraternal twin of my great-great grandmother, Samantha. He flipped the car's seat down. Samantha Herrera and her mother, Priscilla, climbed out.

Another ghost car, one I recognized, rolled to a stop behind Cecil's. The Nova had been my car until a bunch of bullies burned it up. The driver's door cracked open, and a very young man with longish black hair got out.

"Daddy," I whispered and ran to him.

He held out his arms, and I hugged him as best as I could. Usually, he had a smile for me. Not this time. His sad eyes met mine. "It's time for you to meet your destiny."

"You say that like it's the end." I fingered the cold dram of potion hanging on my chest. Would I lose myself in all this?

"It is the end of my little girl." One translucent hand touched my face, sending a chill through my body.

Eddie Kennedy got out of the car's passenger side and approached, young and strong again, but just as see-through as Paul. He carried a huge sword, its blade blue like ice. I tried to hug him, but my arms passed through his form. He laughed.

A van pulled up behind the Nova and parked. The door swung open, and Chase Fischer climbed out. In death, he'd gone back to being a teenager. I ran to him, studied the face I'd once loved with all my heart. He pulled a ghostly sawed-off shotgun out of the van and winked at me.

Heart full, I looked around at all the people who'd come to help me. One was missing. Memaw. Her absence hurt. But she must've had her reasons.

The headlights of another car approached. This one was of our world and looked like a generic rental sedan. It passed the ghost cars and parked behind Finn's truck. I glanced at Tubby to see if this was who he'd called. He shrugged at me and shook his head.

Tanner slowly removed himself from the car and softly shut the door. He stared at me, solemn, so like the first day I met him.

I launched myself at him, unafraid of his rejection, and threw my arms around him. He staggered against the car but wrapped his arms around me. His earthy smell surrounded me, and I was home. I laid my face against his chest.

"You should have stayed away. You're going to get hurt." For the first time, I admitted out loud that I expected to die tonight.

"Bullshit," Tanner muttered. "If I had known sooner, I'd never have gotten on the plane to California."

"I tried to call you." Accusation hardened my voice. If Tanner still cared, why had he ignored my calls?

He dropped his gaze and kicked at the ground. "My phone went missing at the airport." He tried to laugh, but it just came out as a snort. "Before cellphones, I probably had fifty telephone numbers memorized. Now I don't know a single one. No way to tell you what had happened."

"Then how'd you know I needed you?" I hated the note of disbelief in my voice. But a lost phone was too convenient.

Tanner frowned. "I had this…I don't know."

Our eyes locked. The vision of him on the plane. It hadn't been just a dying wish.

"I saw you on the plane with Dave and Neecie. Did you feel me watching you?" My heart sped at the words. I didn't understand how it had happened or why. "You said you loved me. Then Neecie said…"

"It doesn't matter what she said." He cut me off. "When she understood I intended to fly right back to Texas and find you, she confessed to throwing my phone away at the airport in Austin."

I drew in a sharp breath. "Bitch."

He met my angry gaze. "I knew you were in danger. Felt it. I blew them off and got back on the next plane to Texas, rented a car, and..." He gestured at the night sky. He'd just known where to come.

I thought back to the night I'd laid in the back of Tubby's Cutlass, dying. I'd written off that moment when I'd been with Tanner on his flight to California as a dream. It had been something more.

I threw myself at Tanner again. He squeezed me hard, inhaling deeply.

I grabbed his hand. "My daddy is here. Come on. You can meet him."

"Isn't your father dead?" Tanner studied me, maybe wondering if I'd lost my mind.

"Yep." I dragged Tanner over to where I'd last seen my father and the rest of my dead family.

My father's ghost stood near Mysti and Brad. Gripping Tanner's arm, using precious energy to pour some of my ability into him, I dragged him in front of my father.

"Tanner, this is Paul Mace, my daddy." I realized as I said

the last word that Daddy looked like a kid standing in front of Tanner. I guessed he was. He hadn't even lived to be twenty-five.

Tanner held out one trembling hand. Daddy made a show of shaking it, smiling and nodding.

One last beam of headlights cut the night. By the time it rolled to a stop, I'd identified it as a Mercedes. Only one person in the world would drive a Mercedes to a death match. Rainey Bruce got out of the car and went around to the trunk without speaking to any of us.

My uncle Jesse got out of the passenger side and stretched. Jesse, my father's twin, gave me a window into the future Daddy never got to live. Short gray hair, the beginnings of middle-aged thickness around the middle. He hugged me hard.

Tubby hurried over. "Thanks for coming, dude."

Jesse and Tubby did some complicated handshake, and I realized who Tubby had called to help us. He'd told me Jesse came into his billiards hall for a beer most every day. The two men must have become friends of a sort.

Rainey race-walked back to me, a huge pistol in one hand. "I'm furious with you. How could you not have called me the minute this problem started?"

She gave me no chance to answer and instead pulled me to her and held me tight.

Thunder boomed in the distance. Beneath it, the hunt shouted and their hounds bayed. They'd be here soon.

I let go of Rainey and stared into her dark eyes. "Because I didn't want to watch you get killed."

She muttered something tough under her breath but hurried back to her husband. I took stock of the living members of our army. They were under my command. The thought of losing any of them raised a horror worse than any other. I couldn't live with it. We had to win this thing, one way or the other.

I climbed back up on the rock I'd chosen earlier. Cecil's loss swam in my head. He should have been the one doing this. He'd have been better at it. I swallowed the flood of sobs threatening and cleared my throat.

"These last few days have resulted in terrible loss, but we can end it tonight." I prayed I was telling the truth. "Hear that thunder? Oscar and his huntsmen will be here soon. Half of you need to fight off whoever Oscar has with him. I've seen…" But I couldn't make myself call the names of all the people who'd hated me in life and still hated me in death. It was like the All-Dead Asshole Hour. So I just finished with, "Whoever fights them needs to be careful. If they kill you, they'll take your soul and use it to make themselves more powerful."

My gaze fell on my father. The fury I saw on his face gave me an idea. "What if everybody who isn't alive fights the huntsmen?"

Daddy nodded. The rest of the ghosts agreed. They'd hold off the huntsmen and the motorcycle men. Maybe give the rest of us a chance to get that headdress off Oscar. Between us, we had some real magical firepower. Maybe we could combine it to call the hunt, even if I hadn't yet taken the potion to kill the scar tissue spell. It might not be a good plan, but it was better than nothing.

I let out a breath I hadn't realized I was holding. "Okay. Then the rest of us are going to fight for the headdress and the sword."

Plans went fast after that. We talked about disabling Oscar's horse and who would do that.

"I'll get the headdress." Wade, brandishing his nerd weapon, stepped forward. He gave me a flirty smile. "What happens after that, boss?"

I ignored the smile. "I'll put it on my head. We'll band our power together and call the hunt. If I can't, I'm going to drink what's in this bottle." I plucked at the dram on my chest. It was still impossible to move. I'd cross that bridge if and when I came to it.

Tanner leaned forward to stare at the contents of the bottle. He glanced at the horrified faces of my family and friends. He whispered to Brad. They had a short exchange. Horror filled Tanner's face. He pushed his way to the front.

"No. You can't do something that could kill you on a maybe." His words sounded like an order. I prickled.

"If I can't take over the hunt, we're going to die." My words echoed in the darkness. The weight of the lives depending on me pressed hard on my shoulders.

Thunder clapped. I nearly jumped out of my skin. A shadow of cloud had begun creeping toward the bright orb of moon. Thunder boomed again, shaking the night. Excited shouts followed. They were closer than ever. Blood-chilling howls joined the shouts. Those damn red-eared dogs wouldn't miss one more chance to rip us to shreds. The buzz of motorcycles provided background noise to it all.

Heart thudding hard, I breathed in the chilly, humid night. I felt for the black opal. My fingers found the dram instead. The black opal, and the life I'd had with it, was gone forever.

Fingering the dram, I gave it another pull. This time it did move. My heart skipped. Holy guacamole. I could drink it right now. But I didn't dare. Without the root of the scar tissue fixed firmly in my mind, I'd die. Resigned, I waited for Oscar and his hell army to reach us. Maybe I'd figure it out in time.

Tanner came to stand next to me. He had both hands wrapped around a long-handled axe.

"I'll swing for his neck. Probably take several blows. You shake the head out of the headdress and put it on. Then snatch that sword." His voice trembled, and the smell of his fear hit me.

From the other side of me, Wade said, "Won't take *me* that many blows to chop off Oscar's head. You swing once, hard as you can, Tanner, then I'll finish it."

The two men glared at each other like dogs with their hackles raised. They slowly nodded at each other. Right now, they were allies. Maybe tomorrow, enemies to the death. I hoped I didn't have to see that fight.

Thunder rolled again. The roar of the motorcycles shook the earth. Lightning popped nearby. Someone, probably Hannah, let out a short scream. Tubby laughed. I knew that laugh. He wasn't amused. He was scared.

I drew inward. Deep in my mind, I found a door with cracked white paint. It rattled, and light streamed from behind it. I drew together my courage and reached for the doorknob. My hand was small and unscarred with smooth, pale skin, a child's hand. It closed around the doorknob and twisted the cold metal. The door cracked open, and the light burned my eyes.

The shouts of the huntsmen vibrated in my ears. The horses' hoofbeats hit the earth hard enough for me to feel them through my boots. The hounds' excited, grunting pants underlay it all. Their odor, the perfume of death, fouled the crisp chill air. The motorcycle tires screeched as they hit the road. They were here.

"It's time," I said to no one and everyone.

The horses thundered toward the crossroads, the

horsemen on their backs with swords drawn. Motorcycle headlights blazed behind them.

Tanner adjusted his stance to where he looked like a batter winding up for a pitch.

"Which one's Oscar?" His words came between pants.

"Look for the horns." My voice trembled.

The door inside my head flew open, and bright magic flooded me. It burned the same way my first few sips of whiskey had. My instinct was to strain against it, but I fought the impulse.

The magic circuited through me, faster and faster. The world lightened. I glanced down at my hands to find them glowing. My heart picked up speed.

The hunt raced toward us, shouting and laughing.

Tanner inched closer, stepping slightly in front of me. I gripped his arm, leaned forward, and planted a kiss on his cheek. He almost smiled and winked at me.

Oscar, the tines of his antler headdress silhouetted against the night sky, raced toward us. Gathering my courage, and my magic, I stepped around Tanner and walked out to meet him.

The palm of one hand heated as a ball of white light formed there. I could throw this at Oscar. Knock him off his horse. Tanner and Wade could chop off his head. I'd grab the headdress and win. Oscar stopped a good distance from us, far enough away no ball of fire could hit him.

"Chickenshit," I screamed.

The motorcycles' engines thumped in the night. Their headlights appeared behind Oscar. They shot around him and blasted toward us. Moonlight flickered through the ghostly forms of the dead Six Gun Revolutionaries. King Tolliver rode out front, translucent face set and full of machismo.

The motorcycles formed a straight line in front of us. They shut off their engines but left their headlights burning. King Tolliver dismounted from his iron horse and sauntered toward us. Trench Coat got off the next motorcycle and shrugged into his dark, calf-length coat. He stared at me, hate blazing around his spirit in a dark nimbus.

My mouth went dry. Trench Coat had every reason to hate me. I'd sold his spirit to a sleazy dark being I called Mohawk. Either Trench Coat had escaped Mohawk, or Mohawk was on Oscar's side. Didn't matter now. It was what it was.

Seeing my enemies assembled like this showed me how ill-prepared and outnumbered we were. Terror blasted open in my stomach and began its slow spread through the rest of my body. My vision wavered, and I rocked on my feet.

Winning, no matter how much I wanted it, was unlikely. More likely was the concept I'd die a gruesome death.

A chill wind blew through the old crossroads. It pushed the cloud cover off the moon. Its silvery light bathed my skin and whispered against the mantle. Somehow that let me swallow my fear. These assholes might kill me, but I'd eat fried boogers before I let them see my fear.

I pulled myself to my full height, all five-foot-nothing, and stomped toward the intersection of the crossroads. Tanner walked at my side, eyes slitted like a gunslinger's. Wade took a few steps after us, but I gave him a head shake. It was Tanner who should be at my side.

King walked out to meet us. He hadn't been a ghost for long and still remembered how to walk like a human. But the raw, red wound across his throat testified to his death.

Trench Coat glided next to King. He'd been a ghost too long to even make his feet touch the ground. I wondered again about Mohawk, if he knew where his slave had gone. *Don't think about that. Not now.* I pulled my concentration back into the moment.

Our two groups stopped with a good six feet between us.

"We got a surprise for you," King Tolliver drawled.

"You won the asshole lottery?" My words came out full of bravado, but I trembled all over.

King's smile grew. He bent his knees, leaned back, and released a ghostly wail into the night. It took everything I had not to flinch away. Beside me, Tanner's posture tightened.

Another motorcycle engine screamed in the night. The headlight appeared on the road and zoomed at us. Who'd be coming now?

Then I knew. *Corman.* He was coming for Wade. To settle their grudge. I'd led Corman right to Wade. Desiree's prediction about me getting Wade killed was coming true. And my actions had helped it along. Sorrow stung my eyes and throat.

The motorcycle roared up to us and screeched to a stop. Corman pushed down the kickstand, got off his ride, and sauntered toward us.

I turned to look at Wade. Standing where I'd left him, he watched Corman's approach, face expressionless. The sorrow settled in my chest and swelled. No matter how I felt about Wade's womanizing, he was still my friend. I couldn't just stand here and let this happen. Corman Tolliver could go pound sand. I channeled my power and let the ball of light I'd intended for Oscar form in my hand again. Corman could just die right now. I should have scrambled his brains the first time he attacked.

I raised the ball of light at Corman. "Ready to die, mini-dick?"

"Not here for you, banana slapper." Corman rolled his eyes. "I'm here for Traitor Wade. My club is dead because of him. My daddy is dead because of him. The Six Gun

Revolutionaries are gone because of him. I want to settle it."

Rather than answering, I reared back my arm and adjusted my aim at Corman's head. The ball of energy would fry the doo-doo he called brains and get him out of the way.

"Wait just a minute." King, baring his cheese-colored horse teeth, motioned into the darkness.

A horse's hoofbeats clopped toward us. The horse, silhouetted by the ambient moonlight, had more than one rider. Worry sprouted in my gut.

The horse drew closer, and the feeling budded and bloomed in the space of a few seconds. Michael Gage held Dillon against his chest, a lascivious leer stretching his lips. Dillon twisted in his grip, craning to see behind her. What was back there? My answer came soon enough.

Jadine walked behind the horse, hands bound together in front of her. A rope connected her to the horse. She quit walking just in time to avoid bumping into the horse's rump. My worry grew branches, which wrapped around my heart and squeezed. Where were Zora and Zander?

As if to answer to my question another horse appeared out of the darkness. My mother sat astride it, Zora and Zander gripped against her. As they got closer, I could hear the kids' terrified wails. My entire body went numb and weightless.

"No." My mouth formed the word, but no sound came out.

Barbie gave me a knowing smile and a wink. Her nasty words pushed their way into my mind. *Remember how I treated you? That was playtime compared to what I'll do to these little freaks.*

I couldn't breathe. The sight of my loved ones in the hands of two heartless predators chased away all my strength. My knees buckled, and I would have fallen had Tanner not gripped my arm and held me upright. I stared into his wild, jewel eyes. This couldn't be happening.

Tanner gave me little nod. *Get your shit together,* that nod said. Then he slipped an arm around my waist. His support gave me the push I needed. I glared at Barbie and Michael.

"Let them go." My words grated out, scoring my throat.

"Let me settle things with Wade, and they'll be turned back over to you. I won't even keep the blind girl for myself." Corman, not even waiting for my answer, went back to his motorcycle and detached a nerd axe, not unlike Wade's, from hidden moorings on its frame.

Wade stepped up beside me, dark eyes glittering in Corman's direction. "I'm ready."

I longed to tell Wade to take Desiree and leave this place. But Jadine, Dillon, Zora, and Zander, people I loved, were in danger.

Then a new, even more awful thought hit. Even if I let

Wade and Corman fight, Barbie and Gage might kill Jadine, Dillon, and the kids just for fun.

A sound like a balloon popping came from the darkness. We all jumped. Waterlogged shoes squished across the pavement. Sol flickered into view. His too-white bald head shone like corpse flesh in the moonlight. Cold, wet fingers closed on my wrist. Chill radiated through my body.

Sol's voice slithered into my head. *I'll make sure they uphold their end.*

I took in Dillon's wide eyes and trembling lips. I let her kids' cries wash over me. Stared at Jadine standing helpless behind Michael Gage's horse. Then I glanced at Wade, a man I'd once loved. My thoughts ran faster and faster circuits. I couldn't handle this.

Sol's grip tightened. *You must endure all. I approved you to carry the mantle of the Gregorius Witch because you can rise above this and all other challenges.*

I glanced at Tanner, desperate for security. Just one glance from him, full of encouragement and warmth, was all I needed. I closed my eyes. Yes, I could endure this. And anything else. Not because Tanner had come, but because he reflected my own strength right back at me. He reminded me how tough I was. How tough I could be.

Finally I gave Corman my nod of acquiescence. Yes, he and Wade could fight to the death. I hoped Wade chopped off his stupid, hateful head.

Corman tightened his grip on his nerd axe and said to Wade, "Let's see what you got, you fucking traitor."

Wade, huge hands gripping his axe, moved toward Corman, teeth bared in an awful, violent smile.

"You've gained some weight," Corman told his former best friend. "Sure you're up for this?"

Wade took long breaths through his nose and didn't answer.

Tanner pulled me away from the two men. The rest of my friends and family formed a half circle behind Wade. The ghostly motorcycle riders did the same on the other side, behind Corman. Sol went to stand next to the two horses holding my family. He stared up at them, his needle teeth bared. Barbie took one look at him and turned her face away. Even in death, she was a coward. King stepped near the spot where Wade and Corman glared at each other. He raised one translucent hand.

"Go," rang King's shout.

Corman reared back and swung at Wade, grunting with the effort it took. The axe whistled through the air. Too slow, Wade jumped out the way, bending his back to keep it from hitting him. My chest twisted with worry that Wade really had fallen out of shape. I gripped Tanner's hand.

He whispered, "It's okay. You did the right thing."

My heart ached again at the one-night stand with Wade. How could I have wanted him over the man standing next to me? *Because that man left you.* Pushing the thought away, I turned back to the fight.

Before the arc of Corman's axe stopped, Wade swung. He aimed low, at Corman's legs. Corman, realizing the arc of the axe too late, didn't jump back fast enough. He yelped as the axe sliced his thighs, laying the blue jeans open. Blood flooded out of the wound.

Corman slapped his hand over the injury. Some naive part of me prayed this was it, that he'd give up.

But he raised his head to glare at Wade. "That's the only one you'll get, you cheap son of a bitch."

"Shut up and fight, you little pussy," Wade growled.

Corman let out a yell, raised his axe, and swung it again. This time the blade sang on the air. Wade met it with the handle of his own axe. Metal clanged together. Corman shoved off Wade and swung again with the same result. Wade blocked him, but he stumbled, sides heaving. This was tiring him out. He *was* out of shape.

"Finish him, Wade," Hannah screamed.

Wade slumped away from Corman, axe dragging the ground. The smaller man followed. Wade waited until Corman was close and swung his axe up from the ground, shoulder trembling with the effort. It flew upward in the direction of Corman's face. Eyes wide, Corman tripped over his own feet and fell backward. He'd survived by luck.

Wade lost his grip on the axe. It arced over his head, and

he staggered to one side to avoid its sharp blade. He recovered quickly and raced toward where the axe had fallen. Wade grabbed the axe, spun, and rushed at Corman, a warrior's bellow coming from him. Corman lay on the ground as though in shock.

This was it. Wade would kill Corman. Sol would make Gage and Barbie let Jadine, Dillon, and the kids run away from this. I let go of Tanner and took a step forward to watch the end. That gave me a different view of Corman. He had his hand inside his jacket. What he was about to do hit me like a blast of cold water.

"No," I screamed, tight bands of fury and fear squeezing my chest. I tried to run toward Wade. Tanner grabbed my arm and swung me away. Time slowed down as I watched what I couldn't stop.

Corman pulled a semi-automatic pistol from his jacket. The nickel plating glinted in the light from the motorcycle headlights. Wade, still roaring, ran at him. He raised the axe over his head to deliver the killing blow. He either didn't see the gun or thought he was faster.

"Noooo." The scream tore at my throat.

Fire flashed from the muzzle of the gun. Wade's head rocked back, liquid and brain matter exploding to shimmer in the moonlight before it showered the pavement. Time stopped. The axe clanged to the ground. Wade fell to one knee. He stayed that way for what seemed like a long time, eyes blank. Then he collapsed onto his back. He lay staring at the sky.

I jerked away from Tanner, ignoring his shout, and ran to Wade. I fell to my knees and grabbed at his still body.

"It's my fault. I'm so sorry. Please take it back," I yowled at the empty sky.

Corman moved in my peripheral vision. I turned my glare on him. He took one look at me, and his mouth fell open, his eyes widening. He dropped the pistol and ran to his motorcycle. Tubby and Hannah raced after him, each with pistols in both hands.

"I will kill you now, you fucking cheater." Hannah's voice, guttural with fury, was barely recognizable.

"Go to hell, you used-up bitch," Corman came right back.

His motorcycle rumbled, and tires squealed. Tubby and Hannah ran after it. Gunshots sounded. The vague thought that someone should kill him now, before he got away, flashed briefly. But then the world narrowed back down. All I saw was my dead friend.

I hunched over Wade stroking the soft bristles of the abbreviated beard he had adopted after he left Gaslight City.

"Please take it back," I burbled, tears dripping off my jawbone. I chanted the words over and over, lost in guilt and grief. Sobs tore my throat raw. I didn't care.

"Give me my kids," Dillon yelled from somewhere far away.

"Untie my wife," came Brad's hysterical shout.

Sol's voice rose, and the earth shook beneath my knees.

"Get the babies in the truck," Finn yelled.

A door slammed, and an engine revved. Tires squealed on pavement. The truck roared away.

Sol had kept his word. Jadine, Dillon, and the kids were gone. I wept on.

Caws came from nearby, and Orev perched on my shoulder, his talons digging in. Savoring the slight pain, I stared at Wade's still face. His cheerful rumble played in my memories, as did all the times he helped and protected me. I wept, the pain so big it felt like I was splitting in two, and waited for his spirit and the last interaction I'd have with him.

Horse hooves approached. Oscar's voice came from nearby. "I call the hunt back in session."

He didn't matter. The hunt didn't matter. I'd just gotten one of my best friends killed.

Running footsteps came from behind me.

"Get her up," my uncle Jesse said to someone, probably Tanner.

Tanner's earthy scent enveloped me. His voice was in my ear. "Darlin'? Get up. Lead this fight."

Orev dug in deeper, cawing angrily. I raised my head to see both Jesse and Tanner leaning over me. Tears blurred their faces. I wiped them away.

"I can't," I sobbed. "I can't leave him."

Tanner looked into my eyes. Whatever he saw there brought tears to his eyes. He shoved around Jesse and walked away. It didn't take a genius to understand he'd seen the depth of my feelings for Wade.

I wanted to yell at Tanner to come back, to explain it was nothing, that he was the one I truly loved. But I knew better. I'd known the second I woke up in Wade's bed that it would drive a wedge between Tanner and me. I cried harder as I watched him go. He'd never let me win his heart again.

Jesse leaned in close. "Listen to me. If you don't act now, fight Oscar now, you lose. Do you want to give in to this... this blast of diarrhea shit?"

I shook my head, too flooded with sorrow to do much else. I glanced down at Wade, wishing I had five more minutes with him. I needed to speak with his ghost. I had to tell him it was okay that he couldn't be the kind of man I needed. He'd deserved a better ending.

We all travel our road as best as we can, Wade's voice said from inside my head.

That halted the flow of hurt. It woke up some flicker of connection at the edge of my mind. I tried to pin it down.

Ignoring Jesse tugging at me and his shouts in my ear, I let the thoughts come. Wade had done the best he could. He hadn't been a bad man. Just a damaged one who thought he didn't deserve better.

Like Wade, I had done the best I could. I wasn't a bad person or a nasty supernatural thing. But I often thought I was.

The fog cleared away. I had found the root of the scar tissue. The thought that I was something unwanted, something evil.

It wasn't a new concept. I'd heard it all my life from authority figures, peers, even my own lousy mother. But they'd been assholes. The words and rejections had hurt, yes, but it was all so much hot air.

Yet, I had internalized their hate. Why?

Because it had been reinforced by someone important. Memaw. At home, in the place of comfort and safety, Memaw had taught me to hide what I was. That it was something bad. Something dangerous.

The lessons, presented with love, had wormed their insidious way into the fabric of my being. They had become the toxic story I told myself every day of my life.

Yet Memaw had loved me with all she had. She had given

her life to protect me. How could one person be both champion and tormentor?

Because she'd been human. Flawed and full of contradictions.

She'd done the best she could. The way people do when they're faced with an impossible situation. Just like Wade when he walked out of my life and then succumbed to the one night of passion—even though he knew he couldn't sustain it.

I saw something else, and it broke my heart. It wasn't me who had determined Wade's fate. It was his belief about what he was capable of as a human being. He'd chosen his own fate. I'd never know why he valued himself or his life so little.

"It doesn't matter now." Wade's voice came again. "It's over. Your takeaway is to value yourself more."

My head snapped up to find his ghost kneeling across his body from me. He would let me see him one last time after all.

"Overcome that seed of self-hate, or it'll consume everything you love." He put one freezing hand on my arm.

He was right. If I didn't let go of the self-hate, and right now, I'd be wasting this brave warrior's life. That would be unforgivable.

I called up my memory of Memaw, of her beautiful face, her long hair going from salt and pepper to gray and then to cotton white as the cancer ate away at her. She'd taught me to hate myself. Not to be mean or because she was a bad person. But because she thought it was best.

All this time, letting go of Memaw's teaching had felt like the ultimate betrayal. She had sacrificed so much to raise me and had loved me when nobody else did. But now I understood. I could love her and know she was wrong. Just like I could love Wade, even though I understood he'd been broken and had chosen how he'd lived and died.

"You were wrong, Memaw," I whispered. "But I still love you."

I went back to that door deep inside that I'd opened and walked through. The core of my magic hung suspended on the other side, the mantle and the scar tissue spell still fighting for control.

I closed my fingers around the dram hanging from my neck. It was time to drink it. With my thumb, I flicked off the cork and raised it to my mouth.

"I no longer want my seed of self-hate." My voice came out as a little girl's.

I upended the dram and swallowed its contents in one gulp. Fire worked its way through me. My magical core flamed to life. The scar tissue began to burn, the flames so hot they turned blue. The door I'd opened caught fire, orange and yellow licking over it as the old paint blackened.

My magical core exploded, the blast driving me back outside my body. Orange and blue flames licked over my skin. I was on fire. Burning. What had happened? I'd been so sure I'd done everything right.

My cooking skin sang with pain. Noxious barbecue-scented smoke choked my throat closed. It stung my eyes and blocked my vision. The agony took over my thoughts, turning them into a red haze.

Orev's anguished squawks filled my ears. He was burning too, because he'd been part of me. That hurt worse than anything. I had loved him.

"She's burning," Shelly screamed.

"Use your coats," Finn yelled. "Put her out."

"Get out of the way," Tanner shouted. Something, probably his coat, began to hit me.

I wanted to tell them not to bother. The fire was coming from inside. They'd never be able to extinguish it. But I couldn't make my mouth work. I hunched over my legs as my family and my lover tried to beat out the flames.

Oscar shouted, "Kill them all."

Cecil let out a bellow of rage. The ghosts who'd come to help me took up his battle cry. The sounds of battle began in earnest.

And there I squatted, burning, as my living family battled the fire and not Oscar. This was almost funny. After everything, I'd screwed up anyway and killed myself. I went back over my actions and couldn't figure out what I'd done wrong.

Now I wouldn't get to see what it meant to be the Gregorius Witch. Just my luck.

Blackbirds flitted through my thoughts, beating at the disappointment until it seemed so much nonsense. The pain seemed further away with each passing second.

It didn't matter how I'd messed up. I'd done my best.

Now all I needed to do was die so I could come back as a ghost and finish fighting Oscar. Even though I never quite became the Gregorius Witch, I'd still take the hunt from him. He wouldn't win.

If this was the next thing for me, I was ready to face it.

I let my thoughts break apart then. The pain quit hurting. I let myself fall.

19

I lay in quiet darkness, more at peace than I ever remembered. All the things that had led up to this seemed a war of spun sugar and toy soldiers. I settled in to the soft comfort of this new place.

Hands tugged at me. I brushed them away.

"Get up." Priscilla Herrera shook me.

I searched the darkness for her. Her familiar face came into focus.

"You need to finish it." She tugged at me again.

Though I could have rested forever in this soft darkness, I knew she was right. I sat up and let her pull me to my feet. We stood holding hands in front of my magical core. It was now a fiery red of glowing coals. I'd burned up, so I guess that fit.

"I'm sorry," I told her, even though what I really felt was

peace. The greatest contentment of my life.

"Sorry for what?" She waved one tattooed arm. "You've done it. Look at that." She pointed at a burned-out husk, not unlike snakeskin, lying below my magical core. "That's the scar tissue, the old you."

I stared at her in disbelief. "But I burned to death."

She laughed. "You're not dead. You had to burn away the old useless part so you could take on the mantle of the Gregorius Witch."

"Did you do this? Burn to death?" I couldn't believe it. The pain had almost driven me mad.

"No. Every journey is different. From the day of your birth, you were the one able to ascend to half-goddess." She beamed at me.

For the first time since we started talking about this, I didn't feel ashamed or scared. Instead, excitement stole through me, raising a shiver. "You mean I can still do it? Be the Gregorius Witch?"

She nodded and held my hand tighter.

"What do I do? How do I get away from my burned body so I can kill Oscar?" I glanced around, seeing no exit from this silent, still place.

"Shrug off the burned skin, like an unwanted garment of old, and stand." She came closer. "But before you do, and we merge forever, I wanted to tell you that I'm proud. We all are."

She turned me slightly. Behind her stood many wild-eyed women of all ages and sizes. My tribe. The other witches in my line. We stared at each other. The power rose between us, heady and rich. All mine. I felt myself lifting.

"Go back." Priscilla blew a kiss at me and faded from sight.

I understood without her telling me we wouldn't, couldn't, speak this way again. She'd now be part of me, as would all the other women of my line. Their knowledge brimmed in me, whispers and spells, advice and experience.

My brain shied away from the overwhelm, but I reined it in. This was my destiny, the thing I'd been born for. I listened to what the other witches of my line had to say. They explained to me about the survival of our kind.

And it boiled down to this: *don't give up, you got this.*

I woke to the smell of barbecued flesh. Hannah cried somewhere nearby, loud, braying sobs. Tubby wept too.

Rainey screamed, "Help her, goddamnit."

"It's too late, sweet. Don't worry about her now." Jesse sing-songed the words the way a parent would to an over-whelmed child.

"Nooooo..." Rainey dragged out the word and ended it on a sob.

"*Get up now, baby.*" Memaw's voice came from next to my ear and inside my head.

My heart stuttered. She was here. She'd come after all. Even after I'd decided she taught me the wrong things.

I tried to open my eyes and found that I either couldn't or they'd burned up.

"*It's okay,*" she comforted. "*You don't need to see me. Just know that I'm here and I'm proud of you. You did the right thing.*" A cool hand, which felt great all things considered, pressed to my back. "*But get up now.*"

Caw, caw, caw. Orev's call came from inside my head as well. He wanted me, us, to get up.

I began trying to stand. My burnt skin crunched. Tendons, which had drawn up in the fire, resisted my efforts.

"Oh fuck," Rainey screamed. "Don't let her fall over." She let out a round of hoarse sobs. Jesse spoke soothing words, too low for me to understand.

I wanted to tell her I was okay, that I just needed help standing up, but my vocal chords didn't work.

Feet thumped to the ground and approached me. I felt Oscar, knew him the way I'd know a fart in a car.

"That's that," he said. "I'll take her magical core, unless any of you wants to die for it."

No. He couldn't hurt anybody else I loved. I mounted another effort to stand, this time ignoring the stretching of the cooked muscles. The stench was harder to ignore. I smelled like hotdogs left on the grill too long. I pushed past the pain and began to get to my feet, one arm reaching out blindly.

"She's alive," Tanner choked. He'd been crying. I didn't have to see him to recognize it in his voice. He put his hands on either side of my waist. "It's okay. I got you."

Hannah cried harder.

"Get the burnt skin off me," I rasped at Tanner. Good Tanner. Decent Tanner. Sweet enough to come to my rescue. Once this was over, I'd beg him to stay.

"Oh God, help me. She's trying to speak," he sobbed.

I tried to close my hand. Something cracked and fell away. What I needed to do came to me in a flash. Ignoring the resistance from my cooked muscles, I raised my arms. A silt of ash fell from them. Using both hands, I dug into what was left of my face, and pulled.

Horrified screams met my actions.

I kept right on pulling, digging with my fingers. I finally reached a hard surface, not unlike the shell of an egg. I pushed one finger through it. The crack, right next to my head, hurt my ears.

I gave a vicious yank and felt the hard shell's rip throughout my body. One shrug of my shoulders, and the burned-out husk of the old me dropped to the ground in a pile of stinking ashes. I kicked it out of my way with one bare foot.

The sound of feathers rustling filled my head. Orev and I were one again, for right now.

Oscar Rivera stood not five feet from me. He still had a smile on his thick-lipped mouth, but it was no longer a happy smile. This smile was one of someone so shocked they can't move their face. I walked toward him, aware I was naked and not caring.

"I'm back." My voice carried the thunder of the hunt. I approached Wade's still form. Someone had closed his eyes. His spirit stood next to his body.

Kill this motherfucker for me. Wade's rumble filled my head, and I tipped him a nod.

Oscar began to back up. "We can bargain."

Someone fell into step alongside me. Just as I had felt Oscar, I felt Sol.

"Don't negotiate. He's waged war against you three times now. You must kill him." Sol's grunts and squeals came through as plain as English. He spoke into my ear. "Recall the bargain you made with me some time ago. The time has come to fulfill it. Kill Oscar Rivera. Destroy his soul and all who helped him. Make this a horrible example for anyone else who'd like to upset the balance." Sol was gone before his voice faded in my memory.

No problem. I kept walking toward Oscar. "Give me your headdress and sword, and I'll make it fast."

Oscar ran to his horse and mounted it. He turned the gray

horse to face the huntsmen and the motorcycle men, who'd all frozen, either in terror or in preparation of the shit hitting the fan.

"Get them! Kill them all!" Oscar pointed at my family and me.

The hounds bayed, and a horse whinnied. The phantom motorcycles thundered to life. All the huntsmen charged.

I reached for the mantle, the power that now belonged to me, and found it ready. Vast and infinite, it bent my vision with shadows and color I'd never before noticed. A world to explore.

The huntsmen barreled toward me, all their fears and nightmares hanging over them like clouds. They didn't know enough to shield their bruised psyches from me. Too bad for them.

I centered myself and called to the spirits who'd already come to our aid and any who wanted to join in. They assembled before me. Friends, family, enemies. The hunt rushed toward them. I poured energy into my spirits, made them into the nightmares of the huntsmen.

A cry went up from the huntsmen. The horsemen tried reining in their horses. The motorcycle men braked, back tires fishtailing. But it was too late. They raced through the wall of ghosts and nightmares, screaming. Rather than staying to fight, they fled down the road.

I jumped out of the way and watched them go, mildly

annoyed. They'd have to be found and disposed of. But now wasn't the time. Now was the time of Oscar's reckoning. I turned back to him and raised my arms.

The sounds of feathers rustling echoed in the dark night. I flapped my arms as I walked toward Oscar, kicking up dust. Oscar spurred his horse, but the horse reared up and threw Oscar to the ground. He landed with a rattle of bones and metal, whatever he'd used to fuse together the thing he now was.

I took the last steps running and grabbed his headdress. I pulled as hard as I could. Oscar wrapped gloved fingers around the antlers to hold the headdress in place. He kicked at me with booted feet.

"Get out of the way," Tanner yelled.

I let go of the headdress and took a step backward. This man was the best in the world. Even hurt and angry about whatever he'd guessed about Wade and me, here he was, fighting for me.

Tanner swung the long-handled axe he'd come with, just as he'd planned from the beginning. Oscar put both arms up and screamed. Though Tanner had thought it would take several swings, Oscar's head popped right off. Naked bone gleamed in the ambient light. His sword dulled and rolled away from the body. I'd get that later. First the headdress.

I grabbed the antlers and shook out the skull. It thumped

on the ground and rolled away. I put on the headdress. It clamped down on my head and tightened.

The weight of the headdress should have been uncomfortable, but I barely felt it. I was the mistress of the hunt. Images of chases flashed through my mind, all of them tasting like victory. Bloodlust bubbled through my veins. I stepped over Oscar's carcass and picked up his sword off the ground. A little push of magic made the silver glow as it had for Oscar. Wearing nothing but the headdress and my power, I held the sword over my head.

"I call the Wild Hunt," I shouted. "And these are my huntsmen." I swept an arm behind me. Power sang through my body, eager to fill my command. I was the Gregorius Witch, owner of my own destiny. My first taste of this new power would come in the dish of revenge. I was eager for its taste on my lips.

———

Metal clanged and leather squeaked as my command carried itself out. I found myself seated on a huge black horse. Black leather pants covered my legs. A leather shield covered my chest. The sword, still in my hand, shrunk into a jeweled dagger with a blade in the shape of a flame. Fire winked in its depths. My fire. I shoved it into a leather scabbard attached to my thigh.

Some part of me, probably from one of the witches who'd

come before me, knew how to command the horse. I turned it to face my army.

The people who'd loved me enough to come when I needed them awaited my command. They all sat astride black horses with red eyes. The hunt had clothed them in black leather, and they held swords with flame shaped blades that gleamed like the coldest ice. Behind them stood an army of hounds, black with red eyes, and glowing red-tipped ears. The snarl of the beasts rumbled. They were ready to go. So was I.

"I call the Wild Hunt," I yelled again. "Oscar Rivera is my first target." With a rustle of feathers, Orev and I raised the dagger.

Oscar's headless body shifted. The middle of it roiled and wiggled. Out crawled the mandrake root. It had a pointed, ridged head with a sprig of roots for hair but no eyes or face, root-like arms with no fingers, and legs of a similar fashion. The thing scrabbled out onto the road and took off running.

"Now," I shouted, and we chased him into the night. The clouds moved off the moon and made the mandrake containing Oscar's soul glow.

We raced after it.

Finn and Jesse rode around me to get ahead of Oscar. The hounds followed, baying their excitement. We surrounded Oscar. The weird mandrake man ran from horse to horse, only to have the hounds snapping at him. I slid off my mount.

Sol had told me not just to destroy Oscar, but to make an example of him. I glanced at Mysti.

"I'd appreciate help from both you and Brad." I didn't wait to see if she would comply. She would. That was a given.

"What do we do?" Brad said from behind me.

"I'm going to draw him out of the mandrake..." I began.

"Then we'll need to prepare a ritual." Mysti dug in her pockets.

"I won't need it." Our eyes locked, and hers widened. I'd always wonder what she saw but would never ask.

I spoke to all my huntsmen in a booming voice. "Once the soul is out, I'm going to tear the spirit apart. Each of you will consume part of it." I swept my eyes over my huntsmen. Revulsion, greed, and excitement stared back. "You'll take on part of Oscar's power, which is vast. This is my reward for your help."

I spoke to Mysti. "Once he's out, you and Brad hold him."

Mysti began digging in her pocket again. She drew out a weird little cross with red thread twined around where the wood met. She held it up to me and nodded.

I stalked toward Oscar and held out one hand, palm up. I imagined a hook. I reached inside the mandrake and pulled.

For the first time, I saw the real Oscar Rivera, shed of his beautiful sloe eyes and full lips. He was an ugly little creature resembling a furry frog. He snapped at me, flashing needle teeth. One of them punctured my spirit.

The pain shot through my midsection. I dropped to my knees but kept pushing. My body shook with the effort. One of the dogs whined next to me. I changed the hook into a dog's mouth and latched onto Oscar.

He fought harder than I'd thought him capable. I locked my jaws and let him whip me around, saving my energy and waiting. He stopped to rest. I jerked him out of the mandrake.

Mysti and Brad crowded in, faces pinched in concentration.

"We bind you to this spirit maze

Oscar Rivera

There you'll wander lost in haze

Unable to break free."

They repeated the chant, and I used my will to push Oscar at the red thread. He went screaming. Once on the red thread, he became a white, shifting mist. I pulled my dagger from its sheath.

"Shelly Gregg," I yelled and sliced off a sliver of Oscar.

His scream cut the night, so intense and pain-filled the hounds howled. So did a few coyotes in the distance.

Shelly lapped down the piece of spirit I offered her, eyes dark with greed. I kissed her cheek.

"Finn Gregg," I yelled and cut off another sliver. Oscar's shrieks shook the night. I ignored them.

My cousin didn't welcome his gift as Shelly had, but he took the offered reward without argument. He accepted my kiss and staggered away holding his chest.

"Just let it settle," I called after him. I faced the grouping of people again. "Tanner Letts."

My sweetie came forward, shoulders stiff, eyes gleaming and eager. He understood this ritual and the exchange of power. He put both hands on my wrist and took his bite of soul. He kissed my lips. I kissed him back.

"Hannah Kessler," I called.

My friend hurried to me and hissed, "Corman got away while you were burning."

"I know. We'll get him. I promise." I held out the sliver of Oscar's spirit to her.

She took it, eyes closed in pleasure. Once the extra presence in her hit, she clapped her hand to her chest, eyes widening. Shelly came to take her away.

One by one, everybody who'd come to my aid received what I had to offer, including Mysti, Brad, and Desiree. Then the last and largest sliver of Oscar hovered on my blade. I sucked it down like a delicious bit of candy. Somewhere I heard Sol laughing.

I mounted my horse and yelled, "I call the Wild Hunt. Our target is Michael Gage."

We shared his spirit too, and all the ones after. King Tolliver tasted the worst. My mother's spirit gave me indigestion. Which fit, I guess.

At the end of the night, we went back to the crossroads, stuffed and satiated. We stood in a circle around Wade's corpse. Desiree joined us. Her cold eyes bored into me. She'd always blame me for her brother's death.

"He wanted a warrior's burial." She dropped to her knees next to Wade. I dared not follow suit.

Shelly, the only one who knew what she meant, directed us in cleaning up our mess and wrapping Wade in someone's old sheets.

Tanner worked alongside me. Was he going to stay? He'd kissed me passionately when I gave him his share of Oscar's soul. My heart leapt at the thought, like I'd dodged a bullet. But then I remembered the look on his face when I was crying over Wade. He'd known something. Tears burned in my eyes. I wanted to say nothing and just hope he stayed. But that was the coward's way. Tanner had to know the truth, even if it made him leave. I screwed up my courage.

"I slept with Wade," I whispered when we were off by

ourselves.

"I knew when you were crying over his body," he whispered back.

"Can you forgive me?" I clasped both his hands in mine, wanting to make excuses, wanting to convince him, and knowing I'd better not.

He pressed his lips together and shook his head, brilliant eyes downcast. "I'll help you finish burying Wade. Then I'm going back to California."

Heart aching, I slunk away and picked up my end of the litter we'd built to ferry Wade's lifeless body to a lonely hilltop. All of us carried the still form in silence, save for a few grunts of effort. Wade had been a big man. We got him to the hilltop and set him on the pyre we'd built.

Desiree turned to me, eyes wintry. "Will you?"

I raised my arms with a rustle of feathers. I didn't even have to call the elements. A mist of humidity coated my skin. Breeze rustled my hair. The earth sang at my feet.

"Fire," I sobbed and pointed one finger at the mount on the pyre.

Lightning popped down on it. I gave it a little magical push, and hot, blue fire blazed over the man I'd once loved, the one who'd saved me, and the one I'd let ruin the best relationship I'd ever had.

I inched closer to Tanner and tried to take his hand,

wanting his steady comfort. He twisted away and took off walking down the hill alone. He didn't say goodbye, but I knew that was it. He'd find his car and head back to California. Out of my life forever. Back to Dave, back to Neecie, who'd felt such propriety over Tanner that she took it upon herself to throw away his phone.

A scream built in my throat. In less than two days, I'd managed to lose the three most important men in my life. I might have had the power of a demigoddess, but I sucked at love and romance.

Hollow beyond what I believed possible, I watched Wade's shrouded form burn. Tears rolled down my cheeks and dripped off my chin. My chest ached as though something inside had been cleaved in two. Though I'd fallen out of love with Wade, I had loved him as my friend. Nobody would ever replace the man who'd saved my life, over and over, just because he liked me. I'd never forget him.

Hannah came and clasped hands with me. We cried together. Howled, really. Knees buckling, yelling our grief at the dull morning sky.

The fire burned hot and fast, but it finally died down. We buried what was left of one the best friends I would ever have in an unmarked grave on a nameless hill.

I walked to the largest stone and called my magic. I traced a *W*, turning the stone permanently black beneath my finger. I had to mark this place as special, even though I knew this was the last time I'd step foot on it.

20

Hannah and I walked down the hill together in the new dawn, Tubby trailing close behind. We reached the bottom. I glanced around for Tanner. Sure enough, he and his nondescript rental car were long gone. I bit back a crying jag.

"I'm going to kill Corman," I said to nobody in particular.

Desiree came abreast of me. "Revenge won't bring my brother back. Otherwise, I'd kill you."

I lit a cigarette and stared her down. I could scramble her brain with barely a push. "I take it you don't want to help us."

"Hell no. I've got a daughter still in high school and a grand baby. This is your clusterfuck." Desiree brushed past me and stomped to her car. She got in and started it. Backed up. She glanced at the seat beside her, face sour and disgusted. She rolled down the window and held out something.

"It showed up on my kitchen table about an hour after you left," she yelled.

I hurried to see what she had. It was the spell book I'd always thought was Priscilla Herrera's. Now I understood it went back much further than that, to a time so old I couldn't even fathom it.

"Thank you." I took it with eager hands, excited to see what new information it held for me. Feeling Desiree's eyes on me, I quit staring the book.

"I'll be in touch." She drove off without waiting for my answer.

Hannah had come to stand beside me, also staring at the spell book. We exchanged a smile.

"Do you want to help me kill Corman?" Voice casual as if I were talking about making monkey bread, I raised my eyebrows at Hannah.

She turned to Tubby. They had a silent conversation.

Tubby shrugged. "He's coming for us one way or the other. Best get him first."

"We'll help," Hannah said.

We? I smiled at them, happy for them in spite of losing Tanner.

Mysti and Brad approached.

"I'm in," Brad said. He had liked Wade, even though they argued sometimes.

"Griff and I are in," Mysti said. She and Wade had shared a special relationship, full of respect disguised as insults. She had to be feeling his loss. Griff had found in himself a man not unlike Wade, one who operated on brute strength and used violence to send a message.

Griff stood a few feet back, brow pinched in worry. "Tubman's right, you know. Corman will come for all of us."

"We'll have to watch our backs." Tubby put his arm around Hannah.

Griff nodded. "I'll put out feelers. People owe me favors."

"Same here," Rainey and Jesse said at the same time.

Everybody watched me. It took several seconds for me to understand they were waiting for my yes or no. This new station was going to take some getting used to.

I nodded. "Find him any way you can."

I could have found Corman with the wheel of life, but it had burned back at that hotel with the rest of my supplies. Or were things like that indestructible? Perhaps they simply moved on to the next owner when it was time. My new knowledge about the way the universe worked suggested I had it right.

We took over a tiny roadside motel outside San Antonio. From there, I got used to my new position in life as I caught up with the business of the Gregg family.

The mantle of the Gregorius Witch reminded me a lot of the forests of East Texas. Shadowy, vast, and full of things with sharp teeth.

Orev and I ruled over a meager group of psychopomps who helped spirits of those who died too early into the afterlife. I now had the power to open those gates myself. Approvals and denials ran in the background of my mind, almost on autopilot.

My witchcraft changed from spells and rituals to a simple moving of energy. Mysti coached me through the worst of it. I didn't mess up too many things.

And the hunt. It belonged to me until another worthy leader came forward. In one year, either at Samhain or Yule, I and my court would take over the skies. Like Santa Claus, only with weapons in our hands and death on our minds.

The business of the Gregg family was almost as complex. Cecil had left elaborate plans with his lawyer about my takeover of the family. I signed the papers he sent and emailed them back.

He called when he got them. "You people left a hell of a mess at that RV park over in Atascosa County. There's a warrant out for the arrest of just about everybody in the Gregg clan." He paused and chuckled. "If you want to surrender to the police, I'll go with you."

"Send your bill, and I'll let you know." A few seconds later, his bill came. I paid it and fired him in an email. I turned to Rainey and said, "You're hired. Do your magic."

Within twenty-four hours, the police were no longer seeking anybody in the Gregg family for questioning, and insurance papers for our destroyed RVs and vehicles had been filed. Rainey showed me my bill. I wrote a check on the Gregg family trust to pay it.

Rainey and Jesse left that afternoon for Gaslight City. She couldn't leave her one-woman law practice for very long.

Everybody who had any kind of connections put out feelers for Corman. He seemed to have vanished. After a week, Mysti and Griff went back to The Woodlands, Texas. After two weeks and a very intense affair with Hannah, Tubby went back to Gaslight City to tend to his various illegal businesses.

What was left of the Gregg family checked out of the little roadside motel. We tried to make plans, but our days of traveling together were over.

Brad and Jadine went back to Summervale Carnival. They'd made friends with some other young couples and wanted to enjoy themselves. To my complete surprise, Shelly stayed with us rather than going with her daughter and son-in-law.

"You'll need me," she said to my unasked question of why.

Hannah and I had had enough of the carnival lifestyle. So had Finn and Dillon. They had children to raise, and doing it in an RV was putting a strain on all of them.

The six of us traveled west of San Antonio in a rented van and stopped in a tiny town's soda shop. By the time we finished our frappes, we'd agreed to look for temporary lodging. None of us quite knew how to move forward.

Cecil would have known exactly what to do. I missed him wildly and spoke often with his ghost. He refused to give me advice.

Shelly rarely spoke. She spent her days smoking and staring out the window at the dusty street that ran in front of the old two-story hotel where we'd rented rooms.

One day, Hannah walked up to me holding out her phone. "What do you think of this?"

I studied the screen. "Mountains. Desert. What about it?"

Her lips stretched into one of her rare smiles. "Those are the Christmas Mountains, one of the best places in Texas."

I squinted at the picture, not sure what the point was.

"It's beautiful out there." She started talking fast, which meant she wanted something. "Big Bend National Park is nearby. Balmorhea State Park is less than a day's drive away. So is Marfa. Maybe we could go see the Marfa lights.

That's where they filmed *Giant*. The best part: nobody knows us. We could just disappear."

I took another look at the way blue clouds hung over the mountains and the way deep, impenetrable shadows pooled at their base.

"There's five hundred acres for sale." She showed me another picture, this one of a little ramshackle house. "The property was a hunter's retreat. There's this house and another one. Both houses have solar power, electricity, *and* plumbing."

We sat in comfortable silence. I let out a sour burp. My stomach had been bothering me more than usual lately. I ate an antacid and offered them to Hannah as though they were candy.

Hannah shook her head and named the price of the property. I looked at the pictures again. There was something special about the empty space. I could see myself out there building something worth keeping.

"I'll put in what I can on the purchase," I finally said.

Hannah squealed and hugged me. We did the jumping up and down thing for the first time in a very long time. It felt good.

We told Shelly, Finn, and Dillon over supper at the town's only diner. We'd eaten there so much we knew the nightly specials by heart, and the waitress knew what to bring us without asking.

For the first time in weeks, Shelly sat up straight. "I'm ready to go. Get it started."

I'd have eaten a rat out of a rat trap before I turned away Cecil's wife. The idea of rats and rat traps made my stomach do a queasy somersault. I needed to get away from this greasy, diner food.

Finn and Dillon exchanged a glance. She nodded at her husband. He cleared his throat, olive skin darkening over his cheekbones.

"You remember me marrying Brad and Jadine?" He played with his tea glass.

I nodded. He'd been competent and amusing, his natural talent for public speaking coming through.

"I'm thinking about doing old-fashioned tent revivals with faith healings." His dark eyes, so like my father's, so like mine, settled on my face.

I tried to work out the logistics of the faith healings. Dillon could persuade people of a lot of things, but it wore off fast. Then I glanced at Zora, their daughter. She gave me a smile much older than her years.

When I'd first met her, she'd been able to bring small creatures back to life. But as she matured, her gifts changed with her. Her ability to resurrect had lessened to healing abilities. But they were strong.

My muscles tightened at the idea of my baby cousin becoming a faith healer. It could be dangerous for her. But

I couldn't argue against it. We were Greggs. Travelers who made our gifts work for us. I did have one question.

"You're going to do that without traveling around?" I saw the dangers, but I also saw the draw.

Finn shrugged. "Lotta land out where you two are going. I thought we could find a place nearby and..."

"Hide with me on my five hundred acres?" I smiled, and Finn smiled back.

That huge property would come in handy. I'd use my magic to make it a place people didn't see and didn't get curious about. The energy crackled inside me, eager for such a great task.

The next day Hannah called the realtor and started moving forward on a purchase.

Griff called a few days later. His voice was high, nervous. "Get on your laptop and look at the latest news from Gaslight City."

I typed in a search. The headline came up.

"Gaslight City Sheriff, Dean Turgeau, Shot to Death by Former Biker Gang Leader." The shooting had happened earlier that morning.

Underneath the headline was Dean's campaign photo. Next to it, a mug shot of a roughed-up Corman.

Throat tightening, I skimmed the article. Corman had walked right up to a car Dean was sitting in and shot him through the window. He'd died before the ambulance could get there. I wondered what would become of his wife and new baby. Tears brimmed over and streaked down my face.

Wade wasn't there to save him this time. And neither was I.

I read who Corman went after once he killed Dean, and my blood went cold.

Hannah ran into the room, gasping and holding her phone. Our eyes locked.

"Is he dead?" I asked.

Hannah, who saw deaths accurately, shook her head. "But we have to go."

———

Hannah and I spent the rest of the day driving too fast. I practiced the dimness spell I planned to use on our ranch in the mountains. We passed many black and white Texas Department of Safety cars, but not one of them turned on their bubble lights.

We sped into the Gaslight City Hospital parking lot and squealed into a parking place. We raced into the hospital.

I stopped at the reception desk. "Tubby Tubman."

The young woman manning the desk goggled at me.

Hannah leaned into her face. "Thomas Earl Tubman." She rattled off his Social Security number.

Had I not been so worried, her knowing Tubby's social would have interested me more. She and Tubby had gotten mighty close indeed. Good for both of them. They were both wonderful, fierce people who deserved equals.

The woman tapped a few keys. "Mr. Tubman is still in emergency surgery. His lawyer is in the waiting room."

Rainey. We got directions to the waiting room and took off running.

"Don't run in the hospital," the receptionist called after us.

"Lick me where I pee," Hannah muttered and kept running.

Rainey stood as soon as she saw us. My uncle Jesse bolted out of his seat and threw his arms around me.

Tears I didn't even realize I'd been holding in came, and I sobbed in his arms. I'd been doing a lot of that lately. Maybe buying the new place and getting settled would help my emotions settle down.

Rainey, Jesse, Hannah, and I spent the next hours in the waiting room talking about everything but Tubby.

"I hate Corman Tolliver. That nasty bastard shot Tubby four times. He only stopped because he ran out of bullets." Her lips trembled, but her eyes stayed dry. "Tubby's been my client almost as long as Jesse." She squeezed her husband's hand.

"That's the toughest little son of a bitch in the world. He's gonna pull through." Jesse cradled his wife's hand in both of his.

Hannah sat twisting her fingers and watching the door.

Several hours later, a female doctor came in with a chart. "You all must be here for Mr. Tubman. He was lucky. He's resting..."

Our cheer drowned out the rest of whatever she said. Hannah rushed at her and hugged her. She begged to see Tubby until they let her. I let her go alone. Tubby and I had turned a corner, and it was no longer my place to butt into his life.

I sat in the waiting room with Jesse and Rainey and told them what I planned to do about Corman Tolliver. My uncle, who'd spent all his adult life in prison, listened carefully and helped me flesh out my ideas.

I waited until three a.m., the witching hour, to approach the Gaslight City Sheriff's Office. Rainey had been able to determine a transfer bus would come for Corman the next morning. Tonight he'd still be in one of their few holding cells. It would be our last chance.

In the parking lot of the sheriff's office, I used flying ointment on my third eye and at the base of my neck to help me into a meditative state. I leaned against the building.

Within seconds, energy crackled through me. The elements came—a fine mist coating my skin, soft wind full of magic, the earth thrumming at my feet. Fire lit and began to burn inside me. I did a chant more because I missed the ceremony of it more than because I had to.

"By the power of the elements

The power of three

Let me blend with my surroundings

Blessed be."

I repeated the chant until I felt lighter.

"Oh dear," Rainey whispered. "You still there?"

"Yes." It felt as though I were speaking from within a long, dark cave.

"Shall I tell Hannah it's a go?" Rainey held her fingers over her phone, waiting for me to call it.

"Do it." Without waiting to see if she did, because a good leader doesn't have to, I slipped toward the door of the sheriff's office and waited.

Hannah's car careened around the corner. The tires squalled to a stop. Hannah bailed out of the car and raced for the door of the sheriff's office, sobbing. She never even looked my way, probably didn't see me. I followed her inside and slipped along the wall.

"There's a man following me," Hannah gasped at the officer on duty.

The officer's face never changed expression. "What's going on?"

"I stopped at Twenty-Four for cigarettes. He came over to me in the parking lot, trying to get me into his car. I told him to fuck off and..." Hannah spoke faster and faster, the hysterical edge in her voice quite believable for a woman who'd only landed one acting role in her whole life.

I crept through the office and to the door leading to the cells. I put my hand on the card slot, fascinated at how my skin blended with the stainless steel, and gave the mechanism inside a little jolt of fire. The green light began blinking. I pulled the door open as little as I could.

Hannah began to yell in earnest. "Oh my gawd. I think that's him."

She ran to the door. The officer stood to watch her. I opened the door leading to the holding cells a little wider and slipped through the crack, muscles wire tight, heart slamming against my breastbone.

I crept down the narrow row of cells. Rather than the stereotypical iron bars, each one had a heavy steel door with a tall, narrow window of security glass. I peeked inside the darkened cells, searching for a presence I knew well. I found Corman in the last one.

I passed my hand over the door, and it clicked open. I went

inside, pointed at the surveillance camera I knew was in the upper corner, and whispered, "You don't see me."

"I knew you'd come," Corman said from the darkness.

"That so?" Waiting for my eyes to adjust, I kept my distance.

"I was waiting." The bed rustled as he moved around.

I tensed, pressing my back against the wall. I still couldn't see him. A dark shape rushed toward me. When I saw the whites of his eyes, I danced away.

The room cooled to freezing. A rumbling voice filled it. "Not so easy, little man."

Flesh slammed against the concrete block wall. Corman let out a pained yelp. I poured magic into my vision and finally got a good look at him. Corman, shirtless, tattoos on display, panted as Wade's ghost pressed him against the wall. Corman held some kind of sharp weapon. He tried to stab Wade, but his arm wouldn't move. Wade had him pinned. And it didn't matter anyway because Wade was dead.

"*This is it,*" Wade's voice filled the room and my head. "*Do it, and move on with your life.*"

"Cheating bitch," Corman grunted.

I darted forward and snatched his knife out of his hand. "Aww...does that mean we can't be friends anymore?"

Corman struggled against the ghost holding him still.

I slashed his throat open in one smooth motion. Wade let go of him and winked at me. I used my new power to find the shining ball of white that was his soul. I washed away the darkness that had followed him through his life and opened the gates of the afterlife. He streaked through. I sent a wish of goodwill after him.

Corman slid to the floor, gagging, trying to hold his throat closed. His soul brightened in preparation of exiting his body.

I watched, fascinated, but backed away, determined not to let the blood spreading around him get on my shoes.

"I'll witness your final seconds," I told him.

The anger I'd held for Corman drained away, and I saw him for the sad little man he'd been all along. Angry at the world. Angry at himself. Behind that was enough loyalty and passion to drive an army. The waste saddened me, but not enough to take his hand and comfort him.

The life drained out of Corman's cold eyes. His spirit, brighter than ever, edged away from the now useless shell and stood before me.

He'd died too early, and I held the keys to his soul's final fate. I made my decision in less than a second. Corman had been too destructive in life not to be that way in death. But that wasn't what made up my mind. He'd cost me too much to show him any final kindness.

I moved toward his spirit. Sensing my intent, it shrank

back and tried to dart away from me. Something inside me latched onto his scrawny spirit and sunk curved barbs into it. The gate between this world and the next opened with a clang that shook the entire building. I reared back and slung Corman so far into the dark outposts he couldn't even haunt.

"May you walk there forevermore," I whispered.

I walked back through the sheriff's office, using most of my energy to make myself dim. I didn't have the power of invisibility, but I could do the hell out of dimness. Even so, I still had to stick close to walls. I soundlessly slipped back into the main room of the sheriff's office.

Hannah waved her hands, still explaining her horrible night to the poor officer on duty. He dutifully took notes. I tapped her shoulder. She jumped as though a goose had walked over her grave and wrapped up her story.

"I'm sure he's gone." She let out a fake laugh. "I'll just go straight back to my boyfriend's." Hannah stood.

"Who's your boyfriend?" The officer followed suit.

"Tubby Tubman." Hannah gave him the sweetest smile.

The officer's face stilled. He saw Hannah to the door and forcefully told her to have a good night. She drove around the block and picked me up.

"It's done." I slid into the car.

She started driving. "You don't sound thrilled."

"In the end, he was just a pathetic turd who died a lonely, horrifying death." I leaned back in the seat, nausea swimming in my stomach. A few blocks later, I had Hannah pull over so I could vomit on the curb in front of someone's house.

The next morning, the story of Corman's murder was all over the news. The camera had picked up only Corman's shadow in the darkened cell. Authorities were saying he'd killed himself. Considering he'd killed a sheriff, they probably didn't really care.

Tubby was still in the hospital, and Hannah refused to leave town. We stayed at Rainey's. My uncle's residence there had facilitated a few changes. Gone was the austere white carpet. In its place was wood stained a warm color.

"You like it? I cut, stained, and installed the flooring myself." Jesse reclined on the formerly nice leather couch, now covered with scratches. Rainey's dog, Ugly, sprawled in his lap.

We spent two weeks with them while Tubby regained his strength at the hospital. Hannah went to be with him every day and forced him to do his physical therapy. Their cussing arguments were the talk of Gaslight City's medical personnel.

Jesse and I took long walks through Rainey's fancy neighborhood and talked more than we ever had. The year was guttering, and the weather had turned into what passed for winter in Texas. Our breath puffed out in vapor with our words, making them seem more important than they were.

I told Jesse everything about what had happened with Wade and Tanner's reaction to it. He laughed at how I'd screwed things up. I surprised myself by laughing too.

"Things are going to be what they're going to be, aren't they?" I stopped while Ugly peed next to a tree.

Jesse nodded. "Can you live with that?"

I thought about his question as we circled the block endlessly waiting for the dog to finish his business. We went back to the house. We started supper. Finally I had an answer for him.

"This might sound crazy, but I'm proud of where I've ended up. It might seem like I've got nothing left, but I came a long damn way. I feel like I have everything." I took a sip of my ginger ale. My stomach felt worse than ever.

Jesse stir-fried chicken, intent on the bubbling food. "You finally learned to love who you are."

"I did," I agreed. That peace I'd found in the dark place between my life and death stole over me. That night, I slept harder than I had in my life.

A few days later, Hannah and I stretched Tubby across the long back seat of a used panel van she'd just purchased.

"It stinks back here," he whined.

"If you don't shut up, I'm going to shoot you again." She

doubled up one fist and shook it at him. "Kill you this time."

They smiled at each other. I swallowed my envy and felt good for them.

We drove west and south. On a blustery December day when the clouds hung over the mountains like an avalanche of ash, Hannah and I closed on the property we'd bought together.

That night we celebrated in a rustic steakhouse. It seemed funny to get a table for eight instead of twenty. But then Finn and Dillon's kids ran wild until their mother used her power of persuasion to convince them to sit down and shut up. Tubby and Hannah ordered champagne and laughed too loud. It seemed like old home week.

"I call a toast," Shelly yelled over our din in her Yankee accent.

We held up champagne flutes. Mine was the only one filled with water.

"To new beginnings," Shelly said in a softer voice. "I love you all."

We clinked glasses and made too much noise until they kicked us out so they could close.

21

A week later, sitting at the brand-new table in the kitchen of my run-down little house, I stared at the pregnancy test I'd finally taken. Two lines, a positive, stared back at me.

My heart thundered in my chest, and excitement uncoiled in my stomach. A baby. And after I thought I'd never have one.

I'd known, of course. I knew the first day I felt green around the gills for no reason. That's when I threw away my cigarettes. That's why I'd agreed to the purchase of this huge property. Wade's and my child needed a safe place to be born and grow up.

No question it was Wade's. I'd known in the back of my mind that he'd healed all of me that night in his little house. He'd even tried to tell me in his way.

A little sadness stabbed at me. Wade hadn't lived to meet his child. This baby might have been the thing to break whatever curse he'd placed on himself. A tear slipped down my face, and the sobs came. I let myself cry until it passed.

Because that was how life worked. You let the sad come when it needed to. Then you let it go. Otherwise life turned into a one-man shooting gallery where every target had my face on it and carried a lifetime's worth of blame. Things were what they were. I was what I was—the Gregorius Witch, a spectacularly flawed woman of power.

I wiped the tears off my face and sipped my Gatorade. Hannah and Tubby needed to know. Maybe Hannah and I could do that thing where we jumped up and down and squealed. I finally understood why it was important do that sometimes.

Right now, Tubby and Hannah were the only people sharing this five hundred acres of nowhere with me. Shelly, Dillon, and Finn had taken the children Christmas shopping in Odessa and wouldn't be back for days.

I shoved the pregnancy test in my back pocket and crossed the creaky wood floor. We'd found the wood under the nastiest carpet I'd ever smelled, and the possibility of it, how beautiful it could be, gave me hope and made me love my first real house in a way I hadn't expected.

Just as I got to the door, someone knocked. I drew back my hand. Neither Tubby nor Hannah came without calling. And their house was the first one visitors to the property came to. There shouldn't be any surprise visitors back here at my isolated little house.

I had done the spell I'd planned on the property. Only family, close friends, and one other person could even see the property. And that one person would never speak to me again. I'd stomped on his heart too bad by sleeping with Wade.

Tap tap tap.

Orev cawed from outside. His warning caw.

I took a step back from the door and called up my magic. A low hum filled the room.

"Peri Jean? You in there?" The voice was one I'd been hearing in my dreams for almost seven weeks now.

I yanked open the door.

Tanner stood on my crumbling concrete steps. I'd thought of him at least once an hour since he'd stormed off that last time. But now that he stood right in front of me, I didn't know how to react.

What on earth could he want with me? There weren't many possibilities. He'd forgotten something and hoped I might still have it. He wanted to tell me he hated my guts. He was here on business. The last one made the most sense.

I took a good look at the man I still loved. The weak December sun shone off slacks made of some smooth, expensive material and rippled shadows over a white shirt that looked softer than anything I owned. His long hair fell in graceful waves over his shoulders. A man-style. His new California look. It agreed with him.

I wanted to be angry at him, to scorn his fancy clothes. It seemed the right thing to do. Look at the way he'd left me. But I couldn't work up any anger. My love for him welled up, so big I couldn't tell it no. I closed the space between us and hugged him. He returned my hug, laughing. He even smelled expensive.

I drew away. "You look great."

"Not as great as you." He hugged me again and kissed my neck.

The familiar thread of desire worked its way through me. I stared into his wild eyes. It was like facing down a jungle cat.

He glanced over my shoulder. "This your house?"

I stepped away from the door. "Yes. Sorry. Come in."

Pregnancy test still in my hand, I showed Tanner the two bedrooms, one bathroom, and Eisenhower era kitchen. Tanner threw the test several pointed glances, but I pretended not to see.

Instead I swept one hand over my living room. "It needs work, but it's got potential."

He finally pointed at the test, eyebrows raised.

"Nothing for you to worry about." I stuffed the test in my back pocket.

Tanner recoiled as though I'd slapped him. His eyes, swimming with hurt, searched mine for answers. But he was out of luck. This baby was none of his business. Time to get Tanner out of here. "This visit is a great surprise, but I've got…"

Tanner turned toward the door, even walked a few steps, but spun back to face me. The hurt was gone, replaced by determination. He strode to the kitchen table, sat down, and settled his gaze on mine.

"I didn't come here just to turn right around and leave. Sit with me and talk. Please?" He held out one hand, and the tail of a new tattoo peeked out of his rolled-up sleeve. For all the world, it looked like bird feathers.

My heart picked up speed. Had he taken on the Gregg family mark? Surely he didn't think he was coming back after the way he left. I caught myself. No need to put the carrot before the rabbit. The tattoo was probably some trendy thing his friends Dave and Neecie had turned him on to. Organic tattoos, done in the style of the ancients with an authentic antique hammer. That made me smile again. I sat down.

Tanner cleared his throat. "I owe you an apology."

"It's done. Let it go." Conversations like this made me want to barf. Most things made me want to puke these days. But conversations like this made it even worse.

He held up one hand. "Let me say my piece. I'm a shithead for leaving. I was scared, so I let Dave and Neecie's offer serve as the perfect excuse."

"Scared of what?" I couldn't even look at him.

He took my hand. "Every day we spent together, I loved you a little more. I could see our lives stretching out ahead of us. To the end. And endings hurt…"

I glanced up to see tears standing in his eyes.

"It almost killed me to lose Bea and the girls. I thought if I ran away, then I'd never have to face losing you." One tear rolled down his cheek. He pulled his hand from mine and swiped it away.

I started to say something, to make some forgiving noise just to get him out of my house. He held up his hand to stop me.

"There I was in California, with nothing and nobody to hurt me. But then Nichole and I settled our differences." He took a deep, quivering breath. "I found myself with another chance to have fun with my sister and her children. After I thought I'd lost them forever." He sat up a little straighter, seemed to gather his courage. "So I came back to Texas to find you. To tell you I'm sorry I ran off like a coward."

"You broke my heart. I loved you too." Loved? Was I done with him? The ache in my heart said no. I still loved Tanner so much it hurt.

He stared across the table, leaning forward in expectation. He'd eaten roasted donkey nuts. Now he probably wanted to hear me apologize. My pride spoke up first. *He doesn't deserve an apology. He kicked me to the curb like a box of rancid garbage.*

But then I remembered the conversation with Hannah right after Tanner left the first time. I swallowed my super-sized pride and forced out the words.

"I'm sorry I hated my existence so much. It made being with me scarier than it had to be." Saying the words stung worse than a sunburn on the ass, but Hannah had been right. Tanner needed to hear me admit it.

He leaned back in his chair and regarded me. "We both had to die and be reborn so we could end up here."

His words punched into me. Queenie's tarot reading flashed in my mind. Maybe all that upheaval had been going on for Tanner too, and I just hadn't known. But now the storm was over. We'd both survived, and it was time to start a new chapter in life. One where I admitted my wrongs even if it kicked my pride right in the ass.

"While I'm apologizing, I'm sorry for having a one-night stand with Wade." I pulled the pregnancy test from my pocket and turned it where he could see the positive. "But I will never be sorry that this happened. I conceived the night Wade healed me."

For the second time, Tanner flinched away from me. His brilliant eyes dulled. He dropped his head to stare at the scarred wood table. My face heated at the baldness of my statement but not the honesty of it. Tanner had to know this baby wasn't his. If he left now, I'd find a way to live with it. At least I wouldn't be a liar. Tanner raised his head.

"About Wade..." Redness crept over his broad cheekbones. "If I had called your phone and gotten a disconnected message...especially after I told you to call if you needed me, I'd have felt betrayed. Abandoned. The way I felt when I got back to California."

Understanding passed between us. He'd tried to get back at me, or maybe just forget me, in California. Yet here he was. The most decent guy in the world. My chest tightened.

"And the baby?" I swallowed hard. My pulse picked up. Was I hoping he wanted to stay? Silly. Things didn't work out like that. Not for girls like me.

"I'm excited for you. You'll be a great mother." He said it the way people wish each other luck when they're never going to see each other again. I didn't blame him. Tanner was a special man, but raising another man's child? Who was I kidding?

Almost on cue, Tanner pushed his chair back and began to stand. He stopped midway up and dropped back into the chair. Brow crinkled in a frown, he stared at his fancy slacks, his inner turmoil so great it made my stomach hurt. Finally, he let out an angry snort. He raised his head and rolled his sleeve up to his elbow, eyes on mine. A new raven tattoo, very like mine, graced his forearm. My chest tightened. I'd been right. He'd taken the family mark.

"Give me another chance." His raspy voice barely rose above a whisper. "Let me be your partner and a father to this baby."

I started to remind him this baby wasn't his. He'd be raising another man's child. But he talked fast, his words running together.

"I know this baby is not mine. But Wade isn't here to help you. I am. I want you, and now this baby is part of that package." He stretched one hand across the table, reaching for me. "Just say I can stay. I don't promise to be perfect. But I do promise to love both of you the best I can."

The world seemed to stand still. I couldn't take his hand. I couldn't do anything. Now, after everything, Tanner wanted a second chance. For us to ride off into the sunset together.

It was my wildest fantasy come to life. But fantasies are just that. Not real.

In reality, Tanner had run off like a dog with a scalded ass. How could I trust him not to leave next time he got scared? Or started missing his old life, the one he could never have with me? Even better, could he trust me?

The questions were good ones. And I needed to think hard about them. In seven months and some change, I'd have a baby in the mix. Despite Tanner's promise to love it like his own, what if he left again? A baby didn't need that kind of upheaval. I got ready to tell him no, that it just wouldn't work. But what I saw in Tanner's eyes made the words lodge in my throat.

I saw fear. Vulnerability. But behind that, hope. Hope that I would say yes. And love. I saw his love for me.

He was willing to take a chance on having his ego crushed and his heart broken. Maybe his nose bloodied for good measure. But he'd loved me enough to come back. To chance it.

Now I held the key to the rest of my life in one breath. I could send the man I loved away. Spend the rest of my life guarding my heart like a crown jewel. Waiting for absolute proof I could trust.

But I'd be cheating myself. The baby too. I wanted my baby to have a father. Tanner would be both a good father and a good partner.

The fear tried to rise up again, a flurry of what ifs. I gave it a rude shove. Fear would not hold me back. Because I understood now.

The secret of living, and living well, was to jump. To take chances. Not wait for things to be perfect.

Perfect didn't exist. There would never be proof things would be okay forever and ever.

Life was a ride at your own risk deal. To be lived as it came. A second at a time. Cry tears of joy when it worked out.

Mourn when it didn't. Love like it was forever. And fight the monsters when they came.

"What if I tell you no?" My voice came out choked.

Even with tears running down his face, Tanner smiled. "I'll keep trying. I'll beg. Do tricks. One day you'll change your mind. Because this—us, you, me, and the baby—is worth it."

I shoved my chair back, stumbled around the table, and kissed him. He kissed me back, hard, his citrusy cologne strong in my nose and his lips hot against mine. I broke the kiss.

"Did I show you my bedroom?" I knew I had.

The corners of his eyes crinkled as he smiled. "No. I don't think you did."

He held out his hand, and I took it.

Life would never be perfect. No sure deals. But sometimes fate dealt you a good hand. I followed Tanner into the next chapter of my life.

———

Two weeks into the new year I sat in my uncle Jesse's truck outside Hooty's church in Gaslight City. An impossibly bright sun beamed down from one of those early January deep blue skies. Gorgeous day, but only thirty degrees.

Which is arctic temperature in East Texas. I rubbed the chill bumps scattered over my bare arms.

"You cold?" Uncle Jesse adjusted the heater vent to blow on me.

I turned the vent back toward him. "I'd rather be cold than puke on my dress."

Jesse smiled. "Wrong time of year for that sleeveless dress."

The dress had been Hannah's when she married her first husband. Esther Bruce, Rainey's mother, had altered it to fit my much smaller frame. It was nicer than anything I'd have bought for myself.

"I know. But I wanted to do this before I really started showing." Even though it was my second marriage, I wanted a church wedding. Walking down the aisle with a beach-ball stomach sticking out didn't sound very glamorous. "Maybe I should have waited until after the baby comes."

My uncle threw back his head and laughed. "You'd never get it done then. If you want to do this, you're going about it the right way."

Jesse's phone buzzed. He put on his reading glasses and stared at the screen. "All right. My father-in-law says it's time." He got out of the truck and came around to my side.

"Is Hooty a good father-in-law?" I asked as Jesse helped me navigate the four feet to the ground without getting tangled up in my yards of dress.

"He's almost over a guy he went to high school with marrying his only daughter." Jesse gave me a wink and held out his arm.

I took it, and we walked down the sidewalk in front of the church, past the naked January trees, the stiff, sleeping shrubs, and the empty flowerbeds. Dormant, all of it, waiting for another spring. Over the sparse months of winter, even one as short as winter in East Texas, it was easy to believe renewal would never come.

But the perfect blue sky and blazing sun promised something different. Spring would come, and everything would be alive and vibrant again. Life worked the same way. In spite of all the deaths and the ends, a new beginning waited not too far down the road.

My new beginning started in a few minutes. Other than taking on the mantle and becoming the Gregorius Witch, I had never been so sure about anything. Marrying Tanner Letts was the first day of the rest of my life.

And it was going to be a good one. I knew because Tanner and I were good people. Good people don't always get happy endings, but Tanner and I had gotten lucky.

Uncle Jesse opened the door. Guitar playing drifted out. Hannah sat on the church's small stage, strumming her guitar and singing "Storybook Love." Tubby leaned against the wall nearby, one hand on the cane he'd probably use the rest of his life.

Hooty waited in front of the pulpit. His dark eyes shone

with tears. Tanner stood next to him. He broke into a smile as soon as he saw me. On the other side of Tanner stood a flickering figure. My father, Paul Mace. Forever young.

A huge rumble went through the room as everyone stood and turned to watch Jesse walk me down the aisle.

Faces of my loved ones, both living and dead, passed by too fast. Griff and Mysti stood near Jadine and Brad on the second row. Jadine reached out to let her fingers trail over my dress as I passed.

The front row seemed empty until I let my sight waver. Memaw stood next to my grandfather, George Mace. Both were younger than me. Cecil stood next to them, hands clasped in front of him, face solemn. Next to him, Shelly stood in the spot reserved for the mother of the bride, elegant in a mauve dress. Rainey stood with a little space between her and Shelly so Jesse could join them after he gave me away. Beyond her, Dillon and Finn struggled to hold their kids still.

Then Jesse and I stood in front of the pulpit, our backs to the congregation. Paul moved from his place beside Tanner to waver on the other side of me. He'd have been the one giving me away had he lived. But having Jesse, his twin brother, do it was just as good.

Hooty asked, "Who gives this woman in marriage?"

Uncle Jesse said, "Her aunt Shelly and I."

Jesse let go of me and went to stand between Shelly and

Rainey. He put his arm around his wife and kissed her on the cheek. The room rumbled again as everyone sat.

Hooty took a deep breath. "I've performed many weddings over the years. Hundreds. But marrying a woman who's been like a daughter to you is..." He pressed his lips together and shook his head. He wiped a tear from his eye and swallowed. "It's an indescribable honor."

Hooty went through the standard wedding vows, which Tanner and I both had requested. But after we'd said our "I dos," Hooty said something I hadn't expected.

"The miracle of life isn't the fact that we live. It's that we weather life's storms and survive them. I won't wish you luck, Peri Jean and Tanner; I wish you strength and love. It's those two things, mostly the latter, that keep you going." He paused and smiled. "You may kiss the bride."

I looked into my husband's wild jungle eyes and felt the world opening up for us, paving a new road for Tanner and me to travel together. Together we'd find a way to fishtail through the sharpest curves and speed up the steepest hills. Not because we had so much horsepower, but because we'd learned the secret to winning.

Knowing that we could.

THE END

Keep reading for a special note from Catie.

AUTHOR'S NOTE

Dear Peri Jean Mace Fan,

Ever heard the saying, "A lady knows when to leave the party?" I'm no lady, but I did know—deep in my gut—that it was time to end the Peri Jean Mace Ghost Thrillers series.

Peri Jean deserved to go out with a bang and not a whimper.

Though I know I'll never please every reader, I hope you got a kick out of Last Exit. It was a blast to write.

Which brings me to the reason I sat down to write this letter.

Thank you for accompanying me on this journey.

Writing these books has changed my life. It took me from an adulthood of dead-end jobs to realizing what I want to be when I grow up.

(I actually suspect I'll never grow up. How can you and still do this job?)

The Peri Jean Mace Ghost Thrillers is far from perfect as a series. But this series will always hold a special place in my heart as the catalyst for huge change in my life. It's the series that taught me I could.

But none of this would have been possible without you—Peri Jean's fans. **You** brought the *Peri Jean Mace Ghost Thrillers* series to life.

Your interest let me know someone out there gave a shit. That I wasn't just spinning my wheels.

And when you told me how real Peri Jean Mace felt to you? That was when I knew I wasn't crazy.

Because all the characters in these books, all the settings, feel as real as anybody I've known or any place I've been.

And that brings me to my second reason for writing this letter.

Every thread in this story and every character came to the end that felt most natural and made the most sense. Not all of those endings were happy. But not all of life is happy.

Rising above adversity—finding your inner Six of Wands—is one of the themes of the Peri Jean Mace Ghost Thrillers series.

Life throws us curveballs. The point is not giving up. You

throw that damn ball back and hit life right in the nuts. Hard. And then you holler, "You can't beat me."

It's one of the most valuable lessons I've learned. You see, I'm not so unlike some of the people I write about.

And on that note...great, fun things are coming in the fictional world of Catie Rhodes.

(See how I did that? Talked about myself in third person like Tubby Tubman? Yeah, I'm the boss.)

What kind of stuff is coming, you ask? A new series. And another new series after that.

Still sad—or mad—about saying goodbye to the Peri Jean Mace Ghost Thrillers? Don't be.

You're not saying goodbye forever to these characters. Or this universe.

The Peri Jean Mace Ghost Thrillers introduced you to one character's experience in this story world. There are many unexplored facets—and stories—still to tell. These new stories just might have cameos of the characters you loved from the Peri Jean Mace Ghost Thrillers.

New books mean fun extras. Maybe even a few new short stories.

Interested? Here's how you can keep up with me.

Join my email list.

"Like" my Facebook fan page. (Be sure to subscribe to notifications.)

Just want to know when the next book is coming out? No problem. Follow me on Book Bub or Amazon.com.

Now we're coming to the end of this little "goodbye for now" letter.

Thank you one last time for being a Peri Jean Mace fan. You changed my life.

Never surrender and never retreat,

Catie Rhodes

Visit Catie's website:
www.catierhodes.com

Find Catie on Facebook:
http://www.facebook.com/catierhodesauthor

Follow Catie on Book Bub.
https://www.bookbub.com/authors/catie-rhodes

Join Catie's email list:
http://smarturl.it/lrdenewsletter

ABOUT THE AUTHOR

Catie Rhodes writes southern-fried urban fantasy with a strong dose of horror and a side dish of humor.

She is the author of the Peri Jean Mace Ghost Thrillers. Her short stories have appeared in *Tales From The Mist, Let's Scare Cancer to Death, and Allegories of the Tarot.*

Catie was born and raised behind the pine curtain in East Texas. She comes from a family of world champion liars.

Their tall tales molded Catie into a purveyor of her own brand of lies and legends. One day, she found the courage to start writing down her stories. It changed her life forever.

Catie Rhodes lives steps from the Sam Houston National Forest with her long-suffering husband and her armpit terrorist of a little dog.

Find Catie online:
www.catierhodes.com